The Hook

A NOVEL

The Hook

A NOVEL

ELISA GIOIA
TRANSLATED BY HILLARY LOCKE

amazon crossing

Text copyright © 2015 Elisa Gioia
Translation copyright © 2016 Hillary Locke
All rights reserved.

Previously published as *So che ci sei* by Elisa Gioia through Kindle Direct Publishing in Italy in 2015. Translated from Italian by Hillary Locke. First published in English by AmazonCrossing in 2016.

Published by AmazonCrossing, Seattle

www.apub.com

Amazon, the Amazon logo, and AmazonCrossing are trademarks of Amazon.com, Inc., or its affiliates.

ISBN-13: 9781503935495
ISBN-10: 1503935493

Cover design by Shasti O'Leary-Soudant

Printed in the United States of America

To all those who believe.
Always and in spite of everything.

Prologue

Things had gotten out of hand.

That helpless heap you see on the bed, her face smashed against the pillow, her legs wrapped in the duvet like a Thanksgiving turkey—that was me.

I had always been a couch potato. First-place winner at the sport of couch diving, my gym card happily neglected in my wallet. Champion of laziness.

But in two weeks I had gone from couch potato to larva.

A larva writhing with heartache.

Yup. Things had really gotten out of hand.

At first, I thought the hammering in my head was just my brain protesting. It felt like an AC/DC concert in there. As soon as I tried to open my eyes, a blinding fit would force them closed again. I couldn't remember much about the night before, just that karaoke was involved, and that I'd belted out some song by Vasco Rossi. And that this blond boy was breathing on my face. He wasn't even cute.

Then nothing. Total blackout.

Way to go, Caputi.

I shoved my face under the pillow again with a moan.

This wasn't me. The real me had it together. I'd always been the queen of order and reason, maniacal about it like an obsessive-compulsive serial killer.

From the outside, my life must have seemed perfect. I'd wake up at seven on the dot, check in with my social networks, scan WhatsApp for those three all-important words—LAST SEEN AT—then I'd spend the whole morning, from the bathroom to the metro stop, wondering who he had been chatting with after he'd said good night to me. I'd arrive at work, chipper and in love, but on the inside, I'd be swimming in doubt and jealousy.

In one day, I went from living in London and having the best boyfriend in the world to betrayed and single back in Italy.

I heard the phone ring somewhere in the apartment.

I threw off the sheets with a sigh and peeled myself out of bed very slowly. My throat was as dry as the desert, and I badly needed the bathroom. At least the shots I'd done the night before had numbed me to the point that I hadn't replayed the prior weeks in slow motion before collapsing into bed. On any other night, I would have spent the hours curled up in the fetal position, annihilated by grief.

Yes, things had gotten out of hand that night before Christmas Eve, in the arrivals terminal of Venice Marco Polo Airport. I'd managed to cram six months of my life into two suitcases and one bag, and had lugged it all ecstatically through customs, knowing I'd find him on the other side, waiting for me with open arms.

I wasn't looking for a declaration of love on a banner, a heart-shaped balloon. He was enough. He had always been enough.

But the bastard hadn't even shown his face. There was just my father, mortified, his downcast eyes focused on the tips of his Clarks sandals, and his Panda 4x4 parked outside in the loading zone.

The phone was still ringing incessantly, yanking me back from my painful memories.

"Coming," I mumbled.

My mouth was sticky and my breath could have knocked some-one out. I ran my fingers through my hair, but they got stuck in its tangle of knots. I knew I must have raccoon eyes from my mascara and eyeliner. I could hear my mother's voice: "Never go to bed with your makeup on!"

She was right. Alcohol and makeup were a deadly combo, and that—paired with not sleeping—meant I was basically a hopeless case according to the *Guide to CoverGirl Skin Until You're Fifty*.

I fumbled for the light switch and stubbed my little finger against the bed instead.

Shit!

Gasping for breath, my finger throbbing, I switched on the light and squeezed my eyes shut. Again. I massaged my temples. The concert in my head was playing in the key of the evening before.

Someone give me a gun—quick!

My room wasn't in much better shape than I was. It looked like a refugee camp. Last night's dress was balled up on the floor by the bed, and my stiletto was . . . on the desk? What was it doing there?

The contents of my bag had been dumped all over the floor. Makeup, tampons, and candies were strewn everywhere. My dirty socks were crumpled at the foot of the bed.

I frowned. How much had I drunk last night?

I limped over to the armoire and pulled on my Uggs. The apart-ment was freezing, but I persevered in my bra, panties, and boots, fol-lowing the sound of the ring.

I felt like a *Baywatch* lifeguard, except I had so much cellulite that only Photoshop could have saved me. Not to mention the map—oth-erwise known as stretch marks—that was etched across my inner thighs and hips. And I didn't even have kids. *At least my bra and underwear match,* I consoled myself, rubbing my arms to stay warm.

When I got to the kitchen, I had a second shock. One too many for that morning.

My phone was on the counter, and it wasn't ringing. But then I heard the ring again.

Oh. My. God.

Who was in my house?

I couldn't remember anything from the night before. Nada. Zilch. What if I'd let that blond kid come home with me? I wanted to die.

The phone rang again, and I jumped.

Jesus! I was in the kitchen, half-naked, my phone in my hand, listening to a phone ring somewhere else. And there might have been—*might* have been—an unidentified man in my apartment.

I dialed 911 on my phone, got ready to press "Call," and reached into the drawer under the oven to grab a rolling pin. Then I crept down the hallway, ready to pounce.

But when I turned on the light, there wasn't anyone there—just my other patent-leather stiletto. I smacked my forehead with my hand. I must have had quite a night. I shook my head, exasperated, and gingerly tiptoed to the only room I hadn't checked: the bathroom.

Here goes, Gioia!

I flattened myself against the wall and held my breath, gripping the handle of the rolling pin. Then the doorbell made me jump again.

Stupid, stupid, stupid!

There was no phone. It had been the doorbell all along.

"Gioia!" shouted a woman's voice on the other side of the door.

I frowned. I was in no mood to take orders.

"Gioia, open the goddamned door!"

I gave a halfhearted military salute and, covered by mere inches of fabric, wielding a rolling pin, my stubbed finger still throbbing, and wearing my best Instagram smile, I opened the door for my very best friend.

"Bea."

"Gioia!"

There she was, her red down jacket perfectly matching her high heels, her untamed blond curls, and her ocean-colored eyes boiling with rage. Beatrice Turani.

"Good morning to you too," I snapped.

"Why the hell didn't you answer your phone? You know, that thing we all use to keep in touch? I thought I was going to have to call in a SWAT team."

She assessed me from head to toe, from my split ends down to my woolly boots, skipping my lingerie ensemble. She snorted.

I crossed my arms, ready to be scolded.

"Jesus. Christ."

Nope, not even Christ and all his saints could have gotten me out of this.

"Gioia!"

"Bea."

"You're half-naked and . . . Oh God! Are you in the middle of something?"

Bea, goddess of the hunt. Diana was an old spinster in comparison.

Hunting season was open 365 days a year for her. She collected men like I collected snow globes; she was an unrelenting feminist and committed to "single" as her permanent legal status.

"No one's here," I sighed, relieved I hadn't slept with that walking toilet from last night. If I had, I would've tattooed a giant *L* for "Loser" on my own forehead.

I opened the door, and she tiptoed in like she was afraid of getting Ebola from my apartment. I had to admit the kitchen was in even worse shape than my room. Stacks of dirty plates in the sink, open cereal and cookie boxes on the breakfast bar, Post-its layered over Post-its everywhere, and a rancid stench wafting through the air.

Bea picked up an empty milk carton as if it were some kind of forensic evidence and threw it into the sink.

"My God, Gioia! Why do you insist on living in a Dumpster?"

I ignored her and went into the living room to collapse on the sofa. I could hear her moving around the house.

"You can't go on like this. I know you feel like shit, but you're hitting bottom here. Gioia, I'm your friend. I love you. But I'm beginning to wonder if you'll ever come out of this hole you've dug for yourself."

She wasted no time in telling me the truth. That's why she was my best friend, along with the other two Graces: my sister Melissa and Ludovica Valenti.

I had no excuses. I lifted myself half an inch off the sofa. What I needed was coffee.

I dragged myself back to the kitchen and lit the burner under some day-old coffee that was already in the percolator. I found my last clean cup and cleared some space for it on the counter as Beatrice continued to patrol the apartment.

Then I went back to the sofa and let my eyes close again, hoping that the hammering in my head would taper off. I needed quiet, some painkillers, and a gun in case nothing else worked, but Bea didn't care. She opened the garbage can and slammed it shut again, clattered the dishes in the sink, and snorted with disgust every three seconds. The princess who didn't even know how to read an expiration date had suddenly transformed into Cinderella.

"Gioia . . ."

"What."

"You haven't answered your phone in days. I'm guessing you haven't even taken your mother's calls."

It was true. Over the past few weeks, my patience had hit an all-time low, and let's just say I didn't need to hear my mother spouting her usual *I told you so*.

"I've been busy."

"Busy accumulating garbage to drown yourself in?"

"Did you come here to judge me?"

Beatrice sighed and turned off the burner under the coffee. "We're all worried about you."

We're all. In other words, the three Graces.

"I've been hiding in case I'm contagious," I mumbled from under the cushion. Too bad they didn't sell Band-Aids for your heart. I imagined Bea was giving me one of her are-you-kidding-me looks, so I relented and offered up some reassurance. "I'm fine." Maybe hearing myself say it aloud convinced me a little. "Some coffee and a pill, and I'll be good as new."

There were pills for everything: carsickness, airsickness, stomachaches, headaches. But there was nothing for heartaches; no one had found the cure.

"Get dressed or you'll catch a cold."

My eyes still closed, I reached for an old oversized sweatshirt that I had left on the sofa.

"You're such a slob!"

"Gee, thanks."

"It's true! You're gross, you stink, and your hair is like a rat's nest. Your apartment looks like a bomb went off, and you're ignoring your family. And for what? Because of some asshole rocker boy?"

The rocker boy in question was my ex. The unnamable. The asshole. Not too skinny and not too fit, five foot eight, and 150 pounds. He was cute, charming, and understated in his jeans and T-shirt, the kind of guy that made women hurl their underwear onto the stage. He was the cause of the pain I had been feeling down to my bones, the pain that was always present like the extra pounds around my waist or the cellulite on my thighs.

I sat up as she handed me the cup. "I'll get better," I murmured into the coffee.

"Has he called you?"

"After the first week? No, radio silence. He's always on WhatsApp, but I'm not going to contact him first. Actually, pass me my phone so I can delete his number."

That way I wouldn't even be tempted, like I was with Facebook. I had spent an entire Saturday afternoon in my pajamas with a pint of double-chocolate ice cream looking through his photos. I'd told myself I was only going to glance at them, but three hours later, I had worked my way from 2007 to 2014.

Thanks, Mark Zuckerberg! Thank you so much for sending millions of Italians running to their therapists with your Facebook and your WhatsApp read receipts!

That afternoon, I'd discovered that the unnamable had deleted all our photos together. He had moved Gioia Caputi to the trash with a single click and then emptied the bin.

Asshole!

He was like a virus in my database. Gone was the practical, happy Gioia, with her t's crossed and her i's dotted. She had been replaced by a ghost of herself. And now I'd let the first blond boy who happened along breathe on my neck in a dirty bar, for Christ's sake! I felt like Miley Cyrus or Britney Spears when they said good-bye to their fresh-faced Disney personas.

And that was exactly the point: Disney.

I had stopped believing in my Mr. Right. I was like Jennifer Aniston without Brad Pitt, Brenda without Dylan. And what about Tom Cruise and Katie Holmes? Just look how they turned out. They jumped off Oprah's couch and landed directly in a courtroom.

"I don't want a boyfriend ever again."

Bea burst out laughing. "You're twenty-five. Do you even know how many more of these losers you'll have to go through? Cowards, serial cheaters, mama's boys. And we've known for centuries what men think with. Are you sure you don't want to become a nun?"

I shoved a cookie into my mouth, hoping to soak up the alcohol in my stomach.

"Nuns have a better social life than I do."

Bea nodded, thinking. "Actually . . ."

"Screw it. I don't need a man."

I was back in control.

I was over him.

I would rise up from my own ashes.

Why, then, did I feel the need to make a big bonfire with all his photographs?

"You know what you should do?" Bea said. "Get revenge!"

"An eye for an eye? That's real mature."

She waved me off. "Hear me out. Men don't know what they've lost until someone else has it. Like when they trade their fantasy football players. Do you follow me?"

I nodded, wary of where she was going with this. When Bea had a plan, it was better to keep a safe distance.

"That pile of shit needs to know what he's missing now that you're gone. You need to increase the value of your shares on the market, but you can't do that sitting at home. So enjoy your last day of freedom, leave a good ass imprint on the sofa, destroy yourself with junk food, and watch a *Sex and the City* marathon. But starting tomorrow . . ." she said, pointing a finger in my direction, "you'll be under my supervision. You'll get your ass out of this house and have a minimum of five hours of fresh air, and we're going to make ourselves look gorgeous. Then you'll go kick his cheating ass."

The plan didn't sound half-bad.

It wasn't perfect—we'd have to change the last part—but at least it was a plan.

A few minutes before, I'd been in an alcohol-induced coma. He'd cheated on me; I'd needed time to lick my wounds.

But Bea was right. I couldn't be a shut-in forever—or be with a gross rebound blond boy—just because some asshole couldn't keep it in his pants for six months.

"Fine," I sighed.

Beatrice raised a victorious fist, triumphant. She leaned forward and placed her hands on my shoulders, smiling sweetly.

"And for the record," she said in a gentle voice, "don't think for a second that I'm going to help you clean up this mess. Your house is a cesspit. I'm your friend, I'll love you forever, but you can wipe your own ass." She slowed down on the last sentence to make sure I got the message.

I rolled my eyes, exasperated. Too tired to respond, I gave her a thumbs-up and a copy of the keys to my apartment, and then plopped back down on the sofa and turned on the TV to some movie with Robert Downey Jr. But not even his biceps could excite me. Not one hormone budged.

I was a bad case.

RIP Gioia Caputi, 1989–2014.

How had it gotten to this point? It wasn't just the hangover. How had I let myself deteriorate to this state over a guy? How on earth had I gone more than two days without washing my hair—all for a dumb guy?

My seemingly perfect life had changed in the blink of an eye.

I felt like a loser, bitter and jaded.

But it's true what they say: right when you stop believing in love, right when you stop looking for it, that's when it comes looking for you.

Chapter 1

Four months later . . .

I was late for work. Fantastic.

It was only Monday morning and I was already hitting the "Snooze" button twice. I knelt down and looked under the bed. Nothing.

"Bea!" I shouted, jumpy with nerves. "Have you seen my work folder?" Where the hell was it? I shifted through the pile of dresses on the chair. Not there either. "Bea?"

I walked into the kitchen, breathless, car keys in hand, shirt still open, and my hair gathered up in some semblance of a bun. Beatrice was perched comfortably at the bar, playing with her phone and listening to Paolo Fox's horoscope at full blast.

"Have you seen my work folder?" I asked desperately.

No reply. She was probably more interested in whatever boy she was chatting with. I rolled my eyes and switched off the radio, finally getting her attention.

She gave me a confused look.

"The folder," I said for the hundredth time. "Have you seen my folder?"

"It could be by the TV."

"Could be?"

"Hey, you're the hot mess. Don't look at me!"

"I'm just a little frantic here. That folder is how I make my living."

For two months, I had been working at an ad agency as a copywriter. Preying on my fellow Italians with deceptive commercials had become my bread and butter. I rummaged around among the boxes that I hadn't unpacked yet and, finally, under a pile of papers, I found my folder.

"Did you need me to wait for you? I'm running late already . . ." I grabbed a croissant and shoved it in my mouth.

"It's not even eight!" she said.

"Keep in mind when you hit the office at nine that I've already been at work for half an hour."

"I'm so impressed."

"Okay, I'm going."

I grabbed my bag and threw my makeup kit inside. I needed it after the long night Bea and I had spent at a local bar. She was already in great shape, her skin luminous without any makeup at all. I, on the other hand, needed a miracle to hide the circles under my eyes—and maybe a liver transplant. It wasn't fair.

"Wait." She rested her elbows on the bar and pointed her phone at me. "I booked Barcelona."

"You did? For when?"

"Next week."

"I'm so jealous. It'll be so warm!"

I held the rest of my croissant between my teeth and slipped on my ballet flats. I would have given anything to get away for a few days. Only with great effort had I managed to avoid the unnamable since he'd left me. Eighteen thousand people in this town, and I hadn't bumped into him once by following the *rules for not running into your ex*, which included: don't go to the same bars; spend Saturday evenings at home with a pint of ice cream and a tearjerker movie; and pray that you don't make a fool of yourself.

"Let's all go."

"Hmmm?" I said, my mouth full of croissant.

"Let's go to Barcelona. All four of us. Me, you, Melly, and Ludo."

I burst out laughing. "For a second there, I almost believed you. How'd you learn to lie like that? I was never any good at it."

But then I saw her expression and my face fell.

"You're not serious, are you?"

"We'll have so much fun. We'll drink a ton of sangria and meet beautiful Spanish men. Hot, tan, fit, and gifted in other departments too. You need to get out of this cloister."

"And I have to go all the way to Barcelona to do it? First of all, I can't ask for any time off. I've only been working at Dreamstart for a few months."

"We thought of that. Next week is a long weekend. You can't get out of this, Gioia. You've used up all your excuses."

I thought about the last four months. I had done nothing but work, work, work, and avoid my mother's sermons. I had spent nearly every Saturday on the sofa watching romantic comedies with their stupid, predictable endings. Could someone please tell those filmmakers that life wasn't really like that? My own most romantic encounter had been at karaoke with that blond boy again, who asked why I had never called him back.

Maybe a few days in the sun would help tame my homicidal instincts against the male population.

"Barcelona?" I asked.

"Barcelona.

"Well . . ." I drawled. Bea took a deep breath. "Now I just need to figure out how to fit my entire wardrobe into a carry-on."

I gave her a peck on the cheek and left to the sound of her giggles.

Thirty minutes later, I parked my Mini in the only available free parking space and ran to the office, trying not to trip on the cobblestones that I nearly broke my ankle on every morning. I looked at my watch. Eight thirty already.

I could totally make it. Just four flights of stairs, sneak into the office, and nonchalantly sit down at my desk. Dreamstart was in the historic city center, on the top floor of a peeling eighteenth-century building that seemed ready to collapse in the slightest breeze.

Inside, though, the agency was a modern mecca of design and technology. A riot of white, black, and red décor and futuristic furnishings welcomed you to the fifth floor. Each employee had an ultramodern computer *and* a tablet so they could take work home. Sabrina, the boss, was demanding, and there was one rule that could never be broken: every Friday at five on the dot, you had to send out your completed project by email. Otherwise, she always said, there was a line of people waiting who would give anything for your job.

Exhausted, I breezed past reception and MTB. That is, Margherita the Bitch, Dreamstart's receptionist. She was a poster child for women that like to stab other women in the back. She generally didn't even bother to look at me, unless it was with disdain, but she never missed a chance to take me down a peg.

I passed the other offices and took my place at my desk, logged onto my computer, and looked out the window.

All I could see was a red brick wall.

"Gioia, honey." The desk creaked under Marco's weight. He was my colleague and the agency's art director.

Yes, he was a good guy. No, he wasn't available. He was happily gay—not to mention taken by a lovely guy named José. I could erase "workplace affair" from my to-do list.

"Hi, Marco. Is Sabrina here yet?"

"I haven't seen her. We would have smelled her perfume by now."

Every day, before we even saw her come through the door, the sound of Sabrina's high heels against the parquet floors and a storm cloud of Chanel would announce her dreaded arrival.

"What are you working on?" I asked him, checking my email.

"You don't know? We've been summoned by Her Majesty the Ice Queen."

"*We?*" I went pale.

Ever since I'd been hired, I had only been thrown the leftovers, the most tedious projects. I had never worked on a launch with Marco, and I wondered why it was happening now. Maybe Sabrina had finally taken notice of my talent?

"Margherita said," he whispered, "that we're getting an international campaign. Sabrina wants us all on it. She canceled all her meetings for the week to be here in the office and oversee everything personally. So prepare yourself to work 24/7 with someone breathing down your neck."

I shivered. Sabrina Kent bossing me around 24/7 was my definition of a nightmare.

"Of course I-I didn't know anything about it. She hates me," I stammered.

"Who?"

"Margherita," I said, nodding toward reception.

The telltale clacking of high heels made us both jump. She was here.

Marco sprang up and I straightened in my chair, hurriedly opening the graphics program on my screen. We both involuntarily looked up to admire her triumphant entrance.

It was as if she were walking the red carpet. She concealed her small stature with a pair of dizzyingly high black stilettos, her makeup was impeccable, and her Armani dress seemed as though she'd been sewn into it. Even though she was over fifty, she seemed to have made some deal with the devil in exchange for an elixir of youth. No bloating, tapered legs, a wispy waist, and dewy skin. Her bun was so tight that all the lines on her face were pulled taut—no Botox needed! She adjusted her glasses at the end of her nose and didn't deign to look at Margherita, who was already running behind her with a cup of coffee: black, no sugar. Even I knew her order. She barked it every morning like a rottweiler.

She took the steaming cup and slammed her office door shut behind her, causing all the glass dividers to shudder.

Her Majesty did not wish to be disturbed.

I gulped. "She said the meeting was today? Because I just remembered I have a doctor's appointment and—"

I didn't manage to finish my sentence, because her door swung open again and she barked my name.

"Caputi!"

Holy shit!

I threw Marco a desperate look as he gave me a thumbs-up for encouragement. Trembling, my hands sweating, I tucked a strand of hair back into my bun and practically sprinted to her office. I just arrived at her door when she barked, "Caputi, come in!"

I took a breath and entered. The air conditioning slapped me in the face.

She really was the Ice Queen.

"Caputi, sit down. Don't lurk there in the doorway, I don't have all morning."

"Yes, Sabrina."

Unsteady, I made my way to the armchair in the center of the room. Thank goodness I was wearing ballet flats.

"So, for next week," she went on, staring at her computer screen, "I want some proposals for Sound&K. It's an international record company. You'll be working with Marco and the rest of creative. Margherita will give you the file with all the details."

I thought she actually looked up from her computer screen to glance at me, if only for a millisecond. Maybe I imagined it.

"This project is very important to me," she hissed.

I was frozen in the chair, having forgotten to breathe.

"I want original ideas, unique. Above all, winning. The client presentation is in two weeks. Everything must be in my inbox by next Friday. Then I'll schedule a briefing with the media and production department. This ad campaign could be huge for our agency. Do. Not. Screw. This. Up. Understood?"

But I didn't really hear anything after "Friday."

Shit! Friday! Barcelona. Girl time. Rottweiler!

The devil on my shoulder was flashing images of bars along the Ramblas, glasses of sangria, and plates heaped with paella. On the other shoulder, the angel was shaking her head no. Absolutely not!

I would absolutely not forgo a weekend with the girls. But I couldn't exactly risk getting fired either.

"Something wrong, Caputi?"

I had probably gone pale, or maybe she had spotted the beads of sweat that were forming along my forehead.

"Of course not," I said. "I'll get right on it, Sabrina. Thank you for the opportunity—"

"I'm doing it for the agency, Caputi, not for you!"

"Of course," I mumbled.

"Good. You can go. Don't waste any more time."

Her ring-laden fingers immediately began hammering at the keyboard.

"Sorry, Sabrina? One thing."

Please don't let this piss her off.

She raised an eyebrow, inviting me to continue. Quickly.

I blushed, my cheeks aflame and my hands sweating.

"I just realized that the office will be closed this Friday, so I'll have to turn in the project early."

She must appreciate my initiative. Of course she does . . .

She shot me a look through her tortoiseshell glasses, snatched the calendar from the desk, and slammed it back down where I could see it.

"Do you see anything about a holiday here, Caputi?"

I shook my head, too terrified to open my mouth. She wasn't buying it.

"I only honor the holidays honored by God. In other words, the ones labeled 'holiday.' That includes Christmas, New Year's Day, and Easter. Nothing else exists. You have a tablet and you're paid to work from home. The office will be closed, but I want everything on Friday. Not before. And certainly not after. Is that clear?"

I imagined getting up and saluting this glamorous dictator. Instead, I mumbled a yes and left her office. As soon as I closed the door, I realized I had been holding my breath.

Shit!

I felt like I was walking on hot coals. My throat was dry at the thought of living up to Sabrina's expectations.

At least I wouldn't have to skip the trip. I just needed to find some Wi-Fi in Barcelona so I could connect long enough to send the email. That would be easy. I ran back to my desk and got straight to work.

There was no time to waste. I still had an entire wardrobe waiting to be crammed into an impossibly miniscule carry-on.

Chapter 2

Any teenager in the world would have killed for a fake ID to get close to the lead singer of the Sounds. The band was all over the radio with their number-one hit single.

Not me.

I had never been one of those screaming girls, pulling out my own hair, painting "Backstreet Boys" across my face.

I had managed to avoid that phase, and now my freaking karma was out for revenge.

After ten hours of SWOT analyses, PowerPoint graphics, and marketing strategies for the new ad campaign, I left the office and went to meet the girls at Smile, the fast food joint where we always stuffed ourselves full of junk at the end of the day.

I put on my headphones and scrolled through the songs on my phone as I walked. Timberlake, Rihanna, Lana Del Rey. And Justin Bieber—*how had that gotten there?* For the most part, I had stopped listening to Italian music. Just international rock, pop, and hip-hop.

It was all part of the Gioia rehab program. No dangerous songs that would feel like a punch in the stomach or a tightening of my chest.

Have you ever thought about how crazy it is that different combinations of seven little notes can make us feel things? A little like the letters in the alphabet. Certain combinations have the power to hurt, kill, annihilate you.

Ever since the bastard had left me, I'd fallen into a kind of limbo, a stupor that numbed all my feelings. I had shoved all my emotions into a remote corner of my heart, and there they would stay.

I turned up the volume on Pharrell's "Happy." It put me in such a good mood, I could have jumped around on the sidewalk in my own personal dance of ecstasy—a clear sign that my recovery was well underway.

Yes, I was almost over him.

And it's then, when your defenses are down, that destiny comes for you. Call it fate, call it karma, call it Lady Luck. All three were against me.

As I turned the corner, I felt my pulse quicken. I spun around, ready to knee a potential attacker in his nether regions, but instead I just froze.

Shit!

The blood drained from my cheeks, my stomach churned, and my heart jumped into my throat. My legs, at least, kept obeying orders, keeping me on my feet.

I was face-to-face with the person at the top of my blacklist. The executioner who had administered a lethal injection to the muscle pumping in my chest. Now it was fighting to keep moving.

I stared down the unnamable, incredulous.

The asshole.

Matteo Perri, my ex.

I had imagined what it would be like to run into him. I had stood in front of the mirror and practiced what I might say to him. I wasn't going to let him off easy.

But then a wave of memories rushed over me. I staggered backward, painfully aware of his eyes on me. He appeared to be speaking, but Pharrell drowned him out.

I took off my headphones, not breaking my stare.

Neither of us spoke.

I felt myself blush as he studied me, and hated it.

I could see his green eyes glistening like emeralds in the dark; I could feel their power over me. He was wearing a leather jacket over one of his usual gray T-shirts, and his toned legs showed through his ripped jeans.

He was gorgeous . . . and dangerous. I had to remember that. He should have been required by law to walk around with a skull and two crossbones blinking over his head wherever he went.

There are two types of people: those who fight, who keep getting back up; and those who instantly give up, overwhelmed by life's injustices.

I was the latter.

I had two options: I could kick his ass, or I could tell him off for being such an ass that he'd dumped me with a note.

But I chose a third option—the fastest and the most painless. I continued on my way.

I walked quickly. Very quickly. I was practically running. The girls were waiting for me at Smile, and you should never keep a lady waiting, much less three.

I felt his eyes on my back.

"Gioia, wait!" he shouted, running after me. "Gioia!"

How could he possibly say my name like that when all I wanted to do was chop his balls off?

I sped up till I was moving faster than Usain Bolt at the London Olympics.

"Gioia, we need to talk," he begged.

That was the last straw.

I stopped, my spine rigid and my hands itching to slap him across the cheek. *We need to talk?* I turned to face him and exploded.

"Now you're telling me that we need to talk?" I yelled.

I had stopped listening to our songs, tried to forget his voice, avoided the places we used to go, and hadn't as much as glanced at WhatsApp. And for what? Nothing. Everything had just been on pause, and now that I was standing across from him again, it was as if someone had hit "Play." It was as if not one damn second had passed since that day at the airport.

No!

I pointed my finger, almost touching his chest.

"Did it ever cross your mind to tell me whatever it was you had to say months ago?" My voice was rising. At least I didn't have an audience for this free sidewalk show.

"I'm sorry, I messed up. But at least let me explain."

He stepped forward. I stepped back.

He had always been breathtakingly beautiful.

Tousled chestnut hair and tired green eyes. His nose a little crooked from when he broke it in a soccer game. He was a night owl: always out late with the band and sleeping until noon, when he'd get up and play his guitar. After a few hard years, the band had gotten good enough to record their first album, and it had exploded all over the country.

He stepped closer. Too close.

You can do this, Gioia!

I held my breath. I didn't want to feel the way I was feeling.

No!

I gazed into his hypnotic eyes. "The girls are waiting for me. I have to go," I said with resolve.

I turned to leave, but Matteo grabbed me by the wrist.

God, those hands.

I knew them well: rough, solid, strong.

How many nights had I spent watching him stroke his guitar, among other things?

We stared at each other, both of us panting.

"It's always so nice to see you," he said with a timid smile.

I swooned at the two dimples at the corners of his mouth.

He jammed his hands into his back pockets and shifted his weight from one foot to the other. He was nervous too. At least he did care, after all.

I sighed loudly and composed myself. Standing up taller, I repressed all the feelings that were resurfacing: sadness, disappointment, bitterness, and maybe even some love.

"I'd better go," I said quietly, looking down.

And without another word, no ciao, no wave, I walked as fast as I could in the direction of the bar, a little disappointed he didn't try to stop me.

◆　◆　◆

In high school, Matteo had been the classic beautiful bad boy, and girls went out of their minds for him. Ramones or AC/DC shirts, ripped black jeans, matted hair, dimples, and a smile that melted more than one heart.

It had taken me longer than most to surrender to his charms.

He never noticed me in school, of course, and I didn't see him around for a few years after graduation, but then I ran into him at a party at a bar in town. Bea had already gone off with some jerk, my sister was chatting with a friend, not even aware of the line of men behind her, and Ludovica was waiting for a special someone to ask her to dance.

But I was a wallflower. I'd gotten so used to going from home to school and back home again that my social life consisted of intimate evenings with marketing books and a few dates with *Gossip Girl*.

"What are you waiting for?" I had asked Ludo, who kept scanning the room frantically.

"Francesco should be here any minute," she said, hearts practically floating out of her eyes.

Suddenly, the lights went out and everyone began to scream Matteo's name.

His electric guitar cut through the dark, and one at a time, the band members chimed in. Then the spotlight came up on him, front man for the Sounds, and the music exploded along with the crowd.

I couldn't take my eyes off him. Matteo was up on that stage in his tight jeans and a shirt that lifted at every movement to reveal his toned abs. I scarcely noticed when Bea, having shrugged off the jerk, dragged me and Ludo onto the dance floor. He was so good at singing and playing the guitar—and gyrating his pelvis—that as everyone else raised their hands up and moved and sang with the band, I stood frozen, mesmerized.

I felt intimidated by his bad-boy gaze, and all the courage I had gulped down in the form of two beers completely evaporated. I unglued my eyes from his body and looked up to his face, only to discover he was staring straight back at me. I wanted to look away. Normally I would have, but I just couldn't. There was something hypnotic about his eyes.

I turned my head.

"How beautiful is Matteo?" gushed Bea, jumping up and down and splashing her beer everywhere. "Ladies, this one knows how to use his voice."

Matteo went into a guitar solo.

"And he's not bad with his hands either," she added.

I wish she had been wrong.

The way he held the guitar so close to his chest, the way he stroked the chords, his eyes lost somewhere in the melody . . . He was like a snake charmer, and all the girls were under the spell of that sound, that voice, those hands. He was just so cool.

"Rock star charm," I said, trying to justify my paralysis.

I finally peeled my eyes off of him and joined in the dancing, but I could still feel him looking at me. Song after song, and two more icy beers later, I let go of all my inhibitions and dared to dance near the stage.

By the end of the band's set, everyone was putty in their hands. Myself included.

The girls were shrieking and making eyes at the band, especially Matteo. The men were running around with pints in hand, beer sloshing everywhere.

When the stage lights went off, I dropped into a chair, drenched in sweat, my hair matted to my forehead.

"What a night!" Beatrice panted, gleaming. "We need to do this again."

I gathered my hair into some semblance of a ponytail; my clothes were clinging to my body like a second skin.

"Where's Ludovica?" I asked.

"She was dancing with Francesco, didn't you see?" asked Melly, the only one of us who still looked impeccable after jumping up and down for an hour with a bunch of elbowing drunks.

"No."

"Maybe because your eyes were glued to the stage?" She smiled.

"Who needs another drink?" I asked, ignoring her.

I went over to the bar and tried to get the bartender's attention. All of five foot three, I got swallowed into the crowd of drunken thugs, who didn't hold back from making vulgar comments in my direction.

Five minutes later, I was about to give up all hope of ordering when I heard a deep voice behind me.

"Let the lady through."

Then I turned and saw the singer of the Sounds inches away from my face. The only time I had seen a rock star so close was when I was ten and used to practice kissing techniques on my Nick Carter poster.

But he didn't give me time to think; he just took my hand and led me through the crowd. He was like Moses parting the Red Sea. Except that instead of water, it was a sea of tattooed, drunken dudes.

My first red carpet walk with a singer!

Romantic.

When we reached the bar, he placed his hand on the small of my back, guiding me ahead of him so I could lean against the wood, which was damp with beer.

"Joe!" he called, raising his hand. His voice made my ear tingle. I could feel the strength of his arm, his cologne mixing with sweat after two hours of singing. "Three beers for me. And for the lady?" He threw me an inquiring look.

I swallowed, acutely aware of his hand on my back, his other arm resting on the bar. I was trapped by his body.

I was too embarrassed to look him in the face, so I looked down, my cheeks burning, and said, "Two beers."

I ran a nervous hand through my hair. I was a sweaty mess, while all the other girls looked like they'd just stepped out of a shampoo commercial.

"So, did you like the concert?" The voice of the Sounds snapped me out of my self-pity and took me by such surprise that when I lifted my chin to look up at him, I bumped straight into his dimples.

And that's when I fell in love.

There was a playful light in his eyes, his scruff accentuated his jaw-line, his hair was disheveled and sweaty—at least I had company in the messy hair department.

I blinked a few times to be sure I wasn't seeing things. He was there, right in front of me, a funny look on his face.

"You were . . . you were amazing," I stammered.

I had never been the kind of girl who stammered.

"You know, at the beginning, I saw you just standing there on the dance floor and I thought maybe you didn't like us," he said, still smiling that mischievous little smile.

My heart did a somersault.

"No, the music had nothing to do with it!" I said, gesticulating wildly. How could I tell him I had been awestruck just looking at him up there onstage? "I'm not a very good dancer."

I omitted the fact that I never missed an episode of *Dance in the UK* and that I could do a damn good Harlem Shake.

"You looked pretty good out there to me," he said as Joe set our beers down.

Another somersault.

I blushed scarlet, grateful for the low lights. I tried to stop my hands from trembling as I took out my wallet to pay, but Matteo's hand closed over mine to stop me. An electric shock jolted me from head to toe; my fingers felt like they were on fire.

Stupid, weak, stupid heart!

"Let me get this. It's the least I can do to thank you for the ego boost." He smiled again and put the money down on the bar. "Thanks, Joe!" he shouted over the delirium.

"Thanks," I said. The word barely escaped my throat.

Please ask me out! Please!

I took the beer and offered up a shy smile to all five feet eight inches of him standing over me. "You didn't . . . I . . ."

He took my hand in his. "What does a guy have to do around here to get your name?" he asked, tracing circles on my palm. "You already know mine."

Good one, Gioia . . .

I was so busy drooling over him that I'd forgotten the basic rules for meeting another human being.

"Gioia!" Bea called. When she saw me holding hands with the Sounds' lead singer, she glowed bright enough to light up all of Italy for a month. "Matteo," she purred. "Great show. You certainly know how to woo the ladies, if you know what I mean." She winked.

I had to do some damage control. Fast.

"Bea, we should go—"

"Are you kidding me?" she slurred dramatically. She grabbed my beer and took a swig. "I'm not tired."

Matteo was clearly entertained. "Beatrice, you haven't changed one bit."

Bea didn't notice the hint of mocking in his voice, or at least she didn't show it.

"Hey, Matteo!" someone shouted from the stage. "Lay off the pretty girls and bring us our damn beers."

"Ladies, I have to go." He excused himself with a little bow. He kissed Beatrice on the cheeks as she made eyes at a blond kid standing near us.

Then it was my turn.

Breathe, Gioia!

He took my hand, pulled me toward him, and gave me a lingering kiss on each cheek.

"My self-esteem and I are eternally grateful," he whispered in my ear.

With one last mischievous wink, he took the beers and left.

Oh. My. God.

I grabbed a coaster and began to fan myself with it. That man had absolutely demolished my self-control.

I turned to Bea, but she had already disappeared again with my beer. *What a piece of work,* I thought, rolling my eyes. I called to Joe like we were old friends and ordered another two beers.

I was drumming my fingers on the bar when I felt a hand on my back again. I turned and it was like déjà vu. Matteo had reappeared behind me, those incredible dimples just inches away again.

"Call me. You owe me a beer."

He gave me a peck on the cheek and, dumbstruck, I passively accepted the napkin he slipped into my hand. My gaze chased him back across the room as he vanished into the crowd.

Call me. You owe me a beer . . .

He was gone and my brain had left with him.

I looked down at his number and when I looked up again, I already had it memorized.

◆　◆　◆

So Matteo had asked me out with a napkin, and he broke up with me with a letter.

Women always complain that their partners don't write them little notes, that they're too busy playing video games or watching sports.

Two notes, like two tickets, had passed through my hands. The first was an invitation to ecstasy. The second was a one-way passage to the Broken Hearts Club.

At least he'd written it by hand and spared me the pain of getting dumped in Courier New twelve.

Chapter 3

In addition to hating men, I also hated airports. We had compatibility issues.

After a never-ending line at check-in and another at security, where I kept setting off the metal detectors for some mysterious reason, we discovered that our flight to Barcelona had been delayed for an hour. But at least God invented duty-free.

After trying out the new Marc Jacobs makeup collection and spending nearly all our money on miniature perfumes, the girls and I sat down at a café in the terminal.

It was my third espresso of the day; I was still trying to wake up. I'd been up all night going over the Sound&K project. All the files were loaded onto a USB stick; I had double-checked my tablet, phone, and chargers before I left; and I'd set my phone alarm for four thirty in the afternoon with a five-minute warning.

I couldn't mess this up! Sound&K was the biggest recording company in the US, with offices in Milan, London, and Tokyo.

I had this. Perfect timing and email would save my ass. I repeated it like a mantra.

"Gioia. I'm sorry, but you're doing it wrong."

I yawned. Another lesson on how to conquer a man from *The Gospel According to Beatrice*. For months now, she had been telling me how dull my existence was, that my social life was appalling and my love life nonexistent.

"I've said it before and I'll say it again: there's a bomb in you just waiting to explode."

"You have me mistaken for someone else."

"You don't get it. You're not living, you're surviving. You're just skimming the surface of life, and one day you're going to explode. God, Gioia, can't you hear the ticking?"

"No." I shook my head. "I . . . ear . . . m . . . stom . . . owli . . ."

"What?"

I swallowed a mouthful of chocolate muffin and washed it down with a sip of coffee.

"I hear my stomach growling."

"You need to grow a pair, my friend. We need to find the right man for you. One who knows how to trigger your detonator."

I rolled my eyes.

"Do you want to end up like them?"

I followed her gaze to a group of nuns sitting behind us.

I cleared my throat and launched a mayday look in the direction of Melly and Ludo, who were absorbed in the Barcelona guidebooks, dog-earing the pages with the monuments they wanted to see. They were so used to Bea's sermons that they didn't even look up.

"I'm not saying you have to do online dating, Gioia." She was using her most condescending tone, the one that preceded a coup de grâce. "But you've been out of the game for five months now, and if you let yourself get too old, you'll be completely out of the running."

"It's not like I don't know how to have a good time!" I protested.

She gave me a skeptical look. "Are you sure about that? You really look like you've given up. You absolutely must change your shitty OOTD."

"My what?"

"Your outfits of the day!" She laughed. "Your wardrobe. Look at yourself. You look like a widow in mourning."

I looked down at my black shirt, black pants, and belted leather jacket. Black. Like the boots on my feet.

"You have to capture a man's imagination. Surprise him. God gave them the balls and us the brains. We can outsmart them by wearing a push-up bra and showing a little skin."

"I have nothing to show off," I replied, looking down again.

I was the classic pear-shaped woman: Mediterranean from the waist down, German from the chest up.

Thighs and ass, yes. Breasts, forget about it.

Bea snapped her fingers in front of my face to get my attention. She leaned back in her chair and crossed her arms. Then she cocked her head to the right and left, studying me.

Help!

"When was the last time you had sex?"

I almost choked on a chocolate chip. I looked around to make sure no one had heard her and slunk down in my chair, mortified.

"Bea! Do you want the whole airport to know about my sex life? Maybe they'll let you broadcast it over the loudspeakers."

I snatched a menu off the table and pretended to read it.

How embarrassing!

It was then that I spotted a man sitting two tables behind us. He was listening to his iPod with Ray-Ban Wayfarers on his head and his face buried in a book.

"Oh my God! I knew it!" Bea wasn't going to let this go.

"Knew what?"

"How long? Please tell me someone has been up in your business since Matteo."

"Stop it, Bea!" Melly erupted, covering her ears with her hands. "I don't want to know. I'm going to get a newspaper, and when I get back, I want the interrogation about my sister's sex life to be over!"

She gathered the guidebooks from the table, and I watched her disappear up the escalator with Ludo.

"So?"

"Jesus Christ, Bea! Just drop it already. He only left me five months ago."

"Only? Only five months? We need to do something about this." She brought her fist down on the table, spilling a cup of coffee. "No more chastity. I got you off the couch, but that's not enough. From now on, your prescription is fun. I order it as your life coach. If you're not down to have some fun, men will think you're the kind of girl who's just dreaming of diamond rings and a bun in the oven. You need to be a little more"—Bea stopped to find the right word—"generous, damn it!"

Have you noticed how much she swears? It's her trademark.

"Generous?"

"Generous. I'm not saying you have to give it up on the first date. You want to keep them interested. Make him sweat, but not too much. Wait too long and you'll have to start getting Botox down there."

Jesus, Mary, and Joseph . . .

I was absolutely mortified. I slunk down even more, until I was practically under the table. I wanted a sinkhole to open up and swallow me whole.

Bea was so caught up in Operation Save Caputi: Give an *O* to Gioia that the elderly couple sitting next to us was fully up to date about my sex life.

That's when I saw the man sitting behind us close his book, pick up his bag, and begin to walk toward the escalators. For a split second, our eyes met, and then he put on his sunglasses.

He was beautiful. He would have been perfect for Dolce & Gabbana's spring/summer collection. Had he smiled at me? *Impossible.* He couldn't have heard Bea with his headphones on.

Thank God!

"We need to make this our project," Bea went on, undeterred, as I followed the dark, handsome stranger until he disappeared from my sight.

"*We?*"

Fortunately, they announced our gate over the loudspeakers; I walked over to rejoin Melly and Ludo on planet earth, dragging my carry-on behind me and ignoring Bea, who still hadn't stopped talking.

"I'm going to run to the bathroom," I said.

I parked my suitcase next to my sister's and followed the signs for the restroom, but then I saw the guy from the café entering a souvenir shop.

There were still a few minutes before we had to board. I was dying for a closer look—I just had to be careful not to get caught.

With his black leather jacket, jeans, and white shirt, he looked like he'd just walked out of *Vogue*. He was pretty tall—maybe six feet—and towered over me. He had broad shoulders, flat abs, and toned legs. His dark hair—not too short, not too long—was disheveled to perfection, as if he had just run a hand through it. I relished the sexy way he fingered the collar of his jacket—just as I ran smack into him.

Shit!

Standing ovation for me.

After he turned, his frown morphed into an amused smile.

Oh. My. God! What a smile.

I normally would have just excused myself and fled, but I was rooted to the spot by eyes that made my whole body tremble. My brain wouldn't respond to orders; my mouth was incapable of articulating a simple apology. I just stood there gaping at him as he looked back at me, entertained.

That smile should have been illegal for my heart and my *you know where*. After months of depression, my hormones had finally snapped to full attention.

I swallowed hard and came out with an "Oops." Then I broke eye contact and moved faster than anyone has ever moved in a souvenir shop.

"Oops?" What the hell was that? Maybe I did need to take a lesson or two from Beatrice. I nonchalantly picked up a snow globe and didn't look over my shoulder, not even when I felt him pass behind me.

When I finally turned around, Mr. Cover Boy was at the cash register. I watched the cashier gaze longingly as he left. I was pretty sure I had the same dazed expression on my face.

I quickly bought the snow globe and hurried back to the gate.

"Hey, where were you?" asked Melissa.

"There was a line." I shrugged.

I took out my ticket and ID to give to the attendants. Then I froze.

The guy was right there.

In line for the same flight.

What were the chances that Mr. Cover Boy would be on the same two-hour flight as me? After all I'd been through, maybe fate, karma, and Lady Luck were finally on my side.

Mr. Cover Boy's seat was at the back of the plane, which meant I spent the entire flight straining my neck to get a good look at him in all his glory. On our way out of El Prat, I took one last, hungry look and caught him staring at me.

Then the girls and I got into a taxi with an Egyptian driver who didn't speak a lick of Spanish and made our way to the hotel.

"I can't believe you guys convinced me to go out dressed like this!" I exclaimed, catching a glimpse of myself in a shop window.

After an afternoon of sightseeing like exemplary tourists, we'd freshened up at our hotel in the Gothic Quarter and were headed back out to feast on paella and sangria.

I tugged at the hem of the microscopic black lace dress.

"What are you talking about? It's a gorgeous dress," insisted Bea, who had stuffed herself into a golden dress, her hair up in an immaculate bun.

"A few feet of fabric that barely covers my ass isn't exactly what I'd call a dress," I snapped.

It was too tight across the chest, too clingy around my soft hips, and way too short. I had paired it with black Louboutins—the only high heels in my entire shoe collection of ballet flats and sneakers.

"Stop it," my sister interjected. "You look beautiful."

I looked again at my reflection. I actually didn't look so bad. I wore my hair soft and loose down my back and had opted for minimal makeup—just a little mascara and some lip gloss.

"Why are you lugging such a huge bag around?" my life coach asked.

"For someone with more style rules than *Cosmopolitan*, you of all people should know that this bag isn't *a bag*, it's *the bag*, and it cost me a kidney." And a diplomatic crisis with my father, who was horrified by what I spent on purses.

Barcelona's oldest streets weren't the best for stilettos, so Melly and I held hands for support, while Bea strutted like she was on a catwalk. Ludovica trailed behind us, busy on the phone with her other half.

She had been with her boyfriend, Francesco, for four years now. They were the perfect couple, the kind you read about in romance novels. He looked at her like she was the only woman on the planet.

Was I jealous? Hell yes.

"Why isn't this guy messaging me?" Melly said. "He's online."

Like Bea, Melly was impossible not to notice, with her cascade of perfect chocolate-colored curls, bronzed skin, and super-toned physique thanks to the hours upon hours she spent at the gym. In spite of being my sister, she was my total opposite: dark-eyed, tan, and thin. I was pale with green eyes and spaghetti-straight hair—and, like I've already mentioned, a world-champion couch potato. Jealousy is an ugly beast.

"I know that tone, Melly," I said, struggling to stay upright on my heels. "Don't start. He's probably chatting with the guys from the gym."

"But if he's online, he could at least take the time to say hi."

"Oh God. Are you turning into one of those emoticon women?" Bea snorted as she continued her one-woman runway show down the Ramblas. "I can't stand those dudes who wink at me on WhatsApp and then take ages to actually ask me out. Put your phone down, pick your ass up, and ring my doorbell. It's easier. Alex needs to act like a man so you don't make yourself crazy trying to figure out what a dumb smiley face means."

"All I want is a simple 'hello' from my boyfriend when he sees me online," Melissa countered. "I'm not looking for a marriage proposal."

She smiled faintly, but I knew that behind the smile was a suffering heart. My sister was a traditional kind of girl, dreaming of the perfect boy, a ring on her finger, and children.

Unfortunately for her, Alex Basso was the opposite.

After years of back and forth, tears, canceled holidays, and slammed doors, Alex had finally taken the plunge. He'd given her keys to his apartment and single dresser drawer. But he was still too focused on his work, his friends—and lately, extreme sports—to put a noose around his neck. He was looking for a thrill, just not the kind of thrill Melissa had in mind.

"I bet he's dying of jealousy knowing you're here without him, with three other awesome women, in Bea's dangerous hands," I joked, throwing an arm around her.

I actually was convinced that Alex loved Melissa, but he took her for granted. He needed a little jolt.

"Tonight, after we've had a few drinks, we'll take a picture and send it to him," Bea said, swaying her hips back and forth, knowing how many men were watching her.

Yes, I was jealous of Bea too . . . especially of her brazenness.

After a dinner of Catalan paella and a few rounds of shots, we walked back to the Gothic Quarter.

"Hey—look!" Beatrice yelled.

Ludo, Melly, and I looked where she was pointing: a lit-up sign across the street.

"There's karaoke tonight!" She clapped her hands. "I love, love, love karaoke."

Her exuberance was probably the combination of sangria and shots. Not that I was much better off. I crossed my arms and stared at the river of people flowing into the bar.

"I love it too, but I've humiliated myself enough recently."

"You don't know anyone here."

"No. Not happening. I'll just make a fool of myself and, even if I don't remember afterward, you jerks will make sure there are photos and videos to remind me."

I looked back to the bar and the neon sign: "Touch Music."

No! I couldn't risk a repeat of that night with the gross blond boy.

And that's how I ended up sitting in the corner of the karaoke bar, alone, clutching a martini.

Bea, Ludo, and Melissa were already up near the stage, trying to get their names on the list, ready to play rock star.

The outside of Touch Music reminded me of a Las Vegas casino, but in reality, it was just a modern bar with tables scattered in front of a stage lit with blue spotlights. To the left, there was a long bar with bottles of liquor on display along a wall lined with LED lights.

I played with the olive in my drink and then decided to look busy by texting Andrea, a good friend of mine from college who'd moved to New York just over a year ago to work as an intern at a weekly paper.

I fished around in my bag and finally found my phone. There were five missed calls from the office, one from a private number, and two unread messages.

A shiver of terror ran down my spine. The alcohol in my body suddenly evaporated as if by magic. What could they be calling about? I had sent the email with the completed project to Sabrina at five on the dot from a Starbucks near the Sagrada Família.

Five exactly. Not one minute before, not one minute after.

I was sure of it.

I frowned and opened the first message. It was Marco.

```
Gioia, where the hell are you? Call me
the second you see this.
```

I looked at the time. It was after eleven.

I read the other message.

```
MS. CAPUTI, WHY DIDN'T YOU SEND THE
SOUND&K PROJECT AS REQUESTED? DON'T
BOTHER WITH EXCUSES.
```

No, no, no. I was sure I had sent it.

Only someone as sure of herself as the Ice Queen would write a message in all caps. Madame Rottweiler.

All the missed calls had been made five minutes apart.

Oh shit!

But I'd sent the email! I had entered my password, opened my inbox, and sent out the draft I'd so carefully prepared.

I fished my tablet out of my bag. It would be okay. It had to be. I'd check my inbox again, make sure the email had gone through, and Sabrina would be forced to tear up the notice of dismissal that must have been sitting on my desk already.

I nervously drummed my fingers on the table as I waited for Google to load. I rubbed my forehead as if it were Aladdin's lamp and I could make a wish on it. It was probably just as shiny.

Shit! No roaming data on the tablet and Wi-Fi access denied. I absolutely had to get the bar's password.

If I didn't, I'd be out of a job by Monday.

I launched myself halfway over the bar and asked an inked-up, muscular bartender for the Internet password. She didn't even look at me as she continued to shake cocktails and pour shots for a bunch of suits at the end of the bar. I tried another bartender, but then the room went black and a spotlight hit the stage, where there was a microphone and a huge screen on one wall.

The games had begun.

As I stood there on tiptoe, clasping my phone in one sweaty hand and my tablet in the other, I felt someone tug at my arm.

"Come dance!" Ludovica, so tipsy she was about to fall over, dragged me toward the dance floor.

"I can't," I said, squirming to free myself from her surprisingly strong grip. "I'm in deep shit," I started, but realized I was talking to myself.

Melissa, Ludovica, and Beatrice were already on the dance floor, applauding and egging on the first victim of the night's karaoke competition.

Perfect!

I went back to the bar, where Ms. Tattooed Biceps finally deigned to look at me and, with an annoyed look, asked what I wanted to drink.

"The password . . . I mean, a martini and the Wi-Fi password . . . please!" I mumbled nervously.

I had a funny feeling about the email. Had it really not gone through? Was my luck that bad?

"Yes," chimed fate, karma, and Lady Luck in unison.

"Our Internet's out."

Damn it. I had found the only bar in all of Barcelona with no Internet.

Shit. Shit. Shit.

I looked over at the girls, who were onstage singing "Like a Virgin." They rolled their hips and clapped to the beat, and Bea blew kisses to the men she'd met at the bar. There was no way I was going to get them out of there.

I went back to our table and downed the second martini in one gulp, trying to numb my nerves.

Frantic, I went into the drafts folder stored on my phone and found it: the stupid message that was going to cost me my job.

Argh! How could it not have sent? I wanted to scream.

I moved around the whole table in the hopes of catching a signal.

Nothing.

I raised my phone up in the air, praying that one tiny bar would appear.

Still nothing.

I grabbed my bag and went on the hunt for a signal. I kicked off my shoes to save time, and also because the martinis had already hit my legs.

Meanwhile, my friends were giving their own little concert: after Madonna, they opted for Beyoncé's "Drunk in Love." Judging by the cheers, the men in the bar were enjoying it very much.

The email, Gioia! Send the email!

If anyone had seen me at that moment, they would have thought I was insane: I was carrying my shoes, holding my phone up to the ceiling as if it were Harry Potter's wand, and stalking around the karaoke bar on tiptoe like a mental patient.

At least no one noticed me—they were all too focused on the three wild girls onstage.

I was about to retreat to my table, defeated, ready to get wasted and celebrate my unemployed status, when a data signal finally appeared on my screen.

Thank God!

I raised my phone up again and the signal went away. So I lowered it. Still nothing.

Had I imagined it?

After a few attempts, all in vain, I headed toward the dead center of the room—the only place I hadn't tried.

That's when I slammed right into someone. A very muscular and warm someone.

"Sorry," I muttered, not looking up. The signal was back! I scrambled to send the email.

"Do you have it out for me or something?" The voice was so deep and sexy that it pulled my attention away from my phone, even though the email still wouldn't send.

I looked up and stopped breathing. My senses went on alert as my body ran out of oxygen.

Come on, Gioia! Inhale, exhale.

I dropped my shoes and bag to the floor, spilling all its contents. I noticed his pristine white shirt pulled over his muscular chest, his tapered waist, and his tanned arms protruding from his rolled-up shirtsleeves. I stared mutely into a pair of eyes that were dark like chocolate, and a smile that still should have been illegal.

"Hey—everything okay?" he asked, mildly concerned.

I staggered and two hands grabbed me by the waist, preventing me from making a bigger fool of myself than I already had.

What the hell?

Mr. Cover Boy from the airport was towering over me again. His perfume, a mixture of citrus and Acqua di Giò, tickled my nose. Cover Boy was truly beautiful. His leather jacket and jeans had been replaced by a suit tailored for his body, and his white shirt set off his tanned face. If this morning he'd looked like he had stepped off the cover of *Vogue*, tonight he was ready for an issue of *Elle Wedding*.

And I just stood there gaping at him like an idiot.

He was the one to break the spell.

"Everything okay?" he asked playfully. His Italian was perfect, though with a hint of an accent I couldn't place.

I followed his gaze. With my hand still reaching toward the ceiling, clutching my phone, my other arm loose against my side, and "Dancing Queen" playing in the background, I looked like Agnetha from ABBA.

"Sorry," I stammered. I stepped back, and Mr. Cover Boy let his hands slide away from my waist.

I owed my dignity an apology as well. I was such an idiot! I had literally thrown myself at this man twice now.

"It's your lucky day," I joked. "Twice in just a few hours."

He knelt down next to me and helped me collect the contents of my purse. "You can say that again," he murmured.

I looked up to see that perfect face again: chiseled features, sculpted jaw, mouth made for kissing. A few strands of hair fell over his forehead.

So the famous Greek gods really did exist. There was one kneeling across from me, handing me a tampon.

Shoot me now!

"Thanks," I muttered, my cheeks burning.

A smile spread across his face that scrambled my insides like a cocktail shaker.

I leaned against the bar to slide my shoes back on, but Mr. Cover Boy took them from my hand.

"Let me help."

He wrapped his long, straight fingers around my bare ankle. I was on fire.

"I admire you girls for enduring these heels."

That smile was a weapon of mass destruction.

"You seem like the kind of guy who likes women who wear heels."

He slipped on my other shoe, stood up, and leaned on the bar. "I do, huh? What kind of guy do you think I am?"

A roar from the crowd gave me a second to think of an answer in this conversation that could have been taken from a *Cosmopolitan* quiz. Bea was singing the chorus to "It's Raining Men," while Melly, Ludo, and the audience were dancing at the edge of the stage. The men in suits and ties were laughing, downing martinis, and dancing.

"Oh, like the rest of them. Your brain goes to mush as soon as you see a pair of tits in a push-up bra, a short skirt, and legs that seem long in a pair of heels." I turned and gestured toward the men drooling over Beatrice. "Look at them. They're like starving hyenas."

My brain-mouth filter was definitely on the fritz. The second martini had been a bad idea.

"I'm glad you hold the male sex in such high esteem. So young and already so cruel." He brought one hand to his heart as if mortally wounded. "So you expect me to drool over that?"

I followed his gaze.

"That" was Beatrice. My best friend. The woman who'd held my hair back as I vomited out my heart over Matteo.

Oh, you're throwing shade in the wrong direction, Cover Boy!

"Just because a woman goes to a bar alone doesn't mean she's looking to give it up. The clothes do not a woman make, Mr. Big Shot!"

"Mr. Big Shot? Well, at least I don't dress like I'm in mourning!" His eyes burned into me, appraising every inch of exposed skin. "Though I must say you're hardly in mourning tonight," he added in a husky whisper.

"What?!" My skin crawled and a cold shiver ran down my spine. He had overheard my conversation with Beatrice at the airport!

He sipped his beer, assuming the classic I'm-hot-and-I-know-it bar pose, his elbows resting on the counter.

"Do you really believe that stuff? That all it takes is a push-up bra and some skin? Going around half-naked doesn't leave much to the imagination, and your friend is living proof. There's not much left to fantasize about when the gift is already out of the box."

Oh. My. God.

I knew I should be defending Bea's honor, but I couldn't get past the fact that he'd heard her lecturing me on how to snag a man. And all about my nonexistent sex life. I wanted to dig my own grave and crawl into it. The color drained from my face as a wry smile spread across his perfect one.

Fantastic!

"You know it's rude to eavesdrop on other people's conversations, don't you?"

"It was impossible not to hear it."

"Weren't you listening to music?"

"Don't you know better than to stare at people?"

His melty chocolate eyes won hands down over my green ones any day.

"Hey, boss." A stocky drunk man in his fifties stood up on a chair near the stage and yelled to Mr. Cover Boy in English through teeth clenched around a cigar. "Get over here! You don't know what you're missing."

Great. The starving hyenas were apparently his employees.

"Excuse me?" I asked with a hint of irony. "Maybe you'd like to introduce me to one of those hyenas?"

He flashed a playful grin. "Touché!" he said. Then he extended his hand. "I'm Christian, friend of the hyenas."

I shook it, hoping he wouldn't notice my sweaty palm. "Gioia," I responded, flashing a smile. "Friend of '*that*.'"

And an eternal loser.

I noticed he wasn't wearing any rings. So he probably wasn't married, unless he had hidden his ring in his pocket. Maybe he was gay.

"What can I get you?" asked Ms. Tattooed Biceps, clearly more interested in Christian than our order.

"I'll have an electric," he said. "What about you?"

"I'll have the same," I said, in no condition to stand there and contemplate what to order.

The man standing before me had managed to annoy me with his playboy allure. Yet somehow I was still swooning.

"Now, what brings a nice Italian girl like you to a Barcelona karaoke bar?" he asked with a mischievous grin as the bartender set two drinks in front of us, her eyes locked on Christian.

"Vacation," I replied, sipping a glass brimming with blue liquid. I could distinctly feel the rum and vodka burning their way down my esophagus before their warmth spread to my belly.

It was disgusting.

"And what brings you and your American hyenas to a Barcelona karaoke bar?" I asked.

He laughed.

God, that mouth.

"Music," he said, fiddling with his straw. "I work for a record company in the US."

Well, at least I hadn't tried to sing in front of him.

"You're on the hunt for new talent? At a karaoke bar?"

My girls certainly wouldn't be candidates, the way they were butchering Lana Del Rey's "Young and Beautiful."

"Let's just say karaoke attracts some interesting characters." He gave me a long, intense look from under his lush black eyelashes. "Not all of them are singers."

I flushed again, my heart in my throat, and tried to cover my embarrassment by taking a long, disgusting drink of my electric.

"So, have you found your next hit singer?" I asked, looking in the direction of the stage.

Now the girls were out on the dance floor, while the guys had begun a drunken interpretation of "Piú Bella Cosa" by Eros Ramazzotti.

It was a sing-off, Spain versus Italy.

"Well, your loud friend isn't bad," he said with a little wink.

I glared back at him.

"She needs to work on pitch, but she has a great presence. Think she'd go out with me?" He threw back the last of his blue swill.

I turned away and managed to choke down another sip. When I turned back, he was still there, but closer, and the pheromones hit me all over again. My heart jumped into my throat and my knees began to shake.

Mr. Cover Boy held his head at a dangerous tilt and brought his mouth an inch away from my ear.

Breathe, Gioia!

"Gioia . . ." he began, his breath on my cheek. If I had turned an inch, our lips would have touched. "I'm just teasing you," he concluded flatly, and then drew back with a smirk.

Jesus Christ!

I had never felt so scrutinized, embarrassed, and turned on all at once.

It had to be the drinks. Yes, it was definitely the alcohol's fault. It had lowered my guard or I wouldn't have let myself be taken in by such a pretty face. Not again.

I looked again at his illegal smile and felt myself begin to slip. *No!* I absolutely would not be seduced by his charms.

My phone interrupted us with a beep. Thank God, or I might have thrown myself at this joker.

I looked at my phone and swore. The email, I still had to send the email! I panicked, shaking my phone around in all directions.

Damn it, signal, where are you?

"Everything okay?" asked Christian, cocking an eyebrow.

Okay?! Not only was I humiliating myself in front of the world's hottest guy, I was on the brink of being fired.

Inhale, exhale.

Inhale, exhale.

My cheeks were burning again, but I clung to a thread of dignity.

"I absolutely must send an email and I don't have reception. I'm in the only bar in all of Barcelona with no Wi-Fi. And yes, I really do have to send it right this second because it's for Sabrina Kent, aka the Ice Queen, also known as Madame Rottweiler, to whom all projects have to be delivered by five on Fridays. I was supposed to send the documents for our Sound-and-something campaign today, and believe me, I was 100 percent sure I had. But apparently it didn't work because this fucking email is still here in my drafts and it refuses to leave my damned phone!" I caught my breath, surprised I had spilled my entire sob story to a stranger. "I might as well consider myself fired," I moaned. "I should probably cancel my return ticket and stay in Barcelona to sell tin cans on the beach."

"Calm down."

Two strong arms came to rest on my shoulders. I looked up to meet Christian's gaze, and that Cover Boy smile made me forget about Sabrina again for a fraction of a second. I wanted to tell her to go to hell, along with the Sound-and-something project and the entire agency.

"Breathe."

Butterflies filled my stomach, though it might have just been the electric.

"Your boss sounds like a nightmare," Christian murmured, then sipped beer straight from the bottle. God, I never knew a simple gesture could be so sexy. "So you have to send this email to Madame . . . ?"

"Rottweiler," I breathed, defeated. "That woman will devour anyone in her path. She has an iceberg for a heart." Tears clouded my eyes.

"Hey there, everything's going to be okay," said Christian, taking my empty glass from my hands and replacing it with a napkin from the bar—a napkin which, for the record, I didn't really need.

"Sorry," I whimpered, dabbing at my eyes. "I don't know what's wrong with me."

Fantastic! Now he could add "weepy drunk" and "crybaby" to my description, which already included "nun-like" and "angry man-hater."

"I usually make girls cry when I don't call after the first date, but not the same night!" A coy smile tugged at the corners of his mouth. He was clearly restraining himself from laughing in my face.

What a player.

"This isn't a date," I snapped, trying to wipe the mascara from under my eyes. But on the inside I was screaming, *Please give me your number! Please bring me back to your hotel!*

Matteo and gross blond boys everywhere could go to hell. I was finally having a conversation with a real man. A bizarre conversation, sure, but it was an improvement on our silent encounter in the souvenir shop.

He stepped away, and I thought I might have offended him. But after exchanging a few words with a guy behind the counter, he came back with a bag.

"So, Hurricane," he said in that husky, reassuring voice, "do you want to send this thing or not?"

49

What did he call me?

He pulled a laptop from the bag like a magician.

I looked at the laptop, then back at him, then back at the laptop, as awed as if it were the Holy Grail.

He moved behind me and trapped me between his arms, moving his hand dexterously on the touch pad. I could feel his hot breath on my neck, his toned chest against my back.

Do not fall for it, Gioia. He's a Casanova. He's like this with everyone.

My heart beating, my mouth dry, I saw him type in a password, and his background—a picture of New York City—was replaced by a Google homepage.

"Here we are. I have my own data connection," he said in a low voice close to my ear. Too close.

"Th-thank you!" I stuttered. I hoped he wouldn't notice my trembling hands as I typed in my username and password. The message sent. "I can't believe it," I gushed, clinging to Mr. Cover Boy's arm.

Maybe I wouldn't get fired after all!

In an ill-advised bout of euphoria, I went to give Christian a peck on the cheek. But just as I was about to kiss him, he turned toward me unexpectedly.

I heard him groan as he pressed his mouth against mine. He tasted like mint and beer.

His lips are so soft, I managed to think, my head, heart, and senses in a tailspin. Why had I denied myself this kind of pleasure for five whole months? Beatrice would be proud of me.

I pulled away from him, panting. "Sorry. I swear I didn't mean . . ."

I hadn't finished my sentence before I found myself pinned between the bar and his body. Christian took my face in his hands and pressed his lips back into mine.

This time the kiss was long, frenzied. Brutal.

Everyone around us was singing "Love Story," but there against the bar it was just the two of us, fireworks bursting behind my closed eyes.

Christian pulled me closer still, one hand on my neck and another on my waist. I arched my back, our bodies fitting together as if they'd found their missing halves. He groaned again when I ran my fingers through his hair.

I felt like I was having a heart attack. My heart was in my throat and there was no more air in my lungs. Maybe I'd die, but at least I'd go out happy.

"Maybe you didn't mean to, but I did," he whispered against my mouth.

He pulled away from my lips and rested his forehead against mine. He was panting, his chest rising and falling to the rhythm of my own. I grabbed at his shirt to steady myself. My legs were like putty, unwieldy.

He meant to kiss *me*? My heart did a triple flip and raised its arms in triumph. Meanwhile, rational Gioia kept repeating, *Danger! Stay away!*

I was in trouble.

"Hey, Gioia!"

What miserable timing. After ignoring me for an hour, why did Bea have to choose that moment to remember I existed?

I jerked away from Christian like I'd been caught red-handed.

I smoothed out my dress and pulled up my collar. Christian leaned on the bar and ran a hand through his hair. At least he seemed rattled too. Thank goodness I wasn't the only one.

"Gioia!" Bea screamed at a decibel level that far exceeded human tolerance. "Where have you been all night?" She rolled her eyes. "You absolutely must sing in the contest. We put you down for the *Notting Hill* song. You're next!"

She kept blabbing, seemingly unaware of what she'd just interrupted. Then, like a hunter tracking her prey, she zeroed in on Christian.

"No! Please, Bea, please don't make me sing," I whined. *Not in front of this sexy record company president.*

"Don't fight it," she insisted, her eyes glued to Mr. Cover Boy. She took me by the wrist and dragged me onstage, everyone cheering and shouting.

I was about to make an idiot of myself for the umpteenth time that night, only now it would be recorded for posterity on everyone's phones.

I looked to Mr. Cover Boy.

Christian was leaning with his back to the bar, his hands in his pockets and a sexy little smile on his lips.

I blinked pitifully at him, begging to be saved.

He mouthed his reply: "I love karaoke."

Chapter 4

Okay, so it wasn't exactly the MTV Video Music Awards.

I was pale and my hands were clammy as they clung to the microphone like Leonardo DiCaprio's character held onto that piece of the *Titanic*.

I tried to ignore the stadium roar inside the bar and the shouts of encouragement from the girls.

I wanted to die as soon as I set foot on that stage. My dress was too short to hide my curves, I'd had way too much to drink, and one of the most beautiful men I had ever seen—and now kissed—was watching my every move.

God, how my heart leaped when I saw him mouth the word "love."

I closed my eyes and tried to concentrate. The spotlight fell on me, but at least that meant I couldn't see anyone's face.

I lowered the microphone and cleared my throat. I owed it to my dignity to put on a memorable performance.

When the soft chords of "When You Say Nothing At All" came on, I took a deep breath and pointed my gaze toward where I'd left him at the bar.

I started to sing the list of things that were better than a million words: smiles, looks, touches. Someone who could light up the dark.

I never took my eyes off that spot, hoping Ms. Tattooed Biceps—aka Ms. I-only-have-eyes-for-Christian—didn't think I was singing for her. I couldn't see him, but I could feel his eyes on me. Every cell in my body could feel him.

The thought of his illegal smile and melty chocolate eyes made the crowd vanish and stirred the depths of my heart. Or maybe just my libido.

When the song ended, the crowd erupted, and I descended from the stage into the arms of the girls.

"Wow, I've never heard you sing like that!" Bea shouted in my ear.

"How much have you had to drink?" I laughed, freed myself from her grasp, and fell into Melly's arms.

"I didn't know I had a rock star for a sister!" she gushed.

"It was fun."

I stood on tiptoe to look for Christian, but I couldn't see him through the crowd massed by the stage. I wanted someone else to start singing so I could sneak away. I had to get my bag.

Right, Gioia! Your bag. It has nothing to do with the six feet of hunk you left unattended at the bar.

Feedback screeched through the speakers. Beatrice was holding the microphone, tapping to make sure it still worked, and after a few "Testing, testing, one, two, three," she cleared her throat.

She was drunk.

"Hellooooo Barcelonaaaaa!" The crowd exploded in thunderous applause. "Are you having fun?" she asked, obtaining a chorus of yeses in response.

No, she was plastered.

"My friends and I," she said, looking over at us, "are here on vacation to have a little fun. Especially my friend Gioia, who is still hopelessly in love with her singer ex-boyfriend."

Everyone in the room turned to stare at me.

I wanted to die. How many times had I already died and come back to life that night?

"But he, ladies and gentlemen, left her for someone else. With a note. Asshole! But not before he cheated on her."

A chorus of whistles and boos.

So freaking plastered.

"Gioia," she said, turning to look at me, "that asshole didn't deserve you. Isn't that right, boys?" The entire room erupted in a single unanimous shout of approval. "So I'm going to ask Gioia to come back up here and sing, with all her rage and love, a beautiful rendition of Cher's 'Strong Enough.'"

"Gioia! Gioia! Gioia!" The entire room was chanting my name.

I hated Beatrice.

I hated her with all my heart.

God only knows what Christian was thinking. That I was so heartbroken I threw myself into the arms of the first stranger I saw at a bar?

I added "loose" and "pathetic" to his hypothetical description of me. It was getting long.

I threw Ludovica a desperate look, but she was as excited about the whole thing as Bea was. I looked to Melly for the unconditional support she should have offered as my flesh and blood. But alas, I still ended up back onstage belting out Cher with Bea, Melissa, Ludovica, and all of Touch Music in an attempt to convince everyone—myself not least of all—that I really was strong enough to live without Matteo.

Even though I'd have given anything not to be up there, I found myself screaming with all the rage and bitterness in my body. It felt liberating.

I kept looking for Christian, but the place was too packed and the lights were too bright.

My exhibition ended with an exaltation to goddess status by the entire bar, plus whistles and cheers from all the men.

"This was the most beautiful night of my entire life," said Ludo, breathless, as we exited the stage.

"I'm proposing a final toast." Melissa grabbed my arm, too wobbly to stay upright on her own. "Shall we?"

"I'm in!" said Bea, ignoring two of Christian's colleagues who had been tailing her all evening in vain.

Still singing, the threesome set off to claim a sofa. I got stuck in the crowd of people coming and going, people headed toward the bar or away from it, people who didn't know where to go because they didn't even know where they were.

I had to go get my bag.

Not to mention my Cover Boy.

By the time I managed to push my way through to the bar, there was no trace of Christian. His computer was gone, but my bag was right where I'd left it. I stood on tiptoe again to see if I could glimpse him somewhere in the chaos, but to no avail.

"Excuse me?" I asked the bartender. "Excuse me?" I raised my voice so she'd hear me.

She barely looked up, too busy serving beers and flirting with a group of guys.

Shit!

I spotted Christian's colleagues leaving in a herd, so I elbowed my way to the exit, my blood alcohol content through the roof. I staggered out onto the sidewalk and found that Barcelona's nightlife was still hopping, even though it was already Saturday morning. The cool air hit me in my dress that barely covered my crotch. I shivered and rubbed my arms.

I saw some of the hyenas getting into a taxi; others were loitering on the sidewalk smoking. Still no trace of Christian. He had disappeared into thin air.

I sighed, sad I hadn't at least said good-bye. How many millions of Christians were there in the world? I could forget about looking him up on Facebook.

I peered around one last time and, despairing, went back inside so I wouldn't catch pneumonia. I moved slowly, taking small steps, achy from all the hours spent traipsing around in heels.

Catching sight of my reflection in a mirror near the bathroom, I jumped.

My hair was a mess, my makeup was smudged, my skin was as white as a ghost's: I looked like the Corpse Bride.

I decided to take a quick bathroom trip to try to settle my stomach, refresh my face, and clear my head.

"Gioia!"

I turned and there they were: Christian and his illegal smile.

"Thanks for the show," he said, tucking a strand of hair behind my ear.

Then he leaned in to kiss me. One of his hands slid around my waist, pulling me tight to him. I found myself responding to the kiss in spite of myself, the rational Gioia nowhere to be found. Maybe she had missed the flight.

I groaned slightly as Christian broke away.

He gently touched my cheekbone with his thumb, then lifted my chin, forcing me to look into his eyes. His face was still very close to mine, too close for my sanity.

"I don't need to use my imagination with you, Hurricane," he breathed into my ear.

He kissed me gently on the temple, and then I watched him turn and walk out of the bar and out of my life.

What was he trying to say? That I was some kind of whore?

"Oh my God," I moaned, pressing my head into my hands.

I hadn't even gotten his number!

I wanted to scream.

Maybe one last drink isn't such a bad idea after all, I thought as I walked to find the girls. I just wanted to flop on the corner sofa with my friends and gouge my eyes out, but I found myself being dragged back onstage. Again.

I had to claim my karaoke contest prize.

The next morning, I was awakened by the phone.

There was nothing I hated more than to be brought back to the real world by its ring. I grunted from under the pillow. Everything was sore. I felt gutted, and as I groped around to turn off the phone, my legs got tangled in the sheets and I fell to the floor.

My face was smashed against the carpet, my knee was throbbing, and the room was spinning.

What a way to start the day . . .

"Turn off the fucking phone!" screamed Bea from her bed. She pulled the duvet over her head.

Melly and Ludo were still completely passed out.

Dizzy, I found the phone and answered without checking the caller. Big mistake.

"Gioia?"

"Uh-huh?"

"Gioia!"

"Mom," I hissed. I was in too much pain to speak any louder. "It—it's eight in the morning!"

"Sweetie," she squealed, nearly rupturing my eardrum. "I called to see what you wanted to eat for lunch."

"Mom, I'm in Barcelona, remember?"

"We're trying to sleep over here!" barked Bea. She was in her underwear with all the blankets piled over her head.

I threw a blanket around my shoulders and slipped out onto the terrace.

Even though it was only mid-May, it felt like summer in Barcelona. The sun was high, but—from the looks of the nearly empty square—it seemed as though the entire city was still asleep. The offices were closed and shops were shuttered. There were only a few Japanese tourists milling around, snapping photos.

"Not today, honey!" she huffed into the phone. "Sunday! When you get back. Who do I hear there with you?"

"Bea, Mom." I sighed, exasperated.

"Don't tell me you're all still in bed. You didn't go all the way to Barcelona to sleep. You could have stayed home for that."

I leaned against the railing and looked to the sky, praying for some kind of divine intervention.

"Mom, it's Saturday morning. Everything is still closed. Not to mention we're on vacation. Va-ca-tion. So no alarms, no early mornings, no schedules."

"Modern youth. So, about lunch. Your dad wanted to grill."

I could hear him yell across the room, "The ribs you love so much!"

Just the mention of food made me want to puke my guts out.

"Melissa is bringing Alex," she went on, oblivious to my physical state. "And what about you? Have you met anyone new to bring home yet?"

For the first time in months, it wasn't Matteo I thought of but two melty chocolate eyes and an illegal smile.

Gioia! Wake up!

Blame it on the electric. I still wasn't thinking straight.

"Didn't I tell you I was becoming a nun?"

"Gioia . . ."

"I'll be married to Jesus. You wanted a wedding and now—"

"Gioia Alessia Caputi."

Middle name. Uh-oh.

"Yes, Mom."

"Single yes, nun no."

I couldn't suppress a giggle. "Fine, Mom. I'll see you Sunday."

I hung up and closed my eyes, letting my skin be caressed by the Mediterranean breeze and kissed by a warm ray of sunshine.

Oh God. Just the thought of kissing made me think of Christian. The taste of his lips on mine. His hands on my body . . . It all surged up inside me.

Unfortunately, the mix of sangria, martinis, and blue electric also surged up, and I sprinted to the bathroom, heaving.

After ten minutes of clinging to the toilet, I took a hot shower. I could finally feel my limbs again. I braided my hair loosely, put on some makeup, and entered the room wrapped in a towel.

"Are you sick?" Melissa was awake, sitting up in bed. She glanced at me as she tapped at her phone. "You're usually good at holding your alcohol."

"It must have been the paella," I said, picking up my dress and shoes from the floor. "I'm getting older. I just can't absorb it all like I used to."

Ludovica was moving like a robot in the direction of the bathroom.

"Did you ever hear from Alex last night?" I asked, pulling my clothes on.

A smile crossed her face. "Yeah. He called me right after he saw the picture of us all onstage."

"See? I told you." Bea lifted a vindicated fist from under the covers.

"Hey, sleepyhead! How about getting up?" I said, pulling off her covers. "We should go see the city some more."

"Ugh! I feel like I'm going to die . . . Make the room stop spinning."

"Come on, Bea. You're our tour guide! There's no way we're going to spend all morning holed up in here. Get moving!" I said.

An hour later, the four of us were lying on the beach in Barceloneta, lulled back to sleep by the sound of the waves, too wrecked to face the frenzy at the nearby Maremagnum shopping center.

Chapter 5

Monday morning at 8:30 sharp, I was at my desk with my computer on and my hands pressed together in prayer.

I had gotten home from the airport late, showered, and spent the rest of the night going back over the Sound&K campaign, eating an entire chocolate bar in the process.

I knew Madame Rottweiler would find a way to make me pay for sending the email late. She'd be looking for the tiniest flaws in my project.

If she didn't fire me on sight, of course.

At 8:32, I heard the unmistakable sound of her heels, followed by a whiff of Chanel No. 5.

I spied on her from behind my monitor.

Her hair in a bun and wearing a tailored blue suit and open-toed shoes dyed perfectly to match, she marched straight to the office without glancing at Margherita, who had already fallen in step behind her with a steaming cup of black coffee.

I didn't know whether to fly after her, apologizing, or just sit there and wait for the end like a prisoner on death row. I decided to eat some chocolate and ruin my figure while looking through my emails.

I clicked on the sent folder and there it was!

The email from Barcelona. I looked at the date and time and knew they'd be forever stamped in my memory. I touched a yearning hand to my lips like a teenager with her first crush.

The phone rang.

"Dreamstart, good morning. This is Gioia. How may I help you?"

"Ms. Caputi, you've worked here for two months, and you still can't tell the difference between internal and external calls?"

It was Madame Rottweiler. Operation Destroy Gioia was officially underway.

"I-I'm sorry, Sabrina."

Blessed Mary, pray for me.

"Come to my office," she ordered. "Now!"

Through the line and across the office, I heard her slam down the phone.

I grabbed my notebook, two pens, and the tablet, and practically catapulted myself to Sabrina's door, telling myself I had to learn that phone stuff once and for all.

I stared at the brass plate embedded in the door: "SABRINA KENT."

"Employee Killer," it should have read.

I took a deep breath, exhaled slowly, and knocked.

"Come in!"

Saint Mary, please.

As soon as the door closed behind me, I realized there was no one at the desk.

What the?

"Caputi, what are you standing there for?" Sabrina appeared from behind the door of an open cabinet in the corner. She sat down at her desk with a stack of papers and began typing. "Ms. Caputi, how is it that you managed to be late on the Sound&K campaign?"

Her tone was eerily calm. Too calm. The calm before the storm.

"I-I sent it. On time," I stammered. "But somehow it didn't go through."

She raised an eyebrow, skeptical. She didn't believe me.

I waited for a response, but none came. Did she want me to burst into tears all over her blue décolletage?

"Don't let it happen again. If it does, you can consider yourself fired," she warned, continuing to stare at her screen.

"Of course!" Maybe it wasn't time to box up my things after all.

"And as for your proposals, they're good. We already sent them to the company. The meeting is set for tomorrow morning."

"Tomorrow morning?" I could say good-bye to my evening of ice cream and *Grey's Anatomy*.

"To-mor-row," she said, looking me in the eye for the first time. "Sound&K wants to meet as soon as possible. They'll be here first thing."

"Okay, I'll go take care of the final details with Marco—"

"Wait!" She got up. Not that it made much difference whether she was sitting or standing. She took off her glasses and gave me a look I'd remember until I retired. "I'm going to present with Marco myself. Don't come in until nine."

"But—" I protested.

"I'm not asking permission. You work for me, Caputi, and I'm going to be in that room tomorrow. Sound&K is our best client, and I don't want anything to go wrong." She dismissed me with a wave.

The discussion was over.

Back at my desk, I closed my eyes. She was making me pay for that email. I had worked day and night on that project for an entire week. I had walked barefoot in a Barcelona karaoke bar, burst into tears in the arms of a handsome playboy, even kissed him. (Not that I minded that part.) I'd ditched rational Gioia and belted Cher at my ex in front of a bar full of strangers. All because of that damn email.

Now, after forcing me to slave away at that project, she wanted to take credit for it?

I crouched down behind my monitor and held out my middle finger in the direction of Sabrina's office.

Chapter 6

The conference room door was still closed.

I looked at the time on my computer: only one minute had passed since the last time I'd checked it.

I had come in early to defy Sabrina. I wanted to see her dumb face in the conference room with the Sound&K execs and test whether she really was cold enough to ice me out of my own project.

But when I arrived, everyone was already in the conference room—everyone except for the copywriter.

Yours truly.

I prayed that the meeting would go well, even though I wasn't in it, that Marco would make a good impression, and that Sound&K would approve of the proposals.

Tired of waiting and pissed that I had been excluded, I decided to get my revenge by shopping online.

I was about to add a pair of leopard-print shoes to my shopping cart when Marco came running over, breathless.

"Gioia, hon, you need to come right away," he panted. He leaned against the doorframe to catch his breath, two halos of sweat under the arms of his blue shirt. *He's out of shape,* I reflected. "They want you in the conference room."

"What happened?" I snapped to attention, worried. "Is something wrong with the video presentation? Is Beatrice's junk on the USB stick? I told her not to touch it."

Marco kept shaking his head, trying to catch his breath. "The Sound&K execs want you to present."

"Are you serious?"

It's not that I wasn't confident in my abilities, but they didn't even know me.

"Your name is on the materials," he explained. "You need to come. Now!"

"I'm coming!" I grabbed my tablet, gathered my notes on the campaign, and with Marco on my heels, rushed to the conference room.

Inhale, exhale.

I prayed for courage and knocked on the door. An assertive knock, despite my trembling hands.

After a few seconds of silence, I turned to Marco. "Did you hear them say 'come in'? Because I didn't."

"Gioia, get in there already!" With one hand on my back, Marco opened the door and pushed me into the room.

Caught off guard in too-high heels, I face-planted on the carpet.

Good God, Buddha, and all the saints in heaven, please tell me this isn't happening.

My face was smack against the ground and my ass was in the air, right in front of every single Dreamstart department head, the Sound&K execs, and Madame Rottweiler.

A silence fell over the room. Then Sabrina cleared her throat.

If yesterday I had redeemed myself, today I could once again consider myself fired. I tried to estimate how many boxes I'd need for my things.

Marco's shoes appeared at eye level, and then I saw him kneel down and mouth, "Are you okay?"

I gave a little nod as I took the hand he offered to help me up.

I wasn't physically hurt. But my pride wanted to leave my body and punch me in the face.

I kept my head down and straightened my shirt, smoothed my skirt, and tried to put my hair back in place. Then, despite an uncontrollable urge to run away, I looked up and flashed my best fake smile. Ten heads were watching me, motionless, breathless, as if they had been placed on pause.

"Ahem, good morning," I mumbled.

As soon as I greeted them, they restarted the film. They all started breathing again, and I took my seat by Marco. I still hadn't dared to look at Sabrina.

I arranged my tablet and notes on the table, pressed my lips together, and looked in the direction of my boss.

Oh. My. God.

Two melty eyes were staring straight at me.

And that illegal, smirky smile . . .

Thank God I was already sitting down because otherwise I would have done another face-plant.

Holy shit!

Mr. Cover Boy was sitting right next to Sabrina.

I opened my mouth and closed it again like a puffer fish.

This couldn't be happening.

Maybe I was imagining things. Maybe my blood sugar was low.

Never underestimate the importance of breakfast!

Christian. *That* Christian.

Right in front of me. Smiling.

The Christian who had kissed me and saved me with Internet access in that dingy Barcelona bar. The one who had seen me pour my heart out into a microphone. He was the head of Sound&K?

Someone put me out of my misery!

"Caputi." Sabrina cleared her throat again. "Can we start?"

It was not a question. It was an order.

"Of—of course."

My brain was short-circuiting. My eyes were glued to the brochure, but I was aware of his gaze on me. My stupid traitor body was acutely aware of it.

Asshole! He'd known all along the email was for him!

"Ms. Caputi," murmured Christian in a velvety voice, "I'm sorry we called you in so unexpectedly, but I saw you were the copywriter on this, and I think the creative team is fundamental to the success of an ad launch." He leaned forward and gave me a smoldering look through his long eyelashes. "Could you tell me about the slogans you proposed for our record company, Ms. Caputi?"

He was perfectly composed, his hands resting comfortably on the wooden table. Dressed in another pristine white shirt, now with a dark-gray suit and matching tie, he was the embodiment of sexy confidence.

I could totally do this.

I can totally conduct a public conversation with him without thinking about his lips on mine. The way he made my body feel. No problem.

I cleared my throat and imagined a fat, bald man looking back at me. "We wanted something short, simple, and effective. Something that says 'music' and evokes young people's dreams of breaking free."

I took a deep breath, refusing to break eye contact. He'd pulled one over on me, but I'd show him what was what.

"That's why Dreamstart," I went on, "proposes 'Let It Be.' It's a phrase as internationally recognized as your company, just three simple words that sum up a dream. A hope. The promise—"

"Yes. I've read your proposal," he interrupted. "And what about distribution, Ms. Caputi?"

Oh, it was on.

"The target demographic is quite young, which is why we think a short, immediate slogan will be most effective. Young people want everything to be a click away: Facebook, Twitter, Instagram. So we'll run a few short video ads at high-traffic locations, like subway stations, train stations, and bars."

He studied me closely. He was impressed but trying not to show it.

I glanced at Sabrina, who was writing something on her tablet. Marco gave me a little nudge of encouragement.

Christian flipped through the brochure and looked back at me. His eyes were ravenous.

"I'm seeing something unusual on this list of distribution points. Can you clarify for me, Ms. Caputi?"

I should have known he'd go there. "Excuse me?" I pretended not to understand.

He wanted to play cat and mouse? Then we'd play.

He smiled. "Hmmm . . ." He pretended to search for the item. "Here it is. Karaoke bar. Don't you think that's a little strange?"

I felt myself blush, my throat went dry, and my heart was bursting inside my chest. But I was determined to rise to the challenge.

I cleared my throat. "The campaign is aimed at young people, but also music lovers. You're on the lookout for new talent, and based on some very recent personal experience," I said in a firm and detached tone, "I can confirm that karaoke bars are full of interesting characters. Don't you think, Mr. Kelly?"

Score one for me! Ball back to the center.

"I agree that beautiful discoveries can be made at karaoke bars, Ms. Caputi. My compliments to your imagination. It's essential in your line of work."

I wanted to tell him where he could stick his "Ms. Caputis."

"If I may interrupt," said Marco, coming to my rescue, "we have a few stats we'd like to share."

I let him explain our market research data.

With nothing left to prove, I gazed thoughtfully at my tablet, which wasn't even on.

In all my daydreams about us finding each other again, a face-plant on office carpeting and coded banter about distribution points had never crossed my mind.

Christian grilled Marco for the next half hour, but Marco held up admirably. I kept my eyes averted, even though I could feel him studying me every now and then.

"Okay, I think that will do it for now. Great work, guys." Christian Kelly closed the brochure and turned to consult with his colleagues.

I smiled at Marco, who winked back at me. Christian kept glancing at us out of the corner of his eye, so I made sure to lean into my 100 percent gay colleague and give him an even bigger smile.

Take that, asshole!

Christian's jaw tightened and he sat up in his chair.

Gioia, 2; Christian, 1.

"So, Sabrina," he said, "I think we're ready to close whenever you are. I'm happy with your work, so I don't see any reason to waste time. Go ahead and draw up a contract."

No one had called her, but Margherita the Bitch swooped in with a tray of glasses and a bottle of champagne to celebrate the meeting's success. Had she been listening at the door?

While everyone sat back to talk business and swig expensive French bubbly, I slipped out unnoticed.

My work there was done. Now I just needed to go to the one place in the office where I felt like myself so I could process everything that had happened that morning.

Chapter 7

My reflection in the mirror wasn't exactly heartening.

I was white as a ghost again, my makeup was smudged, and my hair was totally flat. How did I look like this in front of him again? And despite it all, my eyes were so bright it scared me. I hadn't felt so alive since before Matteo left me.

Not that things had been all that great before we broke up.

Matteo had been completely caught up in the upcoming album release and the tour, spending most of his days and nights at the recording studio, while I sat around waiting for him. Heading off to London for my marketing internship had been sad, but it wasn't like I was seeing much of him at home anyway.

I splashed some water on my face, gathered my hair into a ponytail, and spread a layer of gloss on my lips. I could still feel Christian's sweet and salty mouth on mine.

What was I thinking?

Mr. Cover Boy was way further out of my league than Matteo had ever been.

I locked myself into one of the floor-to-ceiling stalls and held my head in my hands. Of all the people I could have made out with in Barcelona, did it really have to be the president of Sound&K? And did I really have to sing a big "fuck you" to my ex-boyfriend right in front of him?

I wouldn't have been surprised if he'd wanted me off the project. I wouldn't have trusted an important campaign to someone I saw drunkenly singing Cher.

I could forget about Christian Kelly. File him away. No grounds for appeal.

Through the stall door, I could hear heels clicking against the tiles out by the men's and women's shared sinks. I sat there on the floor, silent, my knees curled into my chest.

"My God, did you see that man?"

"See him? I devoured him with my eyes. So glad I came to work today. That's the first time Sound&K's bothered to come in."

It was Chiara and Giulia from accounting.

"He's usually at his New York office, but I read in a magazine that he had some love troubles there."

"Yeah, he's always with some gorgeous woman."

"And never the same one. They say he's a hopeless playboy."

"I read that he's one of the most influential men in the music world."

"The world of women too."

"Wasn't he dating an Argentine model for a while?"

"I have no idea, but I'd line up for a turn with someone like that any day."

They giggled and left the bathroom.

I wanted to bang my head against the cold tiles.

I looked at the back of the stall door, counted the tiles on the walls, then looked up at the ceiling.

Enough! I had to get out of there. I couldn't hide out in a bathroom stall all day. If I ran into him, I'd just ignore him.

But then I opened the stall door and found myself standing two feet away from Mr. Stealthy Cover Boy himself.

Not exactly the most romantic setting.

He had taken off his jacket and rolled up his sleeves, revealing his bronze biceps; his hands were folded and he leaned against the sink, the embodiment of a man who wants what he wants when he wants it.

And it was sexy. Too sexy.

I couldn't think—a recent but distressingly recurrent phenomenon—so instead I locked myself in the stall again.

"You know I saw you, right?" he asked. He planted himself in front of the stall where I was futilely trying to hide.

I didn't answer, praying he would take the hint.

"Gioia, I know you're in there!"

"Wasn't I 'Ms. Caputi' a few minutes ago?"

"Come on! You know that was work."

"Fine, Mr. Kelly. My work is done, so could you please give me a little privacy in the bathroom?"

"You have to come out of there sooner or later, unless there's some magical escape route through Dreamstart's plumbing."

"No."

He huffed, impatient. "Gioia, if you don't come out, I swear to God I'll break the door down!"

"Go ahead!" I knew he'd never do it, or he'd end up on the front page of perezhilton.com.

"Don't try me," he hissed.

Christian Kelly was the classic presumptuous asshole who couldn't take no for an answer. And God could strike me dead if I was going to let myself fall at his arrogant feet.

More high heels came through the door.

"Mr. Kelly." MTB's voice was sugary enough to induce diabetes.

"Margherita. Can I address you by your first name?" he replied in the smoothest voice I've ever heard in my life.

"Of course," she drooled. She must already be a puddle on the floor.

"Margherita, I think Ms. Caputi is having some issues with the lock on the stall door. Could you inform Sabrina of the problem?"

Bastard! Bastard! Bastard!

He knew I was terrified of Sabrina.

"Wait, let me try again!" I silently cursed Christian Kelly's name. I pretended to jiggle a stuck lock and then opened the door.

Christian smiled, satisfied. MTB shook her head—I was already a lost cause.

"Problem solved, Margherita," he said, lightly touching her arm. "Thanks anyway." Margherita was about to faint. "Ms. Caputi looks quite alright, doesn't she?" Those chocolate eyes locked onto mine.

I couldn't breathe.

A butterfly can flap its wings in one part of the world and cause a hurricane in another. The butterflies in my stomach were causing an apocalyptic storm.

I looked away and said, through clenched teeth, "False alarm."

MTB glanced at me disapprovingly, gave Christian one last adoring look, and then spun on her heel to leave.

"Thanks anyway," I called after her, mimicking Christian.

I was about to follow her out, but he clamped his hand around my wrist.

"Hey, not so fast, Gioia."

His tan looked so dark against my pale skin. I shook him off as if his touch were burning me alive.

"Am I just some big joke to you?" I said, not turning to face him.

"I never lied about anything."

"Right. Totally failing to disclose information isn't a lie. Is that it, Mr. President?"

"As I recall, you weren't in any kind of state to learn who I was."

"You asshole! You thought it was hilarious."

I could feel his body at my back. A tingle of excitement went up my spine. I turned and tried to give him my best look of disgust, but all I got in response was the beginning of yet another amused smile tugging at his lips.

Asshole.

I looked to the ceiling, praying for the strength not to slap that smirk off his face.

"You were drunk, Gioia! Drunk and crying."

He took a step forward to grab my arm again, but I dodged. He wouldn't get the satisfaction of winning this round with that smile and the sex appeal he used on women like a weapon.

"I wasn't that drunk."

Otherwise I wouldn't remember every last thing that happened. Everything you made me feel.

Worry lines appeared across his forehead.

"Is there anything else you forgot to tell me?" I said. "Is this agency yours too? Are you partners with Sabrina? Are you my boss? Maybe the *K* is for Kent and not Kelly after all?" I knew I was being hysterical and childish, but I couldn't help it.

He bit his lip, nervous. "The *K* isn't for Kent, no, but I am her nephew, Gioia."

My vision blurred. "What did you say?"

"Madame Rottweiler is my mother's sister. She's my aunt."

"Tell me you're joking."

I looked around for the camera. Because I must have been on candid camera, right?

I thought of the terrible things I had said about Sabrina on karaoke night. What had I called her? The Ice Queen. Madame Rottweiler.

Oh God! I really was going to be fired.

"Gioia . . ." For a split second, he had the upper hand again. He took me by the elbow to get my attention. "Let me explain."

"No." I jerked out of his grip and stormed out of the bathroom. With the last shred of dignity I had left, I marched back toward my desk.

I stomped past MTB and denied her my usual polite smile. She didn't look up anyway. Then I heard her cooing at Christian like a geisha and realized he was still right behind me. Damn it!

"Gioia, just listen to me."

"I don't want to discuss it, Mr. Kelly. You can go now."

It was time for some boundaries. Not calling him Christian was the first step.

"You're so stubborn—"

"I'll take that as a compliment." I finally reached my desk. I was on my own territory now, but as soon as I crossed the threshold, I cursed the architect for not putting doors in every doorframe. I wanted to slam one in Christian's face.

"Would you hear me out for one second?" His tone was impatient. He was probably used to dealing with more compliant types. He grabbed my elbow and turned me around. "Please, Hurricane—"

"Do not call me Hurricane, Christian!" I faced him, shaking off his hand. My last-name policy had already gone out the window. "Did you have fun that night? Did you have a nice laugh at my expense knowing we'd see each other again? I don't have any interest in hearing you out. Now, if you'll excuse me, I have a campaign to work on."

My heart was pounding.

"Are you done?" He sighed and ran a hand through his hair. He must have been frustrated that I hadn't just thrown myself at his feet.

"Don't you get it?" I said, sitting at my desk. "This conversation is over. Please go. Now."

Someone coughed.

We had an audience: one of Christian's hyenas.

"Sorry to interrupt, Christian," he said, "but Ms. Kent and the others are waiting for you in the conference room."

I hoped the hyena wouldn't recognize me, but from his look, I could tell all he saw was the drunk karaoke girl whose ex had cheated on her.

This just got better and better.

"I'll be right there, Thomas."

I cleared my throat and waited for them to leave my office. My eyes were glued to the shopping website that was still up on my screen.

"I'll let you cool off, Gioia. But we're going to talk eventually, whether you like it or not." His calm voice was both assertive and foreboding.

Why did I have a feeling that I hadn't won the war with Christian Kelly?

◆ ◆ ◆

"What?" Beatrice's eyes grew wide and she nearly choked on a mouthful of hamburger. "Mr. Cover Boy is the president of Sound&K?"

"And Madame Rottweiler's nephew?" added Ludo, incredulous.

Melly just shook her head.

I took a sip of Coke. I had called an emergency lunch meeting at Smile. I needed the girls and I needed junk food. My basic emergency protocol.

"That's how I felt when I saw him in the conference room. Bam! My composure crashed right to the office floor."

"So does this mean you have to see him every day?"

"Make him suffer," said Bea, bathing her fries in ketchup.

I envied her metabolism: she could eat whatever she wanted and still look like a model.

"I actually don't think I'll see him again." Too anxious to eat, I pushed away my plate of chicken wings and leaned back in my chair. "He's probably on a flight back to New York by now."

"I bet he was bummed not to find the same submissive girl he kissed in Barcelona."

"I wasn't submissive, Bea."

I had told the girls all about Mr. Cover Boy the next day at the beach. Melly had listened wide eyed, Ludo had already been making a movie about it in her head, and Beatrice had glowed with pride that I had finally thought about someone besides Matteo for more than a second.

"But that doesn't take away the fact that he is still an enormous asshole," I said. "He could have told me everything, but he decided to ambush me instead."

Bea took my tablet from my bag and Googled "Christian Kelly."

"So, here it says he's thirty years old. He inherited the company from his father, Mr. Maxwell Kelly, who died young from an illness. He reigns over his multimillion-dollar empire from New York, where he lives, and from other offices scattered around the world. He's known for his personality, professionalism, passion, and tenacity."

"Thanks a lot. This is even more embarrassing now that I know he has his own Wikipedia page."

"And who is this?" Ludo passed me the tablet.

Christian looking adoringly at an exquisite woman. Shiny black hair, amber skin, her enormous eyes gazing back at him. On Google Images, the same woman appeared in photo after photo of Christian. Galas, premieres, benefits. I didn't need to read the caption to know who it was.

The Argentine model, I thought.

My stomach seized with jealousy.

Stupid! You're jealous over a man you've spent a whopping three hours of your life with?

"Okay, lunch is over." I placed the tablet facedown. "I don't care who it is or who he dates. Karaoke night was just an embarrassing little parenthesis that is officially closed."

I got three doubt-filled looks in return.

"Plus, I'm not ready to fall in love again. I still need more time," I declared, trying to convince them—and myself.

Chapter 8

When I got back to work, Marco was lounging at my desk with his mouth full of chocolate and a wide smile across his face.

"You know that chocolate's for emergencies, right?" I said.

I hung up my bag and sighed. I couldn't wait for this day to be over so I could go home, snuggle into some pajamas, and start channel surfing.

"Gioia!" Marco jumped up guiltily, popped the last chocolate into his mouth, and began picking at imaginary threads on his sweater. "I was looking for you. We have to get straight to work on this new Sound&K campaign. Sabrina wants a draft by tomorrow morning."

"Tomorrow morning?"

"Kelly's request. By the way, what did you think of him?"

I thought the president of a record company would be fat and bald, but instead he's the god who I kissed drunkenly at a Barcelona karaoke bar. When I saw him sitting there at the conference table, my entire being dissolved into the floor.

"He's young."

"Young?" He wasn't convinced.

"Yeah. Didn't you think he'd be a little older?" I shuffled papers in an attempt to seem disinterested. *Pathetic!*

"Young," he repeated. "Okay, hon. Now look me in the eye and tell me what happened in that conference room. And don't lie to me. Because as soon as I said his name just now, you turned as red as my sweater."

I shrugged. "It's hot as hell outside."

Marco got up and started tapping his foot, one hand on his hip. "Gioia, I'm gay, not blind. There was so much tension between you two, I could barely move."

"Fine, he's cute," I huffed.

"Just cute? Gioia, you can do better than that."

I folded my arms on the desk and buried my face in them. I felt like a mass of nerves. "What do you want me to say? Sexy? Godlike? The height of perfection?"

"A walking testosterone bomb?"

I nodded, demoralized.

I could hear that bomb ticking, and like an idiot, I wanted to be the one to hit the detonator. "Whatever. Who are we presenting the draft to?"

"No idea. The Sound&K execs already left. We might do a videoconference with one of the higher-ups. Maybe even with your sexy president."

Marco gave me a sly look. He watched too many soap operas. When I'd told him about how Matteo and I broke up, he'd spent days fishing for juicy details. He loved Matteo and harbored a faint hope that he might turn out to be gay.

"He's not 'my' sexy president."

Marco frowned. "He didn't take his eyes off you the entire meeting, and when you touched my arm, he wanted to murder me."

"He's the client. He's very influential and important for Dreamstart. It ends there. Can we get to work already?"

"If you say so."

We worked for three hours straight, and it was just after six when I finally felt satisfied. The Sound&K campaign was winning, original.

I'd dare Sabrina and Mr. Cover Boy to say otherwise.

After Marco left, I collapsed in my chair, exhausted. Time to run home, throw off my heels, and peel off my itchy tights. I'd pull on a pair of sweats and stretch out on the sofa to watch some Hollywood movie.

I had concentrated as hard as I could on the project, but my mind kept drifting to six feet of muscles, an illegal smile, full lips, and tousled hair with a little rebellious wave in front. And don't even get me started on the way he walked.

The phone on my desk pulled me out of these daydreams.

"Dreamstart, good evening."

"Have you calmed down yet?"

Christian's playful voice induced its usual heart attack.

I brought my hand to my heart, a stupid smile spreading across my face. So he hadn't left without saying good-bye.

Stop it! I gave my head a shake to snap myself out of it.

"You're wasting your time, Kelly."

"I always have time for you, Hurricane."

Even though it was only over the phone, his low, husky voice made my skin tingle.

"Well, I don't." I hung up and turned to check my email.

I wasn't nervous. Of course not! There must have been some other reason why I was furiously biting my nails.

The phone rang again. This time it was my cell.

I fished it out of my bag and saw an unknown number on the screen. It must have been a sales call.

"Hello?"

"Don't be shocked if you end up single. Do you treat all men this way?"

"Just you, Kelly." How did he have my number?

I could hear his smile on the other end of the line. "That's the first time a woman has ever hung up on me."

"You're used to women who do whatever you say, Mr. Kelly. I'm happy to be the first and the second woman to defy you." I hung up again, silenced the phone, and threw it in my bag.

To hell with him!

Maybe I was jeopardizing our contract with Sound&K, but if he really was one of the most influential men in the world, he should know how to be a professional about it and evaluate our work on its own merit.

I shut down the computer and rubbed my aching feet. I straightened my desk and left the office. I was one of the last ones out.

I said good night to Giulia from accounting, the one ready to line up for a one-night stand with Christian, and gave MTB a wave. For the first time, I was grateful for the four flights of stairs ahead of me. Maybe, by the time I reached the ground floor, my heart rate would have returned to normal.

When I walked outside, I noticed a shiny black Maserati Ghibli parked directly in front of the building. I had never seen a Maserati in real life before. Just in ads. I wasn't surprised when the passenger's side window lowered and I saw the driver's illegal smile.

"Gioia." How was he able to make my name sound so sexy? "Why don't you take a ride with me?"

"Don't you have an empire to run, Kelly?" I kept walking.

Don't let him win!

Do. Not. Let. Him. Win.

"I have people to do that for me." Undeterred, Christian drove two miles an hour following me. He looked ridiculous. "Give me a break, Gioia, get in! We need to talk."

"I have nothing to say to you, and I don't want to hear anything you have to say, Kelly."

I could hear a laugh escape him, which pissed me off even more. The flashy car passed me and then slowed down again until I caught up.

"Just please let me explain. Then you can go home and I won't bother you anymore."

I stopped.

A smile spread across his face and his eyes gleamed, victorious. I could tell from the look on his face that he thought he'd won.

I reached for the door and pretended to try to open it. Then I smirked and started walking again. He hit the gas until the engine was as revved up as he was.

I hoped to lose him by crossing the street, but, pathetic rule follower that I am, first I waited for the walk signal.

I heard a door slam; then Christian grabbed me by the elbow and spun me around to face him.

"You're more stubborn than a mule!"

He had shed his suit for a collared shirt, leather jacket, and a pair of distressed jeans that clung to his legs divinely. I had never seen such a beautiful man before. His stubble was the perfect length on his chiseled face; his mouth seemed more sculpted than real.

Michelangelo's *David* didn't hold a candle to Christian.

Run away!

"Comparing me to a mule doesn't exactly win you any points!" I spat. I looked him in the eye, my face mere inches from his.

"Gioia—"

"I don't want to hear it."

"I want you to understand why I didn't say anything sooner."

"Understanding is one thing, forgiveness is another."

"Please, Hurricane."

The nickname and his pleading tone almost gave me pause. Almost. "What if you're dangerous, some kind of psycho?"

"Gioia, I'm a nice guy," he replied with a smile.

I stood up straight. "Nice guys are always the most dangerous ones. When a guy does anything horrific, everyone always says, 'He was such a nice guy.'"

Christian burst out laughing. His smile lit up his handsome face.

Run away, Gioia, run away while you can.

We walked toward the car; he opened the door for me.

"I never said I was getting in," I said.

"You never said you wouldn't."

"Is this how you rule your empire? By wearing down your opponents?"

Christian frowned. He leaned in close and stroked my bottom lip with his thumb. "Do you really want to know what it feels like when I try to wear you down?"

My lips swelled at his touch.

I huffed. "Christian . . ." The air was charged with tension.

"Gioia," he whispered, his lips so close to my ear I could feel them. "I just want to talk to you. After that, if you choose to get out of the car and never see me again, I'll understand."

We stared at each other in silence. It took all my self-control not to melt under his gaze.

"Let's make it fast," I said, getting into the car that cost more than four times my yearly salary.

Christian breathed a sigh of relief. He lowered himself next to my door, his face hovering close to mine.

"You're not my opponent, Hurricane," he murmured. He smiled and pressed the door shut.

My heart was beating out of my chest.

I had just won myself a one-way ticket to self-destruction.

As soon as Christian climbed in beside me, I felt dangerously close to him. The car was too small, or maybe his presence was too big. Maybe this hadn't been such a good idea.

As if to prove there was no turning back, he locked the doors. Now I really couldn't escape.

I scooted over in my seat, practically hugging the door.

"I'm not a monster," Christian said, reading my mind.

The engine roared as he pulled onto the road.

"Where the hell are we going?"

"To get dinner." He turned and smiled. "I haven't eaten since this morning and I'm starving." His expression said he was starving for more than food.

I looked down. "Weren't we just going to talk?"

"I prefer to dispose of my victims on a full stomach. But I think you can consider yourself spared, Ms. Caputi. Your work is efficient and original. You're a great asset to Sound&K."

"Hilarious."

He winked. This jerk was still laughing at me.

I sighed and leaned my head against the glass, the opening notes of "Stay with Me" breaking the silence. Every time he changed gears, his arm would brush against my leg, making my whole body tingle.

I looked at his profile silhouetted against the orange light, the sun a low fireball in the sky. He was focused on the road, his strong hands firmly gripping the wheel.

The Ghibli was powerful and luxurious. It was stealthy, agile, ready to face any opponent in its path. It reminded me of Christian's description on Wikipedia.

"You're looking at me," he said, his eyes still on the road.

"I'm still waiting!" I crossed my arms and glared at him.

He raised an eyebrow.

"I agreed to listen to your excuses, so talk. I can't believe you let me to say all that crap about your aunt. You could have stopped me, but no, you let me humiliate myself singing in front of all your colleagues. You knew that whole time I'd see all of you again at the meeting, and you didn't even warn me. That hilarious ambush this morning could cost me my job. And anyway, I'm not the kind of girl who goes around kissing guys in bars. I was drunk and stressed out over that stupid email. But whatever, we kissed, and now we're here. You're my client, but every time I look at you, all I can think about is Friday night. And that's not okay. So spit it out already, will you? Then you can feel better about yourself, and I can get back to work."

The words came out in a torrent; my voice sounded shaky and breathless.

Now I was the one who seemed like a psycho. I wouldn't be surprised if he stopped the car and kicked me out.

When he didn't respond, I looked out the window and cursed myself. *Idiot!*

"If I had told you who I was, you wouldn't have wanted anything to do with me," Christian said quietly. "And I didn't want to let you get away."

He was embarrassing me. "Can you just turn it off, please?"

"Turn what off?"

"Your bullshit generator."

"Hey, I'm not bullshitting you. And I don't have any more surprises up my sleeve."

"You better not!"

He smiled. "I didn't mean to embarrass you. Believe me, Gioia. It wasn't like me either. I wanted to kiss you desperately. But please. Don't insult your own intelligence by blaming it on the alcohol. I know you felt it. We both did. Don't ask me to diminish that. Please, please forgive me for not telling you who I was. I wanted you to meet Christian, not the president of Sound&K."

I bit my lip, nervous.

Self-preservation, Gioia! Self-preservation!

"Okay."

Brilliant response!

"Okay? You're giving in that quickly? Because I spent all morning preparing my rebuttal."

"I said I'd listen to you, Christian; I didn't say I could forgive you." I couldn't tell him that if I did forgive him, I'd end up doing something stupid. Again.

"I thought you might say that. So I wanted to take you somewhere special."

The car had come to a stop in a parking lot.

"Where are we? I don't want to be on a date with you," I protested weakly. I wanted to be on a date with him so badly, but I had to protect my battered heart.

"Who said anything about a date?" he asked, serious. He got out and came around to open my door. "I'm taking you to see how we work at Sound&K. I thought it might help you with your campaign. But if you'd rather go home . . ."

Stupid! I had been building my castle in the clouds all along.

"No, I . . . that is . . . I didn't mean 'date' in the romantic sense . . ." I was stammering. When would I learn to hold my tongue?

He touched my cheek.

"You're cute when you blush, Hurricane." He smiled. "No one ever blushes anymore."

He was making fun of me again.

"Shall we go in?"

He took my hand and led me inside. I loved having his hand over mine. It felt strangely . . . familiar. As if he'd been holding my hand all my life, as if the life lines on our palms were aligned.

Rational Gioia—prudent, pragmatic Gioia—was telling me to call a cab right away to take me home. It was my spirit of self-preservation, which had been curiously malfunctioning over the past several days.

It was on the fritz again now as I let Christian lead me into a typical English-style pub, with a bar and beer on tap, soccer on TV, and simple wooden tables scattered around.

I was confused. This was supposed to show me how they worked? Plus, I'd assumed Christian was used to eating at five-star restaurants, where they served caviar and rivers of champagne. But instead, I saw waiters with trays spilling over with burgers and fries. My empty stomach jumped for joy.

"You have the look of ketchup in your eyes," Christian teased. He was still holding my hand as if we were a couple or something.

I reminded myself that this was a man with a Wikipedia page who all the tabloids said was a terrible playboy—someone used to having a woman on his arm at all times. I wondered what had happened with the Argentine model.

I dropped his hand and held onto my bag strap.

"Maybe you're used to women who only eat salad," I huffed, annoyed by what I'd overheard in the bathroom that morning and the way all the women in the bar—and some of the men—kept turning to stare at him.

A ghost of a smile crossed his face in the pub's dim light. "So tell me, do you have it out for all men, or am I the lucky winner?"

"What the hell did you mean that night when you said you didn't need to use your imagination with me?" I asked him point-blank. "It's true I wasn't exactly wearing a burka, but I'm definitely not like the girls you're used to dating."

"And where did you get that idea?"

"E! Online, People, USA Today, Page Six. Should I go on?"

His jaw tightened. "So instead of working on my ad campaign, you spent all day reading garbage about me online?"

I shrugged. "It was work, Kelly. I needed to understand who my famous music-industry client was."

"Well, it's all lies."

"Yeah? You seem too smart to date women like that."

"Hmmm . . . was that a compliment, Ms. Caputi?" he asked. "I thought you had already written me off as all balls and no brains."

I grimaced. "Seriously, Kelly. I don't know what this whole thing is about. I'm obviously not like the other women you've dated."

"Oh no. Believe me, Hurricane. You're an original." He studied me too intently. "But please tell me, what is my kind of woman?"

"The kind who's all glamorous and skinny as a toothpick, the kind who cries out, 'Take me now, I'm yours!'"

"And what do you cry out?"

Be gone, Satan!

"I don't. Not for men like you anyway."

I'd scarcely managed to finish my sentence when Christian's mouth was on mine with a kiss that was gentle and firm all at once. He held my neck with one hand, while the other slid languidly down my side. Caught off guard, I nearly surrendered to it, but then jerked back and felt myself teetering on the edge of a precipice.

"Every time you start talking nonsense," he murmured, "I'm going to kiss you. So if you don't want me to kiss you again, you'd better hold your tongue. Not that I mind."

I gave him a hard shove. "You pig!"

"That night in Barcelona, I was trying to say that I don't need to use my imagination with you because you already fulfill my every desire without it."

Relentless!

"I thought we agreed that you'd stop bullshitting me," I said to ease my embarrassment.

Amused, Christian led me to a secluded table in the corner of the pub.

It was then that I noticed the small stage.

"Did you bring me to a karaoke bar?" I said.

"I admit I was tempted," he said with that smile that made my heart skip. "But no. I think your performance in Barcelona will stay with me for a while."

"Hey, I won that contest! You should consider yourself lucky to have seen that performance."

"I do." He gave me a look that burned me to the bone.

"So, live music, then? Who is it?" I asked to change the subject.

"A group we've been following for a while. We're going to ask them to sign with us, so I wanted to come hear them."

"Do you really personally listen to all your musicians before you sign them?"

Much to my chagrin, I found myself curious to know the work habits of Mr. Christian Kelly, music magnate.

"You ask like that's so hard to imagine," he said. "You know, I just sleep, eat, and work like everyone else. I check out our artists myself whenever I can, but sure, I have employees I trust cover a lot of them as well. Otherwise I wouldn't be able to be in New York for so much of the year."

"I love New York," I sighed. "I'm literally in love with that city."

"I was hoping you only had eyes for me," he breathed.

"Will you stop it? No more kisses for you, Mr. Playboy."

"Okay, you caught me!" he said, raising his hands. "Score one for Gioia."

"Maybe, but the fact that I'm even here," I said, gesturing at the pub, "is a big point for your side. I shouldn't have let you get home-court advantage, Mr. Kelly."

Embarrassed, I turned toward the stage, where they were setting up the instruments and checking the sound.

"Better for me." He rested his elbows on the table and leaned in toward me. "I'm not someone who likes to lose."

What a blowhard.

Was it time to say I found him conceited, self-centered, and too damn charming for his own good—though not necessarily in that order?

"You're used to women who let you win." I glanced at the trays of greasy fried food flying back and forth across the room. "Though I have to admit, this place is a surprise. I pictured you as more of a champagne-and-white-tablecloths kind of guy."

"I have a weakness for french fries. In New York, when I have to eat dinner at work, I always get a burger. Please don't go blabbing it to the tabloids. We wouldn't want to ruin my playboy reputation." He threw his head back and laughed.

Relaxed, without his ruler-of-the-world mask, he looked like any other thirty-year-old in a pub with a girl. Except "any other" didn't really belong in the same sentence as Christian Kelly.

Chapter 9

After some greasy food and coffee, I finally felt relaxed.

Or maybe it was the two beers I had downed.

"The concert is starting. Want to go upstairs?"

Christian took my hand, and we went up to the loft, where the acoustics were better. He leaned rakishly against the wooden railing and studied the stage in full record-producer mode.

Sensing himself observed, he turned to look at me.

Caught with my hand in the cookie jar, I quickly turned away.

"Are you looking for trouble, Hurricane?"

"I'm just doing my job. Observing Sound&K personnel in action. Isn't that what I'm here for?"

Christian stood up straighter, the corners of his mouth curving into a smile that would have melted the most hardened heart. "Right, I forgot you're here for work. What was I thinking? Gioia Caputi would never go on a date with someone like me."

I took a few steps back as he crept toward me like a panther. "You're not so bad, you're just not really my type."

And I certainly wasn't his. I thought of Ms. Argentine Model and began to tense up again, my self-esteem bleeding out.

"We're making progress," he said, putting his hand to his heart in feigned shock. "I never thought I'd hear a compliment come out of that pretty little mouth of yours."

"I'm like Paganini performing for the governor, Kelly. I don't give encores." I felt the railing against my back.

"Are you sure I'm not your type?"

He caressed my cheek and then my neck, brushing the sensitive skin behind my ear with his fingertip.

I trembled. The man actually made me tremble.

Luckily, the lights went out, announcing the band's entry and hiding my face, which was surely broadcasting the truth in bold seventy-two-point font.

I wanted him.

He should have been a controlled substance! How could one man be so beautiful and charming? God should have divided the riches so more women could have been happy instead of just one Argentine who probably didn't fully appreciate him, considering that she must have all male beings at her feet.

My neck was still tingling so much from his touch that I didn't even focus on the band until familiar acoustic chords cut through the room and the front man started singing.

I closed my eyes.

Please don't let it be him.

What were the chances that Matteo and the Sounds would be playing that very night in that very pub?

In slow motion, I turned toward the stage, where Matteo, my Matteo, was holding court. He embraced his guitar seductively as he sang one of their best-known songs in his throaty voice. The audience was in a frenzy over being at an intimate acoustic concert with one of the hottest up-and-coming bands of the moment.

With his black shirt and faded, snug jeans, he was just as gorgeous as ever. Even from the balcony, I could still see the dimples around his mouth, those sparkling eyes, the tousled hair that I had run my fingers through so many times.

I clung to the railing with both hands, afraid of drowning in a sea of memories.

All the feelings I'd tried to erase rushed back to the surface. I had put them in a corner of my heart, but they'd never really gone away.

"Do you like them?" Christian touched my arm, but my eyes remained glued to the stage.

"Mmm hmmm."

I knew every word—every damn note—of these songs.

More than half of them had been written for me.

Christian and I sat in silence for the duration of the concert. He was focused on his next deal, and I was captivated by Matteo. The man who had been the center of my world for four years. The crowd became more delirious with each song. There were the usual swooning women, bewitched by Matteo. I had forgotten how sexy he looked onstage.

Oh Lord!

I felt Christian's eyes on me before he spoke.

"If they have the same effect on everyone that they have on you, I'll give them a contract tonight!"

"What effect?" I turned. Christian was studying me.

"You look . . . hypnotized by their songs."

"Yeah," I sighed.

I really was hypnotized. And fucked.

All the lights went out—first onstage, then in the whole pub. The place fell silent as a small spot from the foot of the stage came up on Matteo, who now sat at the piano.

"I hope you're having fun!" he said. The crowd roared. "We're going to close this evening with a song that's close to my heart, an acoustic cover of 'Every Breath You Take' by the Police. Thanks, everyone. Good night."

Our song.

I had goose bumps.

Matteo began to play, his body curled over the keys, his voice soft and biting at the same time, his eyes full of emotion and regret.

When the song ended, the spotlight faded and the pub lights slowly came on. The audience was near delirium as the Sounds stood to receive their deserved applause.

I was still hanging onto the wooden railing, my hands aching, my heart racing. I turned to Christian and realized I hadn't glanced at him once the entire concert.

He turned to me and winked. "They're exceptional! It would be stupid to let this one get away, right?" Pleased that he had discovered a band that was ready to explode, he took my hand. "You want one last beer?"

"Maybe I'd better go home. I'm really tired."

In truth, I just didn't want to run into Matteo. I should never have gone to the pub in the first place.

"I won't make you sing or anything." He smiled. "Scout's honor."

"You're not exactly a Boy Scout, Christian. But seriously, I need to get home."

He peered at me quizzically, then took my hand. "Okay, let's go."

We were almost home free when he stopped a few feet short of the exit.

"Sorry, I just want to talk to him for a minute," he said, pointing to Roberto, the band's manager, who was sipping his usual scotch at the bar.

"Okay, I'll be in the bathroom."

He studied me again for what seemed like an eternity, then let go of my hand and smiled.

I slipped into the bathroom before Roberto could see me. I fixed my hair, tried to clean up my makeup, and leaned against the sink.

I looked at myself in the mirror. My life was such a disaster. I sent a group message on WhatsApp to the girls with about three thousand desperate smileys.

At least they'd have a laugh in the morning.

When I emerged from my bunker, I saw Christian still at the bar with Roberto. I mimed to him that I'd wait outside.

As soon as I reached the Ghibli, I started to pace back and forth.

Of all the bands in Italy, Christian wanted to sign the Sounds? I should be happy for the boys, for all their years of hard work and sacrifice. But no. I wanted the contract to fall through. I hoped Christian would never get to meet Matteo.

I was a terrible person. Terrible and cruel. A bitch.

The parking lot was empty now. I picked up the phone and sent an emoticon of Munch's *Scream* to the girls.

"Gioia?"

Lady Luck hated me.

I spun around and collided with two dimples. Matteo was standing right in front of me, his guitar case on his back and a cigarette in his mouth.

I wanted to run, but there was nowhere to hide. If I went back into the pub, Matteo would follow me and we'd run into Christian.

I was trapped.

The cigarette nearly fell out of his mouth. "Were you at the concert?" he asked.

I nodded and hid my trembling hands in my jacket pockets. "You guys were fantastic, but you always are."

"Who are you here with?" he asked, looking around. "The girls?"

I shook my head. "No one you know."

He ran his hands through his hair, hesitant. "Gioia, I know this isn't the best time or place, but . . ." He advanced slowly as I backed up against the sports car. "I need to talk to you. I owe you an explanation."

My confusion turned to anger. *Need?* He'd dumped me with a pathetic letter. He didn't get to impose his stupid emotional needs on me anymore.

"I'm not in the mood, Matteo," I hissed through clenched teeth.

I braced myself against the hood of the Maserati. Naturally, the alarm went off, a siren ripping through the quiet night.

I swore to the sky, but the worst was yet to come.

"Gioia." Christian placed a hand on my side and, keeping me pressed to him, deactivated the screeching alarm.

My ex looked back and forth between us in disbelief.

Christian put the car keys back in his pocket and held out a hand to Matteo.

"Pleasure to meet you. I'm Christian Kelly," he said, tightening his grip on me even more. His eyes met mine. "Gioia's boyfriend."

He did not just say that.

He did not just say that.

Matteo went pale with shock, though I was sure I didn't look much better.

I tried to ease away from Christian, but I could tell by the way he pulled me closer that I shouldn't say a word, much less move.

"Hi," said Matteo coldly, giving me a who-the-fuck-is-this look.

Christian continued to study him, his jaw clenched. "You're Matteo, from the Sounds."

The testosterone in the air was so thick you could practically see it.

Finally, Matteo deigned to shake Christian's hand.

"I am. A pleasure."

They studied each other for another tense moment like I wasn't even there. All they were missing was a pair of helmets and swords, and they would have been ready for battle.

"Congratulations on the show tonight. I already talked to your manager. Now, if you'll excuse me, Gioia and I have to get home. Right, sweetheart?" He took my hand and kissed the inside of my wrist slowly, a delicious agony.

Sweetheart?

"Mmm."

If I opened my mouth, I couldn't be responsible for what came out.

Matteo stiffened. "Oh yeah. I'd better go too. The boys will be wondering what happened to me. It was a pleasure to meet you. See you soon, I hope."

Of course he hoped.

His seething eyes came to rest on me. "Bye, Gioia."

"Bye," I said breathlessly, still too shocked by Christian's display to even think about damage control.

Matteo gave me one last look before slinking back into the pub.

I got into the car, not bothering to wait for Christian to open my door.

I was spitting mad.

"What the hell was that?" I raged.

"Calm down, Hurricane."

"Don't you tell me to calm down. And don't think I don't know what you were trying to do putting your hand on my waist in front of Matteo! My *boyfriend?*"

"Why are you so mad?" he asked, putting the car in gear.

"Oh, I'm not mad. I'm furious! You were marking your territory, just like a dog."

I sat as far away from him as I could manage. I needed to keep my distance, otherwise I'd throw him out the window.

"What else should I know? First I find out you're the president of Sound&K, then you're Rottweiler's nephew, and now you're my boyfriend? That's a good one. How dare you say something like that?"

"Oh, I thought you'd already changed your Facebook status."

I clenched my hands into fists and counted to ten. "Stop. Joking. Around. I was perfectly at peace that night in Barcelona. Drunk but happy. I was having fun until I realized that my work email hadn't been sent, and who did the universe send to my rescue? A playboy who's used to treating women like property. And on top of that, not only was the email for you, but you're also the nephew of the Ice Queen who's probably going to fire me because you made me fuck up at that meeting. I'll never—and I mean never—be your girlfriend. Not even in your imagination."

My chest was rising and falling; I was short of breath and my face was on fire.

"You know you should stop to breathe every once in a while?"

"No!" I said, pointing at him. "You do not get the last word this time. You've already said too much for today."

I turned on the radio to shut him up and closed my eyes, my face pressed against the window.

We stayed like that all the way back to where my car was parked, the silence broken only by the suffering sounds of Damien Rice.

"Gioia. A jerk like that shouldn't get to have a girl like you."

My hand was on the door handle. One click and I'd be out of there.

I closed my eyes and drew air into my lungs.

"I'm not a business deal, Mr. Kelly," I said through my teeth. "I'm not anyone's territory or a prize that goes to the highest bidder."

His face was hidden in the shadows, but his heavy breathing cut through the air.

Maybe he wasn't used to not having control over someone. Maybe I was an interesting challenge for him.

But I had already been through enough when it came to my love life. Christian Kelly didn't get to be yet another disappointment.

I opened the door and got out without saying another word.

As I closed the door on having him in my life, my eyes clouded with tears, I thought I heard him say, "Sorry."

I mechanically made my way home, my body on autopilot.

My mind was drifting between two planets called Matteo and Christian.

I dropped my shoes at the door, stripped off my clothes, and jumped straight into the shower. There, all the tears I'd held back came pouring out, mixing with the stream of scalding water that fell against my face. I sat on the shower's cool marble floor, hugged my knees to my chest, and let out all the sadness, pain, and anguish that I'd been carrying around for months.

They say time heals all wounds.

Bullshit.

Instead, day after day, my pain had grown silently inside me like a cancer.

I thought about how my father looked that day at the airport, his eyes fixed fearfully on the ground, not knowing how to tell me that Matteo would never be there to pick me up. I thought about the note where he said he was leaving me for someone else, that he'd already been cheating on me, the girls hugging me silently as I cried, how badly Beatrice wanted to murder Matteo, my mother's worried looks, the way she asked me twenty times a day if I was eating enough, the sleepless nights I spent crying and studying so I could finally land a job at Dreamstart and try to pull my life together.

Sure, I was employed and no longer living in my own filth, but I was still a mess. It was hard enough to stop thinking about Matteo. Why did Christian Kelly have to come along and make everything even worse?

It was almost four in the morning when I finally fell asleep on the bed, my hair clinging to my face still wet with tears.

Chapter 10

Online.

LAST SEEN AT 7:30 A.M.

Great! Christian had been on WhatsApp but hadn't bothered to say "Sorry, Gioia. I was a jerk." Not even a bouquet emoticon.

I dropped my phone on the bed.

Better luck next guy.

Yep, story of my love life.

My list of suitors wasn't exactly as long as the wait list for Birkin bags. I could count my relationships—official and otherwise—on one hand. Obviously not counting the crush I'd had since childhood on Dylan Mile-High-Forehead McKay from *Beverly Hills, 90210*.

Mr. Cover Boy did not make the cut.

I studied my reflection in the bathroom mirror and stuck out my tongue.

My eyes were still a bit swollen from the crying; my face was drab and lifeless. After applying a layer of foundation and more than a little concealer, I was reasonably satisfied with the result. Thank goodness for YouTube makeup tutorials.

I grabbed my keys and my purse, and went downstairs to the street.

Before starting my car, I picked up my phone, entered the group chat, and told the girls I wouldn't have time to stop by the café for breakfast. I peeked at my list of favorites. I had saved Christian as "Mr. Cover Boy."

Like a junkie taking a hit, I clicked and saw that he was online.

I threw the phone down like a hot potato, my heart pounding, those butterflies flapping their wings in my stomach.

Idiot! He can't see you looking.

I slapped my forehead and turned on Radio Deejay as I slipped into the stream of traffic.

When I got to Dreamstart, the Ghibli was already parked outside.

I clawed at my chest as if my heart were hurting me. After everything with Matteo, I couldn't risk being infected again by the love virus.

"Gioia, you look like you haven't slept a wink. Someone keep you up all night?" Marco closed his gossip magazine and followed me to my office.

I threw my bag on the desk and plopped into my chair.

If only!

"Like who?" I muttered.

"I don't know, your ex?"

"The answer lies in the word 'ex,' Marco."

MTB's shrill, hateful voice made us jump.

"Sabrina wants to see you both," she sniped from the hall. "Now."

"Good morning to you too, hon," Marco said. He got up from my desk and straightened the collar of his spotted shirt. Was he primping for Christian?

I nervously sprang up, and all my papers fell to the ground. I collected them and, with trembling hands, smoothed the white silk shirt that I had paired with simple black jeans.

I looked up and saw Marco looking at me skeptically. "What?"

Marco looked around, put his hands on the desk, and leaned forward. "What is *up* with you today?" he whispered, an intrigued smile on his face.

"Nothing. Everything's fine."

"Gioia, in the two months you've been here, I've never seen you flustered like this."

I shuffled my papers, batted at my hair, and fussed at the already-tidy sticky notes on my monitor.

Organization as therapy, one of the many dysfunctions I inherited from my mother.

"I'm not upset."

"Uh-huh. And I have two heads."

I pressed my head in my hands. "Can you imagine Sabrina and Kelly in the same room? It's like being catapulted into a circle of hell."

"Seems more like paradise. Pity Kelly doesn't share my tastes."

I couldn't even muster a smile. "Maybe you can convince him."

He grimaced. "No chance. I can tell by the way he looks at you."

"Marco, it's not really about me," I snorted. "He's just a flirt."

"So flirt right back! What do you have to lose?" He herded me toward the conference room. "Nothing."

Or everything, I thought.

"So I'll knock, you enter first, and I'll follow. Oh, and no sudden stops, or I could trip on you and fall again. And stop laughing," I said, giving him a shove.

He raised his hands in surrender.

I knocked firmly.

"Come in!"

Was I wrong, or did even the door tremble at the sound of Sabrina's voice?

Jesus, Mary, and Joseph.

I let Marco pass and practically hid behind him as I entered.

The large conference room was nearly empty. Sabrina was sitting at the table, but Christian was standing over near the window. He was on the phone, speaking English at lightning speed, looking into the distance. In his jet-black suit, he emanated power. He held the phone with one hand, and the other was shoved confidently into the back pocket of his trousers, displaying his butt.

"Nice view!" Marco whispered.

I glared at him, pressed my notes into my chest, and took my place at the table.

Rottweiler and Mr. Cover Boy together, right in front of me.

It was like being in a lion's cage.

Breathe, Gioia!

As I looked over the notes with Marco, I tried to eavesdrop on Christian's conversation.

I didn't catch much, and if I leaned any more in his direction, I would fall off my chair. I didn't know American slang, but I did understand the word "dear." It was one of the first words in English I'd learned in kindergarten, along with "The cat is on the table" and "What's your name?"

Dear.

From his soothing tone of voice, I was convinced he was talking to a woman. Had he been talking to her online earlier too?

Christian turned and caught me staring at him. Yet again.

Shit.

He whispered something I couldn't hear and hung up.

"Sorry about that."

He took a seat next to Sabrina, fiddling with the phone as he picked up the campaign brochure. His tone was professional, authoritative. He seemed to have left his smile at home.

Fine! He was Mr. Asshole today.

"So, Marco, can you walk me through the changes you made?"

He listened to Marco's proposals with his arm resting on the mahogany table, hand tapping impatiently, eyes fixed on the screen.

Marco held up brilliantly through thirty minutes of questions and concerns.

I had been deliberately sidelined.

"Enough for today." Christian closed the documents, turned to Marco, and said, "There are enough great ideas to work with here. Let's update everything this week."

Marco and I got up to leave, my colleague with his head bowed. Maybe he was rethinking that crush.

"Ms. Caputi?"

My heart accelerated at just hearing Christian say my name.

Okay, just a sec. How pathetic was I? He had lied to me, he had embarrassed me, he had pretended to be my boyfriend in front of my ex, and then he had shown up at the office in a sour mood, offended, and ignored my contributions to the campaign. And I was still lusting after him?

The kisses had been awfully nice . . .

I looked up, and those two chocolate-colored eyes lit a little flame of new hope before his tone extinguished it like a cold shower.

"Can you tell Margherita to bring me the contract documents? Thank you."

I could hear an imaginary audience booing, just like in those American sitcoms.

Boo! Boo!

I stood there gaping like an idiot. What was I? His secretary?

"You're welcome," I said in a glacial tone.

I closed the door firmly behind me and pouted all the way back to my office.

Mr. Cover Boy was rallying.

Gioia Caputi, 2.

Christian Kelly, 2.

◆ ◆ ◆

You know where men have one up on us? They excel at making us feel guilty.

You want an example? Your man leaves his phone on the bathroom counter. Your curiosity and jealousy get the better of you. So you pick it up, peep at the call log, their messages, and WhatsApp. Apparently, he's been spending all his time talking to "Samantha," whose profile picture is a half-naked selfie with a duck face.

You burst out of the bathroom in a rage and mute his sports program just as they begin to discuss his team. You face him and show him the phone. Clear evidence of cheating.

But what does he say? Not "My love, I'm sorry. It's not how it looks." He says, "Stop blocking the TV" and "Why are you looking at my phone?"

He says you're invading his privacy.

And what do you do? Instead of throwing him out on his ass and telling him to iron his own soccer jerseys from now on, you say you're sorry.

Yes, you say you're sorry. Because men hardly ever admit they're wrong.

Why am I saying all this? Because I refuse to let Christian make me the jealous girl in the bathroom.

After being ignored at the meeting this morning, I hid out in my office and worked through lunch. I threw myself headlong into new campaigns, piles of marketing books, strategies, and papers stacked up on my desk.

There was nothing that captured my mind like work. It was gratifying; the pressure and the challenge of a new project electrified me. It was fabulous to see my ideas come to life on a label, in a commercial, in a newspaper.

I was intently focused on a SWOT analysis when I felt the familiar tingling through my spine. I felt the heat of his gaze on me even before our eyes met.

There was Christian leaning against the door, his hands in his pockets, five o'clock shadow on his face, a jacket and tie that fell much too perfectly.

How is he so handsome?

"What do you want, Kelly?" I picked up a stack of papers and began to leaf through them. I would rather learn them by heart than face his gaze.

Come on, Gioia, you can do it!

I could not make eye contact under any circumstances or I'd be lost. He would see all my anger, disappointment, bitterness, and hatred.

And you know what they say about hatred: it's the other face of love. But I wanted to be indifferent.

Totally indifferent.

Immune to the Kelly virus.

He advanced with confident steps, hands in his pockets. "We need to talk."

"I have nothing to say to you."

"Well, I do."

"Not now."

"Now."

I rolled my eyes. "Can't you hear yourself?"

"If you'd let me speak, I might."

It was a shame I had a wall outside my window, otherwise I would have picked him up by the balls and tossed him into the street.

"Hurricane . . ."

I jumped to my feet. "Let's make one thing clear, Kelly. My name is Ms. Caputi or Gioia, not 'Hurricane.' Your 'I command because I can' attitude doesn't work on me. You're an important client for this agency, but I'm not your employee or your pet."

I congratulated myself for how assertive I sounded.

"Gioia—"

I put up my hand. "I earned this job with years of study and internships. I will not allow you to ruin it. You're used to getting your way with your smiles and your cheesy lines, but it won't work with me. You'll never be able to count me as a member of your fan club, Mr. Ego. Never."

It was my moment of glory. I could hear a stadium crowd chanting my name.

Gioia! Gioia!

I crossed my arms and waited for his reaction.

Christian cocked his head to one side, his eyes still locked on me. "Have you finished with *The Gioia Caputi Show*?"

Oh, if I had been wearing a pair of stilettos, I would have skewered him with them.

"It's not a show, Kelly. It's reality. I'm sorry, but that's just the way it is."

"What is your problem with me?"

What an ass.

"Christian, I want you—"

"Finally!"

I leaned across the desk, my face mere inches from his.

"—to get out of here."

I said it extra slowly so the message could enter his brain loud and clear.

"Actually, I'll go and leave you here to absorb your defeat."

I took my bag and marched out of the office. "I'll see you tomorrow, Kelly."

Gioia Caputi, 3.

Christian Kelly, 2.

Chapter 11

Bam! Bam! Bam!

I hit the FitBox bag again and again, trying to concentrate on the exercises my instructor was barking. But my mind was all on Christian "Mr. Cover Boy" Kelly.

Oh God, how conceited!

Bam!

Asshole!

Bam!

Pig!

Right hook, pivot, kick.

"Good God, Gioia!" Melly said, catching my bag. "I don't even want to know whose nose you're thinking of breaking."

I looked up and saw her surprise. Little as she was, she could hit pretty hard herself.

"No one's," I panted, still poised for another punch.

I was out of breath, sweat running down my back, and horribly thirsty. But I needed to keep going.

"So you're not imagining his face?"

I threw another punch.

"I'm not thinking about Christian at all."

"Maybe I was talking about Matteo," she teased.

Great!

"No."

"Whenever you get too quiet, it means you have something on your mind."

"God, Melly! I just came here for twenty minutes to work out some frustration."

"Do you like him?"

"What?" I kept going under the instructor's watchful eye. "I invited you here to box, not chat."

"Okay, okay. No need to be so touchy."

"Stop!" I gave the bag a sudden kick, making it fly backward.

My sister got the message and returned to her own bag, trying to match my rhythm.

I concentrated on the sequence, and with each hit I cursed Christian's name and his stupid face for showing up in my office as if it were no big deal. In just a few days, he had humiliated me at work twice.

Left cross, pivot, roundhouse.

And then he went and pulled that possessive alpha male shit in front of Matteo. Why? And why me? He'd be gone in a few days, back to New York and his toothpick women. Why was he messing with my life? With any chance there might be for Matteo and me? For what? A few kisses?

God, that man knew how to kiss.

I pummeled the bag with all the fury in my body. I felt freer with each punch.

"Um, Gioia." Melissa smiled, amused. Even after a workout, her hair was always in place, her face fresh as a daisy.

"What?" I replied. I threw another merciless right hook.

Melissa looked around. "The class is over."

Exhausted, I accepted the bottle of water she handed me.

"Are you sure you don't like him? Not even a little?"

"Shut up."

"Or else?"

"Or else I'll have to *break you*," I said, doing my best Ivan Drago voice.

"Yeah . . . you don't like him at all." She burst out laughing while I unleashed another kick.

What ticks faster than a young woman's biological clock? A potential grandmother's. And my mom had two ticking madly: one for me and one for my sister.

Every family lunch, dinner, or celebration was the venue for an airing of grievances. "When are you guys going to make me a grand-mother?" "Your eggs won't stay good forever, you know!" "If you wait till I'm much older, I'll barely be able to lift the baby!"

Obviously, Melly and Alex were under the most pressure: after four years together, they still didn't even have a baby on their radar. For both my parents, it had become a crusade, but my mother took it furthest. She'd already warned us that she was planning to hire an airplane to fly around with a welcome banner for the first grandchild, not to men-tion a giant stork to sit on the roof. It would be like the moon landing. Armstrong planted the American flag on the moon; she would plant a stork near the TV antenna.

After Matteo left me, my parents eased up a little. As the months passed with no potential sperm donors in sight, the flame of hope in their eyes began to flicker. They watched as their stork flew away, its bundle empty.

Now that I was twenty-five and single, my mother had begun to fear I was a hopeless case. My father, on the other hand, was caught between wanting to see me married and not wanting his little girl to grow up.

So you'll understand how I felt when my mother called just after kickboxing, when my nerves were fried and my defenses were low.

"Gioia, why didn't you tell us?" she panted melodramatically.

"Hi, Mom."

"To think I had to find out like this . . ."

I rolled my eyes. "Mom, I just got done at the gym and I need to shower."

"Don't you roll your eyes at me, Gioia Caputi. I can't believe you haven't said anything."

"Mom?" I held the phone to my ear with my shoulder. "What are you talking about?"

"Now I have to change the whole menu for Sunday and clean the house from top to bottom." She sighed heavily, as if she were being dragged off to the gallows. "Do you think we should eat in the dining room and use the crystal, or outside in the garden? Does he like ribs?"

I could hear her slamming cupboard doors.

Keep calm, Gioia.

"Mom, I don't think crystal is quite right for a barbecue. And what on earth are you talking about?"

"Your boyfriend! And I had to find out at the supermarket. From Matteo, of all people! And then I discover he's a millionaire. Gioia, when were you planning on telling us?"

There had been a mistake. A huge mistake.

"B-boyfriend?"

"Gioia!" she scolded. "For the love of God, your record producer! Maybe I'll be a grandmother after all! If I have to wait on your sister, I'm better off trying to get a grandchild using supermarket points."

Ticktock went her clock.

"I should go. There's so much to do! I need to rearrange the dining room furniture and get out the grill. No use asking your father to do it . . . He spends all afternoon in front of those stupid American reconstruction shows. Oh Gioia, do you think we should invite your grandparents over so he can meet them too?"

Ticktock . . .

"I can't wait to meet him, honey." She was in top gear. Nothing could stop her now. "If he loves you, he must be a good man."

Ticktock . . .

My jaw was hanging open, and I was so occupied with trying to find a logical connection between the words "boyfriend" and "record producer" that I didn't even notice my mother had already hung up, off to organize the barbecue of the century.

With my millionaire boyfriend.

I was screwed.

◆ ◆ ◆

"Are you done laughing yet?"

"Sorry . . . but I can't stop imagining Adelina giving your pretty president the third degree. He'd surrender after ten minutes. It'll be a short relationship, don't worry!"

"Oh shove it, Bea!" I scooped up a slice of pizza from the box and sank my teeth into it. "There will be no relationship because there is no boyfriend."

Ever since things had ended with Matteo, Beatrice and I had a girls night once a week: junk food, a nice bottle of wine, and movies we almost never watched to the end because gossip was always more interesting.

After the bomb my mom dropped on the phone, I needed to talk to someone. Ludovica was too busy planning her fourth anniversary with Francesco, even though it wasn't for another month. Melly was exhausted after kickboxing, and talking about Mom's baby rabies would just make her stressed out about her relationship with Alex. So I called the only person I knew who would run over for an emergency briefing: Beatrice.

Sitting on the carpet, legs crossed, our backs against the sofa, we were half watching the episode of *Sex and the City* where Berger leaves Carrie with a Post-it.

I knew something about that.

"Why not?" she said, painting her toenail with one hand and attacking a piece of four seasons pizza with the other. "Having a hunk like that as a fake boyfriend doesn't seem so bad to me."

"I can't ask him to do that."

"Why not?"

"Because this very afternoon I said to his face that I would never, ever be his girlfriend. Plus, he's the agency's most important client—I can't risk the work we're doing. Otherwise you'll be reading my obituary in the newspaper: *she died a swift yet gory death at the hands of one Sabrina Kent.*"

"Caputi, you astound me!" Bea looked at me in amazement, standing up. "You're totally hot for this guy, but the thought of getting to play his girlfriend for one day is horrifying."

She opened the fridge and found another can of beer.

"I mean, I get it. He's pretty repulsive," she teased. She closed the fridge with a flick of her hip and sat down next to me.

"Stop it." I snagged her can of beer and took an icy swig.

"Come on, lady. If it's that bad, can't you just tell your mother there was a misunderstanding and leave it at that?"

"Ha! You know how my mother is, Bea. If I try to explain what's been going on, she'll probably spin out. And maybe this would get her off my back for a little while. She's so annoying she could wear down a band of terrorists if she wanted to."

"Okay, so just invite him already! Gioia, it's only a barbecue."

I hated her pragmatism. "And after that? What do I say?"

"Say he went back to New York for work. Then after a while you can say you broke up because of the distance. I doubt your mother would book a flight to the Big Apple just to chew him out."

"Never underestimate Adelina."

"This is all assuming you are willing to pretend," she sang.

"Of course it would be pretending with someone like Kelly!" I responded too vehemently.

"Of course."

"I'd never want someone like him as a boyfriend. Especially after what the last one put me through."

She looked up from *Sex and the City* and put an arm around my shoulders. "If you're even comparing a man like that to Mr. Matteo Perri, you're clearly not feeling well, my dear. I have no idea what you still see in your rocker boy."

"Beatrice, stop."

"Hey, y'know, the Adonis of Manhattan was the one who started this whole boyfriend charade. Make him cook in his own broth!"

"I'm sorry I asked you to come over."

"And if Matteo ran straight to your mom to tattle about you and Christian," she went on, undeterred, "it means that it bothers him, and you should totally go on with the whole farce for that reason alone. Don't you want to make the bastard jealous?"

I nodded.

"Don't you want him to gnaw off his own limbs with the anguish of knowing he let you go? Don't you want to make him feel like the biggest loser on the planet?"

I nodded again.

"So. You should absolutely make this enormous sacrifice and bring Mr. Cover Boy to your parents' house—just to make Mr. Perri's head spin."

I felt a familiar tugging at my stomach. "I can't do it, Bea. I just can't."

Chapter 12

It would be fine.

I'd go in assertive, decided. I wouldn't crumble before his sex appeal. I wouldn't melt at his illegal smile. Everything would go according to plan . . . even though I'd be dying to slap the smile that would surely appear off his face after I finished spewing the bullshit of the century.

Him. Me. Dating.

Not if he were the last man on earth.

Gioia, you can do this.

I had been repeating it like a mantra over the past few minutes, just outside the conference room door, my trembling hand frozen in midair.

I wouldn't let myself be demoralized by Melly's phone call that morning.

"It won't work," she'd said about my plan. "You're not a good enough liar. You're the one who hides in the bathroom at Christmas when Aunt Elvira brings over presents so you don't have to pretend to like them."

"I know! But she gives me Barbie furniture every year. I'm a freaking adult and I've never owned a Barbie in my life!"

"Remember when we were kids, with the tree? Or that thing with your purse last year? I can go on if you want, Gioia."

"Okay, fine, so I'm not Meryl Streep," I answered. "But you know Mom won't let up until she meets him. It'll just be for the barbecue, not one second more."

"Even if you somehow could fake it, what if you can't convince Christian? Will you do a casting call for a fake boyfriend? Look, I have to get to work. Call me if you need anything."

She hung up, leaving me with a thousand doubts.

There is nothing that could go wrong, I told myself there at the conference room door. Nothing.

"Gioia Caputi."

I jumped at the sound of MTB's voice behind me.

"What exactly are you doing?" she asked, glaring at me.

"I need to speak with Mr. Kelly. It's urgent."

"Do you have a meeting with him?"

I've had lots, witch!

"I need to discuss an idea with him," I said.

Which wasn't a total lie.

"I'm sure you know that Mr. Kelly is very busy," she replied tartly, looking me up and down. "He's not receiving anyone without an appointment."

She'd convinced herself that Christian was her own private property. She was delusional.

"Yes, I know. But it's really very important that I see him." I could hear my mother breathing down my neck. "Now."

"Perfect, because Mr. Kelly also wants to see you. Immediately."

Was she joking?

"Wh-What do you mean, he wants to see me?" I stammered. This hadn't been part of my plan.

Margherita spun on her heels and went back to her lair to cast some more spells.

I took a deep breath, like a Buddhist monk. "Abandon all hope, ye who enter here" might as well have been written above the door. I knocked and walked right in, not waiting for an answer. Christian was perched on the edge of the table in the middle of the room, his blue dress shirt stretched over his powerful shoulders, biceps protruding from rolled-up sleeves. His tousled black hair brushed his collar; his black suit jacket was draped over his chair. His back was turned to me, yet he still exuded power and magnetism from every last inch of his body. A goddamn Greek god.

"Gioia."

My eyes locked onto his and I nearly lost my balance. I swear I heard my heart sputter out and come to a halt inside my chest.

"Sit down, Gioia."

Why had I let Bea talk me into this?

All my confidence was shattered by his icy tone. Maybe I should have asked him to be my fake boyfriend on WhatsApp instead.

I could have seen the "Message Read" icon with zero response from him and spared myself the embarrassment of being laughed at in person.

I walked to the table, thanking my trembling legs for not collapsing and leaving me sprawled across the carpet with my feet in the air—again. I cleared my dry throat as Christian slid some documents into a folder.

"I know you wanted to see me," I said, staying on my feet in case I had to make a fast escape. "But I need to talk to you."

"Me too, and I have a videoconference with New York in half an hour, so sit down."

"I have work to do too, you know? I don't just sit around all day twiddling my thumbs!"

"Now that we've established that we're both busy with work, will you sit down and listen to what I have to tell you, please?" He nailed me with his gaze.

I huffed and sat down in the closest chair. What nerve! Even when he was arrogant, he managed to be unbelievably attractive. A defiant lock of hair fell over his forehead. His strong jawline, thick eyebrows, full lips, and hypnotic eyes under long black lashes all made his face unbearably perfect.

"I know what you want to tell me," he said.

"Really?" He knew? I crumpled up my mental script and tossed it in the trash.

"Yes." He sighed, seeming exhausted, and ran his fingers through his hair. *I want to run my fingers through that hair,* I thought. "You and me, the kisses, the boyfriend stuff—"

"Speaking of, Christian—"

"Let me finish!" He raised his hand to silence me. "You made your-self clear yesterday. We got off on the wrong foot, Gioia. Let's forget everything and start from the beginning. Like nothing ever happened."

I widened my eyes in surprise. "Nothing?"

"Nothing. Barcelona, meeting your ex, yesterday at the office. I've been a jerk."

Yes, he had!

Christian got up and looked out the window, his gaze lost some-where over the city. His jaw was clenched, his mouth a fine line across his sculpted face.

"So, starting over. Totally professional from now on. What did you want to say to me?" he asked, sounding afflicted.

Where am I supposed to start now?

"Um . . . do you like ribs?"

I didn't know how a sentence like that managed to escape my mouth. *Idiot!* My brain-mouth filter must have called in sick again.

Christian turned, his eyebrow raised, confusion all over his face.

I sighed, ready for him to add another description to the list.

"I need to ask you something, and you're going to think I'm crazy, but I think you'd understand if you knew my mother. She's worse than a bloodthirsty vampire or a hunting dog. She's tenacious and won't release the bone—that is, me—until she gets what she wants—that is, you. I know what I said yesterday, but—"

"Gioia, I have to be on the phone with New York in a few minutes," he said impatiently, looking at his watch. "Get to the point."

He sat down and began drumming his fingers on the table.

I wanted to ask him to stop because it was making me even more nervous.

"Well, this is vital for me, otherwise I wouldn't be here asking you to come to my parents' house this Sunday." I took a deep breath. "As my boyfriend."

There, I said it.

"Excuse me?" Christian snapped his laptop shut and looked at me, aghast. Now I had his full attention. "I'm a little confused."

He wasn't the only one.

"Matteo told my mother that you and I were dating, and she invited us to come over for lunch on Sunday."

He frowned. "Are you bipolar or something?"

"No," I replied.

"Did you hit your head? Are you sick? Because as of yesterday, you hated my guts, and now you're asking me to eat ribs at your parents' house?"

I rolled my eyes, trying to rein in my frustration and resist planting a sharp heel in his shin.

God, give me strength!

"Hey, you were the one who told my ex you were my boyfriend. If you had been able to bridle your alpha-male shit, I wouldn't be here begging you to be my fake boyfriend for a day."

He walked around the table and sat on its edge in front of me.

Now we were just inches away from each other. Not enough inches.

I didn't need to see his pants stretched across his thighs, the veins running along his tanned arms; I didn't need to smell his scent, already so familiar to me.

Look up, Gioia!

I gulped and looked him in the face.

"What was it you said yesterday? Something about a fan club?"

"Oh stop!" I jumped up, exasperated. I crossed my arms and gathered my courage. "You remember very well what I said. I'm sorry I hurt your feelings."

"Seemed like you were kind of a fan in Barcelona."

"You're an asshole to bring that up!"

Christian stood up and came forward until he just brushed against me. We locked eyes, challenging each other for a few long, tense moments.

Then I raised my hands in surrender. "I knew it was wrong to come to you. I'm sorry if I wasted your precious time. Go back to your important business."

"Gioia, wait!" He moved forward, and I stepped back.

"Do not touch me, Kelly!" I was pretending to be confident, but inside I was actually praying for him not to touch me, afraid my nervous system would give out.

Shit!

"You are exasperating when you argue."

"I'm exasperating because you are im-pos-si-ble," I said, pointing a finger at him.

Christian grabbed me by the wrist and pulled me to him. "We're not done, Gioia."

"New York is calling, Mr. President. Don't make them wait."

"You're exhausting."

"And you should review your seduction techniques, because they leave a lot to be—"

He silenced me with a kiss.

Oh, how I had longed to taste his lips on mine again. Infinitely.

I responded, pressing myself against his shirt. Christian took my face in his hands. I opened my mouth and moaned when our tongues met and danced together.

He was kissing me as if it were our last kiss, as if I were his last breath of fresh air before he died.

And that was the death of rational, strategic Gioia.

I stood on tiptoe and grabbed the back of his head, our lips at first urgent, but then melting into something slow and tender. The butter-flies in my stomach were doing high fives. I had lost all sense of reason. My brain had ceased to process the world around us. Completely. So when Christian broke away from my lips, I had to hold on to his shirt for balance.

I followed his gaze, and my jaw dropped. The last person I ever expected to see in that conference room was standing at the door.

Adelina Caputi.

"Mom! What are you doing here?" I practically screamed.

I tried to compose myself, smoothing my suit jacket and stepping away from Christian, but he put his arm around my waist and pulled me close. I glared at him, while my mother lit up like a Christmas tree. How could I blame her?

"I'm sorry, Mr. Kelly." Margherita burst into the room, panting. "I left for a second to make a photocopy. I didn't think she'd barge in here unannounced."

"No problem at all, Margherita, you can go. Thank you." He dis-missed her with one of his striptease smiles. He kissed my hair and held out his hand to my mother. "Ma'am, it's a pleasure to meet you. Now I know where your daughter gets her looks."

"Oh, you're too much," gloated my mother.

What a load of horseshit.

I couldn't believe my mother had caught me kissing this creature. "Mom, I didn't know you were coming today."

"Sorry if I interrupted. I know it's hard for you two to be apart."

Oh Lord, help me. I could already hear the wedding bells in her head!

"Mom."

"No need for explanations, sweetheart!" she interrupted, her eyes still on Christian. "Your father and I were inseparable for the first few months. Now I have to beg him to get off the sofa. You'd think he was stitched to the cushions!"

I had to guide the conversation into safer waters. "What are you doing here, Mom? Don't you know you can't just show up at my office like this?"

She ignored me as usual. "Mr. Kelly, I wanted to personally invite you to lunch at our home this Sunday. I think Gioia may have mentioned it to you?"

"Please, call me Christian." He gave me a squeeze and an adoring look, to my mother's delight. "I was just telling your daughter how much I love barbecue. Right, honey?"

He took my chin between his thumb and index finger and lightly kissed my lips.

"That's right," I said, giving him a sideways look. "Mom, why don't we continue this conversation in my office? Christian has a conference now."

Christian nodded, checking his watch. "Unfortunately, work calls."

"Oh, but of course!" Adelina pressed her hands together with excitement. "It was a pleasure to meet you, Christian."

"The pleasure was mine, Mrs. . . . ?" he replied, extending his hand.

"Call me Adelina. You're family now, sweetie." She ignored his hand and went in for an overly enthusiastic hug.

Ding-dong, ding-dong, ding-dong, ding-dong went the wedding bells in her head.

"Mom," I said, interrupting the Hallmark-card display. "Why don't you wait for me outside? I just have to tell Christian something."

I managed to push her into the hall and headed back inside to face him. I was in a fury. "What was that?"

Christian calmly returned to the table as if nothing had happened. "What?"

"That little scene. Your arm around my waist, calling me honey, the adoring gaze, the kiss."

"You asked me to pretend to be your boyfriend, remember?"

"I did not ask you to stick your tongue down my throat!"

At least not in front of my mother.

"Didn't Matteo kiss you in public?"

"What does Matteo have to do with it? Don't bring him into this. We're in this mess because of you. Thank you."

"Don't thank me too much, Hurricane," he sang.

"You have no idea what you've done. Can't you hear it?"

"Hear what?"

"The wedding march! After your over-the-top display, my mother will be arranging the priest and the catering right about now."

He frowned, one hand on his laptop and another on his Bluetooth headset. "Don't you think you're blowing this a little out of proportion? She's adorable."

"Adorable" was not a word I would use to describe my mother, who never let a single detail past her. I began to object, but a beep from the computer interrupted me.

"Chris, dear . . ."

I froze at the sound of a woman's voice.

We both turned toward the computer, but Christian minimized the window and turned on the Bluetooth in a flash.

What was that gnawing feeling in my stomach? It couldn't be jealousy. How could I be jealous of a playboy who had no intention of ever retiring his illegal smile?

I cleared my throat. "I should go before my mother informs the entire office of our imminent nuptials."

"Gioia."

"Your meeting is waiting for you," I said, dying to snatch the computer and see who was on the other end. Why was I so jealous? "I'll see you Sunday?"

He nodded but quickly looked away when his eyes met mine.

"Gioia?" he called out as I reached for the doorknob. "Is there anything I need to do for Sunday?"

Why did he sound so annoyed? I was the one who had to put up with Adelina "Bulldozer" Caputi.

"Think about how many kids you want."

A hint of a smile on my lips, I left the room without turning to look at him.

Chapter 13

I felt terrible about lying to my parents.

Pretending Christian was my boyfriend was just supposed to get them off my case, to make them stop worrying about my heartbreak over Matteo. It was a little white lie, and it was only for one Sunday.

But I still felt bad, especially when I returned to my office and my mother gushed, "I saw more real emotion between you two today than I saw between you and Matteo in four years."

I mean, sure, Christian had given an Oscar-worthy performance, but had I really spent years with someone who didn't love me very much? Had I been so blind?

Back home, I opened the fridge, and my stomach growled in protest at the salad waiting there. I was hungry, but I didn't feel like eating. How could I have let things get so far out of hand? Even an episode of *Friends* couldn't lift my mood.

Nor did it help to know that Christian had been on WhatsApp multiple times that afternoon. Yes, I kept checking. ONLINE. LAST SEEN. ONLINE. LAST SEEN.

Once I saw he was typing something to me, but he didn't send it.

Fed up, I switched off the TV and turned on the stereo. Snow Patrol's "Chasing Cars" came blaring through the speakers. Disconsolate, I took a bowl from the cupboard and was beginning to prepare my sad dinner when the phone rang.

I dried my hands and sighed. Adelina, no doubt. Nothing made my mother happier than cooking, bringing out the good china, and rearranging the furniture for a family lunch. Even better if her daughter's new boyfriend would be in attendance.

I was tempted to ignore her, but I knew she'd just call back. I picked up my phone and jumped when I read the name on the screen.

MR. ASSHOLE COVER BOY

I had added the "asshole" after lunch.

I immediately made sure my hair was in place, even though I knew he couldn't see me. *Stupid!* If this was how I reacted to a simple phone call, I couldn't imagine how I'd survive an entire day with him and my family.

"Christian," I said.

"Hello, Hurricane. How was your day?"

The usual tingle went up my spine at hearing him say my nickname in his low voice. "How'd you get my number?"

"Margherita let me look through her files. The powers of my charm."

"Don't be so sure of yourself."

He laughed. "I called because I was thinking—"

"Wow! Stop the presses!"

There was a moment's pause. Now I was antagonizing him on purpose.

He sighed and went on. "I was thinking that I can hardly pretend to be your boyfriend on Sunday if I don't know a thing about you."

"Want me to send you a summary of my life on WhatsApp?" *Since you're always online.* "There's not much to it; your life is certainly more interesting than mine."

"I don't have time for social media."

"Liar," I muttered.

"Excuse me? Did you say something?"

"I said welcome to the twenty-first century, Christian. A hip music producer should probably learn to keep up with the times."

A car honked and Christian swore. He must have been in the Maserati.

"How did we meet?" he asked.

"Do you have amnesia?"

"No, what do we tell your parents, Gioia? About how we met. We have to tell them something on Sunday. I doubt you want to tell them about Barcelona."

I saw myself barefoot and drunk, sucking face with a stranger in a dark room. My parents would have disowned me.

"How about we just say we met at work?"

"Let's have dinner tonight and talk about it." I heard the sound of a door slamming. "I found a place that does great burgers."

"Christian, we don't need to have dinner. I'll send you an email with my version."

My official statement.

"I didn't imagine you could resist hamburgers and french fries swimming in ketchup. Do you have plans with someone?"

Oh yeah, a romantic getaway with Mr. Right.

"No, I don't have plans," I replied as the doorbell rang. I figured it must be Bea, hungry for the latest episode of *Gioiafall*.

I had already changed into my pajamas. *All I want to do is stay home tonight,* I thought, opening the door.

I found myself confronted with an enormous takeout bag from Smile, my favorite place. Christian's smile radiated from behind it. He took off his Bluetooth headset.

"Burger delivery," he said with a disarming smile.

"Wha—what?" I looked down at my phone and then back at Christian.

"Power of the twenty-first century," he whispered in my ear, passing me on his way inside.

In a simple T-shirt and broken-in jeans, he looked good enough to eat. His hair was damp from the shower; the first signs of stubble already framed his face. It was then that I remembered I was in my pajamas. In boxers and a shapeless T-shirt, with a messy ponytail coming loose and my thick, black-rimmed glasses on. My outfit was the ultimate boner killer.

Not that I was thinking about his—!

I frantically pulled down the hem of my boxers and smoothed loose strands of hair behind my ears. All the while, Mr. Month-of-May-Pin-Up-Calendar was making himself at home in my kitchen.

Oh my God!

Christian Kelly was in my kitchen. In my kitchen, in my house! He was invading my sacred space, my antiman mecca.

I watched as he hung his leather jacket on a chair and looked around. His presence filled the room.

Look at this place! What a fantastic hostess I am!

"I'm not even going to ask where you got my address." I closed the door and joined him in the kitchen.

"I hope you haven't eaten yet because you absolutely must try these."

He pulled out two still-steaming burgers and two heaping cartons of the city's best french fries.

My stomach danced a jig. I ignored it. "She likes you."

"Who?"

"Margherita." I took two beers from the fridge and set them on the Ikea table in the living room. "And she has it out for me."

Christian followed me with the burgers and fries. "I'm her boss's favorite nephew and the agency's most important client."

"And she likes you."

"Because I'm rich."

"And good looking," I said, returning to the kitchen for a bottle opener.

"You aren't reconsidering your interest in the Christian Kelly Fan Club, are you?"

I turned and found he'd followed me. My heart rate soared. He stepped forward, and I stepped back. Our usual dance. I could already feel the drawer handles prodding my back. Christian put his hands on the counter. I was trapped.

Jesus. I was going to die of a heart attack at this rate.

"I could put in a good word for you," he whispered.

He leaned forward, and I could see tiny flecks of gold in his eyes. How long could I hold my breath without passing out?

I shook my head. "I'm not joining," I panted.

He cocked his head to the side and touched his thumb to my lower lip.

Breathe, Gioia!

I had read that more young people were dying of heart attacks these days.

He drew even nearer, and his melty chocolate eyes focused on my lips. "Gioia . . ." He let his lips brush against my ear and whispered, "The burgers are getting cold."

Oh, what a sorry sight I must have been. I had practically melted at his feet.

Stupid Christian! Or stupid me . . .

I took refuge across the kitchen, where I was safer.

When I turned and saw him laughing, I thought I was going to choke him. *Damn it!* He enjoyed toying with me.

I had to compose myself. I took two glasses and walked away from him. "Why are you even here?"

"I thought you might have had a rough day and wouldn't feel like going out, so I thought, if Gioia won't come out to play—"

"If this is about Sunday, I think we have time to discuss it tomorrow at the office," I said, sinking into the couch. "Assuming you're not too busy on the phone with New York!" *And talking to your "dear."*

"Actually, I'll be away for two days as of tomorrow, which is why I'm here tonight."

"Oh." So I'd have two days of peace.

"I'm not some kind of stalker, if that's what you're thinking." He sat on the ground, his legs crossed and his back against the sofa. I looked at him as if he were a circus animal.

"What?"

"It's weird to have a millionaire in my living room."

"I already told you I'm not a champagne-and-caviar kind of guy. Come sit."

He patted the floor next to him. I took the beers and slid down to the carpet, where the two of us sat like an old couple, eating burgers and fries. Mr. *Financial Times* was eating junk food on my floor!

"So?" he asked me.

"I'd kill for these burgers."

"I mean, so what are we going to tell your parents?"

I took another huge bite of my burger as I tried to open a ketchup packet with the other hand. "Oh, that . . ."

"Yeah, that. Is your mother so bad?"

"You only met her for five minutes. I am twenty-five years old and I'm under constant fire."

Christian took the ketchup packet from my hand and squeezed it onto the fries. "Are you an only child?"

"No, fortunately, Melissa absorbs some of my mother's attention. But I'm the baby." I took a handful of fries. "She was in Barcelona with me, didn't you see her? Mediterranean beauty, thin, tanned?"

"I was probably distracted by someone else," he murmured smoothly. He got so close we could have touched noses.

I gulped. "I wasn't exactly at my best that night."

"I was actually referring to your friend Gloria Gaynor." He wiped a smidgen of ketchup from the corner of my mouth with his thumb and then licked it off. "Unforgettable."

Oh Christ!

"Stop that. Idiot." I elbowed him away and threw a fry at him.

"Ouch! That hurt!" he said, bringing a hand to his chest.

"You'll live."

"Bitch," he said, and threw the fry back at me.

I burst out laughing.

I liked joking around with him. Seeing him so relaxed, sitting with his legs crossed on my carpet eating french fries made me forget that our lives couldn't be more different. I collected snow globes; he collected women.

Christian polished off his burger. "What does your friend have to say about this whole farce?"

"Bea? She's a fan. She thinks I can use you to make Matteo jealous."

Christian lowered his beer and frowned. "What a bastard."

"You don't even know him."

"But he cheated and left you for another girl. With a note."

I hoped he had forgotten Beatrice's karaoke speech. "With a letter, to be precise. Yes, he left me for another woman, but I imagine you've dumped people before."

Christian locked his jaw and looked at me intensely. "Why are you defending him?"

"I'm not." I stood up. "I just don't understand why he bothers you so much."

He got up and walked toward me. His eyes were piercing my chest. "Incredible!"

"What?"

"How could you possibly still like such an asshole?"

"Now you're being ridiculous, Kelly. What—are you jealous?"

"I'm not jealous of anyone who doesn't have the balls to break up with his girlfriend in person."

"You are the last person who should be talking about how to treat a woman."

He huffed. "I'm not even going to dignify that with a response."

"I didn't ask you to."

"So we finally agree on something."

"I'll mark the date for posterity."

"Great," he said, teeth clenched.

"Great!" I replied.

Mature!

I was sitting there painting ketchup on my plate with a french fry when Christian broke the awkward silence.

"Did you just move?" He pointed to all the boxes piled up in the corner.

I shook my head. "That's all my stuff from Matteo's house, mostly CDs. I haven't unpacked them yet." And I didn't know when I would. It would be like taking the lid off of Pandora's box.

"Can I take a look?" he asked. Without waiting for an answer, he began to paw through the stacks of CDs. "I want to know what kind of person is working on my company's campaign. You know what they say: tell me someone's taste in music and I'll tell you who they are. It would be a low blow to discover that the woman on the Sound&K campaign likes artists from other record companies like . . . Justin Bieber? Really?" He raised an eyebrow, skeptical.

"It was on sale," I said defensively.

"Well, he sells." He pulled out the other albums. "Let's see . . . this is ours, we have this one, we missed these guys . . . What's this?" He showed me a CD with no cover.

"A CD with all the songs Matteo wrote. For me. He gave it to me before I left for London. He said I should listen to it whenever I missed him."

"Maybe he should have listened to it."

I huffed. "Will you drop it already?"

He sighed, shaking his head. "We have Pharrell, we don't have Lopez. Florida Georgia Line?"

"Do you have something against country?"

"I just didn't have you down as a banjo-and-fiddle type."

I got up to get two more beers from the fridge. "Country isn't just banjo, yodeling, and a jar of whiskey, Kelly. I might as well resign from the campaign now that I know you don't love Florida Georgia Line. Well, go on! I'm afraid of what your final verdict will be." I waved him on with my hand.

"Wow." He jumped to his feet and went over to the stereo. "Let's say the level of music in here just went up considerably."

He grabbed the remote, and the sounds of "This Year's Love" by David Gray invaded the open space.

"I went to his concert in London," I said, excited, sitting back down on the carpet. "He's even better live. His raspy voice, the piano . . ."

Christian came over and took my hand, pulling me up to my feet.

"What are you doing?"

"Ms. Caputi, may I have this dance?" He gave me a longing look, along with a breathtaking smile.

"I'm a disastrous dancer."

"Just follow me."

I looked at him, hesitant.

"Trust me!"

His illegal smile inspired anything but trust.

I took his hand and suddenly found myself dancing barefoot in his arms to one of my favorite songs.

Christian held me close to him, his hands on my hips. I laced my arms around his neck and let him guide me. Of course Christian Kelly was a perfect dancer—on top of everything else.

Relaxed, I laid my head on his chest. I felt the beating of his heart that slowly synced with mine, until our hearts finally beat in unison.

I made the mistake of looking up and got lost in his smoldering eyes. I took in the small wrinkles along his brow, which was half covered by a rebellious lock of hair.

I raised my hand to brush it aside.

Christian grabbed my wrist midair and pressed himself even tighter against me. He turned my hand over and softly kissed the back of it.

"Gioia . . ."

The power of this gesture hit me right in the chest. I should have stepped back; I shouldn't have stayed there, pressed against him, frozen in the living room. I felt like a butterfly trapped in a jar.

"Christian . . ."

"When I said you could trust me . . . well . . . I was lying." He lifted my chin with his finger, forcing me to look into his eyes. "I'm going to kiss you, Hurricane."

Oh Jesus!

"No, Christian! We can't . . . I can't . . ."

He pressed his lips hungrily to mine.

The diet, the gym, Mr. Cover Boy. Maybe I wasn't as in control as I thought I was.

I hung on his neck with my arms; his lips left a fiery trail along my neck, my jaw, my chin.

"Gioia," he whispered, his lips lingering at the corner of my mouth. "If you were with me, I'd kiss you constantly, in front of everyone, just so they'd know you were mine."

I grabbed him by the shirt and pressed myself up on tiptoe. "Less talking, more kissing, Kelly!"

I buried my fingers in his hair like I'd wanted to do from the first time I saw him. I let myself be transported by his kisses and his touch as David Gray's voice filled the room with a song about placing your heart in someone's hands. I felt him tremble as I pressed my tongue into his mouth to find his. Hot, wet. Our bodies fit together like puzzle pieces.

The kisses were sweet, but also frenetic and confident, just like the man I was kissing, the man with a seven-figure bank account, the man with a garage that would be the envy of any luxury car dealer, the man used to CoverGirl women and a penthouse overlooking Central Park.

And he was kissing *me*, a thinner but no less desperate or complicated version of Bridget Jones.

"Gioia." He worked his hand under my shirt and touched my belly. I was on fire, completely unprepared for the emotion I felt at the touch of his expert hands.

"Gioia? Oh shit!"

Record scratch!

My life coach was standing in the door, frozen, her eyes glued to the ground. "I'm so sorry, guys! I didn't mean to interrupt!"

Bea was better than a Swiss watch. She was an expert at choosing the wrong moment to make an entrance. I cursed my decision to give her a set of keys.

I stepped away from Christian and turned off the stereo.

"Bea?" I pulled down my shirt and smoothed my hair. "What—" My voice cracked. "What are you doing here?" I said, trying to get myself under control.

She held up a bottle of red wine, her eyes still on Christian.

He was studying her, amused.

Damn him and his perfect mouth!

"Bea, do you remember Christian?"

"I'm Christian," he said, stepping forward and holding out his hand. "Great show in Barcelona."

"Bea." She looked at him straight in the eye and shook his outstretched hand. "Her best friend. And if you fuck her over, I'll serve you your own balls on a platter."

Christian raised his eyebrows. He freed himself from the handshake—not without some difficulty—and threw up his hands in surrender. "Message received."

Bea continued to look back and forth between Christian and me.

"Christian was just leaving, right?" I said. "He has to get up early tomorrow."

"Right, I was just leaving." He smiled, shaking his head. "It was nice meeting you, Bea."

"I'm sure," she mocked him.

I glared at her. "I'll be right back." I accompanied Christian to the door as he stared at my lips, which certainly wasn't helping. "See you Sunday?"

"See you Sunday." He leaned down and kissed me on the temple.

Like some kind of mute idiot, I raised a hand to wave good-bye like the Queen of England. Christian was already at the bottom of the stairs.

"Wait!" I shouted. Between the burgers and the kissing, we hadn't decided which version of our story to give my parents on Sunday. "What do I tell my parents?"

"Tell them what a good kisser I am," he replied without turning back. He waved his hand. "Night, Hurricane!"

That man was making me lose my mind.

I closed the door and went back into the living room, where Bea was waiting with her arms crossed and a Cheshire cat smile across her face.

"What?"

"That man, my friend, is as dangerous as he is beautiful!"

"Go easy on me, Bea."

I cleaned up what little was left of dinner and threw it in the trash.

"A little getting to know each other, huh? To be honest, I'm proud of you. The student has surpassed her master."

She raised her fist in victory.

I gave her the finger. "Give me back my keys!" I joked.

Chapter 14

Friday morning, I got to work with a headache worse than any hangover.

I had spent the entire night tossing and turning in bed, touching my lips. I could still feel the tingle left over from his kisses. Instead of worrying about the time bomb that would explode on Sunday when my mother grilled Christian like we were in an episode of *Murder, She Wrote*, I had done nothing but think about Christian's eyes and his touch.

Then, to make matters worse, I had checked WhatsApp at three in the morning. And he was online. What was he doing awake at that hour? Who was he chatting with?

I was getting as paranoid as Melissa.

I could have written to him and said that the kiss had been a mistake and couldn't be repeated. I actually did. But then I deleted it.

Write, delete.

Write, delete.

In the end I had launched the phone to the end of the bed and tried to get a few minutes of sleep.

As soon as Marco saw me come into the office, he followed me and sat on my desk.

"So, hon, do you want to tell me about your very special meeting yesterday? Your mother was entranced by Kelly," he said.

"She ambushed us," I sighed, spinning in my chair like a child. "Kelly and I were arguing when she came in. You should have seen Margherita's face."

"Everything okay?"

"I think after yesterday MTB hates me even more than before."

"I meant between you and Kelly."

"There's no me and Kelly," I objected, knowing how unconvincing I sounded. "It's just that he told my ex he was my boyfriend, and then Matteo told my mom."

"He said he was your boyfriend?! Okay, girl, you have to tell me what's going on."

I sighed and told him everything.

When I was done, he said, "You need to be careful. Men like Kelly are dangerous. Sexy, but assholes. It's in their genes. They're used to getting what they want, and it looks like Christian Kelly wants you!" Marco wouldn't stop pacing around my office. "He's dangerously handsome and rich, and I understand why you're attracted to him. I mean, I'd do him, as much as I love my boyfriend. But for God's sake, he's Sabrina's nephew."

"You don't have to worry about me, Marco." I covered his hand with mine. "We're only going to put on a show for one day, and it will be at my parents' place. No one at work will be the wiser."

"He'll chew you up if you let him."

"I won't let him! Now, can we get to work?"

We worked straight through the morning on the Let It Be campaign graphics. I had just collapsed at my desk chair when the office phone rang.

"Dreamstart, good afternoon," I answered.

"There's someone on the line for you," said Margherita.

Obviously, I still hadn't learned to recognize an inside call from an outside one.

"Did they say who it was?" I asked.

"Yes, it's a Matteo Perri."

The abominable bastard. I began to sweat and instinctively looked around as if he might be watching.

The phone on the desk sounded again. I waited a few rings so I wouldn't seem desperate to hear his voice.

"Dreamstart, good afternoon. This is Gioia."

"Gioia, hi. It's Matteo."

I gripped the receiver tightly. "What do you want, Matteo?"

My matter-of-fact tone caught him off guard. I had always been a geisha with him, attentive, willing to do his bidding—until the day I decided to go to London for a six-month internship. For the first time in four years, I'd made my own life the priority and, instead of waiting for me, he'd cheated at the first opportunity.

No. No more Geisha Gioia!

"I know you don't want to see me, but we need to talk."

I sighed as I played with the phone cord. "I have nothing to say to you," I replied, my voice stern.

"But I do," he pleaded. "Thursday night we're finally playing at the Gotha, and I want you to be there. We need you."

The Gotha was famous for being frequented by plainclothes record company execs. Performing there was like a rite of passage, and to do it you had to wait months. It would be a great showcase for them.

"I'm happy for you, but I won't be there."

"All our friends will be there. You can bring the girls if you don't want to go alone."

"No, Matteo."

"Please, Gioia. I'm not asking for the two of us to go out. I'm just asking you to come. It's a crucial event for the band, and after everything you did for us all those years, it's only right for you to be there to share it." He lowered his voice to a soft whisper. "I need you to be there."

I put my head in my hands and began to thump my foot against the desk. "I don't know. Let me think about it."

"Please."

"I'll let you know—I've got your number," I snapped. "Now, I'm sorry, but I have to get back to work. Bye."

I hung up quickly, as if the phone were burning my hands. If I had let him go on insisting in his sexy voice, I knew for sure I'd give in. It was already in the script.

I put my head on the desk and drummed my fingers on the table. Then the phone rang again.

"What is it now?" I snapped, annoyed.

"Good afternoon to you too, Hurricane."

Just hearing Christian's voice made my stomach flip. I realized how happy I was to hear from him. Just yesterday morning we had been at each other's throats—and now I was smiling like an idiot.

"Sounds like you had a hard morning. Did you miss me, Hurricane?"

"So you have my office number too. Why does that not surprise me, Kelly?"

"Not even a little?"

"Actually, I worked all morning on the Sound&K campaign. I was told that the president is very demanding."

"I know the type. Bastard." I heard the sound of a fax machine and the creak of a chair in the background. "So who did you think I was when you answered the phone?"

The whole Matteo thing was tricky: I knew Christian didn't think much of him, and with a record contract on the line for the Sounds, it would be better not to mention it.

"My mother," I lied. "Once she sinks her teeth into something, she's worse than a rottweiler."

"Speaking of Sunday, that's why I called. I don't think I'll be able to pick you up. I'll meet you at your parents' house."

"You're not calling because you missed me?"

"Are you flirting with me, Ms. Caputi?"

"What part of 'I'll never be part of your fan club' did you not understand?"

"That's not the impression I got last night." His low growl made me tingle.

"Don't get any ideas in your head." This was coming from someone who hadn't slept a wink all night. "Unfortunately for you, I have a date in five minutes, so I'll go now."

"A date? Is that how you talk to your boyfriend?"

I smiled. "I'll see you Sunday, Kelly. Happy working." I hung up, my legs shaking and my stomach clenched.

Chapter 15

"Helloooo? Earth to Gioia!"

Melissa poured me a glass of chilled white wine. It was a beautiful sunny day, and I had managed to duck out of work for lunch with the girls at a small bistro near the office.

"You've been playing with that mozzarella for ten minutes and you still haven't touched a single bit. Spill it!"

I inspected my battered mozzarella. "I'm just stressed," I replied.

"She's busy with Mr. Playboy," said Melly. "So stressful!"

"What? With Kelly?" Ludo lit up like London on New Year's Eve.

"You know?" I asked, looking at Melly.

"Bea gave me the update this morning."

I gave Bea a look.

"Believe me, girls. Things would have gotten totally out of hand if I hadn't shown up." Bea smacked the bottom of the ketchup bottle. "Girl, you don't need me to teach you anything. In fact, I could probably learn a thing or two from you."

"Okay, okay. Wait a second. Someone fill me in here." Ludovica looked to my sister and my life coach.

"You guys should have seen how they held each other. She was clinging to him, pulling him into her. Kelly sure knows his way around a woman. He had his hands on her like—"

"Please, Bea!" Melissa pushed away her plate of salad and took a long swig of wine. "Enough with the details, okay? I'm still her sister."

"It's so romantic." Ludovica smiled. "Ignore her, Bea. Keep going. Did he just come over out of the blue?"

I cleared my throat. "I'm right here, you guys. I can hear you."

Melly leaned back in her chair. "Aren't you running around with Kelly a little too much? How long have you known him? A few days?"

Was that all? It seemed like I'd known him a lifetime.

"I'm not running around with anyone. I know what I want."

"That was obvious!" Bea waved the waiter over and ordered another bottle of water. "In any case, there's nothing like good sex to make you forget about someone else."

"You slept with him?" Ludo squealed, attracting the attention of people at nearby tables.

"Shh! No!" I whispered. "It was just a stupid kiss."

"A kiss with someone you insist is arrogant and boorish," Bea observed.

"Do you write down every word I say or something?" I snapped.

Bea sat up straight. "Hey, I listen to you. And that's what real friends do: they listen to each other."

"It was just a distraction. The music, the beer—"

"The hot guy in your living room," sang my sister.

"What about Matteo?" asked Ludo, the hopeless romantic who always secretly believed love would triumph over all and that Matteo and I would somehow end up back in each other's arms.

"He called me today at the office. He wants me to go see them at the Gotha on Thursday. He said they need me."

"That's fantastic!" Ludo clapped.

I glared at her.

"Uhhh . . . the Gotha, I mean. It's fantastic that they're playing there."

"Of course we're going, right?" Bea couldn't pass up an opportunity to spend an evening on ripe man-hunting grounds.

"I don't think that's a very good idea," I confessed. "But you guys can go without me."

"He broke up with that girl, you know." Melissa, who had been quiet for a moment, dropped a bomb.

"What?!" all three of us shouted in unison.

"The one he left me for? And you're just now telling me?" I snapped.

"Well, they didn't exactly break up," she said. "They're taking a break to think about things. That's what I heard anyway."

"What a load of shit!" Bea huffed. "Breaks are just a way of putting off the end of a relationship. They don't have the balls to end it, so they take a break!"

I raised an eyebrow. I hadn't seen Bea so riled up since the last episode of *Homeland*.

"But this is perfect, Gioia! We'll go find you a new dress, get all dolled up, go to the Gotha, and he, my friend, will be sick with regret that he dumped you! And I'll have a little fun while we're at it."

"I don't know, Bea."

"I thought you wanted to make him jealous!"

I didn't have a clue what I wanted anymore. And it was all because of Kelly!

"Entertain yourself with the American until he goes back to NYC. Punish your ex. When Matteo comes crawling back to you, tell him to fuck off. Simple as that."

"You're saying I should be a total bitch."

"You already are. You're not totally over Matteo, but you're kissing Christian. Not that he minds, from what I saw."

Did I really still want Matteo? Did I want Christian? Was the barbecue going to be a disaster?

Chapter 16

Adelina Caputi was obsessive about Sunday lunches. The dishes from one Sunday wouldn't even be cleared before she started planning the next. On Tuesdays she'd start rearranging the furniture, on Wednesdays and Thursdays she'd shine the crystal, on Fridays she'd recheck her shopping lists, and on Saturdays she'd begin to cook, as if she were preparing for a gala. Melly and I were absolutely forbidden to miss lunch, at the risk of being disowned.

Which sometimes sounded like a good thing.

My father, Mr. Angelo Caputi, took pride in preparing the best barbecue sauce in the neighborhood. He even had his own personal apron that said "Angelo, Grill Master." No one had the heart to tell him he couldn't even cook a pork chop without burning it.

The perpetual guests of honor were our paternal grandparents, Maria and Gianni. My grandfather was deaf in one ear and had to wear a hearing aid, except when he didn't want to hear my grandmother go on about his cholesterol, in which case he'd just turn it off and nod in agreement.

And to top it all off, there was Melissa, Alex, and me.

And now, Christian.

I had spent all day Saturday checking my phone, waiting for a call, a message, an emoticon. After a marathon of *Gossip Girl*, I sent Christian a message on WhatsApp with my parents' address and collapsed on the sofa. There was no message waiting for me when I got up. Just two blue checkmarks to show he'd read it.

As I drove up to my parents' house, I tried to calm down. I was only introducing my family to my fake boyfriend.

I sighed heavily and got out of the car. Christian's Ghibli was nowhere in sight.

"Mom? Dad?" I shouted. I closed the front door behind me and put my bag on the chest near the entrance. "Hello! Anyone home?"

As soon as I stepped inside the house, I was struck by the smells of grilled meat and the white lilies Mom had arranged in the hall. The flowers would come in handy for my funeral if Christian or Melissa spilled something about Barcelona.

They were all in the back garden: Grandma talking, Grandpa nodding, Melly sunbathing, Alex reading the latest issue of *Two-Wheelers*, Mom and Dad arguing in front of the grill about cooking times for vegetables.

"Hello, everybody!"

"Honey! We didn't hear you come in." She ran to hug me. Too bad she didn't remember to take off her kitchen mitts, which were covered in tomato sauce.

"Mom, you're totally covered in sauce. What are you cooking?"

"Oh my God! Lasagna!" She brought a hand to her forehead and sprinted into the kitchen.

"Lasagna?" I asked Melissa, who shook her head as if to warn me I should let it go. "How much food is she making? Hi, Grandma; hi, Grandpa."

I gave them pecks on the cheek.

"Hi, honey. We can't wait to meet your boyfriend. When's he coming?"

"Yeah, where's your 'friend?'" my father chimed in from his station at the grill.

I coughed. "He's coming."

Prick better not stand me up!

My father turned, a sausage at the end of the fork he pointed at me. "What was that, honey?"

"I said he's coming."

Melly got up and took my elbow. "Gioia, let's go into the kitchen and see what Mom is cooking up while we wait for Christian."

As soon as we got inside, she dragged me to the nearest corner. "Where is he?"

"I don't know. I haven't heard from him since Friday." I froze, all the possible scenarios playing out in my head. "What if he doesn't show?"

"Why wouldn't he show?"

"Are you serious? Look around!" I waved my arms around to implicate my father, who was muttering to himself, my grandparents, who were bickering, and my mother, who was banging pots and pans. "Who would volunteer for this?"

"Someone with a lot of patience," she said, leading me into the kitchen.

My mother was mixing the sauce with one hand and fixing her hair with the other—as she closed the oven door with her foot.

"Mom, do you need any help?"

She started to rearrange an already-flawless cabinet, which told me she was in a panic.

"What if he doesn't like what I cooked? What if he's embarrassed at the sight of our home? He's a millionaire, after all; I'm sure he's used to certain standards. This place looks like an Ikea catalog."

Okay, Gioia, stay calm.

I approached Adelina and squeezed her oven mitts in my hands. "Mom, there is no need to hyperventilate. Everything will be fine. Plus, you already met him. Didn't you see how nice he is?"

"Nice? Is that all I am?"

Christian was standing in the door of the kitchen with a bottle of champagne in one hand and a smile that would have knocked out Rocky.

"You can do better than that, babe," he murmured as he strolled in.

"Christian."

You know when corn kernels start to crackle and jump in the air to become popcorn? My heart felt just like that. Not only because I hadn't seen him for two days—that is, since the last time we'd kissed—but also because Christian looked achingly beautiful in jeans, a casual white V-neck shirt, and a leather jacket. Just like the first time I saw him at the airport. He was right: "nice" didn't do him justice.

"Hi."

He approached and pulled me into a snug embrace, then took my chin in his hands and kissed me. I could feel his lips moving slowly against mine and got so caught up in the kiss and all the feelings that came with it that I managed to completely forget that my mother and sister were standing right there.

"You, on the other hand, are stunning," he murmured when we parted.

Oh God!

My jaw must have been halfway to the floor, because Melly suddenly cleared her throat to remind me I was at our parents' house.

"Mrs. Adelina," Christian said, holding out his hand. "It's a pleasure to see you again. I'm sorry I let myself in, but I knocked a couple of times and the door was open . . ."

"Oh, that's alright!" My mom looked like a lighthouse, her eyes shining with hope. She was already imagining pushing a stroller in the park. "It's wonderful to see you again."

"I brought a bottle of champagne to thank you for having me."

"Oh, but you shouldn't have!" My mom was definitely a member of the Christian Kelly Fan Club. "Isn't that nice, Melissa?"

"It is." My sister held out her hand. "I'm Melissa. So nice to finally meet the famous Christian. I've heard so much about you."

"Famous?" Christian turned to look at me, a malicious, triumphant glint in his eyes. "Is that so?"

"Christian, come meet everyone."

I mouthed a sarcastic "thank you" to my sister and dragged him outside to the garden. I was introducing him to Alex and my grandparents when my father materialized at their side.

"Christian, this is my dad. Dad, this is Christian."

"Mr. Caputi. Good afternoon. It's a pleasure to meet you."

"Angelo. Call me Angelo, son," he replied, shaking Christian's hand. "Would you like a beer, or do you prefer wine?"

"A beer sounds great."

"I'll go get it," I offered.

I was about to step inside when Christian took me by the wrist and turned me to face him.

"Are you okay?"

"I've been better."

He frowned. "What's wrong?"

"You disappeared. I thought you weren't coming. And you didn't get back to me on WhatsApp."

"I had to take care of a few things in Milan."

A few things with mile-long legs, bodies like Victoria's Secret angels, and Venus mantrap eyelashes, I thought.

"You were afraid I wouldn't show? Well, how could you blame me, introducing me to your entire family on our first date?" He laughed.

God, he was so beautiful when he laughed.

I furrowed my brow. "This isn't a date! This is an agreement between two parties."

"An agreement? I don't remember negotiating an agreement that was advantageous to both parties, Hurricane." He took a step closer, his eyes lit with a mischievous glint. He pushed me against the wall and took my head in his hands. "I'm not used to negotiating, but I can make an exception for you," he murmured, studying my lips.

I heard the sound of the kitchen door opening.

"Don't do it," I ordered.

"Do what, exactly? This?"

He pressed his lips against mine and kissed me with abandon. My stomach flipped. His hands caressed my face. I couldn't fight it. He could make me lose all sense of reason with just one kiss.

When we parted, we just stood there staring at each other, panting. The taste of him was still on my lips.

Christian stroked my face with the back of his hand. "I'll wait for you in the garden, love."

He winked at me and, with his hands in his pockets, wandered out to join the others as if nothing had happened.

Love? Had I heard him right? I collapsed against the wall, threw my head back, and closed my eyes. That man made me crazy.

Breathe, Gioia!

"Wow!" whistled Melly. "Now I know what Bea was talking about."

"He only kissed me because he saw you were coming."

"If he kisses like that when he's acting, I don't even want to know how he kisses for real. Alex used to kiss me like that, back when we first got together."

"Well, Christian's had a lot of practice," I mumbled, going back to the kitchen.

"Congratulations, Angelo. It was all delicious." Christian hadn't stopped praising my parents' cooking the entire afternoon. They were so inflated with praise they were about to lift off like hot air balloons.

I'd managed to get a few bites down. My stomach was still in an uproar over our kiss and that four-letter word that began with *L*. Not to mention I was on edge at the thought that someone in my family might start the next Spanish Inquisition.

"More lasagna, son?" my mother asked him.

"No, thank you, Adelina. I'm stuffed."

I bit my cheek to keep from laughing as Melissa and I shared a knowing look. Christian lifted an inquisitive eyebrow.

I leaned in closer to him, careful not to touch him, and whispered, "If you keep this up, Kelly, you'll have to start working on your wedding vows."

My mother started to clean up, and when I passed her my full plate, she shook her head.

"Gioia, dear, you've hardly eaten! You've gotten so thin since the last time I saw you. You haven't been eating enough since you started living on your own!"

I grimaced. "Mom, you just saw me three days ago. I eat, believe me."

"She especially likes hamburgers," Melly sang.

"I'll send some lasagna home with you. The last time I was at your apartment, your fridge was so empty it echoed."

I huffed as Melly brought out cups of tiramisu.

"Leave her alone, Adelina. She's living on love," said my grandma. She looked at Christian through her Coke-bottle glasses. "Christian, how did you and Gioia meet?"

The dreaded moment had arrived.

"Yeah, how did you two meet?" Adelina chimed in. "You became a recluse after Matteo left you."

Thanks, Mother!

"That's not true!" I protested.

"It is! I was worried about you. Ask your father."

"Well, Christian and I met . . ." I looked to Christian for help. "At the office."

"At Touch Music," he said at the same moment.

My father lifted an eyebrow, and my grandma and my mother exchanged a perplexed look as Melissa and Alex looked on, clearly amused. My grandpa just nodded with his hearing aid off.

"Where?"

I took a deep breath and tried an emergency intervention. "We met at the office and then we ran into each other again at this bar, Touch Music."

"Fate wouldn't let me escape a woman as wonderful as Gioia." Christian interlaced his fingers with mine and brought my hand to his lips.

Oh, shove it, Kelly!

"My darling," he said sweetly.

"Sweetie."

I gave him a little kick under the table.

"I've never heard of it," said Adelina.

I took a cup of tiramisu and sank my spoon into the mascarpone. "It's a club, Mom! That's why you've never heard of it."

"I'm hipper than you think, dear."

"Tell me, Christian." My father opened a third beer for himself and for my fake boyfriend. "From what I've heard, you're a very talented producer. What exactly does that mean?"

"For the past few years, I've been the president of a record company with a few offices in Europe, but our main office is in New York."

"New York? You mean New York City?" my mother asked, looking at me wide eyed.

"How many New Yorks do you know, Mom?"

"That's not funny, Gioia. Isn't it far? How will you manage to be together? Don't you plan on starting a family?"

There it was! My mother's biological clock.

Ticktock . . .

"Mom!"

Christian didn't blink. In fact, he upped the ante.

"I'm sure we'll find a way. Gioia could come live in New York with me. Right, love?"

Oh God! I was about to faint.

My mother jumped up and nearly took the tablecloth with her; Angelo, on the other hand, took a big gulp of wine.

Think, Gioia!

I was looking for the right words to dig us out of Christian's mess when Melissa stood up and clinked her spoon against a glass.

"Well, since we're on the topic, Alex and I wanted to make an announcement."

"You're moving to New York?" asked my mom, now in full respiratory failure.

Melissa looked at Alex adoringly. "No, Alex and I are trying to have a baby."

And that's how pandemonium broke out in our simple middle-class family one sunny afternoon in May.

Adelina almost fainted in her chair. Too much news for her in one day: her baby was about to fly across the Atlantic and her firstborn would soon make her a grandmother. She knocked over a bottle of wine on the linen tablecloth, which had been a wedding gift from the soon-to-be great-grandmother. Melissa ran to hug her through tears of joy; the tablecloth was beyond repair.

Dad choked on his wine and started coughing while Alex, laughing, pounded his back.

Grandma directed all her elation toward Grandpa, who had no idea what all the commotion was about.

I stayed in my seat. Over the course of one minute, I had gone from likely emigrant to probable aunt. Christian, at my side, enjoyed the entire circus.

Oh, he had no idea what mess he had gotten himself into.

Since all the wine was on the tablecloth, I took Christian's beer and raised it in his honor.

"Welcome to the family!" I mouthed.

Chapter 17

"That doesn't sound so bad," said Bea, sinking her teeth into a cream-filled croissant. "I'm sure your mother will be too distracted naming her future grandchild to even think about what Kelly said."

Monday morning I had to order a double espresso and a heap of pancakes with Nutella from Sweet Bakery just so my hands would be busy eating and not hitting my own head in despair.

Nom, nom.

"I already have three missed calls from her and two messages in caps that say CALL ME NOW—and it's only eight in the morning."

I took another spoonful of Nutella and spread it on my pancakes.

To hell with my diet! Crop tops might be in this year, but next year it'll be bulky sweaters.

"What was he thinking? I asked him to be my boyfriend for one stupid day, not put me on a plane with him to New York. He called me love and sweetie! I hate pet names. I could have slapped him."

"Ah," sighed Ludovica. "Aunt Ludo, Uncle Francy. Doesn't that sound nice?"

"Ludovica! You're not listening to me!" I snapped.

She bit her lip. "Sorry."

"What should I tell my mom?"

"Cite irreconcilable differences. It always works in Hollywood," Beatrice suggested.

I gave her a grim look and bit into a pancake.

"And then he left me with a 'talk to you later.' What the hell does that mean? He'll call me? Should I call him?"

"You're going to call him?" Ludo asked, soaking her pancakes in syrup.

"Of course not."

"Good girl. At least you listen to me some of the time." With powdered sugar all over her face, Bea stood and heaved her purse onto her shoulder. "Whatever you do, don't make his life easy. Absolutely don't call him."

"And if he doesn't call me?"

"Oh, he'll call."

"But what if he doesn't?"

Bea sighed, exasperated. "God, Gioia, don't be ridiculous. Of course he'll call! You haven't gone below the belt, so you're not a notch on his bedpost yet—you're still a challenge!"

That was reassuring. "And when he calls me, what do I say? 'You bastard, what got into you?'"

"Be self-assured and indifferent. Christian needs to be nothing more than a rebound for you. A stage of your grief."

"Um, what grief?"

"Your grief over Matteo! Instead of going around with a funeral veil pulled over your eyes, crying for the millionth time when Taylor dies in *The Bold and the Beautiful*, you need a rebound—or four. It doesn't matter who you do it with or if you do it in Manhattan or here. Do you want to sleep with your FitBox instructor? Do it! I'm sure he'd be up for it. You've always had so many fantasies—now's the time to live them!"

"I'm not an unwavering follower of *The Gospel According to Bea*." I winced.

"Dude, you have an ex who's inviting you to his big show and a millionaire who devours you with his eyes. *The Gospel According to Bea* works!"

She gave me a peck on the cheek and walked away with the girls, leaving me with the check.

I was confused. And sad.

And not because I had to pay for breakfast.

I was proud of myself: I hadn't shed a single tear all week. Still, I was miserable. And sad. And did I mention confused?

I assured myself for the millionth time that I didn't want a thing from Christian. Not one thing.

Sure, I liked him. He was a divine kisser. And of course I loved the electricity that made me short-circuit whenever we were together. He made me feel alive.

But his reputation as an inveterate playboy preceded him.

I wouldn't be anyone's conquest. Just another name on his list.

Chapter 18

At least working at Dreamstart kept my mind occupied.

After days of focusing on the Sound&K campaign, I worked all morning on the launch of a new perfume. There was no sign of Christian; Sabrina, on the other hand, had arrived early and shut herself in her office.

I was about to call Marco to see if he wanted to get lunch when my sister's number popped up on my phone.

"Melly?"

"Gioia, help! I'm already regretting telling Mom that Alex and I are trying for a baby."

"Why?" I asked, amused.

"This morning she wanted to come over and take measurements of the nursery and bring a crib."

"Oh Melly, you know how she is!"

"Yeah, I don't know what I was thinking. I should have waited until I was in labor to tell her. Look, do you have time for lunch? I need to commiserate with someone."

I smiled. "Meet me downstairs at noon."

I hung up and looked at the clock: I had some time to burn. In a moment of weakness, I typed Christian's name into Google Images.

The first page was filled with pictures of him and his famous Argentine.

She clung to him like flypaper: stroking his arm, smiling, gazing at him with those languid eyes.

I enlarged a photo and clicked the link. I found myself on a famous American gossip site with a headline that read "Christian Kelly and Chantal Herrera Together Again?"

In the foreground, Christian was smiling with Chantal on his arm. She was dressed as if she were going to the Oscars, her sparkly nails gripping his arm.

Gold digger, I thought.

I scrolled past other pictures to read the blurb:

> Christian Kelly and Chantal Herrera, who called it quits a year ago, were inseparable at a gala dinner held at the Principe di Savoia in Milan. Now their reunion seems to be official. The happy couple smiled for the cameras, and sources present confirmed that they seemed closer than ever. Is the American tycoon ready to hang up his playboy reputation for good?

My heart pounding and my stomach clenched, I checked the date on the photos.

They were from three days ago. Three days ago, Christian had told me he would be away to sort out some work stuff.

"Asshole," I muttered.

I clicked other links and found more articles and photos of the evening. Then I quickly closed all the pages, my hands trembling with anger and jealousy.

I knew I didn't have any claim over him, but he could at least be more discreet while we were supposedly dating, especially when he was coming to my parents' for lunch the next day. What if my mother saw those pictures? Lucky for him, my mother barely knew how to use a computer.

"Shit, shit, shit!" I muttered. I got up and grabbed my bag to go downstairs. Melissa, like a good older sister, would surely know what to say.

"Honestly, I don't know what to tell you!" said Melissa, looking at the pictures on the tablet. "I hate to say it, but they're a really beautiful couple. They seem like they're made for each other."

"They don't just *seem* like it—they are!" I poured myself some water, distractedly letting the glass overflow. *Clumsy!* I took a napkin and tried to wipe up the spill.

"Gioia, you've been swearing there isn't anything serious between you, that you don't really like Christian that much."

"Yes."

She studied my frazzled movements. "It doesn't look that way to me."

"No, Mel, it's not that! I'm just worried that Mom might see the photos."

"Mom doesn't even know what the Internet is."

"But someone else could tell her about them. What if they get published in some magazine and Mom picks it up in a waiting room somewhere?"

"Gioia." Melissa leaned back in her seat and crossed her arms. "Don't bullshit me. I know you. You like Kelly and you want him. Why can't you just admit it?"

"Because it would never work out," I sighed.

"Because you're too smart and nice for someone like him?"

"And breathtakingly beautiful?" I joked.

"Seriously, Gioia," my sister said, softening. "You get really paranoid and bring yourself down. If Matteo and Christian don't want you, too bad for them. You'll come out on top in the end."

"Thanks for the psychoanalysis, Dr. Caputi." I pushed away my empty plate and rested my chin in my hands. "Now, tell me more about this baby craziness! Last week you didn't even know what was going on between you and Alex. Now there's going to be three of you?"

She blushed. "When we got back from Barcelona, we had a long talk. After four years together, we had to take a step forward—we couldn't just stay in a rut!"

"Yeah, but a baby isn't a doll that you can take back to the store. What about getting married first?"

"We live together!" she interrupted me. "It's like being married."

"It's not the same." I frowned.

"Gioia, you watch too many cartoons. You've been brainwashed by *Candy Candy*."

"Hey, you're the one who used Mom's curtains as a wedding veil when you were little."

"Well, I watched those cartoons with you. And speaking of Mom, you have to call her. She's going out of her mind with the whole New York thing."

"I wish Christian had kept his mouth shut!" *And his lips on mine.* I shook the thought out of my head. "I was hoping she'd forget what he said once she heard about the baby."

"Mom? Forget?"

I could tell from the way Melissa looked at me that this was a patently absurd notion.

"Fine, I'll call her."

She reached her hand across the table and placed it on mine.

"Please. Be careful with Christian. You don't know anything about him, and he'll be back across the ocean in a few days."

◆ ◆ ◆

I went back to the office, my morale somewhat restored after lunch with Melly. I told myself not to think about the photos and instead threw myself into a new campaign. I was so focused on a SWOT analysis for a new product that I didn't even realize anyone was standing in my doorway until I heard a sharp knock.

"Caputi."

I jumped at the sound of my name. Sabrina "Rottweiler" Kent, despite her lack of stature and lean build, filled my small office with her austerity. She was impeccable as always. She drummed her red fingernails on her folded arms.

"Sabrina . . . I-I didn't hear you come in," I stammered.

"How's the Sound&K campaign going?" Her tone was firm, her mouth a straight line.

"Um . . . okay. Graphics is sorting out some final details. I think we'll be able to present the final draft next week," I said.

Sabrina stared at me without saying a word. She didn't move a muscle. I admired her self-control.

"What's going on between you and my nephew?"

Shit!

"What? With Chri—with Mr. Kelly?" *Please don't let this be happening.* "Nothing, why do you ask?" I had broken out in a cold sweat, and it had nothing to do with the air conditioning.

"So you have no interest in Christian." It wasn't a question.

I shook my head and waved my hands. "I could never go out with him. Don't get me wrong," I went on as she glared at me. "Mr. Kelly is fascinating, smart, charismatic . . ." Okay, maybe I was going overboard with the adjectives. "But it wouldn't be appropriate. He's a client."

"So," she said in an icy tone, "I shouldn't worry about the huge bouquet of roses in reception for you."

Oh. My. God.

I was dead. Dead and buried.

I gripped the edge of the desk. Christian was determined to complicate my life. First with Matteo, then with my parents, and now with the Ice Queen.

"No, you shouldn't worry, Sabrina," I said. My throat was so dry my voice sounded like a cross between Brittney Spears and Marilyn Monroe. "Absolutely not."

She stared at me without saying a word. The silence was so thick that I could hear my watch ticking.

"I want those flowers out of here by this evening. The smell gives me a headache," she ordered.

Without giving me time to reply, she marched out of my office in her black patent-leather heels. I knew I hadn't dreamed it all because my office smelled like Chanel No. 5.

I rushed out into the hallway before catching myself and feigning a casual stroll to reception.

Margherita got up and didn't even bother to greet me; she immediately went on the attack.

"They're for you. From Mr. Kelly," she said spitefully. "You must have provided adequate service."

Count to ten, Gioia!

"Why don't you keep your opinions to yourself and try doing your job, Margherita?"

I took the bouquet back to my office. I set it down to take in the smell of the fresh flowers and saw a little card.

I can't wait to do more business with you. Christian

"Oh good Lord," I murmured.

When I got home that evening after my FitBox lesson, I found Bea sprawled on my sofa, munching chips and watching *Friends*.

With my gym bag in one hand, the bouquet in the other, and my keys clamped in my mouth, I raised my chin at her as a hello.

"I started our single-ladies meeting early," she said, her eyes glued to the screen. "I hope you don't mind, and . . . Oh my God! Who are those from?"

I gave her a look that said not to ask. Then I went straight to my room, dumped my stuff, and went to take the hottest shower I could stand. I needed to melt away the tension in my shoulders.

When I came out, Bea was sitting cross-legged on the bed, her face buried in the roses.

"I see we've landed ourselves a sexy millionaire."

"Or maybe it's just his way of saying he's sorry for going out Saturday night with his ex before coming to lunch at my parents'." I had messaged Bea and given her a link to the incriminating photos earlier.

"Those silly pictures don't mean a thing. Maybe they're a red-carpet couple, but I don't see anything wrong with that."

"You're defending him? Whose side are you on?" I snorted.

"Why does it matter?"

"Don't answer my question with a question!"

"You're pathetic—and a hypocrite to boot! You can't pretend that a man who was an infamous *tombeur de femme* until yesterday would stop just because you like him."

I flopped down on the bed and covered my face with my hands. "Should I say thank-you for the flowers?"

"I think that's in the guide to good manners, yes," said Bea, handing me my phone.

"Bea? Do you think I'll ever feel better? Will I ever trust anyone again?"

"Oh honey, of course you will. And if you don't, I'll personally kick your ass."

Beatrice always knew how to make me laugh. "Thank you."

"So, what do you say we order a huge pizza and watch a movie?"

"Why can't I ever seem to stay on my diet when you're around?" I asked.

"Because your mother is relying on me to fatten you up," she said. She was on her way back to the living room when she stopped in the doorway and turned. "Um, Gioia?"

"Hmmm?"

"I'm on your side. Always."

That night at midnight, I was still awake. I tossed and turned, clutching my phone.

I had been monitoring WhatsApp for no less than twenty minutes; Christian's icon, a view of New York from the Empire State Building, had been there the whole time, mocking me.

I sighed, clicked on "Mr. Asshole Cover Boy," and started typing. Like the last twenty times, I deleted what I wrote.

Write, delete. Write, delete.

I needed to thank Christian for the flowers, but he was probably in bed at this hour.

With another woman.

Stop it, Gioia! Stop it this minute!

I sighed and lay facedown, my head under the pillow. Why was I still awake at night, obsessing over an asshole?

I typed "Thank you" and an emoticon of a bouquet of flowers but deleted it immediately.

No! The arrogant jerk would think he'd been my last thought before going to bed. I closed WhatsApp and put the phone on the nightstand.

I tossed and turned for another half hour before finally falling asleep.

Christian Kelly was my last thought.

Chapter 19

"Wake up, sleeping beauty!" A perky Bea bounced into the room and threw open the curtains. I really had to get my keys back.

I buried my head under the pillow. "Pray to your god that it's not as early as I think it is."

"If you don't want the police knocking at your door, I recommend you get up, have some coffee, and call your mother. And not in that order."

I threw my arm over my eyes. "My mom?" I looked at the alarm clock. It was just after six o'clock. "Now?"

I cursed as she pulled off my covers.

"Call her now. She's already called me twice. She's freaking out, Gioia."

I curled up into myself. "No."

"Do it for national security."

"You're not being very nice, Bea."

"I'm counting to five. One, two—"

"Can I at least have coffee first?"

"Three, four—"

"Fine, I'm up," I groaned, sitting up. Bea was already dressed and had done her makeup. "Why do you already look so good so early in the morning? It should be illegal."

"It's you, my friend. You're getting old."

I gave her the finger and dragged myself to the bathroom. After a shower, I took a moment to gather my courage.

Breathe, Gioia!

I crossed myself.

"Hello?"

"Hi, Mom, it's me."

"Gioia Alessia Caputi, do you know how worried we've been?"

My middle name. She was extra pissed.

"I've had some things going on at work, Mom." It wasn't a total lie. Christian, Sabrina, the flowers.

"Why don't you talk to us, honey? We had to find out about your boyfriend from Matteo, and now you won't talk to us about moving to America. Do you know how far away it is?"

"Mom, I'm not moving to America."

"And how do you think your father and I will be able to visit you with such a long flight? Your father has sciatica, and I'll be looking after my grandchild. Not to mention all those things you hear about New York on the news. Does this mean we'll only see you for Christmas and a week in the summer? I don't think any of this is a good idea, honey."

"Mom, slow down!" I lowered the toilet lid and sat down. "I'm not going anywhere."

I heard the sound of cups and coffee bubbling in the percolator. I imagined her in a dressing gown with curlers on her head while she rubbed her eyes. She always did that when she was agitated.

"You're not going to New York?"

"No."

"So your fridge isn't empty because you already bought your ticket and you're leaving? You'd tell us if you were about to leave, wouldn't you, darling?"

She was brimming with melodrama.

"Mom, I'm not moving to New York."

"Do you want me to convince Christian to move here?"

"Mom, Jesus!" I snapped. I got up and paced back and forth in the bathroom. "Don't you dare talk to Christian. He was only dreaming aloud. If things get serious between Christian and me, we'll figure it out together." My performance was so good that even I was nearly convinced. "I need to go get ready for work, Mom."

"I love you, darling."

"I love you too." *But it's not easy when you're breathing down my neck all the time.*

I ended the call and sat on the toilet to count the tiles and catch my breath.

Stupid Kelly! The only thing his big mouth was good for was kissing.

I found Beatrice in the kitchen sipping coffee and fiddling with her phone. Christian's roses were on display on the table.

"Did you know this Chantal woman is a famous model in South America?"

"Don't you have anything better to say to me after forcing me out of bed and on the phone with my mother?"

I poured myself a cup of coffee.

"She modeled for all the top fashion houses before she quit the runway and started working for *Elle America*."

"I don't care."

"I'm not trying to be cruel, honey, but you don't have a prayer."

I pulled up a stool and sat down next to her. "Let me see."

"No, not this early."

"You started it."

"It'll only hurt you."

I glared at her. "Give me the damn phone." I snatched the phone from her hand and looked at the screen full of photos of Chantal Herrera.

She was absolutely beautiful.

So much for my self-esteem.

Tall, thin, olive skin, full lips, and high cheekbones. The exact opposite of me, except for the light eyes—those we had in common. A small consolation.

"Ugh," I said, handing her the phone. "I'm going to see if I can eat something."

"Right." She rocked back and forth on the stool. "Did you thank Kelly for the flowers?"

"I will," I sighed. "I just couldn't deal last night."

Bea was dressed impeccably in a white silk shirt, black skinny jeans, and matching black platform shoes. She had no reason to envy Chantal.

I, on the other hand, was still wearing my oversized Yankees T-shirt and flannel pajama pants.

"Hey, what are you doing tonight?"

"After those photos, I thought I might slink home and hide my stupid face forever."

"Gioia, you are brilliant and amazing and you're going to find your perfect match. I know it."

"Stop trying to give me diabetes first thing in the morning," I joked, trying to swallow the lump that was forming in my throat. "Give me a few minutes to get ready and we can leave for work together, you bitch."

"Hurry up. And don't try to work miracles."

I gave her the finger and headed back to my room to get dressed.

Chapter 20

Back home that evening, I sprawled out on the sofa and contemplated how disgusting I was. My shabby gray shirt and shapeless pants perfectly complemented my mood.

My boyfriend had cheated on me, along with my fake boyfriend, and Morpheus, the god of sleep, was not about to sweep me up in his arms for a restful night.

Sighing, I turned the TV on to an old black-and-white film.

That morning at work had actually been peaceful. Marco and I had worked on the new campaign for a women's perfume, Sabrina had holed up in her bunker all day, Christian hadn't made an appearance, and I hadn't received any more surprise deliveries.

I'd tried to call Christian a few times to thank him for the flowers, but every time I was about to dial his number, I'd hang up and stare at the computer screen, still holding the receiver.

My computer screen that still had a huge picture of Christian with Chantal on it.

He, of course, had not made contact.

No texts. No calls. I had brought my phone with me everywhere, including the bathroom.

I shouldn't have been surprised.

End of script, back to the beginning. Erase everything and start from scratch.

No karaoke. No kisses. No boyfriend.

On the other hand, I had received a message from Matteo that said PLEASE COME TO THE SHOW. I NEED YOU.

Bastard! Now he needs me, I thought bitterly. Not months ago when I'd needed him.

After an hour on the sofa, I was struggling to follow the love story between the two main characters. I wanted to throw the remote control at the screen. All these films about love triumphing over all, the usual Hollywood clichés about living happily ever after. It was bullshit. Bullshit they drill into our heads from the time we're children.

I turned off the TV and got up to get a glass of water.

The red roses sat on the kitchen counter, mocking me. They were beautiful, fragrant, bright red.

I took my phone and pressed the green receiver icon on WhatsApp. I found the person I was looking for.

Riiing.

One ring.

Riiing.

Two rings.

"Gioia," responded a husky voice on the end of the line.

Shit!

I hadn't prepared anything to say. I was terrible on the phone!

I gulped. "Hi, Matteo, is the invitation still open for Thursday?"

◆ ◆ ◆

"What do you think?"

At the office the next day, Marco and I were testing the perfume for the campaign. At least for a few hours, my head was a Kelly no-fly zone. No Matteo either, obviously.

"Just one more sniff." Matteo kept walking back and forth across the room, his nose glued to the bottle.

I smiled. "You've been sniffing that thing for the last half hour. You probably can't smell it anymore."

"Honey," he said, plopping down across from me, "I may date guys, but I can smell an expensive women's perfume from a mile away."

"So you like it?"

"You want the truth?"

I nodded.

"It's awful. Honestly, this isn't perfume, hon. It's man repellent."

I burst out laughing. "Great! Shall we use that as the tagline?"

"Don't worry," he said with a wave of his hand. "You have the king of creativity here with you. Incidentally, that's the same thing I tell José when we're in bed together."

TMI!

"You're terrible. Now whenever I see this perfume I'm going to think of you two doing it!"

"Oh hon, you haven't heard anything yet. Do you want to hear about the night in our bungalow in Sharm?"

I threw a block of Post-its at him. "Oh, shut up."

We were still laughing and chucking erasers and pencils at each other when the office phone rang.

In tears from laughing so much, I answered, "Dreamstart, good morning, this is Gioia."

"Someone sounds cheery this morning."

Inhale. Exhale.

Remain calm.

You definitely have not counted every single hour and minute since you last saw him.

I sat up in my chair. "Hi."

"Who is it?" asked Marco.

I covered the receiver with my hand and mouthed Christian's name.

Marco gave me two thumbs-up in response.

"How are you, Gioia?"

He can be a radio DJ if his company ever goes under, I thought.

Marco grabbed some pens and pencils from my desk and arranged them as if they were flowers.

"Thank him!" he mouthed.

I glared.

"Great," I responded. "Like you said, cheery." I played with the phone cord and thanked him through clenched teeth. "Um, thanks for the flowers. You really shouldn't have."

Who knew how many bouquets he had sent out that day? Maybe he hadn't even ordered them himself—maybe it had been his secretary in New York.

"You don't want to do business with me, Hurricane?"

A tingle went up my spine. I remembered how he had me pinned against the wall outside my parents' house and taken my breath away with a kiss.

I tried to sound detached. "I'm working on a new campaign, Christian. I don't have time to be on the phone."

Take that, Mr. Small-Time Playboy.

There was a pause. A long one.

He was probably absorbing the blow.

Marco, meanwhile, was doing a dance of encouragement in the middle of my office. I threw a pen at him, which he dodged.

"Come have dinner with me." He was using his low, sexy, strip- per voice, the same one he probably used with all the girls he wanted to screw.

"I can't. I'm behind at work. The last campaign took up all my time."

"I still haven't said when," he replied, laughing.

"Well, I'm always busy!"

"Gioia." He sounded impatient.

There he was. The Kelly that couldn't take no from a woman. And to hear it from a little nothing like me! Imagine that! There was nothing he could do to make me say yes.

"Seriously, Kelly. It's not a good idea. And we can stop pretending now. It's over—my parents bought it. Now we just have to fake a fight."

There was another pause, so long I thought maybe we had gotten disconnected. Marco was gesturing at me that I was crazy.

"So right now are we fighting for real, or is this fake?"

"We're not fighting, Kelly."

"What did I miss?"

I'm sure the paparazzi outside the Savoia didn't miss a thing.

I sighed, unnerved by Marco's gestures and confused by Christian. "Nothing, you haven't missed a thing. I just don't see the point of having dinner together."

"Right, you're still in love with your cheating singer."

"What do you want from me?" I spat. "Why don't you go back to your model? Or did she dump you again?" I bit my tongue. Stupid mouth-brain filter.

Marco's eyes almost popped out.

Christian sighed, frustrated. "Stop reading the gossip columns, Gioia."

"Christian, those pictures were everywhere. A blind person would see them. And I think it's in really, really poor taste for you to have gone out with her the night before you came to lunch at my parents'."

"You're not jealous, are you?"

I wasn't jealous. Of course I wasn't jealous.

"No. I'm just upset about the heart attack my mother will have when she sees those photos!"

His tone hardened. "She's my friend, Gioia. You know how those gossip magazines work."

"No, I don't, actually. The last time I was paparazzied, it was for a school newspaper. I was ten." I held the phone between my shoulder and my ear, waving to Marco to stop distracting me from my diatribe. "Anyway, Christian, you don't need to apologize. We played the happy couple for my parents—we don't need to pretend anymore. You can go out with anyone you like, and I'll do the same."

"Gioia, don't be ridiculous."

"Starting now. Good luck with everything, Christian." I hung up and then took the receiver off the hook so he wouldn't be able to get through. Not now and not . . . ever?

My phone rang in my bag. It was him.

I turned off the ringer and launched the phone into the trash.

"At least you aren't jealous," sang Marco.

"Don't you dare even breathe!" I threatened, holding my tape dispenser at the ready.

Fearing a possible rampage, he raised his hands in surrender.

"You look terrible. Bad day?"

I had just gotten home from another FitBox lesson to find Bea in my kitchen concocting something. A nuclear weapon, judging from the smell. I was so exhausted, tired, and nervous from Christian's call that all I wanted was a hot shower, my frumpiest pajamas, and the *Scandal* season finale.

I hadn't planned for Beatrice.

Why oh why had I given her keys?

"You're not such a beautiful sight yourself," I said, eyeing her. She wore an apron with a close-up of the nether regions of Michelangelo's *David* on it. "Very sexy," I teased.

"I'm cooking and trying not to blow up the kitchen—what's your excuse?"

I opened a bottle of white wine and filled two glasses. "What are you cooking?"

"I'm making carbonara. So—get to the point."

I placed one glass near Beatrice while I took the rest of the bottle over to the sofa. "I ended things with Christian."

"You guys never even got started."

I put my feet up on the coffee table and closed my eyes. I had spent all day long thinking about Christian with that model. Maybe he was with her now. Just imagining them together made my stomach hurt.

"He invited me to dinner, but I said no. I told him we didn't need to keep pretending, that my parents are happy, Matteo seems to have taken the bait, and now Christian can go back to Ms. Mile-Long Legs."

Beatrice turned off the burner and came to sit next to me. "So this is what you want."

"Yeah."

"So why don't you seem happy?"

"I am. I am happy. Seriously." I blinked at her. "I'm just confused. It all happened so fast. I need some carbs and a good night's sleep."

"What you need is a good fuck, my friend."

"Bea, please! I don't need any more of your theories about men. The best men are all gay or married."

"No more man talk tonight—I promise! The menu for the evening includes some juicy carbs, the kind that deposit themselves directly onto your thighs as soon as you swallow them. We'll kill this bottle of wine, smother our stress in ice cream, and then root for Liv and her killer outfits. How does that sound?"

Alcohol, carbohydrates, sugar, and adrenaline. The lethal mix I needed.

"Great idea." I gave her a weary smile.

"Perfect." She got up and opened the cabinet, then placed the plates on the counter. "Go shower and get comfortable. You're my guest this evening."

"A guest in my own home? Why, how kind of you!"

I put down my glass and went to get into pajamas. I smiled for the first time since my phone call with Christian.

"But you can't bury your head in the sand forever!" she shouted from the kitchen. "We need to talk about Kelly and what you want to do. Not tonight, but tomorrow."

◆ ◆ ◆

"Does her asshole father have to get in the way every time?"

"Don't tell me you're rooting for Olitz," Bea said.

"What, are you team Jake?"

"Jake has some integrity, at least. Fitz is a whiny asshole."

"He's in love." I took another handful of popcorn. "And he's the president of the United States."

"I don't understand your idea of love, Gioia. Love isn't a weakness—it should be a source of strength. I'm not saying I'm all for Mr. Cover Boy, but Perri destroyed you."

"We were talking about *Scandal*—what does that have to do with my love life?"

"I haven't seen that light in your eyes for months. Kelly seems like he brings it out."

"I thought we weren't talking about this tonight!" I covered my ears with my hands and started singing a Marco Mengoni song.

My phone buzzed. A WhatsApp notification.

Beatrice and I locked eyes and both lunged for it, but Bea was faster.

She scanned the message and then read it aloud to me, disappointed. "It's a message from your group about bio creams. There's a two-day sale on an anticellulite treatment. I can't believe you go to those in-house sales parties. I'd rather have a kidney removed."

And I couldn't believe I was so heartbroken that the message wasn't from Christian. "Melissa got me into it."

I left the group and scrolled to Mr. Asshole Cover Boy.

Just a quick look, Gioia.

LAST SEEN AT 9:00 P.M.

At least he wasn't chatting with anyone else right now.

Maybe because the person he would be chatting with is with him, in person, said the devil on my shoulder. I waved it away and went back to watching TV.

"Maybe you're right. Jake is a badass."

Chapter 21

"Gioia, you look gorgeous!" exclaimed Bea as I made my entrance at the Gotha.

That evening, it had taken me two hours and three wardrobe changes before I had finally been satisfied with what I saw in the mirror. I had followed an online makeup tutorial to a tee, gathered my hair in a soft ponytail, and wore my widow-in-mourning uniform.

Black dress, black leather jacket, black shoes.

I was a vision of happiness.

I wanted to blow off the whole thing, but this was not the night to bawl over a pint of ice cream. It was an opportunity to prove to Matteo that I could live without him. I wanted him to explode when he saw me looking so beautiful, so absorbed in the party, not thinking at all about how he'd dumped me.

"Hey, Bea!" I shouted over the music. "Where are the girls?"

"They're waiting for us in the private lounge. Come!" She handed me a cocktail. "Seriously, though, Gioia. You look absolutely amazing tonight."

"I got in a fight with my closet."

"Well, it looks like you won."

It was only ten, but the Gotha was already swarming with people. On the outside, it was just a rundown brick building, but beyond the bouncers a whole other world opened up, like when Alice goes down the rabbit hole.

The design was modern, the decor exuding the wealth and elegance of the clientele. Entrepreneurs, bankers, undercover talent scouts. Everyone was in bespoke designer clothes.

"You don't look so bad yourself!"

Bea was wearing a tiny gold dress that scooped low in the front and back. She wore gladiator sandals with super–high heels, and her hair was a mass of blond curls. She looked like an ad for hair products. She was divine, but if I dared to dress like that, people would probably inquire about my hourly rate.

"Have you really been waiting for me with a cocktail?" I asked, tasting the mix of strawberry and vodka in my glass.

"I knew you'd need to loosen up a little," she said, guiding me to the lounge. She hugged me tight and whispered in my ear, "You're going to be great."

Bea knew me well: I had never been so nervous in my life.

I knew this evening could be big for Matteo and the guys, and even though I was still mad at him, I hoped with all my heart that it would go well. I had spent years watching them work day and night trying to find the perfect chords, I had gone gigging with them in their rickety van, I had cheered while they played for drink tickets at local bars. Then came some success: the tour, the fans, weeks spent not seeing or hearing from Matteo because he was holed up in the recording studio. In short, I had a stake in the whole Sounds project.

"We're over here!" cried Ludo from a sofa.

As we reached them, the lights went out and the intro music started.

Maybe it was because I was drinking on an empty stomach, but my legs were shaking. I had to sit down, fast.

Breathe, Gioia!

"It's starting!" shouted Bea.

The Gotha exploded as Matteo, Alessio, Jak, and Lorenzo took the stage and started to play.

I strained my neck to see who was in the front row: some of our old friends, Alessio's wife-to-be, and their families.

I looked back at the stage, hoping Matteo couldn't see me. Just the stage and the bar were lit up; the rest of the club was in darkness. The boys were playing all their warhorses and cover songs. Ensconced comfortably on that sofa, I was hearing the story of my entire relationship with Matteo, told live, song after song.

It was like a 3-D movie.

Matteo was an animal onstage. Enigmatic, haunting, mysterious. He had the kind of smile and dimples that could steal a woman's heart and underwear. Looking at him made me lose myself. His T-shirt was stretched across his chest, his muscular arms hung from the microphone. His hair, usually messy, was slicked back with gel. He'd shaved, and his black jeans clung perfectly to his legs. To top off his rock-star look, he was wearing snakeskin boots and a leather bracelet on his right wrist.

I felt his words invade my ear and throb in my chest.

I had to get some distance. I signaled to Melly that I was going to get a drink.

In line at the bar, I moved aside for two men in suits and ties. Then I noticed a familiar face. We both turned to look at each other at the same time, surprised. He was tall, dressed in jeans and a T-shirt. He had the face of someone kind—and fun.

"Hi!" he exclaimed. "You're Gioia, right?"

Wow, he remembers my name! I smiled shyly.

"Your performance in Barcelona was really something!" he shouted, holding back a smile.

Fantastic. So he hadn't been impressed by me, but by my ridiculous display.

"That was quite an evening," I said, embarrassed. "You're Thomas, right?" I asked, holding out my hand. "I wasn't sure if it was you."

I was in a dark bar packed with people and who did I run into? Christian's assistant.

It was full-on war between me and Lady Luck.

"Yeah, I'm here to check out the boys," he said, gesturing to the stage where Matteo, sweaty and more beautiful than I had ever seen him, continued sending all the girls into a delirium.

"Are you here alone?" I asked.

I was determined not to take Christian's name in vain—not even under torture.

"Yeah. Sometimes I scout shows for Sound&K."

"Oh." I looked around. "Kelly's not here?"

I said I wouldn't say his first name, not his last.

"He called me today and said he had some work to do, so he sent me. Not that I mind," he said with a sweeping look. "This is a really amazing place. And the band is fantastic. Do you know them? The Sounds, I mean."

Do I know them? Every fucking song was about me. Not to mention I had damned Matteo to hell in front of a room full of people in Barcelona, including Thomas.

"You could say that," I replied. Better if he didn't make the connection.

"Okay, well, I have to go. I have to talk to the boys during the set break."

I shook the hand he held out.

"It was a pleasure, Gioia. Have a great night. And stay away from the mic." He winked.

"Sure." I smiled through clenched teeth. That evening would always precede me. I should have remembered to check if there were any incriminating videos on YouTube.

At least now I could breathe a little easier knowing Christian wouldn't turn up. Thank God. There was no way I'd be able to handle him, Matteo, and all my emotions at once.

The Sounds took a break and everyone rushed over to the bar, making it even harder to get the bartender's attention. A man in a suit and tie stumbled into me and nearly spilled the entire contents of his glass all over my dress.

I jumped back. "Look where you're going!" I shouted.

"Sorry, love," he slurred. He was drunk. "What's a sexy thing like you doing here all by yourself?"

I took a step back, worried my FitBox lessons would finally come in handy.

"She's with me." Someone stepped between us, gripping me by the waist and moving me to the side. "Get out of here."

The man turned and stumbled away.

"Why do I always have to come to your rescue whenever you try to order a beer?" It was Matteo, gleaming with sweat and red in the face, giving me a huge smile.

"Because I'm not as famous as you are?" I said, recalling our first encounter. Like that first time, he took me by the hand and marched me up to the bar. He positioned me in front of him and shielded my body from the crowd.

"What are you drinking?" He called over the bartender with a single finger.

"Just beer." I didn't move, painfully aware that I was pinned against his body.

Matteo strained his neck forward, his breath on my ear. "Thanks for coming tonight," he whispered in my ear. "I really hoped you'd be here." He spun me around to face him and studied me with his green eyes.

"I'm glad I came," I said.

Gioia, no! Don't let him seduce you with those eyes and his pretty smile!

"Who's here supporting you tonight? I haven't seen any of your family."

"Just the guys from the pub and you."

Don't fall for it!

"What about Georgia?" I asked, detached.

"She's not here." He looked down and bit his lip. "We broke up. She said I spent too much time on my music, so . . ."

"So she left you?" I raised my beer and made a toast. "Welcome to the singles club!"

"I deserved it."

"Yes, you did."

"Where's Christian?" He took a long drink of beer.

Good question. I used Thomas's answer.

"He had work to do."

I tried to erase the image of Chantal in an evening gown from my mind.

He came closer, his face just inches from mine. He eyed my lips and whispered in a husky voice, "What a pity."

"Good thing you don't sing like you talk, Perri."

Christian was suddenly next to me, tense and furious. He was glaring at Matteo.

"Mr. Kelly," Matteo growled.

"Perri," Christian said in a menacing voice.

I should have considered myself lucky to be sandwiched between two sexy men fighting over me. Instead, I was a wreck.

I stared at Christian.

Oh. My. God!

He was breathtaking. He attracted more attention than all the other men there combined.

"Christian? Wh-What are you doing here?" I stammered.

"Hello, love." He cupped my chin in his hands and gave me a quick kiss on the mouth. Then he whispered in my ear, "Don't look too happy to see me, Hurricane."

"Mr. Kelly, I didn't think you were coming," Matteo interrupted us. "Gioia was just telling me you were too busy to make it tonight."

"I'm never too busy for Gioia. I wanted to surprise her." He tightened his grip on my side. "Looks like I succeeded. And not just her." He gave me a quizzical look before glaring at Matteo again. If Christian had been able to shoot fire from his eyes, Matteo would have been incinerated. "I think you're needed onstage, Perri."

"I was just going." Matteo leaned in and kissed me on the cheek. "Thanks for being here for me tonight, Gioia." He lowered his voice, but not so much that Christian couldn't hear him.

Alone with Christian, I squirmed away and turned to go, but he blocked me with his arm.

"Wait a minute, young lady. Not so fast."

"The girls are waiting for me."

"Let them wait."

"Don't you dare tell me what I can and can't do, Kelly."

"Gioia, don't be a child." He took my elbow and maneuvered me to a corner of the bar.

"Oh, so I'm the child! I'm not the one who showed up unannounced to play macho man and beat my chest with my fist!"

"I don't like him."

"I hate to remind you, but you're here to give him a contract."

"Don't remind me, or I'll tear it up." He ran a hand through his hair, exasperated.

I want to run my hand through that hair.

"He's a little prick."

"You don't even know the guy."

He glared at me. "He dumped you, which puts him up there with the top-ten pricks in the world."

I wondered who the other nine were, but now wasn't the time to ask.

"Not to mention the cheating and dumping you with a note," he went on, undeterred. "Which brings him right up to number one."

I crossed my arms and smirked. "You seem pretty jealous over someone you say is such a prick, Mr. Kelly."

"Seriously, Gioia. I don't understand what you see in that trained monkey."

"Stop it, Christian! You have no right to come here and tell me who I should or shouldn't date."

He clasped my waist and pulled me toward him. "That man," he whispered, his face too close to mine, "does not deserve you."

Who does? An asshole like you? "Why don't you go back to your model and leave me alone already?"

"I can't stand you when you're like this."

"I can't stand you ever."

"Perfect."

"Great. At least we agree on something."

Christian stepped back, panting. He ran his hand through his hair again and looked at me as if he wanted to shake me so hard Matteo would just fall out of my head.

I sighed. "Christian—"

He took my face in his hands and kissed me fiercely, as if he were claiming me in front of the entire club. It was a clash of lips and teeth, until I opened my mouth and our tongues met.

I trembled and gripped Christian's shirt. I could feel the heat from his hands, the frenzy of his lips, the power of his body. I was drunk off his scent.

And then Matteo's voice hit me like a cold shower.

In Dolby surround sound.

Guitar in hand, he sat on a stool at center stage. The girls in the club started screaming his name even louder than before. A rebellious lock of hair fell over his eyes, and I was mesmerized watching his hands pluck the guitar strings.

"The Sounds wouldn't exist without my muse for all these songs," he whispered hoarsely. "This song is for you, like all the others."

Shit.

He was looking straight at me.

My eyes widened, my heart hammered in my chest. I hid my face in my hands.

This was not happening. This could not be happening. How could Matteo mess with me like this? This stunt didn't seem like the action of a man who really still loved me. Something had changed since he'd first seen me with Christian.

Before I could stop them, silent tears began to pour down my cheeks. Matteo's voice had found a crack in the wall I had built between us, and all the pain I had tried to bury hit me right in the chest.

I found myself in Christian's embrace, my face buried in his chest.

"I'm sorry," I gulped. "I don't want to ruin your shirt." It probably cost more than my rent.

Christian's face was a mask of rage. "I can hit him if you want."

"You need his face in one piece for the CD cover," I reminded him.

"You're right," he sighed into my hair. He pulled me tight to him, his hands softly caressing my back. "Let it go, Hurricane," he said in a low voice. He brought his thumb to the tears that continued to pour down my cheeks. The dam had opened and it wasn't about to close. "You don't want to seem weak, you always have some witty response prepared, you try so hard to seem confident, but you don't need to pretend with me." He took my face in his hands and studied me tenderly. "So use my shirt to cry on if you want. No one will see you."

"I'm going to ruin it . . ."

I heard him laugh into my hair.

We looked into each other's eyes for a long time, and then he pulled me close again. I buried my face in Christian's chest and let him caress my hair as I poured out all my tears.

I couldn't hear what Matteo was singing, just the beating of Christian's heart. It soothed me until my tears finally ran dry.

"Thanks," I said, my voice muffled.

Christian caressed my cheek. "You'll have your happy ending, Hurricane."

◆ ◆ ◆

"You should stop staring. I'm fine! Seriously . . ." I said to Christian, who gave me a skeptical look.

"And you should stop drinking," he said. "You're drunk."

"It's only a beer."

"She slurred, on her third one . . ." he shot back.

I stuck out my tongue. "I'm buzzed. You've never seen me drunk." I brought the bottle to my mouth and took a long sip.

Christian raised an eyebrow, amused.

"Fine, Kelly," I snorted. "You've seen me more drunk than sober since we've met."

"Should I take that personally? I'm usually the one who makes women go crazy. But you make me crazy for you. Completely."

"It must be my sharp wit." I poked a finger into his chest. "Don't think I didn't hear what you said when I was crying."

During the torrent of tears, Christian had managed to find two free stools near the bar, far from the lounge, from the stage, and from Matteo.

After an hour, we were still there, drinking. That is, I was still drinking. I had an unbelievable headache: tears and alcohol were a potent combination.

"Shouldn't you go hear the guys instead of babysit me?" I gestured to the stage. From where we sat, Matteo was a miniscule dot; inside me, he was an enormous question mark.

"I'm not here for them."

He hopped off the stool and leaned against the bar. He turned and faced me for a long time. The way he studied me said more than a thousand words. The man was impenetrable; I never managed to understand what was going through his head.

"You're not saying you're here for me, are you?" I joked. I brought the bottle to my lips, but I nearly choked after seeing how serious he looked.

"We had our first fight as boyfriend and girlfriend, and then you dumped me over the phone. I couldn't not come say I was sorry, honey." He winked at me as he played with his cocktail straw.

I rolled my eyes. "So we fought and broke up. Deal with it, dear."

I still had all the same reasons for dumping him. Reasons like long, tanned legs in high heels without a trace of cellulite; perfect, voluminous hair; and an exotic name. Chantal.

"Don't make that face, Hurricane. I already told you—Chantal and I are just friends."

Had I been thinking out loud? I shrugged. "You can go out with whoever you want, Kelly. But like I said before, you're lucky my mother doesn't know how to use the Internet, otherwise you'd be dead by now."

I avoided adding that my mother currently saw him as the monster who was going to steal her baby. She had already planned lunches and dinners with me for every foreseeable Sunday just to make sure I didn't end up calling her from JFK Airport.

"So, Kelly. Tell me," I said abruptly. "How come you and Ms. Mile-Long Legs broke up?" I leaned in and rested my chin on my hands.

"Who?" he asked, amused.

"Don't pretend you don't know who I'm talking about."

A crease spread across his bronzed forehead. "I don't want to talk about it."

"Oh come on, Christian! You know practically everything about me. My parents even showed you my naked baby pictures!"

"Are there any other naked pictures of you?" He cocked his head, and his voice made my ear tingle. "More recent ones?"

"Oh stop!" I pushed him and narrowed my eyes. "Spill it!"

I hadn't found anything about their breakup on Wikipedia or anywhere else online.

"If I don't want to talk about it, it's for a good reason."

"Come on, Kelly!" I scooted closer to him on my stool. "I promise I won't blab to the tabloids and ruin your playboy reputation."

"You never give up, do you?"

"I've had a good teacher." I smiled.

"It's a long story."

I leaned against the bar. I knew it wasn't fair of me to keep asking all those questions about his private life, but my curiosity was getting the better of me. "I have all evening."

Christian sighed and rolled his eyes. "Let's just say you're not the only one who's been cheated on."

"She cheated on you? Okay, I'm done, I'll stop prying," I said as he scowled at me.

"I found her in bed with someone else. Chantal was in Miami for a fashion show, and I went to surprise her." He stared emptily at his glass. "In the end, she surprised me."

No surprises, I always used to say. Send a text message or a WhatsApp message, post a photo on Instagram with geotags. But never, ever surprise me!

I rested my hand on his arm. "I'm sorry."

He looked as though he had just been spit out of the whirlwind of memories I had awakened. He shook himself and said with a bitter smile, "That's why I know how you feel. I felt like shit. I completely fell apart. I had asked her to marry me and then found her in bed with a stranger."

I imagined Christian kneeling in front of Chantal and asking her to spend her entire life with him.

Okay, maybe I didn't want to know the whole story after all.

"I punched the guy and went back home to get rid of her stuff, even though she kept telling me that it had been a mistake, that she loved only me."

"And that she only understood how much she loved you once she cheated on you."

Classic.

"I spent months eating my heart out over her. I went out every night; I'd sleep with girls I met and then dump them the next day with a phone call from my secretary. Anything to hurt Chantal. But in the end, I was the one who woke up every morning feeling like shit, betrayed by the only woman I ever loved."

My brain registered only the information it shouldn't have: Christian had dated half of New York City and acted like a colossal asshole.

How recent was all this?

I bit my lip. "How did you forgive her? I mean, in the photos you guys look like you get along well." *Better than well.*

"We work together. She does PR for Sound&K. So we had to find a way to be in the same room together."

"Oh." I imagined Chantal's face in the middle of a dartboard as I took aim at the bull's-eye.

"I didn't know she'd be in Milan last Saturday," he explained. "She showed up at my hotel dressed to attract cameras. She wants to get back together with me, and she's doing everything she can to make me cave."

I threw the dart. Bull's-eye!

"And what about you? What do you want, Christian Kelly?"

Christian started to play with his beer bottle. It was still a sensitive issue. A wound that hadn't closed yet—that is, if he really wanted it to close.

"Sometimes I think it could work, that we could be happy together. But then I think about that day at the hotel . . . She broke my heart. I don't know if I could handle going through that again."

Stop! Enough!

We were entering a minefield. Exes, cheating, getting back together again, fears. Any step could be fatal. We needed to change the subject. My heart was still wrapped in bubble wrap, with a string around the bundle and a sign that said "No Access. Stay Back." Christian's heart was in pieces, and Ms. Mile-Long Legs was trying to put it back together again with her sexy eyes and who knows what else.

We were more scrambled and complicated than a Rubik's Cube.

My phone vibrated in my pocket.

It was a WhatsApp message from Beatrice.

`I'm going home. See you tomorrow.`

I raised an eyebrow and checked the time. It was just after eleven, and Bea was going home? Had they announced the end of the world or something? There were only three reasons why she'd leave a bar this early: there was a terror threat, her house was flooded, or Javier Bardem had announced his divorce from Penelope Cruz and Bea was already at the airport, destination Madrid.

`Are you okay?`

`I'm just tired.`

I frowned. That wasn't like her. I typed:

Do you want me to come with you?

"Is everything okay?" asked Christian, worried.

"Yeah, I hope so. Bea's leaving."

His eyes flashed with amusement. "You mean Gloria Gaynor?"

"That's the one." I smiled.

"Too bad! I was sure she'd get up at the end of the night and sing a duet with your moody troubadour over there! I would have gotten it on video."

"Stop it. That's my best friend you're talking about."

My phone sounded again, and Christian burst out laughing when he heard my ridiculous Sherwood Forest ringtone. I really needed to change that.

I opened the message.

REMEMBER THE GOSPEL ACCORDING TO BEA. SHOW IT TO HIM, BUT TELL HIM IT'S NOT FOR SALE.

I laughed. I'd talk to her about everything tomorrow.

I put my phone away and eyed the cocktail Christian was offering. "A second ago, you were accusing me of being drunk."

"I don't want to get in your way," he sang.

I huffed and accepted the drink. "What should we toast to? Broken hearts?"

He lifted his glass. "I'd say a new beginning." He nailed me to the stool with his low voice and intense eyes.

I felt myself blush, suddenly self-conscious under his soul-searching gaze.

We weren't a good match. We had both been profoundly hurt; we were both disillusioned about love. Two broken hearts didn't always equal a whole one.

I buried my face in my glass, realizing too late that I really couldn't handle any more vodka. I looked around the room, noticing that the guys had stopped playing and that all the people out on the floor were dancing to the house music. I had been so lost in conversation with Christian that I had forgotten why I was there.

Matteo. The asshole.

I blinked, searching the entire room. My attention settled on a corner of the lounge. Matteo and the guys were celebrating the concert with their friends.

Christian followed my gaze. "Do you wish you were over there?"

I sighed. "Why should I?"

"He dedicated the concert to you."

"You know where he can stick his stupid concert?"

"Where's his girlfriend?"

"She's not here. They broke up." I studied his reaction.

He was staring impassively at Matteo, his jaw pulsing. "Come."

Without giving me time to respond, he took my cocktail and led me toward the center of the club.

"Christian?"

We zigzagged through the couples, our hands pressed together.

"Christian, what are you doing?" I nearly smacked right into him as he stopped and faced me in the middle of the dance floor.

"I'm helping you, God forgive me."

"Don't bother teaching me how to dance. My repertoire already includes the hokeypokey."

He wrapped his arms around my waist and lifted his chin in the direction of the lounge. I followed his gaze: we were right where Matteo could see us.

"I'm making him come back to you, Hurricane."

Confused, I put my arms around his neck and pulled him close. "Didn't you just say he's the world's biggest prick?"

Christian pressed his lips against my forehead. "He is, but if he's the one you want . . ." He trailed off.

His breath caressed my neck as the usual tremor moved through my whole body. In that moment, in his arms, I had no idea what I wanted.

Mayday, mayday!

"If he sees us dancing like this, won't he think I'm out of the game?"

"Shh." He placed a finger on my lips and smiled his illegal smile. "Hasn't anyone ever told you that you talk too much?"

We kept dancing to "I See Fire" by Ed Sheeran. The DJ was clearly slowing things down.

I rested my cheek on his chest, closed my eyes, and let myself be guided by his slow movements, lulled by his caresses.

I looked up at him. "You're insane, you know that, Kelly?"

"Gioia," he murmured, "I really would go insane if I had to see you dance with someone else."

God, this was a man who promised heaven in the flames of hell. His eyes gleamed with desire, and I could feel his heat rushing through my veins.

"You leave a wake like an aircraft carrier, Hurricane," he whispered hoarsely.

Then he pressed his lips to mine. He kissed me with infinite slowness. A long, sweet torture.

I clung to him, my hands in his hair, and then grabbed his waist, pulling him against me. Our bodies had found the right combination of colors in the Rubik's Cubes that had been our lives up to that point.

Panting, I pulled away from him. We were in a public place, not in a cheap motel. There was only one thing I could do to ground the electricity between us.

"Are you sure your plan worked? He left," I said, sensing that Matteo was now very far away from me.

Matteo's name worked instantly.

He took a deep breath and closed his eyes. "Give him a few days. You'll hear from him."

I shoved my trembling hands in my jacket pockets. I needed another drink. Now.

"Do you want to get one last drink?" I asked him, even if it would have been better to run back home and escape this man who could cause global warming with one smile.

He tucked a stray strand of hair behind my ear. "You've had enough to drink, Hurricane."

"Just one," I begged.

He studied me like he always did—in silence. Then he said, "Okay, one last drink, and then I'll take you home."

I put my hand across my heart.

Just one drink, just one drink, just one drink.

One hour later, we were still at the Gotha, dancing in the middle of the floor.

More than dancing, I was trying to stay on my feet, literally hanging on Christian's shirt.

All night long, people had been wanting me to let go. First Beatrice, then Christian. And I aimed to please. Yes, I did.

I had officially let go.

"Gioia?"

"Why are you speaking so slowly?"

"I'm not. You're drunk. Come on, the club's closing. I'll take you home."

"Oh no! Come on!" I moaned. "Just one more song!" I latched onto Christian's neck and pressed against him, still swaying and humming to the song.

I could hear him sigh. "Gioia." He removed my hands from his neck and held my shoulders. "Everyone's gone," he said softly.

I frowned and looked around.

I was so wasted I hadn't even realized we were the last two people in the entire club. Besides the bartender, who was cleaning up the bar, and the cleaning ladies, who were giving us weird looks, the Gotha was completely empty. The music I could hear—the music I had been dancing to—had been in my head! I was a musical genius!

I had a vague memory of having gone back to the bar with Christian, ordering a mojito, and spilling it on my dress.

With difficulty, I had reached the women's bathroom, which seemed more like a rugby team's locker room by that time of night. *Disgusting!*

I barely recalled having arrived back at the bar to find Christian speaking English into his Bluetooth headset. He'd been using that sweet and seductive tone that I had already heard at the office. He'd been on the phone with Hello Dear, also known as Ms. Mile-Long Legs, better known to the gossip columns as Chantal Herrera.

Indignant, I had ordered another mojito. And then I couldn't remember anything else. It was all a total blank.

I cocked my head to one side, looking at Christian's mouth as it opened and closed. He was talking to me. "Wha—what?" I stammered.

"I'll get your bag and take you home. You can't drive like this."

I grabbed him by the hand. "No, wait."

I didn't want to go home and be rational Gioia again. I just wanted to have fun and not think. I wanted to be done forever with Geisha Gioia who had spent all those years with Matteo, and Bridget Jones Gioia who had appeared in recent months. It was time to take off the widow's weeds and wear the clothes of a woman who was bold, light, and happy. And also a bit drunk.

"Can we stay for one last dance? Just one more. Please?" I pleaded with puppy-dog eyes.

Christian studied me for a long while, as if he were in the midst of an internal struggle.

Dance, or sling me over his shoulder like a caveman?

He abruptly walked away, making me think he had chosen the third option: go to bed and leave me standing there drunk. Instead, Christian went to the bartender, conferred for a minute, and came back to me.

"After this, Cinderella, we're going home."

I nodded as the sounds of a piano came pouring out of the speakers.

"Ms. Caputi, may I have this last dance?"

I smiled and accepted his outstretched hand.

The notes of John Legend's "All of Me" echoed through the room as I pressed myself back into Christian. I was becoming addicted to his body.

He placed his hands on my waist and we began to sway, guided by the music.

"Kelly, I want to thank you for tonight."

"You're saying that because you're drunk."

"No, seriously."

He caressed my lip with his thumb, stopping me from blabbering. "Shh, I know."

I rested my cheek against his chest, feeling his heart beating as frantically as my own. Christian held me tight to him, drawing circles on my back with his fingers through the thin layer of my dress. I breathed in his scent; he smelled like citrus, like fresh air. He smelled like Christian.

I stood on tiptoe and laced my hands around his neck. Christian never stopped looking into my eyes; his face was lit by the desire that crackled between us. He brushed my cheek with the back of his hand. We gazed at each other for a long time without saying a word.

"Christian . . ." I whispered.

I closed my eyes, longing to feel his lips on my mouth. I was finally prepared to admit how much I wanted him.

Christian moved away. "Gioia," he breathed. "I can't."

Just like John Legend said, I had placed my cards on the table, showing my hearts for one evening, ready to take the risk, even though it was scary. And he was rejecting me.

It's not that I thought I was so irresistible, but I wasn't exactly expecting a two of spades in return.

I looked at him, confused. "Why not?"

"If I kiss you now," whispered Christian, "there'll be no stopping me."

"What if I don't want to stop you?"

"You're drunk."

"I'm not drunk."

"Tomorrow you won't remember any of this."

"I'll take notes, Kelly," I slurred.

He sighed, exasperated by his own struggle with himself. "You're playing with fire, Hurricane."

I bit my cheek to stop myself from laughing at his tormented expression. "But I want to play with you, Mr. Kelly. Are you afraid I'm going to spill it all to the press? I'm not like those drama queens you're used to dating."

"Don't be ridiculous, Gioia. I'm taking you home."

I took him by the arm. "Come home with me," I whispered.

Chapter 22

I could hear AC/DC running through my head.

I kept my eyes closed for a few more minutes, hoping the rock concert would end and allow my brain to make sense of my surroundings.

I opened my eyes and daylight hit me in the face, making me groan.

I buried my head under the pillow, trying to make the room stop spinning.

Then I heard the shower running.

I wasn't imagining things. Someone was definitely in my shower.

Oh God! The night before!

The beers.

The dancing.

Christian. Me clinging to him, begging him to come home with me. Obviously not so I could show him my snow globe collection.

My eyes snapped open, and I bolted up in bed. I looked around and saw my dress on the floor, along with my shoes and bag.

I remembered slow dancing with Christian; then I had gone to the bathroom, and when I came out I had caught him on the phone with Chantal. Then we danced again and I had clung to him like a koala, trying to make him kiss me. *What an idiot!*

Christian had pushed me away and said, "Midnight's long past, Cinderella."

Then darkness.

I looked under the sheet. *Thank the Lord!* I was still wearing my underwear—matching underwear, at that!

The shower turned off and I panicked. I slipped out of bed and pulled on the clothes heaped on the nearest piece of furniture. My oversized T-shirt and Hello Kitty pants. *Sexy, Gioia!*

I couldn't remember anything about what had happened with Christian. Nada. Zilch. I should have been drinking Shirley Temples.

"Morning, Hurricane." Christian appeared in the bathroom door wearing his pants from the night before and on top . . . nothing. Water dripped from his sculpted muscles, his uncombed hair still wet from the shower.

God, he was so sexy first thing in the morning. It was Christmas and my gift was standing in the bathroom door half-unwrapped.

I stood up and swayed. Was it Kelly or my hangover? "Chr— Christian. Hi. How are you?"

Great, Gioia. Bonus points for interesting conversation starters.

"I'm great. What about you?" he asked, amused.

He clearly pitied me.

Cinderella had gone home from the ball and woken up with her hair tangled and her mascara crusted around her eyes. "I feel disgusting."

Smiling that illegal smile, he shifted his weight off of the doorframe and walked over to the bed. "We hardly slept last night," he whispered.

His low voice woke my entire body.

I went pale. "R-really?"

"Really." He brushed a strand of hair from my face; his eyes, two black pools, sparkled with desire. "It was . . . unforgettable." His gaze fell to my lips, delivering the final blow to my nervous system.

My brain was no longer processing information. Was it possible that I had slept with Kelly and didn't remember it?

"Truly unforgettable," he said softly.

A night with a sex god and I couldn't remember a thing.

"Wow . . . you're speechless. I was that good, huh?"

"Oh, look! It's late." I pointed to the bedside clock. I dodged him and headed to the closet. "I need a shower."

"Gioia . . ."

I pulled a random black dress from its hanger. "You can make yourself some coffee. There's skim milk in the fridge."

"Gioia?" I could hear him behind me, his eyes burning into my back.

I opened my underwear drawer and snatched up the first ones I saw. Had I really begged him to sleep with me? Was I that pathetic? *Yes and yes. Oh God!*

"If you prefer, there's also some tea in the cupboard," I babbled, so I wouldn't have time to think. When I turned around, I slammed into a solid, muscular chest.

I flailed back and grabbed Christian for dear life.

He took my chin and lifted my face, forcing me to meet his gaze. "Gioia—"

"I know what you're about to say, Christian. We shouldn't have done it, you're right."

Christian pressed his lips together, amused. "Nothing happened."

I could have killed him. "Nothing?"

"Nothing."

"You tricked me!"

Christian burst out laughing. "I practically had to carry you up the stairs," he went on. "And as soon as I got you into bed, you collapsed and started snoring."

"I don't snore," I said, crossing my arms.

"Are you sure about that? You kept me up all night."

"Listen, Christian . . . about last night . . ."

He caressed my lip with his thumb. "Gioia," he said slowly. He traced a line along my jaw and down my neck. I trembled at his touch while trying to hide the disappointment I felt at remembering how he had rejected me.

"I'm glad you stopped me. I don't know why I jumped you like that, but thank you. I'm sure I would have regretted it this morning. I probably would have given you a kick in the balls. I'm sorry if I ruined your night."

Christian moved closer until I felt the closet door against my back. I hoped my closet would open up and swallow me whole. God, what an idiot I had been, throwing myself at him like that. Christian stared at my mouth; the desire in his eyes made me look down, but that meant a close-up view of his bare chest.

I gulped.

Christian had his hands on either side of my head, blocking my escape routes. "Did you think I didn't want to sleep with you, Hurricane?"

I could smell my shower gel on his skin. Heavenly.

"You said you didn't . . ." I sighed. I could hear his heartbeat. It was fast and erratic—like mine.

I raised my hands to push him away, but Christian grabbed my wrists.

His eyes were nothing but desire.

Breathe, Gioia. Remember to breathe!

His smile had straightened into a serious, straight line. He bowed his head and his lips followed the line of his fingers. He kissed my cheek, my chin, nibbling up to my earlobe.

"Once I make love to you, Hurricane, you'll remember. Once I have you in my arms and kiss every inch of your skin, you'll only want my lips on your body. You'll just want me and no one else."

He stared at me so intensely that I thought I might drown in his eyes. I was frozen against the closet, unable to move or utter a word. I was totally at the mercy of Christian Kelly.

I grabbed him by the neck and drew my lips to his, biting him. "I. Will. Never. Sleep. With. You. Kelly."

The illegal smile returned as his fingers stroked my cheek. "Are you sure about that?"

"I was under the influence last night. I already told you—I will never join your fan club."

Christian laughed and then regarded me. I hadn't even convinced myself, let alone him.

"Don't try to use that illegal smile on me, Kelly." I pushed him away and ducked into the bathroom.

Christian followed me. "You're even sexy in those Hello Kitty pants, Hurricane," he sang from the door.

"Go to hell, Kelly!" I yelled before slamming the door in his face.

I leaned against the sink and grimaced at my reflection in the mirror. My mascara was caked onto my eyelashes, my foundation was not as long lasting as it had promised to be, and my hair was a mass of knots. I shuddered at the thought that Christian had seen me in this state.

I grabbed my toothbrush with one hand, and with the other I entered our group chat and wrote in caps:

BEA, IF YOU ARE READING THIS MESSAGE, PLEASE DO NOT COME OVER. I REPEAT: DO NOT COME OVER. KELLY IS HERE. NOW. DO NOT COME OVER.

I put the phone on the shelf and rocketed into the shower, trying not to have a heart attack rethinking the night before. I was late,

Christian was in my kitchen, and I had a meeting at eight thirty with Sabrina.

I brushed my hair, put on my dress, smeared on some foundation, and went to my bedroom. There wasn't a peep from the kitchen.

There was from my phone, though. I already had a ton of messages from the girls.

Bea: Do you like him better than me?

Melly: Gioia, did you sleep with him? Actually, don't answer that. I don't want to think about it.

Bea: It would be about time.

Ludo: But isn't he with Ms. Mile-Long Legs?

Melly: Gioia, what is wrong with you? You don't need to know his social security number, but you should know something about him!

Bea: How was it? Melly, get out of this chat. I want spoilers from your sister on her night with the American sex god.

Ludo: Easy, Bea. She doesn't have to tell us anything.

Bea: Who put up with her all that time she was depressed?????? We did.

Melly: I don't know, Gioia. I just hope
he's good to you.

Ludo: This is all very *Pretty Woman*.
Rich man seduces poor girl.

Bea: The woman in that case was a
prostitute.

Ludo: Whatever. It's romantic.

Melly: I have a bad feeling about this.
Kelly has a reputation.

I snorted. One minute without me and they had already jumped
to conclusions.

You guys are terrible. I was drunk last
night and he took me home. End of story.
No sex. No seduction. I have to go. The
American sex god is in my kitchen. And
stop bombarding my phone with chats
please. Thanks.

I went to the kitchen and found Christian sitting at the bar drink-
ing coffee. He poured me some.
"Here."
I covered my mouth with one hand and gagged. "I can't drink that."
"You have to put something in your stomach."
I sighed, took the cup, and sat on the stool next to his roses. I
brought the cup to my lips and looked at him. His white shirt, a little

rumpled, was tucked into his black pants; his hair was still damp from the shower, but it looked impeccable as always.

I looked like I had been run over by a truck; he was ready for a photo shoot.

He was occupied with his phone, and I could tell from his eyebrows that he wasn't reading anything pleasant.

"When will I see you again?" he asked, looking suddenly serious. "To follow through on our little charade," he said, noting the surprise on my face.

"Oh, I don't think it will work. Matteo will never fall for it," I said.

But I was falling for it.

"Give him a few days. I'll be in Milan this week for work. Do you want to meet next week?"

He was scrolling through something on his phone. Was he putting me in his calendar? How generous of him.

"Next Saturday is Alessio's wedding—the drummer for the Sounds," I said. "Do you want to come? That way we can carry out our plan."

Yeah, it was only so I could get Matteo back.

"Perfect."

A message notification broke the awkward silence hanging over the kitchen.

What had happened while I had been in the shower? One minute he'd had me up against the closet, devouring me with his eyes. Now he was hardly speaking.

"I have to go. I have three missed calls from the office and thirty emails to read."

"You're a popular guy."

"Yeah," he muttered unenthusiastically. He looked up from his phone and held my gaze, his expression unreadable. He looked threatening, with his back against the bar and his arms folded across his chest.

I sipped my coffee so I wouldn't speak.

He looked at his watch and slid his phone into his pocket. "I'll call you, okay?"

I don't know why my feminine intuition was telling me that he wouldn't call. "Sure. What about my car?"

He had driven me home and left my Mini at the Gotha.

"I already called you a cab."

He had thought of everything. "Thank you."

He took a few steps toward me, and I thought he might try to kiss me. But then he sighed and left the kitchen. A few seconds later, I heard the front door slam.

He was gone. No smiles. No good-byes.

Hell, even a fight would have been better than that.

Something was up, and I had no idea what.

Chapter 23

"I ruined everything."

I was back in my office after my meeting with Sabrina and couldn't sit still. I paced back and forth with my phone. I couldn't figure out what was going through Christian's head.

"What can I help you with?"

"I need someone to talk to, Siri, and you're the only one around."

"That's fine. I just hope you're not doing anything dangerous."

"No, of course I'm not." I cracked my knuckles. "Christian and I have been lying to Matteo and my parents."

"You know what they say: a lie can travel halfway around the world while the truth is putting on its shoes."

I raised an eyebrow, confused, and stopped in the middle of the room. "I don't understand."

"I thought not."

"You're not helping."

"De gustibus non est disputandum."

I swiped the answer away and kept going. "What do you think of Christian?"

"It's nice of you to ask, Gioia, but it doesn't really matter what I think."

"But I need your help," I said impatiently.

"You know I only live for you."

I stuck my tongue out at my phone—it wasn't like Siri could see me. "I know you say that to everyone."

I went back to my desk and held my head in my hands. God, what had I gotten myself into?

"What do you think got into Christian this morning?" I asked Siri.

"I'd rather not say."

"How diplomatic," I huffed.

"I'm happy you think so."

Someone cleared his throat at my office door. It was Marco, looking worried. I waved him in.

"Are you okay, hon?" he asked.

"I'm great! I've never been better in my life! Sorry, I'm just tired."

"Listen to me, Gioia," Siri said. "Put down this iPhone right now and take a nap. I'll wait here."

"Shut up!" I yelled at the phone. "I wasn't talking to you."

"I'm doing my best, Gioia."

I gave the phone a thumbs-up. "Great, Siri. Keep it up."

"It's nice to have one's work appreciated," she replied.

I turned off Siri and shoved my phone in a drawer.

"Marco. Can I help you?"

"Hon, were you talking to your phone?"

"It was Siri."

"Are you okay?"

"I'm fine. No need to call the men in white coats."

Marco took his usual position on the edge of my desk and snagged a chocolate. "You seemed a little off in our meeting this morning. Is something wrong?"

I took the bowl of chocolates from him and stuck it in the top drawer with my phone.

"Well, considering that Matteo is single again, I spent the entire evening flirting with Christian to make Matteo jealous, and this morning I found him in my apartment, so I'd say everything's just fine."

"You slept with Matteo?"

I blinked. "No—Christian! I mean, I didn't sleep with him. He drove me home. He put me to bed. And he heard me snoring."

"No sex?"

"Why do guys only ever think about sex?"

"I can't think of anything else I'd ever do with Kelly."

I snorted and went back to staring at the computer screen. "Anyway, this morning he left my house angry about something. I don't know what came over him."

"He didn't score! That's what came over him." Marco laughed.

I looked up from the screen. "It's not always about sex, Marco. Last night we were feeling each other, walking the same tightrope, in step. We opened up to each other. He told me about his breakup with the Argentine, how bad it was for him. You know he asked her to marry him?"

"You do know that men get scared when things get serious, right?"

"So you're saying I should have run? Me? Ms. Insecurity?"

"Put it this way," he said, crossing his legs. My desk protested his weight. "Kelly is a man of the world. He's strong, confident, fearless. At work, that is. He told you himself he went to pieces over this girl— maybe he's afraid to throw himself back into another relationship. You guys are clinging to each other without taking down the walls you've both built to protect yourselves."

"I'm not clinging to him." I fell back in my chair. "I'm struggling to survive on my own every day, when I should be living. I don't need any more complications."

"Sometimes it's worth taking the risk and following your instincts."

"My instincts have been seriously wrong over the years."

"I don't know, Gioia. Only you know what your heart wants—you just need to trust it more. You should stop thinking so much about what you don't want and start acting on what you do."

Chapter 24

Friday flew by. It was nearly six when I got up to leave the office after a long day of monitoring my phone for calls or messages from Christian.

I had even called myself with the office phone just to make sure my cell worked. I was on my way out when the office phone rang.

I leaped back to the desk, practically flaying my side on its edge.

"Hello?" I replied, sore and out of breath.

"Gioia, dear. What are you doing at the office so late?"

Disappointed, I sighed and slumped in my chair. I checked the time on the clock. I wouldn't be out of there before six thirty—calls from my mother were known for being long and exhausting.

"Mom, hi. I stayed late waiting for you to call me," I replied dryly.

"I just tried calling your cell, but you didn't answer."

I fished my phone out of my bag and checked the ringer. I had accidentally put it on silent when I had gone to the bathroom. I'd brought it along with me because it is a statistical fact that if you want something badly, it comes when you least expect it. Given my luck, I figured Christian would call while I was sitting on the toilet. Except he didn't, damn it!

"I called, dear, to ask what you want to eat on Sunday—roast chicken or tortellini made by me and your grandmother?"

"Mom, I can't come on Sunday. I'm going to the beach with the girls. I forgot to tell you."

The long silence on the other end of the line told me she wasn't happy. "Are you sure?" She was using her dramatic tone. "Is there something you're not telling me? Where's Christian?"

"Mom, I'm going to the beach on Sunday, I swear, not New York. One hour from home. Do you want me to send you a selfie to prove it?"

"A what?"

"Nothing. If you want, I can come sometime next week." I needed to keep her happy.

"With Christian?"

Once my mother started playing *Murder, She Wrote*, she couldn't be stopped.

"Christian is away on business. He's very busy these days."

"As long as he's busy with you too, honey."

I looked at my missed calls log. It was empty.

"He is, Mom, don't worry. He is."

◆　◆　◆

I arrived home, exhausted, dragging behind me Christian's radio silence and my fatigue from the past few days. I dropped my bag by the door and headed toward the kitchen. I needed a nice glass of wine. Bea was sitting on the sofa, her tablet on her lap, the TV on the music channel.

"You really should give me back my keys," I said, taking two glasses from the cupboard. "Don't take it personally, Bea, but what if I was with a guy? Okay, not that it's likely, given that I brought one home and practically fainted in his arms." I took the wine and joined her on the sofa. "Come on, give me one of your usual li—oh God!"

I put the glasses on the table and squatted down next to the sofa. Beatrice, my sun, my smiling, ball-busting life coach, was in tears, her face streaked with mascara.

"What happened? Why are you crying?" I took her by the shoulders.

She sniffed. "I'm an idiot."

"No one's perfect, Bea," I joked.

A stronger sob rose up in her, and she buried her face in her hands.

"Is this about a man? Who do I need to kill?"

"Alessio."

"Alessio . . . Alessio," I said, thinking. "Alessio, the pizza delivery guy?"

She shook her head.

"Did you meet someone new? Does he work with you?"

She shook her head again.

"I need some help because I have no idea who you're talking about."

"Matteo's Alessio."

"Matteo's Alessio . . . The one who's getting married on Saturday? Bea!"

Shit!

"Don't look at me like that, Gioia. I didn't choose to fall in love with the bastard. You of all people should know something about that."

"But he's engaged. And he practically has one foot on the altar."

Silent tears streamed down her face. "Not when we're together, he doesn't."

"You've been together?"

"Will you stop repeating everything I say?"

I sat on the sofa and put an arm around her. "What do I need to know?"

"Alessio and I got together for a few months while he and Serena were on a break."

"Ah."

"I know what you're thinking."

Really? Because I didn't know what to think.

"You think I don't deserve love. You think I'm a slut, a home wrecker. That I'm a hypocrite for everything I said about Matteo's cheating."

"Bea, calm down!"

She wiped her eyes with her sweatshirt sleeve. "I didn't think they'd get back together. He kept telling me it was over, that he wanted to be with me. But then he never left her; he kept putting it off. He always had some excuse, and I was stupid enough to believe him."

"What an asshole!" I spat.

"I was wrong to keep going out with him after he got back with her, but believe me, Gioia, I didn't think it was going to end like this. I didn't think . . . that he'd marry her." Her slender body was wracked with more sobs.

"When did all this happen?"

"While you were in London. I was pretty much alone. You weren't here, Melly had Alex, and Ludo had Francesco. One night, I went to see the boys do some sound tests, got drunk, and we ended up in bed together. It lasted five months."

"Jesus, Bea! What were you thinking?"

"I don't know! I don't know!" she shouted through her tears.

I held her in my arms. The girl who had let me cry on her shoulder for months, who had gotten my ass out of bed so I'd have the strength to find a job. The one who had held me while I vomited my guts out after destroying myself over Matteo.

"Is that why you started partying every night?" I stroked her wavy hair that fell over her shoulders.

She nodded. "To drown my feelings. I thought he'd choose me, I wanted him to choose me, but . . . he just dismissed me. He said, 'It happened, but I'm staying with her.'"

I shook my head, furious. I didn't believe in "it happened." Like those guys who get their mistresses pregnant and then say "oops." It happened. I didn't believe that boxers and heroes suddenly came to life inside random losers, like with Patrick Swayze in *Ghost*.

"You, Bea, need a man who has the goods all year round. Not just on special occasions."

That got a hint of a smile, at least.

"Are you in love with him?" I asked.

"I wouldn't have put up with this shit if I wasn't in love, Gioia." She took a deep breath, filling her lungs. "How are we going to go to the wedding with both of our exes there?" she asked. "Yours will be the best man; mine will be the groom."

I wanted to laugh. "We'll make a perfect couple. We're both screwed up and our exes will be at the altar. And to make matters worse, this morning I asked Christian to come with me. But if you want, we can just skip it. Do you want to skip it?"

"Are you joking? I'm going to be in the front row at that fucking thing, and when the priest asks us to speak now or forever hold our peace, I'm going to let Alessio have it."

"Are you serious?"

"Well, maybe not." She wiped away a tear. "I'm going to get wasted on expensive wine, dance with a cute musician, and make sure I catch the bouquet so I can throw it at Alessio's head. What do you think?"

"Sounds like a plan." I squeezed her hand. "You've made me realize something."

"What?"

"We need to try a new breed of men. I think we've learned that musicians can't play on just one stage."

Finally, her face lit up with a smile.

Although I'd had a busy day, that night I couldn't sleep. I looked at my phone: it was past midnight.

Christian's status said: LAST SEEN AT 12:02 A.M.

But he hadn't called. He hadn't written.

What the hell?

I really wanted to write, "Who are you chatting with, asshole?" but that would have been out of line.

With the patience of Mahatma Gandhi, I pushed off the sheet and—trying not to wake Bea, who had passed out on the sofa—I tiptoed to the kitchen. I turned on the light above the sink and went straight to the refrigerator. I needed a sugar coma to blot out the lack of affection I felt, and there was nothing better for that than the chocolate ice cream that was faithfully waiting for me in the freezer.

I took a spoon from the drawer and sat on the stool, Christian's roses staring back at me.

Dry, lifeless.

A week had passed since he had given them to me; I had been less of a mess then. Just when I thought that I had finally put my life in order, that the pieces were falling into place, he had shown up. With his illegal smile and those intense eyes, he had scattered the puzzle pieces all over the floor.

Not only that, but Matteo had resurfaced.

How had I gone from being single with no prospects to being wanted by two different men? And not total losers, at that. So why was I such a wreck?

I sank my face in the flowers, but the petals just scattered on the kitchen counter. I took the bouquet and threw it in the trash. Then I went back to eating ice cream in the silence of my apartment.

It matched the silence of my phone.

"Good morning, sleepyhead!"

Before I even opened my eyes, I could smell the coffee Bea had brought me.

"Bea, I'll give you one chance to escape. If it's not at least ten, run."

"The sun is shining high in the sky and you're wasting your time sleeping."

I felt the mattress sag under her weight. I opened my eyes and collided with Bea's smile.

I've said it once, and I'll say it again: it wasn't fair for someone to be so put together and chipper so early in the morning. Last night her eyes had been swollen and red from crying; this morning they were perfectly smoky, her skin was glowing, and her hair was curly and soft. She was wearing a yellow dress that showed off her tanned and toned legs, with no trace of stretch marks or varicose veins.

Shouldn't she still be under the covers looking terrible? Shouldn't I have been the one who woke her up with a cup of coffee and a smile?

"But it's Saturday!" I protested, putting my head back under the pillow.

"Let's go shopping."

She sure bounced back fast, I thought. She made me look like I was the one with the ex who was getting married.

"Bea, I want to sleep."

"We need something for Alessio's funeral. We should be stunning, sexy, and unforgettable."

Funeral? Okay, maybe she hadn't quite bounced back.

"I have a closet full of black dresses. They'll be perfect for his last rites." I huffed and sat up.

"Here." She held out the steaming cup. "I'll let you shower and get dressed, then we'll start our man detox day."

"What do you have in mind?" I asked. When Bea had that light in her eyes, there was reason to be afraid.

"Honey, just trust me!"

Uh-huh.

◆ ◆ ◆

"Is this your idea of detox?" I looked up at two stories of escalators rearing up in front of us. "A mall?"

"Honey, believe me. There's nothing better than swiping your credit card when you're feeling down."

I thanked myself for not having requested a daily-limit increase on my card. At the end of the day, Bea would leave this place with more bags than she could carry.

"When was the last time you took an entire day for yourself?" she asked, dragging me into Sephora.

I went over the past several months in my head. It was true—I hadn't been shopping . . . "The last time I bought anything new was before London. I got a raincoat and an umbrella. Things I'd need."

Beatrice looked horrified. She was right: when I was with Matteo, he always preferred me to dress simply, and I hardly wore makeup because he liked a natural look. Then, when I was in London, I never had too much fun when I went out because he was always texting to tell me how he was dead tired and tragically lonely in the recording studio.

Of course!

Now I understood. It was all by design. The tactic of a weak man, one so insecure and jealous that he'd diminish his girlfriend in the eyes of other people. And I, as a woman in love, had put up with it. Because when you're in love, you see it all through heart-shaped, rose-colored glasses. You're incapable of pressing pause and watching the movie you've created in your head as a spectator.

"So, let's start our rehab tour with the fundamental first step: makeup." Bea sounded dry and decided, like she wasn't even expecting me to answer.

"Bea, I don't want to blow a whole paycheck just to distract myself from the messes in my life."

"Messes? Honey, having a rock star who wants to get back together with you and an Adonis who's trying to get into your pants hardly counts as a mess. It's up to you—you can come with me and transform yourself into a sex bomb, or find a comfy bench and wait for me there, and at the wedding, you can hide under the table while everyone asks me to dance—including Kelly!"

"Fine, fine!" I waved my hands in surrender.

Three hours of beauty treatments and shopping later, we were sitting in the food court eating burgers and fries.

"Still no news from the American?"

I shook my head. "Nothing."

"Why don't you just call him?" she said, sinking her teeth into her burger.

It reminded me of Christian showing up at my door with Smile burgers. Ugh. I shouldn't be thinking of a person who had disappeared like a terrorist on the FBI's Most Wanted List.

I shouldn't have been thinking about him, period. The end.

"He left my house so somber you'd think someone had died. He's constantly on WhatsApp, and he never calls me. I don't think he wants to talk to me."

"That could be. That someone died, I mean. You don't know anything about him."

"He never wants to talk about his private life, except for that night at the Gotha. I understand, though—I'm not always that forthcoming myself."

"And you haven't exactly thrown open the doors of intimacy for him, Gioia."

I frowned and pointed at her. "What have you done with my friend Bea? Leave her body now, creature!"

She burst out laughing. "It's still me," she said, wiping ketchup from the corner of her mouth. "I know the rule says if someone wants you, they'll find you, but there are also exceptions, and I really do think you should call him. I mean, you spent a whole night together, and he didn't even try to make a move. Either he's perfect or . . ."

"And perfect men don't exist."

"Or he's gay?"

"And Chantal is his cover?"

"He's not gay." She smiled. "But I do like Gioia AC."

"AC?"

"Gioia After Christian. Not that I'm a big fan of Mr. Manhattan—I haven't been able to get a good read on him yet—but you are different these days. I mean, you're still a total ball-breaker with your moods, but . . . I don't know . . . you seem more alive. Matteo deactivated the bomb in you, but Kelly got it ticking again."

"You know what the real problem is, Bea? It's not that a bomb in me is waiting to be activated—it's that I want forever. I want it so much. And while everyone runs at the mention of it, I run if I can't see how things could work. And with Christian, I just know I won't have my happy ending. But with Matteo, I was so close. If there's the tiniest chance it could still work . . . well, maybe I shouldn't waste it."

"You want forever?" Bea said. "You want to know if you'll still be with him in ten years? Well, here's a news flash, Gioia: you'll never know. There are no certainties in life. It's all so precarious that the only thing you can do is throw yourself back into the game, trust the person at your side, and love them like there's no tomorrow. Every. Single. Day."

"Since when did you become so wise?" A lump was forming in my throat.

"Ever since my best friend became so emotionally unstable. Gioia, you can't let a man or a story gone bad define who you are. Matteo is a dick, and just because things were good for a while doesn't mean you should get back together with him. At the same time, you can't blame every man who ever lived. Look at how Ludo drives! She's a danger behind the wheel, while I'm a fighter pilot in a skirt."

"Um, okay. But what does that have to do with this?"

Bea put an arm around me. "You'll understand in time, my dear. You'll understand in time."

I wasn't too convinced.

After our day at the mall, we crashed on the sofa in sweats, passing a bag of M&M's back and forth.

During a commercial, I peeked at WhatsApp, where the New York icon continued to taunt me. He was online.

I dropped the phone like it was hot.

"What are you doing?"

"He's online."

"Who?"

"Kelly! He's online but still hasn't messaged me."

"God, you're getting as paranoid as your sister. Write to him already!"

"No. He said he'd call me. If I write to him, he's going to think I've been dying to hear from him."

"You have."

I slid over the edge of the sofa to the floor. "Can I send him a poop emoticon? Do you think he'd get the message then?"

Bea took my phone and stared at it. "It says he's writing."

"What?" I bolted upright and snatched the phone out of her hands. "Let me see!"

The writing signal disappeared, then appeared again.

"Why does he keep deleting it?"

"He's checking his punctuation," Bea teased. She took a handful of chocolate-covered nuts and shoved it in her mouth. "He's . . . ing . . . a . . . say."

"What?"

She swallowed. "He's writing an essay."

I gave her a light slap on the knee. "God, he's slow. Oh. Wait. He deleted it and signed out."

"Call and tell him to go to hell."

For the whole movie, I lay with my phone resting on my chest, as if I were guarding the Holy Grail. Christian never came back online.

Shit.

I was desperate to know what it was he had typed and not had the courage to send.

I looked at the blank screen and sighed.

Chapter 25

It was pouring rain on Monday when I left the office at six.

After reorganizing my desk, I greeted the cleaning lady and walked outside. It was then that I spotted Matteo on the other side of the street.

I took a few steps back, surprised, as thunder rumbled through the sky.

Matteo was leaning against the hood of his battered Opel, his hands deep in the pockets of his torn jeans, wearing his usual black Ramones T-shirt. His hair was matted and wet. He just stood there, staring at me, his green eyes glued to my body, oblivious to the rain and his soaking clothes.

I opened my umbrella and rushed across the street. "You're all wet," I said, sheltering him from the rain.

Huddled under the umbrella, I felt the warmth of his body, his scent invading my nostrils. Back when we had been a couple, I had loved to nestle my head in the crook of his neck and pull him to me, calming myself with his smell. I had always felt at home with him, but now my happiness had changed its address.

"What are you doing here?" I asked warily.

I knew I should run, that I shouldn't be there with him, that I was at risk of flushing five months of rehab down the drain.

Run, Gioia! Run!

"I just need a minute." He kept staring at me, his green eyes sleepy and marked by too many hours spent playing, though they still shone like jade. I could just see the scruff on his pale face, along with a hint of a dimple. "Is this thing between you and Kelly serious?"

I frowned. "That's what you came here to ask me? It doesn't concern you, Matteo. Not anymore."

"He's not the right man for you. He collects women like souvenirs—you'll just be another addition to his list."

They both have such high opinions of each other, I thought.

"If you showed up here to tell me I'm just a cheap fuck for Kelly, you might as well leave," I said bitterly.

"You've slept with him?"

"I can't believe this," I snorted, shaking my head in disbelief. "You dump me, completely disappear, and then decide to show up right when I'm getting myself back together?"

Matteo touched my arm and I jerked it away.

"God, Gioia! I was wrong, okay? I got it all wrong with you. Please forgive me." He pulled a hand from his pocket and ran it through his hair, sighing and tightening his jaw. "Every song I ever wrote was for you, Gioia. You're in every damn line of every damn verse. I said it the other night because I want everyone to know what you mean to me."

"That was some seriously manipulative shit, Matteo! I'm sure you realized Christian was there too? I'd like to remind you that you're trying to get a contract from Sound&K."

My anger caught him off guard.

"Why do you think we haven't gotten it yet?" He took a step toward me, and I stepped back, ending up on the curb. "They were supposed to give us a contract and a bunch of money and instead they keep stalling . . . You should tell your boyfriend he needs to separate love from work," he growled, his face inches from mine.

I stepped back again, my heart beating loud enough to make my ears throb. *What was this about the contract?* Matteo reached for me, but in my haste to get away, I slipped on the curb and dropped my umbrella in the street just as a car was coming.

"Gioia!" Matteo grabbed my wrist and pulled me back to him as the car plowed through a puddle and soaked us both.

When I opened my eyes, I found myself in Matteo's arms, my hands on his chest, his heart racing from the scare. One hand was still on my wrist; he used the other to tuck a strand of wet hair behind my ear. We were both soaked, our eyes locked, our chests rising and falling in unison. The air was alive with current from the summer storm.

"Tha—thank you," I stammered, still frightened; his touch felt warm against my skin.

"I miss you." He caressed my rain-bathed cheek with his hand. Then he grabbed me by the nape of my neck and leaned in to kiss me.

Those three simple words would have made my heart do a triple death flip a few months before. But now they just left a bitter taste in my mouth—not to mention I felt like I was cheating on Christian. My fake boyfriend. The one who had disappeared off the face of the planet.

The sound of thunder made me jump.

"No, Matteo."

I turned my head away, and his lips landed on the corner of my mouth, his scruff scratching my wet skin. I pushed him away, gathered my umbrella, and took off, ignoring the pouring rain. My heart was thumping in my chest; my legs felt like gelatin. I ran, trying not to slip on the wet asphalt. I ran without stopping and without turning to see whether he was still standing there or if he was chasing me.

I arrived at my car, gasping, a pain stabbing at my side. With trembling hands, I found my car keys and fumbled with the remote. Once inside the car, I rested my head on the steering wheel and hid my face in my arms.

God! How could he still have that effect on me? All he had to do was show up with his dimples and his tired eyes, and I had a heart attack. I didn't want him to make me feel like that—not anymore. What did he mean about the contract? Christian would never have let a promising act go over something so petty; work was too important for him. Oh Christian! Why did I feel like I'd betrayed him?

What a fool I was. My life over the past few months had been calm; I had been going through the motions, but at least I had my peaceful routine, my friends, a job I was excited about, and a family that was there for me, even if they were a little suffocating.

All until Mr. Cover Boy showed up with his illegal smile, his piercing eyes, and his gorgeous body. But it was his kindness that had delivered the final blow.

I didn't need to speak for him to understand me; he made me tremble at the thought of seeing him, of feeling his lips on mine. He made me breathe even when I was drowning in sorrow.

And now he was gone. It had only been a couple of days, but I couldn't shake the feeling that I'd really lost him.

I jumped at a knock at the window. It was Marco. I dried my tears and lowered the window.

"Hey, hon. Wanna let me in before I get soaked?"

I sighed and didn't respond. I unlocked the doors, adjusted the rearview mirror, and wiped the mascara from under my eyes while Marco went around to the passenger's side.

"I saw you running from Matteo."

"I'm in a tailspin, Marco."

He turned in his seat to face me, his back to the window. "What did he want?"

"He said he misses me."

"He didn't say he loves you."

I ignored him. "And he said Christian keeps postponing the contract."

"Do you think that's true?"

I shrugged wearily. "I don't know, I haven't heard from him since that night at the Gotha. Or, well, the morning after."

"He's a man of the world, Gioia. He's used to conference calls across time zones, business lunches, charity dinners. But that doesn't mean he's used to dealing with his own heart. Or maybe he just doesn't have time to call you."

"Marco, I love you, but it takes exactly five seconds to type hello. I don't want to be with a man who can't find a single second to talk to me. And it's not even like we're together. I'd understand if we were a few months into dating, but if this is how he is with women he's pursuing, then no, thank you. I want someone who will make an effort, Marco. I'm sick of settling, and if I've learned anything from my mistakes, it's that I shouldn't sacrifice who I am for anyone. Not even Kelly."

Marco hugged me. "We're healing, honey. We're healing."

◆　◆　◆

Tuesday morning got off to a strange start: I was sitting at my desk staring at a photo of myself on a music blog.

The headline read, "Is This the Mystery Muse of the Sounds?"

Smack across the page was a photo of Matteo and me from the day before, just as he was about to kiss me down on the sidewalk in front of the office.

The article left little doubt:

The lead singer of the Sounds has been spotted with a mystery blonde. Their unmistakably

intimate body language all but confirms that
this is the famous muse Matteo Perri publicly
thanked at a Gotha concert just days ago.

Shit.

I arched back in my chair and covered my eyes. "How did they
even get this?"

"I don't know, Gioia." Marco was behind me, one arm resting
across the back of my chair, the other hand on the mouse, scrolling up
and down.

"How did you find it? Did you Google my name? Did you see a
link somewhere?"

"Believe it or not, Gioia, I don't wake up every morning and Google
you. José is really into the Sounds and follows their fan page. They
posted the article this morning. You know how fans are, they dig up
everything."

I didn't know what was more shocking: seeing my own face on
a music blog or imagining José and Marco crammed against a stage
singing their hearts out to the Sounds in T-shirts with Matteo's face
on them.

"Shit," I breathed.

I couldn't believe this was happening to me, of all people—a champion of confidentiality. The one who made the girls swear on their lives
not to share our WhatsApp chats. The one who would type and delete
a Facebook status at least five times before posting it, overwhelmed at
the thought of all those thousands of fake friends who might read it. I,
of all people, had found myself in the gossip pages with the singer of a
boy band. And not just any singer—my ex.

"You look pretty good!"

"Yeah, they managed to get my good side. And the light is decent—
no pimples or dark circles. They haven't even photoshopped it." I

snorted. "Marco, if my mother sees this thing, she's going to lose it. I have to find someplace to hide out."

"She won't see it, don't worry. It's just a music blog. I don't think your mother is going to read up on the rock world while drinking her afternoon tea," he said. He started to click around.

"You don't know my mother," I muttered. I couldn't let myself keep looking at the picture, so I turned and began drumming my fingers on the table. "Maybe she subscribes to Matteo's fan page too—you never know."

"Well, the tabloids are starting to follow him around. Look at this."

He showed me a picture of the Sounds followed by a long article.

I rolled my chair closer to him so I could read it better. It was from the Friday before—a whole exposé on the Sounds, from their shy debut to their national success with the last album. Now, the article said, they had sealed their success with their performance at the Gotha, where the lead singer had thanked his muse from all those years. He was visibly in love. Perri, lucky in work and love. It said the band was about to sign a contract with Sound&K, headed by millionaire playboy Christian Kelly.

"Oh shit."

Christian. How would he react to the photo of Matteo and me? Yes, I had rejected Matteo and fled, but anyone who saw the photo would swear the two people were in love. I was gazing into Matteo's eyes; his lips were inches from mine. And then there was the scene: the falling rain, the forgotten umbrella in the street, our dripping hair, and us, ignoring it all, too lost in each other.

It looked like a Valentine's Day card.

◆　◆　◆

"It's what you wanted, right? The return of the bastard rock star." Beatrice sipped her spritzer at the bar where we had met for an *aperitivo* and enlarged the photo on her phone. "If I didn't know any better, I'd say you look desperately in love . . ."

"Why do I have the feeling there's a 'but'?" I played with the olive in my martini.

"If I didn't know you two, if you hadn't told me you ran away, I'd believe the photo. Until a few months ago, you would have thrown yourself at his feet—in fact, you would have lain on the ground and let him trample you."

"That's not true!" I shot back.

"Yes, it is! It was true until two and a half weeks ago, when we went to Barcelona. When a certain Christian Kelly came along."

"Christian's being a jerk about their contract."

Bea plucked the olive out of my glass and ate it. "That's just according to Matteo. He's jealous, Gioia. It bothers him you're with someone like Kelly; it's a blow to his ego. Seriously, why would Matteo decide to show up now, right when you're moving on?" She took my hand and smiled. "I'll be honest because I love you. He wasn't planning to try to get you back. He chose Georgia and she dumped him, and now he wants you back because he's a possessive jerk."

I stabbed at a piece of pizza with a toothpick. "What if he really does want me back? He apologized; he said he misses me."

"Then tell me why you didn't kiss him yesterday. I'll tell you why. Because you were thinking about Christian. You're falling in love with him."

"He disappeared, Bea. Matteo, on the other hand, wrote me two messages last night. Not just one. Two."

"May God forgive me for defending Mr. Manhattan, but has it occurred to you that he might not know how to make the next move? He found his future wife in bed with another man, he's been a jerk to half of New York City, then he meets you, a girl more fucked up than a sudoku puzzle who's determined to convince herself and him that she's just pretending with him and really still in love with her ex."

I bit my lip. "I like being with Christian."

"I know, honey." She reached across the table and squeezed my hand again. "But you have to tell him that. Then we girls will all go out for a celebratory drink."

"A drink?"

"To toast the new couple. And if he really has disappeared, we'll get totally shit-faced. Either way, we'll make sure to get some amazing wine!"

I smiled and gave her a squeeze back. "Thanks for analyzing my twisted head."

"I'm good at cleaning up other people's messes. It's my own I need to work on."

"Do you still want to go to that wedding?" I asked, shifting my attention to her. "If you want, we can always invent some excuse not to go."

"Over my dead body!" She raised her hand and ordered another round, even though I had barely started my first drink. "Alessio thinks I won't show. But his balls are going to retract when he sees his future wife standing at the altar and the woman he screwed over in the first row. Plus, I have to go."

"Why?"

"Because if Kelly really has disappeared, someone has to be your date."

I went back to my apartment with the sinking feeling that I'd never hear from Christian again. He'd probably finally understood the meaning of "I'll never be a member of your fan club."

But then, just as I rounded the corner, I saw Christian sitting on the stairs to my building. My legs almost gave way at the sight.

His shirt sleeves were rolled up past his elbows, his tie was loose, his eyes were tired; he looked rumpled, unkempt, and beautiful as ever. My heart jumped into my throat, butterflies spread their wings in my stomach, and the bitterness I felt just moments ago vanished at the sight of his lazy, sexy smile.

How pathetic! I was furious with myself, so I was furious with him.

"Hey there, Hurricane." Christian smiled.

"Christian." I stepped over him and began searching for my keys.

"I wanted to ask you out to dinner, but given the time, I guess you've already eaten."

Settle down, heart! "Cell phones exist, you know."

"I know I told you I'd call, Gioia . . ."

"No," I interrupted. "Whatever you have to say, I don't want to hear it. And please spare me the usual excuses like your phone broke or you got hit by a truck."

Christian smiled his illegal smile again, amused. Did he think I was joking? "You're mad because I didn't call you?"

"Are you coming in or not?"

Christian got up. "Why are you so mad?"

I huffed and rolled my eyes. "I saw you online."

"What?"

"I saw you on WhatsApp."

"So? I'm here now, with you. Do you want me to go home and message you?"

"I saw you write me something and delete it. Just by chance."

He cocked his head to one side, a smile tugging at the corner of his mouth. "Were you spying on me, Hurricane?"

"Wipe that smirk off your face, Kelly. I was cursing your name for the way you left my house the other morning. You acted like a total asshole."

"I know." He shook his head and took a step back. "That's why I'm here, Gioia. Because of Thursday."

I felt totally confused, totally out of control. I wanted to scream, "Okay, fine, I'll be a member of the Christian Kelly Fan Club!"

Damn it! I'd forget about my happy ending if I could just live in a fairy tale with him, even if it was only for one night. I liked him. So much. He made me happy, angry—I even loved our constant bickering. But there was a side of his life—somewhere in his past, or his present—that prevented me from being able to make the leap.

Christian took a deep breath. "I think the situation got out of hand," he sighed. "None of this should have happened between us. I've thought about it over the past few days, and you're right—we work better as friends. I just got out of a big relationship and you want to get back together with Perri."

I stood there, frozen. I probably looked like I was in shock. "Yeah . . . r-right," I stammered.

Stupid, stupid, stupid!

I had spent the past few days obsessing about him, about what might happen between us, while he had been planning to let me down with the usual "Let's be friends."

"We're just not compatible, Kelly. It's not that I don't like you," I said to defend myself. "In fact, I find you irresistible. You kiss like a god. But you're right, we're always fighting, you keep calling me stubborn, and you're a hopeless womanizer. You're the wrong man for me." I put my hand to his chest. "I can't believe we finally agree on something. I think we just took our first step toward friendship." I wished for a black hole to swallow me immediately.

Christian took a step forward and smiled. "I can't believe what I heard."

"What? The word 'friendship'?"

"First you let me call you babe in front of your mother; now I'm a womanizer who kisses like a god. We're making progress."

"Don't push it too much, Kelly. Remember, we're friends now."

Friends? What a load of crap!

"How's the make-Perri-jealous plan coming along?"

"What? Oh . . . it's not working," I lied.

Christian stared into my eyes, opened his mouth to say something, but then closed it again. "So we haven't been convincing enough. We'll have to work on that."

"But you just said we should be friends."

"I know what I said." He shrugged. "We will, but no one else has to know. I'll take you to the wedding, and Perri will come crawling back to you before you know it."

I nodded. In the end, I knew, I'd be the one crawling home alone, utterly consumed by Christian.

He came up to the door and leaned his shoulder against it. We were very close. If I reached out, I would be able to run my fingers through his hair, feel the scruff on his cheeks, and touch his chest. *Okay, Gioia—enough!*

He rested his head against the door, his eyes never wandering from mine. "I have a problem, Hurricane."

"You have many problems, Christian. But recognizing them is a first step toward healing."

He smiled. "I wanted to invite you out for a drink, but after seeing the effect alcohol has on you, I think we'd best avoid it. How about we go to dinner?"

"I can't."

"Christ, Gioia. It's dinner with a friend, not a date!"

"That's not the issue." Well, it wasn't the entire issue, at least. "I'm on a diet."

Christian shook his head. "Since when?"

"Since I have Jennifer Lopez's thighs and a backside shaped like a Big Mac. I want to be able to fit into my dress on Saturday."

"You know that you won't be able to pull off a miracle in four days."

"Thanks a lot!" I crossed my arms. "You could have said, 'Gioia, you look great as you are. You don't need to lose any weight.'"

"Friends should be honest with each other."

My jaw dropped. "Asshole!"

He cocked his head to one side and whispered in my ear, "You are perfect as you are, Hurricane, but if I said it, you'd think I was flirting."

"Humph!" I looked down at my feet. "Anyway, I only have four days to try to get into the dress, and I have dinner at my parents' tomorrow night. My mother, by the way, has invited you over to eat tortellini, but I told her that you're too busy with work, so you don't have to come."

"Of course I'll come! I wouldn't miss Adelina's tortellini for the world."

I looked at him sideways.

"We haven't put on a fight in front of your parents yet, right?" he asked, amused.

"I thought we could have a big fight after the wedding and the next week you could leave for New York."

"Perfect." He pulled out his phone and fumbled with it.

"What are you doing?"

"I'm putting it in my calendar. I want to make sure I have my roles straight."

I rolled my eyes. "Oh, stop it!"

"I should get going, Hurricane. I have a meeting with Japan tomorrow morning."

He pressed against me, his lips a hair away from mine. I could feel his hot breath against my skin, a fire that spread through my body and down deep into my belly. I lifted my chin instinctively, eyes shut. I could hear the audience in the stands holding its breath.

"You'd better open that door and get inside if you want to stay friends," he murmured in my ear. He kissed my forehead and pulled back.

"You're an idiot." I pushed him away, entered the building, and closed the door on his illegal smile.

"Good night, friend!" he shouted through the door, clearly happy with himself.

I slid down the door until I was sitting on the cold floor of the entryway. The crowd was whistling, "Boo! Boo!" *He's a heartless playboy,* I tried to convince myself. *A playboy.*

Chapter 26

"Friends?" screamed Bea.

We were at Sweet Bakery for breakfast. While Bea and Ludo were stuffing themselves with pancakes, croissants, and cappuccinos, I had black coffee and a whole-grain brioche.

I had started day one of my speed detox.

"You want to repeat that a little louder? The cashier didn't hear you," I said.

"The two of you have never been friends, and you never will be," Bea went on.

"Don't either of you believe in happily ever after?" asked Ludo.

"That's just Disney indoctrination," said Bea, biting into her warm croissant. "They make us believe from an early age that there's a Prince Charming somewhere out there riding his white horse, that the ugliest frogs turn into beautiful princes, and that if you eat a poisoned apple you won't be dead as a doornail. All the men I've kissed have been toads. What about you, Gioia?"

"Well, Christian won't turn into a prince because he's already a god on earth."

"Yuck!" Bea took her bag and stood up. "I'm not going to sit here," she said, pointing at Ludo, "and let you tell me the story of Snow White, who ate the witch's apple only to be kissed by a prince. The first thing they teach you is not to talk to strangers. Or the story of that blonde who falls asleep and waits for a man to come and kiss her. That girl needs to wake the hell up, I say. Once he gets her to the castle, he'll probably settle down to watch the hunting channel and write her a noncommittal message on WhatsApp. And then she'll look for a lover on an online dating site. Ladies, real men are extinct. Ex-tinct."

"You just haven't found the right one, Bea," Ludo insisted. "The love of your life is just around the corner."

"Who are you, the Blue Fairy?" Bea looked at her incredulously. "I don't do long-term plans; all I know is that I have to be at the salon in an hour to get my nails done for Saturday. That's it. Imagine me trying to make plans for *forever*."

She planted kisses on our cheeks and clattered out on her stilettos.

Ludo turned to me. "You don't believe in happy endings either?"

"I believed in the fairy tale when I was with Matteo, and that turned me into Bambi. And even if I wanted to believe it now, Christian made it very clear last night that we don't belong together. So if I tell him I'm thinking about forever, he'll be on the first flight back to New York."

"If you did believe, what would your fairy tale be like?"

"But I don't believe anymore."

"Hypothetically," she implored.

"First of all, I wouldn't eat any apples. I'm allergic and I'd drop dead before the kiss."

"Gioia! Make an effort. Do you want me to dump this coffee all over you?"

"Wow, Ludo. You seem so angelic, but—"

"It makes me mad when I see you and Bea discounting your own futures just because of one crappy man," she said. "So start dreaming. Once upon a time, there was a prince . . ."

"Starting with the prince is a little sexist. Can't we start with the princess?"

"Okay, fine," she huffed. "Once upon a time, there was a princess named Gioia who saw a prince arrive on a white horse."

I didn't have to think about it at all. The picture materialized instantly.

"Prince Christian, Christian Kelly, prince of New York and ruler of my heart."

"Let's not exaggerate."

"This is my fantasy! I can exaggerate as much as I want."

She rolled her eyes. "Go on."

"Christian and I have just gotten married in an intimate sunset ceremony by the sea. Our families are there, and you girls. Melly and Alex bring my niece or nephew, Bea flirts with the best man all night, and you and Francesco arrive with your two newborn twins and a third on the way."

"Whoa! Do you seriously want me to have twins?"

"You love kids! Two in one is lucky. You save yourself some labor."

She nodded, hardly convinced.

"Christian and I live in a simple two-story house in Brooklyn, each window with a view of the New York skyline, and every night we watch the sun go down behind it."

"Wait, are you guys going to live in New York? We'll never see each other. You've erased us from your fairy tale!" Ludo said sadly.

I huffed. "Is this my fairy tale or yours? In my fantasy, New York is super close, and every Sunday we all have lunch in Central Park, and one night each week we leave the kids with their dads and go to a bar in the West Village. We gossip, drink cosmos, and have fun, just like old times."

"Okay, I like that part."

"I work for one of those huge New York ad agencies, in an office with views of Bryant Park. At lunch, Christian and I meet for hot dogs at our favorite truck. And in my fantasy, we all eat as much as we want and still look like Gisele Bündchen."

"I'm liking this fantasy more and more!" Ludo smiled.

"Christian and I spend every free second of our days together. We laugh and listen to music curled up on the sofa, I cook him chocolate-chip muffins every Sunday while he watches the game on TV." Tears clouded my eyes. "We still fight over little things. But it never lasts and we always end up back in each other's arms." I wiped away my tears.

Oh God!

I stood up to go pay.

"Gioia . . ." Ludo pleaded.

"Why'd you make me do that? Your stupid fairy tales are bullshit. Christian is not a forever kind of guy. I should be smart and just use him to get Matteo back."

"Gioia, I was always a fan of you and Matteo, but you seemed like you'd finally gotten over him after he left you. I'm not sure it's healthy to try to get him back now."

I froze. "Maybe it's just that I don't want to throw away four years of a relationship, Ludovica. I'd love to see what you'd do if Francesco dumped you and then tried to get you back. What would you choose? Would you choose him or give in to the passion between you and some guy you hardly know? A guy who has seen more women naked in the past year than a gynecologist? A guy who lives on the other side of the ocean and doesn't want to commit?"

She bristled at my harsh tone. "You can't know whether Christian is the right one if you don't try. If you don't—"

I put up my hand to stop her. "Save it. You asked me what I wanted, Ludo, but it's not just about me. It takes two to have a relationship, and Christian has made it clear that he isn't ready for anything serious."

Chapter 27

When he arrived Wednesday evening, I was a bundle of nerves.

I had gotten ready too far in advance and found myself sitting on the sofa for an hour before he came.

When I saw his headlights stop out front, I rocketed down the stairs and jumped into the car, anxiety gripping my stomach.

"I've come for you, my darling," said Christian in an exaggeratedly gallant voice.

"Save it for my parents, Christian."

"Believe me, Hurricane. There's plenty more where that came from," he murmured hoarsely, looking me up and down. I wore a high-necked dress and simple black leather boots, but under his gaze I felt naked. "You look beautiful."

"You don't have to flatter me, Kelly." I settled back in the seat of the Maserati, trying not to let my bare legs touch Christian's arm when he changed gears. "Photograph" by Ed Sheeran was playing, and I found myself keeping time with my fingers.

"Why are you nervous? We already passed the test." He went through the intersection by my building and turned onto the highway.

"Last time was easy because of my sister's announcement about the baby, but tonight you'll have all eyes on you."

"What exactly should I be worried about?"

"My mother will ask you trick questions. Don't be surprised if she makes you take a *Cosmopolitan*-style aptitude test to see if we're a good match. You might as well start thinking about what we're going to name our children."

"She doesn't waste any time."

"Right." I looked at his profile against the window. He looked beautiful too. He wore a pair of jeans that clung to his thighs and a black shirt unbuttoned at the neck, the sleeves rolled over his muscles, his veins in relief along his arms. He had a hint of scruff on his face. I leaned my head against the window and watched his fingers drum on the steering wheel to the rhythm of the song.

"What about Matteo?"

His voice woke me from the spell he had cast over me. "Huh?"

"How about we call our son Matteo? If it's a boy."

"You are such an idiot. We are not speaking that name in front of my mother; it's already as if she's lost a child. The first week, you couldn't even tell who had been dumped—me or her."

"So I'll save it for the end?"

"If the evening feels never ending and you want to be given the boot, then yes."

He smiled. "I don't have anything planned for after dinner, you?"

Why was he talking to me in that mischievous tone if we were supposed to be friends? I ignored him.

"Then there's my father."

"Angelo, king of the grill."

"He won't be cooking tonight, and there are no big games or races on television, so you'll be his sole focus. Do you like cars?"

"No, but I'm a Knicks fan. I go see them on the weekends at Madison Square Garden. Does he have any other interests?"

"He doesn't listen to music; he used to have Sounds CDs, but he destroyed them after things ended with Matteo."

"If I were your father, I would have destroyed Perri himself."

"His sciatica was the only thing stopping him."

I looked out the window at the world streaming by at the speed of Christian's driving, remembering my first days at the Caputi residence after I came back from London. My father screamed that he was going to castrate Matteo, while my mother tried to calm him down and console me at the same time, even though she was suffering just as much. Matteo had been like a son to them.

Christian squeezed my knee lightly. "What should I say to your father so he'll let me take you out for an after-dinner drink? We've established that, for your mother, the magic word is 'Matteo.'"

I gulped, trying not to think about his hand on my skin and the heat spreading through me.

"Um . . . I'm his little girl. Right now he's conflicted because he doesn't know if he wants to see me married with a baby, or single, happy, and without any men in my life."

"His little girl. Got it." Christian nodded. "But doesn't that work against your mother's dream of becoming a grandmother?"

"I told you it wouldn't be easy. You have to navigate between them. If you want to save yourself, start talking about wine. Do you know anything about it?"

"Are you kidding, Hurricane? In New York, I have a wine cellar that would be the envy of the whole South of France."

"Sounds like you have a few aces up your sleeve, Kelly."

"And you haven't even seen them all yet."

He shot me a look that made my hormones stand to attention. I concentrated on the voice of Ed Sheeran so I would remember to breathe.

After a few minutes, we arrived at my parents' house.

"Are you sure you want to do this? You really don't have to," I said as we got out of the car.

"I don't care," he said. "About the names of our children, I mean." He tucked a strand of hair behind my ear. "I just hope they're as beautiful as their mother." Christian leaned down and kissed me gently. "And smart like their father," he added as his lips left mine.

I was about to shove him when he grabbed my wrists and whispered, "Don't do it, honey."

"And what was that for? Didn't you say we were just friends?" Maybe he had changed his mind!

"Of course we are." He interlaced his fingers with mine and we walked to the door. "That was for our audience."

I followed his gaze and saw my parents' faces pressed against the window.

And they say people mature when they have children.

"Get ready, Kelly. My parents are in top form tonight."

"So, Christian," my father said, "Gioia told me your label has some of the best acts around. But I don't understand music."

It was time for the aptitude test. Like dessert, like icing on the cake after some harmless appetizers and mains.

"We try to produce quality music," Christian said. "I inherited the business from my father, who worked in the industry for years. After his death, I had to learn how to not ruin the empire he had managed to build."

"Well, from what I hear from Gioia, you're succeeding. Did I hear on the radio that you're about to sign some hot young group?"

"The Sounds?" asked Christian.

I glared at him.

"Who?" My father almost choked on a piece of bread.

"The Sounds. Yeah, Perri's band. We're planning to sign them for their next album. Didn't Gioia tell you?" He turned to me and rubbed his thumb over the back of my hand. "Didn't you tell them, sweetie?"

I kicked him under the table in response.

"Ouch!" he whispered. "What was that for?"

I nodded toward my mother, who was preparing to deliver an award-winning dramatic monologue.

"The Sounds?" My mother awoke like a diabetic from a carb-induced coma. "Matteo's band? Why didn't you tell us, dear?"

I sat up straight. "I must have forgotten. I spend all my time these days thinking about my love." I sweetly caressed the nape of Christian's neck until my parents weren't paying attention. Then I gave him a pinch.

"Ouch."

"There will be no after-dinner drink, Kelly. So give it up," I whispered so only he could hear me.

Christian gave me a playful smile and kissed my hand. I was about to jerk it away when my mother turned and lit up like the Rockefeller Center Christmas tree at the sight of us so in love.

"Well, isn't that nice for Matteo," she crooned.

"He's a hack," said my father.

"Don't say that, Angelo. He was always such a nice boy."

"Yeah, until he broke our daughter's heart. Now you're calling him a nice boy?"

I looked over at Christian in distress. He appeared amused by the scene.

"You should have told me he didn't like Matteo," he whispered. "That way we'd have something else to talk about besides wine."

I kicked him again.

"Stop that!"

"You're upsetting my mother," I hissed.

We both turned to look at her.

"Angelo, you're still mad at him because he made our little Gioia leave the nest."

"The nest?" my father echoed. "I'd like to remind you that if he hadn't been so obsessed with those dumb songs of his, we'd be grand-parents by now."

My father was smart—he knew all my mother's triggers.

Adelina gasped in horror at the affront and took a moment to collect herself. She decided to ignore my father and cross-examine Christian instead. "Do you like children, son?"

I crossed my arms, satisfied. It was fun to see Mr. Cover Boy in a sticky situation.

"Very much," he replied. His gaze softened and his eyes lit up. "I have a four-year-old niece in New York who I adore."

"Really?" My mother lit up.

"Really?" I looked at him. "I mean . . . really! I've seen the pictures. She's so cute." I took a long drink of water to keep my mouth busy.

Shit! I really didn't know anything about Christian beyond his Wikipedia bio. Meanwhile, this was the second time he had come to eat at my parents' place, and my mother was already calling him son.

"Her name is Jewel. She's the love of my life; the only girl who's managed to completely steal my heart."

I gave him another kick in the shin. He gasped and kissed the back of my hand, his eyes locked on mine. "Besides your beautiful daughter."

I gulped. My hand tingled where he had put his mouth. His ador-ing gaze struck a chord very, very close to my heart. But it was all an act for our audience. Obviously.

My father interrupted the performance, clearing his throat. He was red in the face, and not because the house was warm. He looked Christian in the eye. "What are your intentions with my daughter?"

Ah, the patriarch, ready to defend his little herd.

"Dad," I said.

"Angelo!" Adelina exclaimed.

"I just want to know what the boy's intentions are. The other one supposedly wanted to stay with her forever and then dumped her like a hot potato."

"Dad!"

"I care for your daughter very much," said Christian, looking serious. "She's a smart girl, not to mention wonderful. She has nothing but lovely things to say about you, and if things work out between us, I would want for us to build a family with the same values you've taught her." He looked at my mother as I gasped for air. "I've only had one important relationship, and I wasn't the one who ended it. But now I'm so grateful because otherwise I wouldn't have met your daughter. I want it all with Gioia. A life, children, birthday parties, dinners with relatives. We still haven't thought of names for our children, but I just want them to be happy and healthy and beautiful like their mother." He looked back at my father. "And I would never take your daughter away from you. Never. Because I know she wouldn't be happy living so far away, and her happiness is my only concern."

There was a long silence, a rare occurrence at the Caputi residence. The American had succeeded where no one had before. We were all dumbstruck.

My father looked at my mother, who was staring at me. I was paralyzed.

Jesus, Kelly!

We had almost made it to the end of the evening, and in that little time we had left, he had managed to seize my heart and wring it out with his hands. His speech had completely blown me away. His delivery had been so measured, as if he really meant what he was saying, as if we talked about children all the time. Then, when he was done, he turned and winked at me, as if to say, "Mission accomplished," and I slammed back to earth.

Christian was a very good actor. Better than DiCaprio.

"This is great wine, Angelo," he said. "What year is it?"

"Nineteen eighty-four."

They started discussing that year's harvest while I went to the kitchen to help my mother with the dishes.

I needed to get ahold of myself.

Adelina took the tiramisu out of the fridge and began to spoon it into little cups.

"He's perfect, honey. Just perfect." She had two bassinets for eyes.

"I knew you'd give him the third degree."

"Sweetie, that's just how we are. If he's really the complete package, he won't let us scare him." She touched my cheek and went back into the dining room.

After an animated conversation between Christian and my father about the Italian soccer championship and the supremacy of Juventus, we departed exhausted and thoroughly proven as a couple.

I reclined the seat in the Ghibli, stretched out, and relaxed to the music of the Civil Wars, watching as my parents' house got smaller in the rearview mirror. I let out a deep sigh, as if I had been holding my breath all evening.

"Are you okay?" asked Christian.

I opened my eyes. "I've had twenty-five years of training. How are you?"

"I think I held my own. Did you see the look on your parents' faces after what I said about us?"

"It was the event of the evening. They were speechless."

And they weren't the only ones.

I went back to looking out the window, my mind far away.

"I think they like me."

"Mmm."

"Why are you so quiet?"

Without looking directly at him, I covered his hand on the gear-shift. "I'm sorry you had to put up with all that nonsense about kids; my parents can be a little over the top. Sometimes I wish I were adopted so my kids wouldn't get our crazy genes."

Christian suddenly pulled over and stopped the car.

"Christian, what—"

He grabbed me by the neck and pulled me to him. He pressed his lips to mine and kissed me. It wasn't gentle. It was decided, eager. His tongue pushed through my lips, muffling the groan that escaped my throat. When he pulled back, my heart was slamming against my chest and I was gasping for air. *Breathe, Gioia!*

"You shut me up by kicking me, I'll shut you up by kissing you. We have different approaches, Hurricane."

He started the engine and slipped onto the dark interstate, lit only by an old gas station on the side of the road.

"Why did you kiss me?"

"I just told you."

"You said you just wanted to be friends."

"Exactly. I never said that I wouldn't kiss you again." He smiled.

"I don't kiss my friends on the lips."

"Good for them," he muttered.

I snorted and leaned my head against the seat, trying to calm down. "Thanks," I said under my breath.

"For what? For the kiss?" he joked.

"For all the nice things you said about me. Even if it was all for my parents, I'm glad you said them. I think my mother will miss you."

After the wedding on Saturday, I knew she wouldn't be the only one in the family to miss him.

"You're kind of amazing," I muttered. Had I really just said that? Oh God, I was thinking aloud. I closed my mouth and went back to looking out the window. *Stupid mouth!*

"You too."

"As a friend, obviously," I said.

"Obviously." He nodded.

Chapter 28

"Let's go eat, honey! It's useless for you to sit there smelling it—it's not going to get any better."

Marco was at the door of my office wearing sunglasses and an amused smile.

I had been sitting in there for two hours, waiting for a brilliant idea to flash into my mind for the perfume campaign. I couldn't focus on advertising copy, though. All I could think about was what Christian had said at my parents' house. Yes, it had all been a part of our act, but damn if he hadn't been convincing. Even I had almost fallen for it. Almost.

I had tossed and turned all night long with the taste of his lips on mine, his words echoing in my head. Eventually, I'd picked up the phone and written him a thank-you note on WhatsApp.

He'd answered almost immediately.

```
You   owe   me   an   after-dinner   drink,
Hurricane.
```

In the office, I closed my notepad and gathered my bag.

"That's the best idea I've heard all day," I said. "I think this will be my worst campaign ever. Why does this designer want to sell a perfume that smells like bug spray?"

"We need a nice Smile burger to fill us up with ideas," he said, taking my arm.

"I still have to fit into the dress hanging in my closet," I muttered. "I can't eat junk food; I'm on a diet until Saturday." *At least.*

"What happens Saturday?"

"Alessio's wedding."

"Who are you going with?"

"Beatrice and Kelly."

"Yikes. I smell trouble, honey." His eyebrows shot up from under his sunglasses.

"Why?"

"A wedding, a romantic setting, slow music, rivers of champagne, emotions running high."

"I know how to be in the same room as my ex for one day," I said.

"I was talking about Kelly, hon," he said. "By the way, how was your dinner last night at your parents'?"

"Fine. My mother elected him Mr. Perfect Sperm Donor of the Year. Unfortunately, every fiber in my body and my ovaries have the same idea."

"What's the problem, then?"

"That man's so full of testosterone that my every fiber also cries *warning, danger zone.*"

"Are you sure you want to go to the wedding with him?"

"It's just for one day, Marco."

"You've been saying that for weeks now. I don't want to see you drowning in a sea of your own tears Monday at the office."

"There will be no tears because I have no expectations. It's clear he doesn't want a serious relationship. So I'm prepared."

"Is your heart prepared?"

I smiled bitterly. "My heart? It is still waiting its turn, like it's playing Monopoly."

"A turn?" he asked, frowning. "Hon, that poor heart's been in prison since rocker boy left you."

I gave him a light punch on the arm. "Saturday will be our last day together," I went on. "Sunday he'll take me home and we'll say our good-byes. He'll go back to his glamorous life and I'll go back to my real one."

"Of course," said Marco, skeptical.

I opened the door to Smile and squinted to adjust my eyes to the interior lighting. When I opened them again, I gasped.

Christian Kelly was sitting in the corner with two other men.

The sound of my heart and the feeling in my legs told me that it wouldn't be easy for my body to go back to real life after Christian was gone.

We spotted seats at the bar. Once my legs had recovered enough to cooperate, I walked briskly to the nearest stool without looking at him. My heart? I hadn't managed to stuff it back into my chest; it was bouncing between my throat and my stomach like a pinball.

I hid my face behind the menu as my colleague looked appreciatively toward Kelly. I was hoping he wouldn't notice me because I didn't know what he would do in public. Matteo and my parents weren't here, so there was no need to pretend. Would he play my friend, the president of Sound&K, or my boyfriend?

"Why don't you go over there and say hi to your . . . um . . . friend?"

"I don't think so." I read the list of sandwiches, even though I already knew that I'd order a salad and a glass of water.

"Fine, but can I?" He turned in Christian's direction and devoured him with his eyes. "*Mamma mia*, just look at that piece of ass!"

"Please stop. Turn around."

"Tell me he's at least bisexual."

"Shut up, Marco," I said, suddenly feeling hot.

I ordered a big salad and Marco a double hamburger. I looked at him and wondered where he put all that food. He wasn't as sexy and fascinating as Christian, but he was a handsome man. Lean muscles in all the right places and not an ounce of fat on him. If I ate a double hamburger, I'd have to run the New York Marathon twice just to get it off my thighs.

"Have you slept with him yet?"

"Why is everyone so obsessed with my sex life?" I poured vinegar and oil over my salad. "For the record, no."

"I mean, you kiss all the time, he's said you don't need to lose weight, he goes to dinner at your parents' house, he's heard all the sermons on you being the baby of the house and the low birthrate in the Caputi family, he spent the night at your place, and he still hasn't tried to sleep with you?"

I shook my head. "I was drunk the night he slept over."

"And he didn't take advantage?"

I shook my head again. "No, I was really drunk. It wouldn't have been okay."

"There was always the next morning!" He glanced over at Christian and then back at me. "My God, he's absolutely heartless. I want him."

"He's not gay," I said. "And what about José?"

"An extra friend never hurts. Plus, I think José would be proud of me when he'd see the friend in question. I mean, it's Christian Kelly, not just some—"

"Hey." Christian's husky voice made us both jump.

The usual tingle ran up my spine. He wore a white shirt open at the neck, revealing a hint of tanned skin; his black tie, the same color as his suit, was loose. As he stood in front of me with his hands in his pockets, his lazy smile pulling at the corners of his mouth, I realized that there was no vaccine against him. Each time I saw him, he looked even better than the time before.

I didn't understand why *People* magazine put Clooney and Pitt on its cover year after year when they could have someone like Kelly.

"Um, I have to go to the bathroom . . ." Marco got up and gave me an enthusiastic thumbs-up for encouragement behind Christian's back.

"Christian," I said, my throat suddenly dry.

"Hey, Hurricane." He took a step toward me. I felt small with him towering over me as I sat. "Were you ignoring me?" He leaned down and planted a kiss on my forehead. As a friend.

"I wouldn't dare. I didn't see you over there. Business lunch?"

"Why is it that I don't believe you? Are you stalking me?"

"You're confusing me with someone else. Smile is my second home. Are you sure you're not here stalking your 'friend' Gioia?"

Christian took my face in his hands and consumed my mouth with a hot kiss that set off every single nerve ending in my body. I had to hold on to his shirt to keep from falling off the stool.

"Didn't we say no kissing?" I panted.

"You had some ketchup on your mouth." He smiled coolly.

I swallowed hard, my heart pounding. "That's impossible. I'm eating a salad." I pointed to my bowl. "I'm on a diet, remember?"

Christian shrugged. "I like kissing you."

"Do you kiss all your friends?"

Not that it made me jealous or anything. Okay—it made me insanely jealous.

Stupid!

Christian slipped his body between my legs and seized my hips. "No, you have exclusive rights, Hurricane," he whispered in my ear.

He bowed his head and kissed me gently. The kiss was slow, tender, the kind of kiss that tastes like sugar and fills your head with cotton candy clouds.

I pushed back into him, my hands on his chest. I knew I should've resisted, that there was no one in Smile we had to convince, but I had become a Kelly addict. I craved the touch of his lips, his hands, the feel of his heart beating wildly in his chest.

"You should stop kissing me, Kelly," I whispered breathlessly.

Christian rested his forehead against mine. He was panting, his eyes misty with desire. "I will live in thy heart, die in thy lap, and be buried in thy eyes; and moreover, I will go with thee to Alessio's wedding."

I pulled back and looked him in the eye. "Is that one of your lines?"

"Did it work?"

Yes.

"No."

He smiled. "I wish I could say only poetry came out of my mouth, but I can't take all the credit. It was mostly Shakespeare. The real one—not Matteo."

"Do your Hallmark lines always work on women?"

"Well, I'm usually playing for lower stakes. Not with you."

"Because you have to respect the rules of the game, Kelly. No kissing and no relationship. We're just friends."

Maybe if I said it out loud, I'd believe it.

"Just friends. Right."

"I don't want people to get any ideas. If your aunt saw us right now, I'd be fired."

"Absolutely," he sang. "People, my aunt. Roger that."

"Will you stop it? You're unbearable. I should have chosen someone else to be my fake boyfriend."

"I seem to remember," he continued, drawing dangerously close, "that an agreement should benefit both parties. I'm helping you with your ex, but what's in it for me?"

With clear symptoms of a heart attack and respiratory failure, I looked up and met his eyes, which were flashing with desire. I squirmed on the stool.

"Don't," I muttered.

"Not that I'm complaining."

I was about to answer when I felt someone staring at me. A blast of air shot through the door where Matteo appeared, looking incredibly sexy, his green eyes burning into us.

Christian followed my gaze. His jaw hardened when he saw Matteo, who was now frozen at the entrance.

"Showtime, Hurricane," he whispered.

"What?"

Christian took my face in his hands and kissed me hard, possessively. He was marking his territory in front of Matteo, just like he had in the parking lot. But of course, as he said, it was all just a show.

I was about to melt in the sweet torture of it all when Christian broke away from me, panting. For a long time we were lost in each other's eyes, our chests heavily rising and falling. I averted my eyes first. Matteo had turned and left, slamming the door.

Is that why Christian had stopped kissing me? Because the scene was over?

"It worked," I muttered. "The kiss. Matteo left."

Christian nodded slowly. He clenched and unclenched his jaw as his usual worry line spread across his forehead. I wanted to reach out and smooth it with my fingers, I wanted him to kiss me again, I wanted to be stunned by his illegal smile. I shook myself out of my fantasies.

He looked at his watch. "I have to go," he said, suddenly serious. His impenetrable businessman mask was back on. "I have clients waiting. I'll see you . . ."

"Saturday?"

"Saturday." He touched my cheek and stepped back, his eyes still fixed on mine. He opened his mouth to say something, but then closed it and walked back to the corner table.

"Whoa." Marco whistled and plopped back down next to me. "I'm sad to announce my hopes have been crushed. He definitely plays for your team—and sends you all the good assists!"

"We're playing a friendly, Marco," I whispered, torturing my salad with my fork.

"I should send José for some training with Christian," he went on, ignoring me. "He could learn a few plays from him."

"Marco—"

"Do you think he has a gay brother?"

I rolled my eyes. "I'm glad to see someone is having fun with this."

Right hook, turn, kick.

Right hook, turn, kick.

"So, Ivan Drago." My sister threw a right hook at the punching bag and studied me as if I were a lab rat.

"Melly, are you here to throw punches or bust my balls?" I panted.

"You seem anxious."

"What do you want?" I was amped up, soaked in sweat. My tank top was drenched, and my shorts were like a second skin.

I had arrived to class agitated by the whole situation. I was in trouble; my life was ruined and it was my own doing. At the last session, I had imagined both Christian and Matteo as my punching bags, but today I was only punching Kelly.

Why on earth did karma want to punish me with six feet of muscles I couldn't even have?

Left cross, guard, left roundhouse kick.

"What are you trying to say?" Impatient, I delivered an extra punch. Melissa stepped back to avoid getting knocked down.

"Nothing," she replied.

I would have preferred getting a full-body wax over admitting she had been right from the start. I was not a one-night-stand kind of girl. I couldn't date a guy without getting involved. If I devoted my time to a man, it was because I wanted to build something.

When I was done with my exercises, I grabbed a towel and made a beeline to the locker room, trailed closely by Melly. Kelly had even managed to infect my FitBox time. I came to vent, to offload all my stress. But now, after an hour-long class, I was leaving with a battered heart and hands.

I opened my bag and took out my change of clothes and shower gel, but my sister intercepted me in front of the shower door.

"Get out of the way."

"You are afraid of being happy."

"I can't hear this."

"But you will."

"No."

"Yes, you're afraid a disaster is waiting around the corner."

Fucking Kelly! Stupid traitor heart!

I sat on the nearest wooden bench and leaned my head back to stare at the ceiling.

"With my luck, as soon as I turn the corner, my prince will have just gone off hand in hand with another woman."

"Try not to be too optimistic!"

"Cinderella lost her shoe; I've lost my hope."

"Here." She reached into her bag and pulled out a little package. "This is for you."

"What is it?" I asked. It was covered in wrapping paper with little hearts. "Are you pregnant? What's with this wrapping paper?"

"It was the only kind they had, silly. Open it!"

I unwrapped the paper to reveal a leather diary with blank pages. "Don't you think I'm a little old for a secret diary?"

"It's not a diary," she said, taking it from my hands. She flipped it open to show me the blank pages. "It's your fairy tale."

I took it back and looked at it. "It's completely blank. I can't think of a sadder fairy tale."

"It's for you to write in every day—it has to come from you, from what you want. Not from the prince that comes to save you."

"What movies have you been watching?"

"The same ones as you, silly. But right now you don't even know what you want. I think you still need some time to find yourself—on your own."

I tried to hold back my tears. I admired my new notebook. "So I need to write what I want, in black and white."

"Elementary, my dear Watson. You're always focused on the happy ending, but the story starts at the beginning, with you."

"How nice to have a shrink in the family."

She got up and took her clothes from her bag. "I always said I should have majored in psychology. You know how much money I would have made off of you by now?"

She bent down to kiss me on the cheek and left me in the smelly dressing room, knowing that I had closed my heart in a double-locked safe and that Christian might have been the only one who knew the combination.

Chapter 29

You know the movie *He's Just Not That Into You*?

I spent Friday evening watching the troubled story of Alex and Gigi, and at the end, I couldn't shake the lesson of the whole damn thing—that there weren't any exceptions about how men treat woman. If they want you, they will stop at nothing to get you, and if they treat you like dirt, well, they *aren't that into you.*

No exceptions, not even me.

There had been no word from Christian on Thursday or Friday night. He hadn't called, he hadn't been on WhatsApp, and he hadn't made an appearance at Dreamstart. I decided he probably just didn't like me enough to defy the rules of our stupid plan to be friends. If only he didn't have that Cheshire cat smile that had knocked me off my feet the first time I'd seen him, catapulting me into his world of contradictions.

And then there was me, a walking contradiction.

Not even the pain of waxing my own legs was enough make me forget the dull beating in my chest, the virus that had invaded my stomach and head.

I had "She" by Elvis Costello blaring in the bathroom when I heard the doorbell ring.

Please let it be Christian, I prayed. *Please, please, please.*

I went to the door in my bathrobe, a towel wrapped around my head like a turban.

How did Murphy's Law go? Whatever can go wrong will go wrong.

"Matteo!" I exclaimed, tightening the belt on my bathrobe. "What are you doing here? We see more of each other now than we did when we were together."

In a black leather jacket and black pants, his hands shoved in his pockets, he looked beautiful—and wrong.

"Can I come in?"

"I don't think that's a good idea," I said quietly.

"Gioia—"

"Please go, Matteo." I was getting anxious.

"It was a mistake for us to break up. I want to get back together."

"Us? You left me, remember? For another woman. With a note, in case you forgot." My voice was rising, sounding more like hysterical dolphin chatter than a person actually over someone. "You didn't even have the balls to face me, and now I'm supposed to stand here and listen to you?"

"I'm not leaving until you hear me out."

"You can't make me do that, Matteo."

He pulled me to him and kissed me. His lips, which had kissed me everywhere for years, found mine in a kiss that grew more and more passionate. I tried to resist and break away, but once his tongue slipped through my lips, I gave in. I clung to him, rejoicing inside myself.

He wanted me. He wanted me over Georgia, and I couldn't deny that the attraction between us was still strong.

It was when I felt his hands trying to open my robe that I came out of my trance and pulled away from him.

"I can't," I said, panting.

What the hell had I been thinking? A whole lot of nothing. That's what.

I hadn't thought. The end.

"You can. I still love you."

I fled to the kitchen, leaving Matteo at the doorstep. I felt like shit. And it was because of Christian.

I had opened the door in a bathrobe, hoping it would be him, and instead I found myself in the arms of my ex. The one who had taken me for granted, who had treated me like a piece of furniture to be dusted occasionally. The one who told me not to forget about him when I went to London, even though he was already with Georgia. The one who always had an excuse for not coming to visit me in England: an album, a tour. The one who hadn't shown up at the airport, sending my dad to pick up the pieces.

And then, the minute I'd moved on, Matteo had decided he wanted me back.

What had I done in a past life to deserve this? Had I been Hitler's lover? Had I tied Joan of Arc to the stake?

Lost in my thoughts, I jumped when Matteo touched my shoulder.

"Get out, Matteo," I hissed. "Get. Out."

"Gioia."

"No!" I shouted. I turned to face him. "Get out—and don't make me say it again!" I pointed to the door, but when it was clear he wasn't going to respect my wishes, I physically pushed him out. "Leave me alone." *Forever,* I added mentally.

I locked the door behind him and collapsed to the floor.

God, what had just happened?

I was still sitting against the door with my head in my hands when I heard the key turn and felt someone trying to enter. I fell forward as Bea pushed her way inside.

"Please tell me that wasn't Matteo just leaving," she said. Then she looked me up and down. "And that you didn't open the door for him half-naked. Don't get me wrong—if it had been anyone else, you'd be my idol."

"Open the window and let me get a running start," I said. I got up and started to pace back and forth.

"Are you okay?" she asked. "You're paler than usual."

"What floor are we on?"

"The fourth. Will you stop pacing? You're making me nervous."

"We're too low. I'd come away with a scratch at most."

Beatrice stood in my path and sniffed me.

"What exactly are you doing?" I asked, stepping around her.

"You're not even drunk! Wow, you really are in a bad place."

"I'm not an alcoholic, Bea." I went to my room and lay on the bed. "I'm just an idiot," I moaned, my eyes closed.

"Well, yeah!"

"You're supposed to say 'That's not true.'"

"That scene has been repeating itself all too often lately." The mattress sank as she joined me. "I came to comfort you and cheer you up with some jokes."

I sat up and brushed the hair out of my eyes. "I'm a total disaster."

"What have you done now?"

I bit my lip. "I kissed Matteo!" I flopped down on the bed and covered my face with my pillow.

"What?" Bea snatched it away. "Gioia Alessia Caputi, what have you done?"

"Don't use Adelina's tone with me," I muttered. "I should revise that: he kissed me. I just didn't resist at first."

"Why? Five months of rehab down the drain."

"Because I felt wanted, not like a runner-up. He wanted me."

Beatrice snorted. "Listen to what I have to say now, because I'm not going to say it again. You can't have your cake and eat it too. First you want Matteo back, then you're infatuated with the American; then, when Matteo comes back, you decide you want Mr. Manhattan. Then what do you do when you're not satisfied with the mess that is your life? You kiss Matteo. Honey, if you keep testing the waters like this, you're going to drown. Again."

I sat up. "I messed up." God, what was wrong with me? I should have been locked up in the nearest mental hospital.

"You keep telling yourself that you and Christian are going to be done for good after this stupid charade. But I can't accept that my best friend is that dumb. It's ridiculously obvious how much there is between you. I'm going to go to the bathroom. You stay here and wallow in your sins."

Beatrice left me alone to face my faults and fears. I was like a fairy-tale princess trapped in a tower. I had to decide whether to wait to be rescued or jump and save myself.

That is, if I weren't hurled out the window by the prince himself.

The next morning, I dragged myself into the shower like a zombie.

Beatrice—and not my phone alarm—had roused me, in crisis over Alessio's wedding. At six in the morning. After collapsing into bed at three.

After wiping away her tears and doing her hair and makeup for the ceremony, I was still in a bathrobe with gigantic bags under my eyes—and Christian would be arriving any minute.

The thought of enduring a weekend wedding on the coast with him and Matteo at the same hotel made my stomach churn. I had to tell Christian everything myself. I just knew Matteo would let it slip. Accidentally, of course.

I was still getting ready when the doorbell rang.

"Bea, can you open the door?" I shouted from the bathroom. I studied my reflection in the mirror. Only Photoshop could have saved me that morning. "It must be Christian!" I wasn't even dressed.

Beating an Olympic record for speed, I finished my makeup and threw on a little black dress I chose at random from the closet. I limped into the living room with two different shoe choices in time to hear Bea say, "Don't try anything funny, Kelly. I'll be watching you. One wrong move and I'll break your legs."

"Bea!" I said. Then I gasped at the sight of Christian.

He was wearing a perfectly tailored tuxedo, a pure white shirt unbuttoned at the neck, and cufflinks; he looked every bit the powerful tycoon, the producer of gold records from New York City. His hair was artfully arranged, a lock gracing his forehead. His jaw clenched when his eyes met mine. A vein began to throb in his cheek as I slipped on my other shoe. My eyes never left his. His gaze was sweet, smoldering. Intense.

I scanned his perfect figure. Broad shoulders, narrow waist, tapered legs. But it was that illegal smile—the one with the strange effect on my head, heart, and stomach—that made me combust.

"Gioia!" Bea broke the spell. "What are you wearing? We're going to a wedding—a celebration of love—not a funeral. Tell her, Kelly."

A corner of Christian's mouth twitched. "It doesn't do you justice, Hurricane."

I looked down at myself. "What's wrong? It's black, it's elegant, and it cinches my waist," I insisted.

"Gioia Alessia Caputi, go and put on the dress you bought for today," declared Bea.

"Jesus, you're just like my mother."

"Today we give our final farewell to Alessio, and I want you looking spectacular. Don't try my patience. I'll wait for you downstairs." She put on her sunglasses and headphones before slamming the door, leaving Christian and me gaping at each other.

Christian raised an eyebrow, confused. "That was some greeting."

I smiled. "It's a long story. She's usually nicer. Much nicer."

"Ah." He nodded, unconvinced. With one model-like stride, he was suddenly close to me. The way he looked at me made me tremble. It was as if his eyes held one end of an invisible thread that connected us, drawing me into him and infecting me with his charm.

"Hi, friend." He took my face in his hands and kissed me gently.

"Hi to you too, friend." My body woke up.

A flash of amusement lit up his eyes. "I hate to admit it," he said, pulling back to examine me from head to toe without taking his hands off my face. "But your friend, champion of karaoke, is right. If you go to church in this dress, you'll look like a nun who missed mass."

"I have no intention of wearing what she picked out for me," I said earnestly. It was too revealing, too tight. "My waist has been nonexistent since . . . forever."

Christian put his hands on my hips and caressed them slowly, his fingers drawing broad circles on my skin. "I like your waist." He pulled me to him and whispered in my ear, "Take off the dress, Hurricane." His smooth voice gave me chills, even though it was almost summer.

I walked away. "No."

"Do it for me."

I huffed. "I will not give in to your charms, Kelly." I pointed my finger at him, walking backward into my room to change. The man had me in the palm of his hand.

I looked at my monochrome wardrobe. The only color in it was the dress that Bea had forced me to buy during our shopping trip. It was a simple silk and chiffon dress, powder pink, with a sweetheart neckline and an empire waist.

"What are these balls?" I heard him ask from the living room. I looked at the pink dress and shook my head, but slipped it on anyway, trying not to stain it with my makeup, which was supposedly no transfer.

"They're snow globes, Christian, what did you think?" I said as I imagined him picking up one of the hundred or so snow globes I kept in the hallway.

"Yeah, I got that part, thanks. Do you collect them?"

"No, I keep them there because I didn't know what else to put on that shelf." I snorted and rolled my eyes. *Men.* "Of course I collect them. My grandma gave me my first one. When I was little, I thought she was some kind of fairy that made it snow. So every time it snowed, I'd get so excited, happy it was my grandma who was dropping the snowflakes."

I looked in the mirror. I gathered my hair into a soft side braid and spread a layer of gloss on my lips.

"I know. I've always had silly ideas," I said, walking into the hall.

Christian was busy shaking the ball and watching the snow fall. It was the one I'd bought in Barcelona a month ago, when we'd met. I'd felt exactly like a sphere with snow that lay still until the arrival of Christian, who had shaken up my life, covering it in glitter.

I cleared my throat. "I'm ready. We can go if you want."

Christian turned and nearly dropped the ball on the ground. His gaze stopped at my neckline. Was it too much? Not that I had much to display.

"Maybe it's better if you do dress like a nun." He coughed.

"It looks terrible, doesn't it?" I said, looking down at myself. "Is it too revealing? I should go change back."

"Shh." He brought his thumb to my lower lip and caressed it. A lump rose in my throat at his touch. "Gioia, in that dress, you are the fantasy of every man alive." His eyes weren't on the dress, but on my abundant curves.

"I feel like the Michelin Man."

I was too much of everything: too insecure, too curvy, too short, too paranoid, too talkative, too pale, too unendowed in the front.

"Why don't you trust me?" he whispered huskily in my ear. "Believe me when I say I can't wait to get you out of this dress. And not for the same reasons I wanted to get you out of the other one."

I shuddered to stop from igniting. I didn't know anything anymore. All I knew was that I was at the mercy of Christian Kelly.

"I know you're probably good at taking off women's clothes," I said, backing away. "How much practice have you had exactly?"

"Gioia . . ." he sighed.

Christian took a step forward as I stepped back.

"I'm sure the training was absolute torture."

The bedroom door handle jabbed my back, a warning that the race was over. There was no way out.

"You know what happens when you start talking nonsense." He trapped me between his arms.

"Don't do it, Christian! I just glossed my lips. Don't you remember the deal? No relationship, no kissing. We're friends."

"I'm beginning to hate this deal," he whispered. His mouth was close to mine. The slightest movement would be fatal. "I've had better ideas in my life."

Breathe, Gioia!

Christian traced the lines on my face with the expert touch of his fingertips. I felt his heat, his breath caressing my face. I parted my lips and our breath merged. I closed my eyes, longing for the softness of his lips, when a murderous rampage on stiletto heels threw open the front door.

Beatrice.

I could see the daggers through her Prada sunglasses.

"The priest and the couple are waiting for you!" she shouted, then slammed the door.

"That was your very nice friend," murmured Christian.

"She's dangerous today." *And not just her,* I thought. I slipped under his outstretched arm and found my purse near the entrance, trying to draw air into my lungs. "Shall we go?"

Breathe, Gioia! Breathe.

Chapter 30

The bride and groom had chosen a venue overlooking the sea. Fortunately, the place wasn't on a cliff, or Bea would have probably pushed the groom off.

The ceremony was going to take place on the beach just before sunset, followed by a poolside celebration with wine, fish, and live music.

The car ride there was quiet enough. Bea sat in the backseat in total silence. The only sounds we heard from her were the music in her headphones and an occasional mumble.

Christian and I, however, spent the whole trip arguing over which radio station to listen to. He had flipped past the Dixie Chicks and Lady Antebellum in favor of blowing out the speakers to Timbaland and Jay Z.

"You seriously don't like country?"

"I'm not the plaid shirt and cowboy boots type."

"Kelly, give up the moonshine and banjo myth. It's like saying all Italians walk around with a pizza and a mandolin."

Christian reached out and turned the volume even higher, drowning out my protests with Timbaland's rhymes.

When we reached our destination, Bea got out and slammed the door.

"I'd like to know which of them had the brilliant idea of getting married by the sea," she muttered.

"I love beach weddings," I said, stepping out of Christian's car. I breathed in the salty air and looked with delight at the three-story villa that would accommodate us until the following day. It looked more like a farmhouse in Tuscany than an oceanside villa. It was all brick with exposed wooden beams and a yard that sloped gradually down to the water.

"The wind that screws up your hair, the heat that melts your makeup, the sand in your underwear. Oh yeah, lots to love. Honey, first get a ring on your finger and then we'll talk." She grabbed her suitcase and dragged it inside the house.

"Sorry," Christian whispered in my ear, "but when will she show us her nice side?"

I smiled. "She's having a bad day."

I picked up my bag and walked with him to the reception area, where Lea, the wedding planner, welcomed us.

"Welcome!" she said with a smile painted across her face. Her eyes were glued to Christian. "These are the keys to your room. Once you get settled, you can go out to the pool for a welcome cocktail."

She handed us two keys: a single room for Beatrice and a double. For Christian and me.

"How are we going to do this?" I asked, walking to the elevator.

"What?" he replied, amused.

"The room. It's double."

"I'll sleep on one side, and you'll sleep on the other."

I snorted. "Hilarious."

"If you want, I'll let you choose your side, if that makes you feel safer. Oh, and I'll try to eat as much as possible at dinner tonight so I won't devour you." Christian gave me a wink and headed for the stairs.

"Gioia?" I turned and saw Bea coming toward me. "Can you take my suitcase up?"

"Why, where are you going?"

She pressed the elevator call button. "To the pool. Free cocktails and single men await."

"Shouldn't you be grieving?"

"In the US, when someone dies, they celebrate all day because they never have to deal with that person again. Isn't that right, Kelly?"

Christian leaned against the railing of the staircase and smiled blankly.

A trill announced the elevator's arrival.

As soon as the doors opened, Bea put her luggage inside. "Thank you, I love you."

She planted a kiss on my cheek before disappearing.

"Are your other two friends like that?" asked Christian. He took our suitcases and started up the stairs. "Because if so, I really am lucky I met you at karaoke and not them."

"Where are you going?"

"To the room?"

"There is an elevator for a reason, Christian."

"I prefer to walk."

"Come on, you're not afraid, are you?" I teased.

But his serious and slightly embarrassed expression confirmed it.

"I can't believe it! How do you get anywhere in New York? Shoot a web like Spider-Man?"

Christian Kelly, *Forbes* cover boy, the man with a seven-figure bank account, was afraid to take an elevator. I really wanted to tweet about it.

"Don't compare New York elevators with these antiques. The ones at my office can travel twenty floors in seconds; that old thing will take twenty years to make it up two floors."

"Wait, do you hear something?" I asked, tears of laughter in my eyes.

Christian sighed. "Come on, spare me."

"Someone's scratching at the walls. It's Christian 'Spider-Man' Kelly, climbing the stairs!" I blocked the closing doors with my foot, wiping away my tears. "Get in here—or are you really going to walk up two floors?"

"Wanna bet I beat you?"

"What are we betting?" I spoke before thinking.

It was best not to make a bet with a man who was used to winning.

"I don't think it will be hard to find something that satisfies both parties, Hurricane."

He winked at me and started up the stairs, while I eagerly pressed the "Close" button.

When the elevator doors opened on the top floor, I saw the door to our room already open and Christian in the doorway, grinning.

"Move over, Kelly," I said, sounding unimpressed. But my heart was doing somersaults.

For once in my life, I had to lose to win.

The ceremony was almost over, the orange light of sunset illuminating the small gazebo where Alessio and Serena were exchanging their vows.

The beach was lit by countless candles scattered here and there, clusters of pink and white peonies graced the whitewashed wooden benches, and the bride's veil was fluttering in the gentle breeze.

Christian and I were following the ceremony from the last row, trying to keep an eye on Beatrice, who was still poolside. She had chosen to stay near the buffet to enjoy a cocktail. Fortunately, the rites didn't include anything about speaking now or forever holding your peace, so the pastor was able to continue uninterrupted. I breathed a sigh of relief, though I was still on edge: the best man's eyes were burning into me the entire time.

As Alessio and Serena proclaimed their love to the tune of "Pachelbel's Canon," I felt my eyes getting damp. They were living their happily ever after. Meanwhile, the man at the groom's side was the prince with whom I had always imagined my happily ever after. I had imagined walking down an aisle of white sand just like this, barefoot, guided by those two green eyes, and swearing our eternal love at sunset. Instead, I was attending the wedding I had always wanted for myself with a totally different dream man sitting right next to me.

The man who didn't want a serious relationship, the man who had already knelt at another woman's feet and asked her to spend her whole life with him.

A silent tear ran down my face.

The magical atmosphere of the sunset, the love that permeated the air, the thought of Christian on a plane to New York and never seeing him again outside of a Google Alert. It was all too much.

I would miss him.

Christian squeezed my hand gently. "You're a sentimental one, Caputi."

"It's the music," I lied.

I already missed him so much it hurt.

"Bea, pace yourself!" I looked at my friend, who had just asked the waiter to refill her wine glass. "Or at least eat something."

We were at the reception dinner. The bride and groom's table faced away from the sea, while the tables for the guests were arrayed around the room, adorned with vases of peonies and illuminated by hundreds of candles. On the opposite side of the hall, a DJ spun discs, the chatter of the guests interrupted by music that ranged from Frank Sinatra to Justin Timberlake.

Almost all the guests had moved to the center of the floor for a slow dance, while others chatted quietly out by the pool with glasses of wine in hand.

"Back off, I'm having fun," said Beatrice. She had just come back to the table after doing a great interpretation of Michael Jackson's moonwalk. "In fact, I have a friend waiting for me by the pool."

"Who?" I asked, worried. I was like my mother with one of her *Murder, She Wrote* investigations.

"I don't know. And I don't want to know. I'll never see him again after tomorrow."

"I said the same thing about Christian in Barcelona, and look how that turned out." I gestured to Christian's empty chair next to mine.

"You hit the jackpot, Gioia! How many times in life do you win the love lotto?" She looked around, clearly searching for someone. "Want me to wait with you until Christian gets back from the bathroom?"

"No, go ahead. I'll live." I watched her as she teetered away and then speared the calamari on my plate. Of course, every male present—except the groom—turned to look at Bea as she passed. The slit at the back of her dress would have made Jennifer Lopez blush.

I grabbed a flute of champagne from a passing waiter's tray and then heard the chair beside me squeak against the floor.

"Christian, have you tasted this calamari? It's delicious." I turned; my fork froze in midair at the sight of two green eyes. "Matteo, you know you can go to jail for stalking people?"

"I need to talk to you."

"Here?" I turned around, hoping Christian would come back soon. "No, forget it."

"You can't pretend nothing happened between us yesterday."

"You pretended for months, Matteo."

"I refuse to believe you didn't feel something."

I pushed my plate away, no longer hungry. "What makes you so sure?"

Where on earth was Christian? And they say women take forever in the bathroom.

"I'm sure, because if you felt even half of what I felt, then you felt a lot," he said with a passion that I hadn't seen from him in a long time.

I was speechless. If he had said all this a month ago, I would have gone crawling back to him, but now I just kept watching the bathroom door.

"Matteo, you finally said the right thing, but way too late."

I got up so I wouldn't have to listen to him, to those words, the ones I had prayed day and night that he would say when we were together, before I left for London and after I came back.

"Gioia, please."

"I don't want to hear it, Matteo. Not now or ever." I turned and rushed out to the pool.

I took off the Louboutins that had been torturing my feet and grabbed one of those evil fruity drinks that go down easy but after half an hour start to have dramatic effects on your legs.

I got absorbed watching Bea and other guys flirting, while the happy couple inside danced to "For Once in My Life" by Frank Sinatra.

I studied the rim of my glass. Was it normal to wish I had a bazooka so I could shoot every happy couple in my path?

"Hey."

I felt the warmth of his body. I gulped down my drink, placed it on the counter, and turned around.

Christian was walking toward me. He had taken off his jacket and rolled up his shirtsleeves, revealing two bronzed, muscular arms. With his hands in his trouser pockets, his hair mussed by the breeze coming in off the sea, he took my breath away.

I'd never know if I would ever have gotten used to the way he could take my breath away with a glance, because he would be leaving soon, and then I'd never see him again.

"Hey." I leaned on the counter and slid on my shoes, averting my eyes.

Do not look into his eyes, I repeated like a mantra. My heart was already pounding, my palms sweaty.

"When I saw you holding your shoes at the bar, I was afraid we'd have a repeat of the scene in Barcelona," he teased.

God, how pathetic was I that night?

I took a stool next to his and sat down. "You saved me that night. Otherwise I wouldn't be here right now—I'd be home job hunting."

He laughed. I'd miss that laugh.

I was already missing him too much.

I was insanely attracted to him: he made me laugh, sigh, shake to the core. But a part of me was completely terrified, scared of everything I didn't know about his life.

I grabbed two glasses of champagne. When I handed him his glass, our fingers brushed, and the usual thrill burned through my body, so much that I gripped the glass so hard I nearly broke it.

"You shouldn't drink too much. You don't want to have a headache tomorrow."

"It's just one glass," I protested, raising it in the air. "I drink to Christian Kelly. To you, for saving me from certain death on a May night in Barcelona. Wasted, barefoot, and above all, without a phone signal."

And for putting together the pieces of a broken, weary heart.

His smile faded, giving way to an unreadable expression. Christian studied me for a long time, his eyes digging deep into my soul, as if he could peel away all the layers of fear and leave me naked, my skin stripped, practically transparent for future falls and bruises.

Embarrassed and unable to hold his gaze, I looked over to the pool.

"I'm right here," murmured Christian, breaking the silence.

Confused, I looked back at him. "I see you, Christian. I'm not that drunk."

"No." He leaned forward and took my chin in his hands, forcing me to look straight into his molten eyes. "You don't understand. I am here for you and I'll always be here to save you, Gioia. Always."

I leaned against the bar. The air seeped out of my lungs and my stomach twisted.

Breathe, Gioia! Breathe.

I closed my eyes. There was so much I wanted to say: that he had already saved me; that I was afraid of drowning in his eyes; but that even as I drowned in him, he was my air, his illegal smile made me melt, his hands had shaped me into a woman I liked, smoothing out my curves, perfecting my imperfections. I could have gone on, telling him I loved how he made me feel safe in his arms and how I'd always felt at home in his embrace. Wherever we were.

I wanted to say what I'd learned in these too-short weeks with him—that it was possible to live after the end of a romance. It was like falling off a bicycle. Some wounds would heal quickly, and others would require time and tears—and still leave an indelible mark. But looking at him reminded me that I had had the strength to get back on the bike.

Yes, maybe I'd fall again, but it was worth the risk.

Love was worth the risk.

It could be as dangerous as walking a tightrope, but as intoxicating as finding your balance, as flying.

Of course I didn't say any of it.

I just swallowed the lump in my throat and took his hand in mine. "I know," I said, my voice breaking with emotion. "I know you're here."

Chapter 31

An hour later, Christian and I were still sitting at the bar, rating the DJ's song choices and watching Bea stumble around with her new friends.

Neither of us had broached the subject of feelings after Christian's declaration, and I had hunkered down behind a glass of wine. Okay, maybe more than one.

Christian frowned when I grabbed another. "You should stop drinking."

"We're at a party," I reminded him. "Wine makes it all so much more exciting."

"Yes, exciting for you. The last time you got drunk with me, I had to drag your dead weight up three flights of stairs while you snored."

"I don't snore. I just want to enjoy myself tonight." I handed him another glass and smiled my best smile. "I think you should too, Kelly. The picture of you on that last issue of *Forbes* was not the real you."

"Will you stop reading about me on the Internet?"

I ignored him. "I understand what you're doing. You've created this image of yourself as a powerful tycoon to keep people at arm's length. You're always telling me to relax, but you're the one who's afraid to jump. Are you afraid to show me who you really are because the wounds Chantal inflicted are still bleeding?"

"Easy, Gioia," he warned.

"You keep everyone at a distance, especially women. You told me yourself that you dated all the Miss America contestants, past and future, and had your secretary dump them, you dog."

"I think you've had more than enough." He took the glass out of my hand and stood up.

I took my glass back, my tongue tickled into action by all the champagne bubbles. "Can I ask you something, Kelly?"

"No."

"What made you fall in love with her?"

"Gioia," he muttered, "whatever is going through your head, keep it to yourself."

"That's what I've been doing all these years, I have a lot of drafts and notes stored up there. Now—boom!—my database just exploded."

"Shall we go?" Christian offered me his hand.

"Where?"

"You'd better continue your explosion on the dance floor before you say something you'll regret tomorrow."

"I can't dance. Plus, they're all waiting for me to fall on my face. They hate me."

"Who hates you?"

"All the women here, and maybe even the one or two men who don't have eyes for Beatrice. They've done nothing but attack you with their eyes since we arrived. They're wondering what a sexy man like you is doing with a Michelin Man in high heels."

He shook his head in disbelief. "How many drinks did you have while I was in the bathroom?" He was amused.

"None." But I could tell he knew I was lying. He must have seen me chug that evil fruity cocktail like a drunk at last call. "I'm barely even tipsy, Christian . . . really," I insisted.

Christian came closer, his hand still outstretched. "You're really hesitant for someone who tells me I have to learn to let go. I know how to let go with a woman. Let me show you now. On the dance floor."

"Are you pissed because I asked you about Chantal? Jesus, Kelly, we've been discussing my private life for weeks."

"Are you going to dance with me, or do I have to throw you over my shoulder and carry you out in front of all those women who supposedly hate you so much?"

"Bully." I snorted. "I need to start keeping better company."

I took his hand and let him guide me to the middle of the floor. I still had a few hours before the stroke of midnight, when I'd go back to being Cinderella. At least she got to dance with a prince.

As Christian was leading me, I realized that all the couples were in each other's arms, dancing to the slow song pouring through the speakers. I gulped, thinking about dancing so close to Christian in front of all those people.

"You know, I'm better at conga lines and getting down to recent hits. Why don't we wait and come back out when the DJ plays 'Brasil'?"

"No." With a tug, Christian pulled me to him. He encircled my waist with his arms and bowed his head, his lips pressing against my ear. "Let go, Hurricane."

Sighing, I wrapped my arms around his neck and rested my cheek against his chest as one song faded and the notes of John Legend's "All of Me" rang out. The song we had danced to at the Gotha.

Our bodies swayed in sync, a perfect match. We fit one another perfectly.

I looked up and fell into two deep pools. I was stunned by how much I needed this man.

I tripped on his feet. "Sorry."

"You okay?" he asked.

"Yes, just that the song . . ." I shook my head. "God, what an idiot I was that night at the Gotha. I practically begged you to come to my house. I should start drinking club soda."

Christian didn't smile; he sighed. Was he relieved he hadn't slept with me? He observed me for a long time. His hands caressed my back though its thin covering of chiffon. I put my hands on his chest; I was short of breath.

Suddenly, I felt his lips press gently against mine. His touch sent me into a tailspin. I forgot about everything: the guests, the DJ, Beatrice, the stinking filthy traitor Alessio, the unsuspecting bride, and especially Matteo. The asshole.

I clung to Christian's shirt and pulled him to me as he muffled the moans escaping my mouth. His hands feverishly caressed my face, my neck.

He wanted me. Not a *Project Runway* model, not a toothpick woman with mile-long legs, and not even a certain Ms. Chantal Herrera.

The butterflies in my stomach rolled out the red carpet and sounded their fanfare as my heart made its triumphant entrance. I melted in his embrace as his hands managed to put back together the thousand pieces of me that Matteo had broken apart.

"The rooms are upstairs, you guys."

Indeed. We did need to get a room. Immediately.

Except the voice that crept between us wasn't Bea's—it was Matteo's.

"Not a good time, Perri," Christian hissed.

I turned to face my ex's stormy eyes.

"The bride and groom should be the focus today, not the two of you, Kelly."

I was about to step back from Christian, but he held me tight against him. They locked eyes in a battle of pheromones.

"So, Kelly. What did you think of our performance for the newlyweds?"

"I'm here to be with Gioia, not to talk about work, Perri," said Christian, his arm still wrapped firmly around my waist. "And we wouldn't want to take any attention away from the bride and groom, right?"

Matteo absorbed Christian's blow as they glared at each other. All they needed to do now was start a burping contest.

"Ah, there you are!" Bea came lurching toward us, holding a glass of an unidentifiable green liquid. "They said we can go sing onstage, Gioia."

Her jaw dropped when she saw how I was trapped between two blazing fires. My ex on one side, seized by fits of jealousy, and Christian on the other, refusing to let me go. I hoped she wasn't too drunk to notice the desperate looks for help I was throwing her way.

"Maybe you should go first, Matteo," I said.

"Why don't we make Kelly sing?" Matteo asked, a diabolic light in his eyes that meant nothing but trouble.

"I think Gloria Gaynor should start us off," Christian shot back.

"Who?" asked Bea and Matteo in unison.

I smiled.

"Bea, why don't you start? You love this stuff. Break the ice and we'll follow," Christian said.

"I want to hear the American," she whined.

"Me too," Matteo said.

"I only sing in the shower, right, honey?" said Christian, kissing me in front of Matteo.

"Why don't you sing for her in front of everyone, Kelly?" asked Matteo. "Why don't you show us all how much you care about her?"

I rolled my eyes. *Why me, God? Why me?*

The whole triangle was standing right in front of me.

A drunken Bea provoking Christian.

Christian provoking Matteo, who turned his anger back on Christian.

"He doesn't have to prove a thing," I replied. Since when had Matteo become such an asshole?

"Come on, Kelly, don't be shy. No one's buying it," said Beatrice.

"Why are you tormenting him?" I asked, glaring at her.

"I'd go sing first, but I want to give Kelly an advantage. Level the playing field," said Matteo.

"Stop it!" I rested my hand on Christian's arm. "You really don't have to do this," I whispered.

Christian pulled me to him and brought his face close to mine. "Get your phone out, honey, and get a video of your Shakespeare singing," he whispered. He stood up tall and adjusted his bow tie. "Is it straight, Perri? My girlfriend has trouble keeping her hands off me."

I closed my eyes, embarrassed. "Christian?" I called to him, but he was already up onstage with an acoustic guitar in hand.

"Whose side are you on?" I scolded Bea. Matteo had already gone to round up the guys. "Why don't you give him a break? I know you don't like him."

"That's not true! I think he's great. Heck, I'd love a shot if things don't work out between you. Even if he can't sing. What I have in mind has nothing to do with singing."

"Bea," I hissed.

"Don't worry, honey, he's all yours. Plus, I wouldn't stand a chance. He's all yours and no one's going to take him away from you now."

"There might be one person who could," I muttered, thinking about Chantal and how Christian was still too hung up on her to even talk about it.

I held my breath as I watched Christian walk to the center of the stage with the guitar. He tuned it, then locked eyes with me and began to sing. He had a beautiful voice, deep and a little scratchy.

He sang "You and Me" by Lifehouse. My heart leaped out of my chest. I watched as he gave himself to me with every word, verse after verse, oblivious to everyone.

"Whoa!" Bea whistled. "He's not bad!"

I barely heard her, just as I barely heard the murmur of the others who'd gathered around the stage, attracted by Christian's performance. I was stunned by the words. Just like the song said, I couldn't keep my eyes off him.

Christian wasn't there to one-up Matteo—he was singing for me, and me alone.

We had knocked each other out, and neither of us could get back up again. My eyes were burning with tears that threatened to spill over.

I wasn't the hurricane. He was.

He had snuck into my life, intensifying his presence every day. He was overwhelming. Upsetting. Puzzling.

Now, our eyes still locked, I silently prayed that he wouldn't hurt me. I wanted him to leave while there was still time, before he toppled my insecurities, before I became convinced that he was the final goal in the obstacle course that had been my life. I silently begged him not to break my heart into a million pieces, not to destroy my foundation like a cyclone.

After Christian sang the last verse, the whole room exploded in thunderous applause peppered with whistles of appreciation. Especially from the women.

"Your American is really good," Bea admitted.

Breathe, Gioia. Breathe.

I didn't know whether to run to him or away from him; I was so gripped by fear.

Fear of failure, and fear of being happy, no matter how short-lived my happiness with him would be.

Christian put down the guitar and joined us, never taking his eyes off me. As he approached, I became more and more confused, overcome by my insecurities. I knew he could read the uncertainty in my eyes, because he knitted his eyebrows together and tightened his jaw as he made his way through all the guests jockeying to compliment him.

I put my hand to my throat. I felt like I was suffocating. Was I brave enough to put my heart in his hands?

I took a deep breath and made my decision.

"I can't."

I turned and ran.

Chapter 32

"Gioia, wait."

I had made a break for it toward the beach. I heard footsteps behind me and a hand clamped around my wrist.

I turned to meet Christian's eyes, shining through the darkness.

"What's gotten into you?"

"I can't." I jerked away from his grip and walked faster, slipping off my shoes as I went.

Christian stopped me. He encircled my waist with his arms and pulled me tight against him. I could feel his rapid heartbeat against my back, his chest rising and falling convulsively like mine.

"What's the matter, Hurricane?" he whispered in my ear.

I closed my eyes and leaned back into his chest, my arms rigid and fists clenched.

"I can't," I muttered. I sounded so weak I wasn't sure if he heard me.

I felt Christian stiffen as he loosened his grip on my body. "Because of Matteo?"

"No . . . no. It has nothing to do with him. It's me. You're going to break my heart."

"I would never hurt you, Gioia."

"I know, Christian," I muttered.

Breathe, Gioia! Breathe.

I sucked air into my lungs and spoke in a single breath before I lost my nerve. "You're going to be on a plane to New York in a few days. You'll go back to your life, and I'll be left here to pick up the pieces of my heart. Like always."

Christian turned me to face him. He held my face in his hands and looked at me with his melty chocolate eyes. I recognized my own feelings in them: confusion, fear, desire.

"You'd have no promise of forever even if I lived here." He lifted my chin with a finger so I'd hear him. "I don't know if we'll have a happy ending, Gioia, but I do know one thing. I don't want to be just friends. I want more. Don't you think I'm afraid of what's between us? I tried to avoid any connections, any feelings, any risks, but then I met you. And I'm tired of running."

My heart was in my throat. I shut my eyes tight. Out of sight, out of mind, they say. It didn't work. I felt this man—his warmth, his desire, and all our spiraling feelings—in every fiber of my being.

"Gioia, look at me."

I opened my eyes. He looked troubled. "Christian . . ."

"No, let me finish." He stepped back and winced for a moment, as if he were fighting an internal battle. "You were the first person to see me for who I am. Not just some famous millionaire. You saw Christian, the guy from New York who was raised on bread and music. When I saw you that night at the karaoke bar, you sparked feelings in me I didn't know I still had. I was scared. I had done nothing but use women for the past year. And I didn't want to commit. That's why I said we should be friends. I didn't want you to become just another faceless number on my contact list. Because you—you're you, damn it! But what I said about being friends was nonsense."

"I don't know if I'm ready," I said. "You're special, Christian. You make me feel more alive than anyone ever has—more alive than I've felt in my whole life. You can destroy me with your eyes, or your smile. Not to mention the fact that you kiss like a god, which makes things even worse." I took a deep breath. "When Matteo left me, I fell to pieces. I wish . . . I wish I could trust you, but I'm scared, Christian. I'm scared to trust you and then see you go. I'd always be afraid you'd just turn around and pull the rug out from under me, just like Matteo."

"Don't make me pay for his sins, Gioia."

"I'm not making you pay for anything, Kelly. It's not about you— it's me."

Christian set his jaw and pointed to the space between us. "So we should give up on this? Don't you think it's the best thing that could ever happen to us?"

I took a deep breath. My head was such a mess. I was walking a tightrope, knowing that any step could be my demise.

"Don't run away from us, Gioia."

I hesitated. Christian was so close I could smell his skin; the sea breeze crept through my bones, making me shiver.

"Hurricane," he whispered, "we didn't choose it, but we can't pretend it isn't there. It's too strong to ignore."

His mouth was an inch from mine, threatening my efforts to rein in my feelings.

"I know you're scared, Gioia."

He touched my cheek and traced his fingertips along my neck, chin, and lips. I trembled at his touch, shaking because I wanted him to keep going.

I took his hand and pressed my cheek against his palm. "If I told you to leave, now, and never look back . . . if I asked you to forget about me . . . would you do it?"

"I would. If you asked me . . . but that doesn't mean you'd be able to forget about me."

I looked away. My inner conflict had reached epic proportions; holding his tormented gaze was becoming more and more impossible.

My willpower was waning. I felt desired with Christian, worshiped with every glance.

I sighed and murmured, "Please don't, Kelly."

Christian ended my protests with a kiss. He grabbed the nape of my neck and pulled me to him, bringing my hand up to rest on his throbbing heart. He was eager, carnal, kissing me as if he wanted to erase any doubts, any fears that still haunted me. He didn't stop kissing me even when some of the wedding guests cleared their throats because we were blocking the path to the beach.

When we parted, Christian leaned his forehead against mine.

"So I kiss like a god, huh?"

I nodded, burying my face in his chest. "You make me crazy."

"So that makes us perfect for each other, because I want to spend all my time making you crazy."

I looked at him and read my own desire in his eyes.

"Christian . . ."

"Stop. No more running, Gioia."

"I already know how it will end."

Christian leaned over and kissed me again. "Has anyone ever told you that you talk too much?" he whispered against my lips.

I smiled. "Yes, you."

He straightened up and looked into my eyes. Then he whispered, "You choose."

He held out a hand.

He was letting me choose.

I could choose to run away from him, forget these past four weeks, avoid what seemed like guaranteed tragedy. He was giving me the chance to go back to my old life. Or I could choose to throw myself into his arms, get swept up in Hurricane Kelly, give my heart a second chance, and let what we felt for each other overtake us.

I reached out and took Christian's hand. I gave him a smile and got an illegal smile in return, making my heart skip a beat.

Christian brought my hand to his mouth and kissed it. "I'll never hurt you, Hurricane."

He intertwined his fingers with mine and we walked toward the house. A gust of wind whipped around us, taking with it every fear, every uncertainty, every doubt that had plagued me over the past few weeks.

We entered the house to the sound of Beatrice's shrill voice belting from the stage.

"I don't know what's worse"—Christian laughed—"hearing Bea sing or Perri speak."

I grabbed his shirt collar and kissed him. "You're wasting time talking about my ex, Kelly. I thought all you wanted to do was make me crazy."

"At your command, Hurricane." He moved me along with a pat on the butt and went to reception to retrieve our room key.

I watched as he leaned against the counter, his jacket over his shoulders, his hair tousled, a smile across his chiseled face. God, he was beautiful.

I called the elevator while I waited.

"What are you doing?" he asked when he returned.

"I called the elevator."

"I know—why?"

"What do you mean, why? I don't want to do two flights of stairs now, Christian. My feet hurt, and this is the fastest way to the room. I don't want to waste any more time."

It all happened in a flash. Christian grabbed me by the legs, flung me over his shoulder like a sack of potatoes, and started up the stairs.

"Christian, put me down! Everyone will see us!"

"I don't care."

"I know how to walk! Put me down right now—please!"

"You can do your begging when we get to the room, Hurricane."

I gave him a slap on the butt. "You may kiss like a god, but you're acting like a caveman," I huffed.

"You're downgrading me that fast?" He took the key from his pocket and opened the door. Then he set me back on the ground, threw his jacket on the bed, and walked slowly toward me.

I suddenly found myself at a loss for words.

The room was shrouded in shadow, the double bed barely illuminated by the dim light of the moon, but I was able to read the desire in his eyes.

"Hey." He put his hand on my cheek. "You're scared."

"Shouldn't I be?" I smiled shyly.

"No."

"I'm not afraid of you, but I thought . . ."

I stopped talking. Christian put his mouth on my neck while his hands stroked my back. I felt the warmth of his hands on my skin.

"You think too much, Hurricane," he whispered.

I dug my hands into his black hair, then ran them down the length of his back, farther down, to his perfect ass. I squeezed him gently.

"Maybe we should close the door," I gasped as Christian left a trail of kisses along my collarbone.

"Are you sure? I'm worried I won't make it back."

I took his face in my hands and kissed him, teasing his mouth with my tongue. He moaned and held his breath when I ran my tongue over his lips and slid it past them.

"You too, Kelly. You think too much."

He kicked the door shut and took me in his arms again. I pressed the inside of my leg against his hip and kissed him hard. I wanted more.

He didn't stop stroking me as he lay me slowly down on the bed. He never took his eyes off me.

"So, Ms. Caputi," he murmured against my lips, "If we both think too much, I guess that means we'd better distract ourselves."

I let out a moan of agreement as his tongue merged with mine and his hands slipped under my dress. I shivered under the gentle touch of his fingers on my belly, which he languidly stroked until he made his way farther down, where I wanted to feel him.

My skin tingled and a warmth spread through my body.

I wanted him inside me, I wanted to feel him closer, I wanted our bodies to merge, so that we no longer knew where one of us ended and the other began.

My hands fumbled with the buttons on his shirt.

"We're overdressed, Kelly."

Christian pulled his head back and smiled. "I agree."

He lifted my hips with one hand and slowly pulled off my dress until it dropped on the floor. He lay on top of me, but I brought my hand to his chest to stop him.

"I want you naked too."

Christian stood up and took off his shirt. My eyes feasted on his bare chest, his chiseled abs, the *V* that ended under his pants.

"Completely," I added in response to his smoldering gaze.

He gave me a little smile and took off his shoes, his pants, and his boxers, leaving them in a heap with my dress.

Oh. My. God. My eyes widened.

Of course Christian Kelly was well endowed.

Christian followed my gaze and gave me a look that sent me up in flames. He crawled back over me and propped himself up on his arms so he could memorize every inch of my body with a gaze that dug deep into my soul.

Contact with his bare skin made me spasm, and my stomach clenched. I grabbed him by the neck and threw myself at his mouth. God, he knew how to kiss.

Christian held me against him. "You're beautiful," he whispered in his husky voice. He pushed his mouth against mine; our tongues merged, dancing and intertwining. He bowed his head and kissed my neck, my chin, the space between my breasts.

With a quick motion, he unhooked my bra, threw it to the center of the room, and brought a thumb to one of my swollen nipples, then the other. Then his tongue and teeth replaced his hands, teasing my nipples longer than I could bear, until they were swollen and sore.

"Christian," I panted. I could feel his erection brushing against my inner thighs. He clutched my back and arched my pelvis, his breathing heavy and rushed.

Breathe, Gioia.

He raised the hem of my panties and slid his fingers under the lace, covering my mouth with his other hand and muffling the groan that erupted from my throat.

He kissed and worshipped every inch of my skin, as if I were some delicate, precious thing. He slowly lowered my panties as I pulled out first one foot and then the other.

He lay back down on top of me, his breathing as hard and fast as my own. His mouth followed the path his fingers had made. He left a trail of kisses down my chest, over my belly, and then even lower.

I gasped when his mouth finally found the part of me that had been throbbing for him, longing for more.

"Christian, please," I gasped.

I arched my back; my hips began to shake uncontrollably. I was overcome with desire. Clinging to his hair, I tugged him hard against me. I pressed my nails into his flesh, squirming against him, against the expert strokes of his tongue.

I was done for.

And so were all my defenses. My breaths grew even shorter and my heart pounded. I hoped I wasn't having a heart attack.

Christian looked up. Our eyes mirrored the other's desire.

"Can you feel it, Hurricane?" He dug his fingers into my skin, making me moan with pleasure.

My legs shook, and I clung hard to the sheets as a spasm rocked my entire body.

Oh. My. God.

I wrapped my legs around him and arched my back in the slow, sweet agony.

Christian crawled on his forearms until his body was back over mine. He bowed his head and kissed me gently, teasing my lower lip. Then the kiss changed. It grew harder, faster, more desperate. He kissed as if he were taking possession of me.

I pulled him to me, my hands following the lines of his muscles. His pecs, his abs. I traced a line down his stomach with my fingers, teasing him.

He moaned at the touch of my tongue, making me feel like the most powerful woman in the world. To know I had that effect on him was worth more than a thousand compliments.

Christian took my face in his hands and kissed me, the taste of me still on his lips. He looked at me as if to ask if I was still with him, if I was feeling what he felt.

I nodded. I felt it to my core, felt it running through my veins and throbbing in my heart.

Then he was back on top of me, his hands everywhere at once, as if he wanted to trace every single line on my body.

"Please, Christian." I arched against him, every muscle taut with desire.

I gasped and let my head fall back on the pillow as Christian thrust himself inside me. He pinned my hands alongside my head, interlacing his fingers with mine. His lips sealed over mine as our bodies pressed together, moving to the beat of our hearts. I wrapped my legs around his back and lifted my pelvis to him so he could go deeper. Our bodies moved together perfectly, as if our life lines had been designed to match.

Christian never lowered his eyes from my face as he pressed himself into me, increasing his pace with each thrust. And with each thrust, I pressed closer to him, welcoming him deeper into my body, into my life.

"I feel you," I whispered against his lips.

A strangled groan escaped his throat.

"Keep feeling me, Hurricane," he whispered, driving his mouth against mine in a kiss that made my heart swell.

I let myself be carried away by the touch of his hands, by his mouth, by the gaze that we shared, thrust after thrust. We moved in unison, and he never ceased to tell me how beautiful I was, or how important.

At last I could feel him readying himself, tensing with pleasure, and I clung to his hands and moaned into his mouth, ready to fall with him.

Or fly away.

I surrendered, groaning, as Christian came with a scream and collapsed with his beautiful face in the crook of my neck. We lay there in each other's arms, the silence broken only by our gasps and our hearts, beating in unison.

Music from the party wafted in through the open window. Christian turned my head and kissed me gently, cradling me in his arms. I looked into his eyes.

I didn't know where any of this would lead; I hadn't found any answers. But I knew my heart had made its decision.

I had chosen him.

I felt him, and only him.

I took his hand and rested it on my heart, relaxing under the warmth of his palm.

The same warmth that I felt over every inch of my body, held tight in his arms.

Chapter 33

I awoke the next morning in the usual tangle of sheets.

Only this time, there was an arm resting heavily across my body.

I opened my eyes to see the Sleeping Beauty beside me and blushed at the memory of the night before.

I freed one of my arms and brushed away a lock of hair that had fallen over his forehead. I traced a line down his nose and along his jaw, now covered in stubble, and then stroked the corner of his full lips. That mouth that had made me feel beautiful with each kiss, as if I were the most important woman in his world. I had felt . . . treasured. I lost myself gazing at him. He was so peaceful, the corners of his mouth tugging upward, suggesting a smile.

Reluctantly, I got up to use the bathroom, slowly lifting his arm and untangling my legs from his, careful not to wake him. I tiptoed around, trying to find something to cover me. Groping, the room barely lit by the rising sun, I found my dress crumpled on the floor. I shook my head. I couldn't go to the bathroom dressed for the Met Ball.

I lifted Christian's jacket to reveal his white shirt and pulled it around my shoulders. I quietly tiptoed to the bathroom, closing the door behind me. Then I caught the reflection of the woman in the mirror.

She was grinning like an idiot, her eyes bright and alive. I ran my fingers through the tangle of hair on my head and imagined they were Christian's fingers in my hair, on my face, all over my body. *Maybe things will work out after all,* I said silently to her. Maybe I was ready for the bomb inside me to explode. And if so, I'd give the detonator to Christian.

But first I need to eat something, I thought, feeling my stomach growl. I hadn't touched any of the food at the buffet the night before. I splashed some water on my face and left the bathroom, pausing in the doorway.

Christian was a vision of beauty: he was lying facedown, a sheet covering him just below the waist, one tanned and muscular leg sticking out from under the covers. He took my breath away. The butterflies began to flutter in my stomach. He was mine.

As I tiptoed to my suitcase to grab some shorts so I could go down to breakfast, a flashing light on Christian's bedside table caught my attention.

It was his phone. Who was calling at this hour on a Sunday morning?

Trust him, Gioia! I bit my lip. *Trust him. Do not snoop on his phone.* It would be an invasion of his privacy.

But his screen kept flashing as if to say, *I'm here, come read me!*

To hell with privacy!

Stealthily, so he wouldn't catch me, I went to his bedside and saw Chantal's name on the screen. What did his ex want on a Sunday morning? What did our exes want from our lives?

I realized with a jolt that I still had to tell Christian about what had happened between Matteo and me before he found out from someone else. He'd understand. We hadn't even been together at the time.

Come to think of it, we weren't really even together now. What were we? Friends with benefits? A couple in training?

I shook my head to ward off any unwarranted fears. *Don't start, Caputi!*

I left Christian sleeping, closed the bedroom door behind me, and went out into the hallway to call the elevator.

As I waited, I buried my face in his shirt, smelling him. I was still smiling like a little girl when the bell rang to announce the elevator's arrival.

When the doors opened, I suddenly jumped back, surprised by what I saw inside.

"Gioia! Were you up all night like I was?"

"Bea! Where are you coming from?"

My best friend was barefoot, her dress still screaming sex, her hair cemented in its perfect updo. I looked like I had just been pulled out of a washing machine; she looked like she had just left the spa.

"From nine," she said, yawning as she stepped out.

I frowned, confused.

"The guy I met at the wedding today—I mean, yesterday . . . In any case, that one."

"You okay?" I asked worriedly.

I had happily gone off to bed with Christian without thinking about what would result from Bea's lethal mix of alcohol and karaoke. I hadn't been a very good best friend.

I got two thumbs-up as a response, partially obstructed by the Jimmy Choos that Bea had chosen to carry rather than wear back to her room.

"Are you sure?" I asked, following her. "Can I get you something to eat? Do you need an aspirin?" I was starting to sound like Adelina Caputi.

"No, Mommy."

I walked her to her room and she opened the door.

"Where are you going at this hour? Why aren't you asleep?"

"Well, I didn't sleep much last night . . . I mean, we didn't sleep."

"Ah." She yawned. Then my words took their delayed effect, joining the rivers of alcohol in her blood. She leaned against the door and her jaw practically unhinged as it dropped to the floor. "Wait, you guys did it?"

"Yeah," I whispered, my cheeks already aflame.

"You and Manhattan?"

"No, me and the bartender. Of course me and Christian!" I snorted.

"Praise God! Praise Saints Dolce & Gabbana! Oh my goodness, I was so worried about you, honey. I didn't think you'd ever experience the joys of sex again, but now look at you. You went from frustrated spinster to Christian Kelly's lover."

"Yes, well . . ."

She took my hands in hers. "You deserve to be with someone like him."

"I thought you said I deserve to be happy."

"Even better if it's with a nice piece of ass like that. Plus, this way I get bragging rights."

"Bea, are you sure?"

"Would you rather be with a total loser?"

I rolled my eyes. "No, I mean, are you sure it's right? Me and Christian. Tomorrow he could be—"

"Stop it! Now I'm going to tell you something very, very important and I need you to hear me," she said.

I nodded and waited for her to continue.

"I haven't slept for forty-eight hours, I'm at my ex's wedding, I need a shower and a long nap. Go downstairs, get your breakfast, and eat it directly off that American man's body. Make him sing you a love song, since we know he can, and then, after I've slept at least ten hours, we'll meet down by the pool and have a chat. I want all the details. But I know you'll find a way to pass the time until then. We don't have to check out until this afternoon."

She winked at me, kissed my hand, and closed the door.

I went downstairs, greeting the receptionist from the night before and the wedding planner with the same smile frozen on her face.

"Good morning."

"Good morning," I said. "Could I take some food up to my boy-friend? He's not feeling well this morning."

"Oh, of course! Can we help you with anything, Ms. . . . ?"

"You can call me Gioia," I said. "I'll just take some fruit and coffee; that's all, thanks."

"If you need anything at all, please don't hesitate to call us, Ms. Gioia."

I gave them a polite smile and went into the dining room. The decorations, candles, and flowers from the night before were gone. Now, at the center of each table, there were little heart-shaped balloons with the letters "A + S."

Maybe it was good that Bea was locked in her room comatose, otherwise she would have been tempted to burst every last one of them with her stilettos.

A long table in the center was laden with delicious food: choc-olate cake, warm cream-filled croissants, yogurt, cereal, and fresh strawberry jam. I was deciding on the most delicious combination of sugar and fat to deposit onto my thighs when a phone appeared under my nose.

I jumped back. "What on earth?"

Then I saw the image on the screen.

I froze when my brain and heart finally recognized the people in the photo.

It was Christian.

And Chantal.

Embracing.

They were glowing. Christian looked elated; Chantal was clinging to him as if he were the newest Hermès bag.

It's not how it looks.

Trust.

Trust him.

I turned and wasn't surprised to find myself face-to-face with Matteo.

"What do you want from me?" I said dryly.

"Open your eyes."

"Maybe I should have opened them when I was with you."

"The photo is from this week. Do you want to see all of them?"

Don't show that you're hurt, Gioia.

"What did he tell you? That he was busy with work? Chantal works at Sound&K, so I guess that's what he meant by 'work.'"

Breathe, Gioia!

All the security I had felt back in the room was now crumbling because of a silly photo on a phone.

"You're one to talk, cheater," I snapped.

I didn't want to give him the satisfaction of knowing that I was dying inside. Because of a man. Again. Except this one was a thousand times worse.

Christian is different, damn it!

"You can't trust Kelly," said Matteo. "When he found out I was your ex, Sound&K stopped the contract negotiations."

"I don't believe you." Christian would never stoop that low.

"We worked for years to get to this point, and you know it, Gioia. And what does he do? He refuses to sign us. I may have gotten it wrong with you—God only knows how much I hate myself for it—but he's playing you."

We were drawing the attention of everyone in reception.

"Let's go outside," I said, resting my plate on the table. I wanted to throw it on the ground for good luck like the Greeks. "That picture means nothing. Just like the one they took of you and me in front of my office."

We walked out on the terrace, where the turquoise pool was set against an achingly blue sea. There wasn't a cloud on the horizon. But on the inside, I felt a storm of emotions brewing: fear, bitterness, disappointment, and pain.

"You never wondered how a photographer knew to wait in front of your office?"

"Matteo, the Sounds isn't just a wedding band anymore. You're at the top of the charts."

"Bullshit! If that were the case, they'd follow me everywhere. How come I don't see any paparazzi right now?"

"What are you trying to say?" A worm began to make its way inside my head.

"Since Kelly appeared, the guys and I are on all the blogs and music sites, I get photographed when I'm with you, they gossip about us on different forums. Did it ever occur to you that the record company is creating this thing between us?"

"There is no us. Not anymore."

"I deserve that." He raised his hands in exasperation and kicked at a pebble. "Betraying you with Georgia was the biggest mistake of my life. But believe me, Gioia, I love you. I never stopped loving you."

"You never stopped loving me?" I shouted. "Who sounds ridiculous now, Matteo? You let me go to London and told me not to forget about you, but you didn't come visit me once—you just left me alone there. You left me alone thinking about you." I pointed at him with each accusation. "And you, meanwhile, were carrying on with someone else!"

"I fucked up. But please give me another chance."

"You betrayed me and didn't have the balls to tell me. And then you dumped me with a note." I pointed my finger at his chest. "With a goddamn piece of paper!"

"I love you," he said, coming closer.

I stepped back. "You don't love me."

"I. Love. You." He took another step.

"You're just jealous of Christian. If he didn't exist, you wouldn't be here."

"That's not true! I would be here, I'll always be here for you." He put his hands on my shoulders and pushed me against the window. "Christian's the one who's playing you," he whispered in my ear.

Christian's name hit me like a punch in the stomach. A tear rolled down my cheek. If Matteo was right, I had been betrayed. Again.

I tried to break away from him. "Let go of me, Matteo."

"No, never." He leaned in and kissed me.

With tears pouring down my face, I gave in to him. Christian had lied to me about Chantal. I felt like a deflated balloon plummeting from the sky.

Matteo's lips pressed against mine as his arms kept me trapped against the window, my own arms helpless at my sides.

But I didn't want him. I wanted Christian.

Christian, who had dispelled all my fears, who had taken me apart like a jigsaw puzzle and put the pieces back together again to make a better one. Christian, who had handled my mother's interrogations with his illegal smile. Christian, who had made me feel like the most beautiful and desired woman in the world, even with all my edges and imperfections.

I opened my teary eyes and looked at Matteo.

The man in front of me was not the one I wanted to see every morning when I woke up, or every night before I went to sleep. I didn't know if Christian and I would stay together, but I also knew we couldn't ignore the feelings that bound us. It wasn't just physical attraction, sexual desire. It was something deeper. Maybe it wasn't love yet, but it was very close.

Oh my God!

I had to get back to the man waiting for me upstairs. I had to tell him everything: how Matteo had kissed me, what I felt for him. I had to tell him that I wanted to be with him even though we had an ocean and a ten-hour flight between us. Because real distance was not measured in miles, kilometers, oceans, or flight times. Real distance was between two people whose roads never converged. Even though they were standing in the same room.

Our hearts had collided.

I struggled against Matteo, pushing him.

"What's wrong, Gioia?"

"Go play with someone else," I said, turning on my heel to go back inside.

That's when I saw two molten eyes burning into me.

Christian.

Shit.

He was standing there fully dressed in a three-piece suit that so divinely fit his body. His face was twisted in disgust; I knew he'd seen it all. The kiss—the fact that I had let Matteo kiss me.

Our eyes met, and then Christian shook his head and walked away.

"No—Christian!" I yelled, running after him. "Wait!"

Matteo ran after me. "Gioia! Don't go—please!"

I turned to face him with a murderous rage. "Stop ruining my life, you asshole!"

Matteo wavered, shocked. I left him there as I ran inside looking for Christian.

He was in the elevator.

"Christian!" I yelled.

The doors closed between us, and the last thing I saw was the disappointment on his face.

Disgust.

I stood in the lobby and held my head in my hands.

I ruined everything, I thought.

I was a very bad person.

Terrible.

Repugnant.

I sprinted up the two flights of stairs, my despair growing with each step. When I reached the top floor, the door to our room was open. I stood in the doorway to catch my breath, watching Christian as he stuffed his suitcase.

"You said you were scared of the elevator," I accused him, as if he hadn't just seen me with my ex's tongue in my mouth.

"That gives you an idea of how pissed I am," he hissed, his back to me. He wore a dark-gray suit and tie, and his white shirt collar brushed against the nape of his neck.

"You're leaving?" I asked softly, trying to hold back tears.

"I'm going away on business. They called me, so I came looking for you. To tell you." He turned and glared at me. "I'm not the one who runs away."

I tried to swallow the lump in my throat. "Christian, it's not how it looks. Let me explain."

"Spare me, Gioia."

"Can I at least come with you in the car so we can talk?"

"I'm going to the airport. Back to New York."

He snapped the case shut, picked it up, and stopped in front of me. Without my heels, I barely reached his shoulders.

I was still paralyzed with shock.

He was about to leave. He was going back to America.

But I needed to know that it hadn't all been just a fantasy, a game. I needed to know whether he had lied.

"I saw the photo of you and Chantal together. What were you doing with her?"

"Not what you were doing with your ex," he snapped.

"Are you still in love with her?"

"Enough with this Chantal business!" He spread his arms in exasperation. "Christ, Gioia! I'm here. With you. At this damn wedding. And you ask me if I'm still in love with her? Since I first saw you, I haven't been able to look at anyone else. Just you."

I jumped. My heart skipped a beat.

It would have been easy to believe him, but that worm had crept into my head, eating away at my confidence like Pac-Man.

"So what about that photo of Matteo and me? I saw it, Christian. And what about all those articles about Matteo and his muse? And the Sounds contract? Why haven't you signed them yet?"

"Do you seriously believe Matteo? Do you trust him more than me?" His jaw hardened. Now he was more pissed.

"I want to know if you were aware of those articles."

"Gioia—"

"I asked if you knew about the damn picture!" I shouted.

"Yes."

That simple word hit me in the chest, shattering the tense air in the room like a bullet. Who knew a three-letter word could hurt so much?

The room spun. "You had me followed?"

"No—Christ! I would never do that!" Christian dropped his bag on the floor and buried his head in his hands. "Someone at Sound&K found out about you and Matteo and sent a photographer to follow you."

"Who?"

"I don't know."

"You're the goddamn president and you don't know?" I asked, growing more and more nauseous.

"Gioia, there are days when all I do is try to protect you from this damn story. I saw the picture of you and Matteo, and I stopped the contract negotiations. If Matteo hit the international stage, the press would have a field day with you two."

I dropped down on the bed, sick. I took my head in my hands, blood pounding in my ears. He had read all the articles; he had seen all the photos of Matteo and me outside my office.

"Is that why you never messaged me?"

"Partly. I never would have used you for a stupid contract, Gioia. But you preferred to believe him. Have you been using me all this time?" He was furious.

I looked up at him. "Never. Believe me!"

"Are you sure? It didn't look like it, the way you were kissing him."

"Do not use that tone with me, Kelly. I could say the same thing about you and your ex."

"The problem isn't me, or Matteo, or Chantal. It's you." He gave me a bitter look, his mouth a straight line, his jaw clenched. "You keep pointing the finger, but you're the one who doesn't know what you want."

I stood up and tried to get close to him, but he stopped me with a hand.

"That kiss was nothing," I whispered.

"That's not true!" Matteo stood in the doorway. He looked me straight in the eye. "I love you."

"Matteo, get out," I said firmly.

"No. You can't say you don't feel anything when we're together. I felt how you kissed me. Today, Friday at your house, the other day at your office. I know there's still something between us."

"Friday?" Christian turned to look at me, confused, hoping I'd deny it. "Something happened with him Friday at your house?"

I stiffened. "I wanted to tell you." I looked away. "But then—"

"Stop! I don't want to hear your shit. I'm not going to stand here a second longer and listen to any more of your lies. I thought you were different." He shook his head and left the room without even looking at me.

"Christian—I'm sorry!" Tears spilled down my cheeks as I followed him out. "Let me explain."

"Get a ride home with your little rock star. I'm leaving." He passed Matteo, but not before telling him, "She's all yours."

His anger ripped my heart to shreds. "Christian—wait."

Outside the room, I saw a sleepy Beatrice wrapped in a bathrobe. We had fought loud enough to wake up the whole floor.

Christian took a few steps and turned.

"Do not follow me. You've made your choice. I chose to trust you, and I was wrong." His eyes were dull, empty. "Good luck with . . . everything." He turned and ran down the stairs until he disappeared from my view.

It was over.

The fairy tale had lasted one night.

I collapsed on the floor and hid my face in my hands.

"Hey, honey." Bea crouched down and stroked my hair.

"I blew it," I whispered through my tears.

"Shh." She wrapped me in her embrace and patted my back. "Come to my room."

I nodded weakly as she helped me to my feet.

"Gioia . . ." Matteo's voice surprised me from behind.

"Perri, get the fuck out of here!" shrieked Bea. "You've already caused enough trouble in your few years on this planet. One more move and I swear I'll cut off your dick. You remember how hangman works, right?"

"Bea, why don't you leave us alone for a minute? Please . . ." I insisted.

She looked at me as if I had two heads. "Whatever. Fine. I'll go get some breakfast." She backed away in the direction of the elevator, drawing her index finger across her neck to indicate what she might do to Matteo when she got back.

I didn't want to deal with him either, but given that this was the worst day of my life, I figured I should make it truly memorable.

I didn't even wait for Bea to reach the elevator before I laid into him.

"I'm not in the mood to argue, Matteo."

"Sorry," he said sincerely. "I'm sorry I hurt you, today and when we were together. You're right, I was an asshole, and I understand you're angry, but I can't stand here and watch you throw your life away."

I wanted to tell him where he could shove his apology.

"Do you even hear yourself? You guilt-tripped me because I went to London, you cheated on me, and now you decide to tell me how much you love me? You can't come here with your puppy-dog eyes and ask me to pretend none of it ever happened."

"I miss you, Gioia."

"I don't love you anymore, Matteo."

When I uttered those six words, I was finally free of the boulder that had been sitting on my heart for months. All the anger and resentment fell away from my body.

"You're in love with him?"

"Please go away, Matteo. Leave me alone."

He tried to kiss me, but I turned my head so his nose landed against my cheek.

"I love you," he said, kissing my cheek.

"It's over. Done. Deal with it."

I heard him sigh deeply before he retreated down the stairs.

I didn't turn to watch him go, but stared at the carpet instead, reflecting on the way Christian had looked when he left.

I had hurt him.

I was still standing there when Bea returned with a tray of croissants. Just the smell of them made me sick.

"Eat one," she said, sitting beside me. "And don't say no, because I went to get them in a bathrobe, and now everyone knows I'm not a sex bomb."

Instead of smiling, I began to cry again.

"Give him some time; he'll be back," she said, yawning. She bit into a croissant and handed it to me.

"I screwed up."

"He'll come back."

"What if he doesn't?"

"We'll go to New York and hold him hostage until he hears you out. Right now, though, we need to find a ride home."

"You really think he'll come back?"

"Jesus Christ!" She shoved an entire croissant in her mouth. "Just shut up and eat. Maybe the guy in nine will give us a ride."

Chapter 34

It had been two days, forty-eight hours, 2,880 minutes since Christian had left. Yes, I was one of those pathetic women who counted.

No phone calls, no messages, no emails.

Bea had told me to wait, to give him time to let off steam, but I was an addict, and I was jonesing for my dose of Christian.

I needed to hear his voice, even if it was just him telling me to go to hell.

I had to see him, even if he would only push me away.

I called him all day Sunday, even though I knew he was on a ten-hour flight to New York. At least he would see the missed calls.

Then I called again Monday.

Silence. The phone was always off. For someone who couldn't live without his iPhone, this was bad.

I pulled the covers over my head and went back to wallowing in my misery.

I thought back to his face disfigured with anger, his pursed lips, his glassy, distant eyes.

God, I was an idiot. I had really screwed things up with my mental seesaws, my fears. I hadn't realized that what I needed had been right in front of me. It had taken me too long to understand. And now Christian was gone. I had lost him.

I gulped. I was a mess.

I had felt something similar just months before, but this time I couldn't even cry.

No tears. My eyes were dry, empty, as if I were in some sort of limbo, enveloped in self-hatred.

I had gone to stay at my parents' house after the wedding and collapsed in tears in my mother's arms. "It will get easier every day," she'd assured me, cradling me and stroking my hair.

I woke up every morning and did nothing but stare at the ceiling of my old childhood bedroom.

Today was worse than yesterday because it was another day without Christian. The knowledge that I'd never see him again was ripping through my body.

Strength, Gioia!

I threw the covers off and crawled into the shower, hoping the burning water would exceed the burning in my heart. No such luck.

I got dressed like a robot, with the faint hope that I might run into Christian at work.

Stupid!

I was sitting on the edge of the bed, putting my shoes on, when my phone beeped.

It was WhatsApp.

I eyed the phone in the middle of the bed.

Please let it be Christian!

I carefully picked up the phone as if it were burning hot and unlocked it with one eye shut.

I entered the chat room and put my hand over my eyes.

What it if wasn't him? What if it was one of the girls?

Damn it, Caputi!

This was not the strong woman I aspired to be.

I held my breath as I read the sender's name.

It was Beatrice asking me to go to lunch at Smile.

I buried the phone in my bag and set off for work. I was almost halfway down the stairs when I heard my parents arguing in the kitchen.

"I told you that American was nothing but trouble!" cried my father.

"Angelo, dear, lower your voice. Gioia will hear you!"

"Only a moron would sign an ass like Perri." I could imagine my father's face flushed with anger.

My mother, who was usually hyperventilating in situations like these, was the quieter of the two. "They'll work it out. You'll see."

My father slammed a cup on the table. "The hell they will! I'll make sure she never sees him again, even if it means I have to lock her in her room."

"Angelo, she's an adult."

"She doesn't seem like an adult to me, judging from the children she's brought home. They're not men. First there's a rocker who leaves her with a note; now it's an American so soft he can't even get through a wedding weekend. Lucky for him, I have sciatica and a fear of airplanes, because that's all that's stopping me from flying over there and castrating him."

Wow. The grill boss had become a mafioso.

"In fact, it's been so long since you and I have gone on a vacation. Book a flight to New York. That Kelly will remember my face like Bush remembers Bin Laden's."

My father, mafioso and terrorist.

I took a deep breath and cleared my throat so they'd hear me coming.

"Good morning." I went into the kitchen and leaned against the counter.

My mom got up; my father sat with the sports page.

"Honey, are you feeling better?"

Better? I feel so shitty I'm going to order a hit man to put a bullet in my skull.

"I'm better, I slept like a rock," I said.

"You want some coffee? Hot tea?"

"No, that's okay." I looked at my watch. "I'm late, I have to get to work."

"Why don't you call in sick and stay home? We could go to the mall. Or go see Giusy."

Giusy was a local hairdresser. The last time he'd cut my hair, I had asked for a bob, and he'd given me a bowl cut just above the ears, Beatles style.

"No, Mom. I can't miss work."

"She's fine!" muttered my father.

"Angelo!" said Adelina.

"Going to work will be good for me—that way I won't think so much," I said with a sad smile on my face, thinking of the certain someone who had already accused me of thinking too much.

"Okay," she said, stroking my cheek. "If you want, you can sleep here again tonight. I'll make lasagna. You know this is always your home."

I swallowed the lump in my throat. "I know, but I think I'm going to stay at my place tonight." I went over and gave her a peck on the cheek. "Thanks, Mom."

I hugged my father from behind, commenting on his Juventus article, then went out into the yard and got into my car.

I started the engine and the radio came on automatically, tuned to Radio Deejay.

When I heard what song was playing, I squeezed the steering wheel hard and hid my face in my arms. It was "All of Me" by John Legend, the song that Christian and I had danced to at the Gotha and at the wedding on Saturday night. Before he had disappeared.

Who knew where he was now. Was he getting any sleep? Was he suffering like I was?

It was two in the morning in New York. Maybe he was in some bar in Soho with his friends, surrounded by beautiful women.

I clutched my chest at the thought.

I backed out of the driveway, berating myself for having ruined everything.

"I blew it," I said softly.

I repeated it all the way to the office.

◆ ◆ ◆

We were at Smile, sitting at our usual corner table for lunch. Me, Ludovica, Melissa, Beatrice, and a newbie—Marco.

Ludovica and Melissa were talking about moon cycles and the best ways to get pregnant as quickly as possible, while Bea continued to pray she never got pregnant by mistake.

Marco just laughed.

He had joined the girls and me for lunch for the past two days, and for him and Bea, it had been love at first blink. They were all honey this, honey that, exchanging beauty secrets and planning a day together at the spa.

I was concentrating exclusively on my burger.

Yes, that's right. My hamburger.

I no longer had to fit into any dress, and my code of conduct for emergencies included saturated fat. I was suffering from post-abandonment stress syndrome. It was an emergency.

"Hey, blondie," said Bea, "you look like shit."

"You always know just what to say," I replied.

"Has he called?" asked Melly.

"As if! It's clear what he thinks of me right now. And he can run right into his ex's arms; I can't even be in the same room as mine."

"Gioia, come on." Bea looked furious. "Matteo had his tongue in your mouth. Even a saint would tell you to go to hell after that!"

Shocked, I froze with my burger midway to my mouth, while Ludo and Melly exchanged alarmed glances. Marco was enjoying the show.

"A saint? Christian Kelly is not exactly a candidate to be the Holy Father's right hand," I muttered.

"Try seeing him through my eyes, not yours."

"I didn't know you were a member of the Christian Kelly Fan Club."

"He came to this godforsaken place to follow a two-bit advertising campaign that he could have sent any old employee to do. And why? For you. He gave you back the dignity you lost when Matteo dumped you, and he didn't even try to take advantage of you after you threw yourself at him, wasted. He went to eat with your family not once, but twice. He accompanied you to a wedding so you could get your ex back, where he sang a song for you in front of everyone. He did all of this for you, and how do you repay him the morning after? By making out with Matteo."

"I did not make out with Matteo. The asshole kissed me; I just panicked."

"Christian doesn't know that."

"So why won't he let me explain?"

"Have you called him?"

"His phone is off," I said disconsolately. I had stabbed my burger to death.

"Well, call him again. If his phone is still off, I can always go to New York to give him a good kick in the ass." She took my phone and placed it in my hand. "Call him."

"It's seven in the morning for him." Not that I was keeping track, of course.

"Try," she growled in a tone that left no room for an argument.

I snorted and went on WhatsApp to see if he had turned his phone back on. When I saw that he was online, I tossed my phone on the table.

"What are you doing?" asked my sister.

Bea, Ludo, and Marco all looked at me, confused.

"He's online. On WhatsApp."

"So? Try him."

"He's seen my missed calls. Why hasn't he called me?"

"Men are strange, honey. Don't you understand that yet?"

"Hey." Marco shot a look at Bea.

"You don't count, you're gay."

Ludo took my hand from across the table. "Stop thinking and call him."

In an attempt to summon my courage, I took a deep breath, picked up the phone, and stood up. "I'll be right back."

I went to the bar, away from the prying ears of my friends. I pressed the green button, knowing that this phone call would change my fate.

My heart began to pound as I waited to hear his voice. His sexy, husky voice.

But the phone didn't ring. "What . . . ?"

I looked at the screen and smiled. There was no signal. Fate could be a real asshole sometimes.

I stood up and walked around the bar, searching for a signal. Anything.

But just as I decided to walk out of Smile, I walked smack into a hot, muscular body instead.

That hot, muscular body.

"You really have it out for me."

My heart was pounding; my lungs collapsed. I looked up and saw the last person I expected to see that day at Smile.

"You should change phone carriers."

I swallowed hard and blinked repeatedly in disbelief at Christian's illegal smile.

I never thought it would have been so hard not to throw my arms around his neck, pounce on his lips, and cling to his body to feel the warmth of his skin under my hands. I had imagined our encounter over and over these past two days, but I could never have imagined the dull pain I felt when I saw him.

I put the phone in the back pocket of my jeans and looked up at his melty chocolate eyes.

Christian was in front of me, his hands in his jeans pockets.

His face was pale and unshaven. He looked tired but also breathtakingly beautiful.

As he watched me in silence, I could see that he was hurting too, that he was fighting the same battle I was.

I broke the silence. "What are you doing here?"

He smiled, but his eyes didn't. "I knew I'd find you here."

"I meant what are you doing *here*," I asked, gesturing around. "I thought you were in New York."

Christian sighed deeply. "I didn't go—I couldn't."

His answer kindled a small flame of hope somewhere inside me.

I went straight to the point. "Why are you here?"

He took a deep breath. "I was wrong not to talk to you about the photos. I should have told you. But why didn't you tell me about you and Matteo? And don't lie to me, Gioia, because I'm fed up with lies. I just got out of a relationship full of lies, and I don't want to start a new one with someone I can't trust." His tone was bitter.

"I saw your photo with Chantal; that's why I didn't say anything. I thought you didn't care about me at all, that you really were just putting on an act for my parents."

He sighed, exhausted. "That day at the airport when you literally plowed into me, you walked right into my life and I was . . . blown away. You changed my life. It had all been work, friends, basketball games. No commitments, just fun. I was with a different woman every night, and I was fine. Then you came along." His eyes burned into me until I felt like my legs might give way. "I fought for you, I tried to have courage for us both. God knows I tried."

Christian dropped onto a stool, as if the words had drained all the energy in his body.

I sat down beside him, wringing my sweaty hands.

"Everything with Matteo has been over for a long time. It just took me awhile to realize it." I swallowed hard and looked up at him.

His head was cocked to one side, and he listened to me in silence, like he always did. He was the only one capable of penetrating my armor.

I let out a sigh before continuing. "I preferred blaming him and the entire male species to admitting that I failed. Yes, I failed with him. I spent four years invested in this relationship, then one day I found myself alone. He cheated on me, it's true, but if the relationship ended badly, that means we were both to blame. And I couldn't figure out what I had done wrong. I still don't know."

Christian wanted to reply, but I raised a finger so he'd let me go on. I had finally found the courage to show him how wounded I really was.

"I'm scared, Christian. I'm so scared of starting a new relationship, getting back into the game, taking risks, trusting another man."

Christian sighed and his tone softened. "You and I fight a lot. Over the littlest things. You think I'm arrogant, I think you're stubborn; you like country, I like hip-hop; you don't want to be complimented, I love to see you blush when I compliment you. We're not the same, Gioia, but we're like two colors that go together. We're on opposite ends of the spectrum, but when we're next to each other, we can be better than ever."

"We can still make it work." I took his hands in mine and looked into his eyes. "It's not too late, it's never too late. You taught me that."

He took my hand in his and placed it on his heart. It was pounding, like mine.

"Hear that?" he asked sweetly.

I nodded. I saw the sadness in his face and knew he wasn't going to say anything good.

"It's not too late, but it's still a little too early."

Fear crept into me, into my bones, my veins, until it reached my heart.

"We both need time," he went on. He stroked my cheek; his eyes never left mine. "Neither of us knows what we want. We're both still wounded and we need time and space to sort ourselves out."

"I don't want you to go."

"I know, Caputi." The corner of his mouth perked up. "But you have to figure out what you really want right now. You have to learn to be with yourself—not with me or another guy."

My eyes were burning. I began to sob. My body knew what was happening before I did. I needed him, and he was leaving.

Christian took my face in his hands. "Look at me, Hurricane."

He bowed his head and kissed the tears from my eyes, showing once again how much he cared for me. How special I was to him. So special that he was letting me go.

"We're not wrong for each other, Hurricane," he whispered in my ear, his voice nearly breaking. "But now isn't the right time. Remember, there's no expiration date for pain. Take all the time you need. Take time for yourself."

"That sounds like good-bye to me," I whispered, shattered.

"It's not."

He kissed me gently and slowly, as if he wanted to leave his kiss on my lips forever. When he pulled away, I felt like I was in free fall. He stroked my face again. Then he dropped his hand to his side and tightened his jaw.

"I have to go now. I have a flight to catch. And I'd better get out of here before Gloria Gaynor kicks my ass."

I smiled through my tears and turned to see Bea, who was standing nearby. Behind her were Melly, Ludo, and Marco. I knew they wouldn't really interfere, that they'd let me fight my own battle. They would always be there to rejoice in my victories or scrape me off the floor when I lost. Or perhaps they were just waiting for my signal, like with Russell Crowe in *Gladiator*.

At my signal, unleash hell.

"You have a whole firing squad at your disposal." He smiled his illegal smile, and the room spun.

We were nearing the end.

"So," he murmured nervously. He shifted his weight from one foot to the other. "I'm going. I'll call you, okay?"

Stay! Stay with me! I wanted to shout.

I nodded. "Good-bye, Christian," I whispered.

"Good-bye, Hurricane."

A sob escaped my chest as I held on to the bar. I looked down, unable to watch him walk out the door, out of my life.

I felt a rush of air and heard the door slam shut.

It was over. Christian was gone for good this time.

"Gioia?"

Through my tears, I turned and saw all my friends lined up side by side.

"Where's Manhattan off to? Do you want us to kill him?"

"If you want, I can hold him still," said Melly.

"I can sabotage his ad campaign," added Marco.

"We're in the middle of an economic crisis," said Bea. "Try to hold on to your jobs."

Instead of smiling, I found myself crying harder, my body shaken by sobs.

I found the courage to look at the entrance. It was empty.

If this had been my fairy tale, Christian would have come running back through the door and said, "Okay, time's up. I'm back. Forever."

Like in all the love stories, like in all the happy endings of the American romantic comedies I loved. In *Pretty Woman*, Richard Gere goes back for Julia Roberts with a bouquet of flowers and a limousine.

But I would have been happy if he had come back empty-handed.

I don't know how long I stood there staring at the door to Smile.

It stayed closed.

Firmly closed.

My nose was stuffy from crying, my eyes were burning, and I had a dull ache in my chest.

For Christian and me, there would be no happy ending.

Chapter 35

You'll survive, Gioia.

You'll get back on your feet.

He'll call—you'll see!

This is what I kept telling myself as I walked from Smile to the Dreamstart offices, putting one foot in front of the other.

I kept imagining the Ghibli parked at the curb, the conference-room door closed, Christian leaning at the threshold of my office.

Damn it!

If I had managed to get over four years with Matteo, why was it so impossible to get over a few weeks with Christian?

As soon as I set foot in the office, MTB called with the acid tone that she only used with me. I had exclusivity with something!

"Gioia, Sabrina wants to see you."

I sighed.

This day could not end soon enough.

"Okay, I'm going to run to the bathroom first," I replied.

"Now." Her tone left no room for arguments.

Yes, sir, at your command!

I had been summoned by Her Majesty Sabrina "Rottweiler" Kent.

Exhausted, I walked down the long hall to her office and knocked on the solid wooden door. The metal tag with her name blurred before my eyes.

I could have sworn it read "Tenth Circle of Hell."

"Come in, Caputi!" she shouted from her lair.

I took a deep breath and entered. Sabrina was on her computer. She was so tiny that I could hardly see her behind the screen.

"Caputi, don't just stand there. Sit!"

"Sabrina." With trembling legs, I crossed the room and sat on a black leather chair. I knew she was studying me, even though her eyes never seemed to leave the screen.

She lowered her glasses to the end of her nose and looked me straight in the eye. "What's going on between you and my nephew?"

Shit.

I bit my lip nervously. "Nothing, Sabrina. Absolutely nothing."

She leaned back in her black leather chair and folded her arms across her chest. "Kelly isn't just my nephew. He's the president of one of the most powerful companies in the world, and they rely on us for their advertising campaigns. Their contracts are worth a lot of money, for us and for them. I'll get to the point, Caputi. If there's a conflict of interest, I need to take you off the project."

I took a deep breath.

What was I supposed to say? That I was in love with her nephew, but then he caught me with my ex's tongue in my mouth? Maybe if I wanted to get fired.

I had spent all of high school watching Sydney Bristow lie for five straight seasons on *Alias*. I had spent Monday nights watching Olivia Pope on *Scandal* lying to protect the nation and her heart.

It was time to put their teachings to the test.

I had to lie.

"There is absolutely nothing going on. Can you imagine your nephew with someone like me?"

She looked at me very, very skeptically.

"Don't get me wrong. Your nephew is clever, driven, committed to his work," I said, "but his life is in New York; mine is here. Not that he isn't charming."

Sabrina sat back and let out a sigh.

I had officially said too much. I had to stop.

Stupid brain-mouth filter!

She finally broke the awkward silence.

"Fine. Now that I know the state of things between you, could you please explain to me why Christian left the country like he was being chased by the FBI and made it very clear that he wanted nothing to do with the Sound&K campaign from now on?"

Breathe, Gioia! Breathe.

"He canceled the project?" I cried.

I wondered how many boxes I'd need for my things. Maybe one would do it.

"No, he didn't cancel it. He's just won't be working on it from now on."

The words barely made sense. I felt like I was going crazy.

"Caputi, are you listening to me?"

"What?"

"I said we're still doing the Sound&K campaign, but my nephew won't be on it anymore. Thomas Brooks will be the point person on it from now on."

So I'd never see Christian Kelly again—not even on a videoconference call.

"I-I don't know . . ." I stammered.

"Never mind," said Sabrina. She sounded cold and aloof.

"Sabrina, honestly—"

"I said that's enough!"

I jumped in my chair.

She stood up and, despite her tiny stature, I felt threatened.

"I don't know what you're hiding, Caputi," she said coldly, her hands on her hips, "but you need to keep your personal life out of this agency. And most of all, you need to stay away from my nephew. Is that clear?"

I nodded. The job paid my rent, and moving back in with my parents was not high on my list.

"You can go. Tomorrow we'll have a videoconference with Brooks. I want you and Marco to prepare everything you need and have it on my desk by five this afternoon."

She dismissed me with a wave of her hand that rattled with bracelets and rings. I stood up, picked up my bag, and left, breathing again as the door closed behind me.

It should have been written into the employment contract as grounds for dismissal: do not fall in love with the boss's nephew.

I smoothed my dress and headed toward the bathroom.

"Gioia, wait." Margherita called me back when I was already halfway down the hall.

I rolled my eyes in despair, asking God's forgiveness for all the sins I had committed in a past life. Maybe he'd go easier on me from now on.

"Yes?" I said through an obviously fake smile.

"Christian was here."

My heart lurched. "Christian?"

She rolled her eyes. "Christian Kelly."

I lit up like a thousand-watt bulb.

Margherita, in her skimpy red dress, shook her thick mass of curly hair in annoyance and gestured toward my office. "He left something for you."

I swallowed hard, my heart in my throat. Had he left me a plane ticket to New York? Richard Gere just brought the girl flowers!

I ran to my office and saw a small gift-wrapped package. I dropped my bag on the floor, grabbed the box, and took it to the bathroom—the only place where I could be alone.

I sat on the toilet and unwrapped the package. Inside was an iPod and a Post-it.

Play.

I pulled off the note and saw writing on the other side.

I never played with your heart.

The word "never" was quickly blurred by the silent tears that had begun to run down my cheeks. I dried them with the sleeve of my cotton sweater and turned on the iPod with a trembling hand.

On the screen, there was a folder called "Christian."

I sighed. Did he really think I'd need a folder named after him to remember him? I hit the "Play" button and the first song came on through the headphones. It was "When You Say Nothing at All," the song I had sung at the karaoke bar in Barcelona. The day I had literally run into Christian twice. With trembling hands, I listened to the other songs.

The second on the list was Cher's "Strong Enough."

I couldn't help smiling, thinking of the standing ovation I got that night when I sang my public fuck-you to Matteo.

I scrolled through the rest of the songs. He had remembered them all, even the ones from the wedding, even the country songs he never let me listen to.

I stopped on "This Year's Love" and closed my eyes.

I could feel his hands on my body as we swayed together in my living room. I was barefoot, dressed like a total slob, and wrapped in his arms until Bea's appearance.

Then the song faded and "All of Me" invaded my ears. I covered my face with my hand, recalling the heartbreak Christian had confessed to that night at the Gotha. And then we had danced to the same song at Alessio's wedding, holding each other tight until Matteo had spoiled the moment.

I went on, my heart seizing with pain at every song. I closed my eyes and heard Christian singing "You and Me"—just like he had done a little over two days ago at the wedding. I could feel the warmth of his hand as he caressed my cheek, his lips as they brushed my forehead and told me not to run away from what we had.

I began to sob, thinking about how things had changed so quickly. How had he become so important to me in just a matter of weeks?

"Hello, Hurricane."

I jumped at the sound of Christian's voice in the office bathroom.

"What on earth—" I took out my earphones but couldn't hear anything. Was I literally delusional now? *I officially need to be committed to a mental hospital,* I thought, slipping the earphones back in. I realized that Christian wasn't outside the stall. He spoke through the headphones in that low voice that made him sound like a radio announcer.

"You're not crying, are you?"

How presumptuous, I thought as I used half a roll of toilet paper to wipe the mascara from under my eyes.

"I didn't want to leave you like this . . ."

"Sure," I sniffed. "You left me with a Post-it."

"No, I didn't leave you with a Post-it. I'm not like that asshole who left you with a note."

It was as if Christian had hacked my thoughts and entered my brain.

"You were a breath of fresh air after months, days, minutes I had spent not breathing, Gioia. I didn't change your life, you changed mine."

His voice wavered, as if he were struggling to find the right words. I pictured him as he ran a hand through his hair, like he always did when he was anxious, a crease spreading across his forehead.

I had to go! I got up to run to the airport.

I had a plane to New York waiting for me.

"But then I realized something, Hurricane. The heart has its time, and no matter how much we want things to work out between us now, it's just not time yet. I might not be ready, and you certainly aren't. We need to step back and let our hearts find their own rhythms. When they do, I hope they beat in time. But if they don't, I want you to live your life, be happy, never be anyone's second choice. And above all, don't be afraid to love. Take risks, love the man whose world you can turn upside down."

There was a pause, and I could feel his breath in my ear, as if he were there with me, holding my hand, stroking my face.

"You'll have your happy ending, Hurricane."

I had used up the entire roll of toilet paper by the time the recording ended. I was sobbing, curled over my legs, my face disfigured by pain.

Guitar chords broke through my sobs.

It was "Photograph" by Ed Sheeran. I knew when we had heard it: the evening we had gone to my parents' house for dinner. I had been too nervous to listen to the words then, but now they took on a whole new meaning.

Sheeran sings about how much love can hurt sometimes, but how it's the only thing that makes us feel alive. The song is for his wife, about a photograph, memories they made together. He asks her to keep it in a necklace near her heart. That heart he never broke when they were together. He asks her to wait for him to come home, and to keep the photo as a reminder of the love that they found and lived together.

He would come home. To her.

I closed my eyes and relived all the moments Christian and I had shared.

There was not one frame of the movie in my mind where Christian didn't smile his illegal smile or when he didn't look at me with an amused grin whenever I teased him.

Christian was smiling in every scene of my personal movie. I'd huff, roll my eyes, but then he'd always make me smile.

Christian had come into my life with the force of a hurricane, leaving in his wake a trail of memories.

Permanent as a tattoo.

Engraved on my heart.

He was asking that same heart to heal itself. He wanted it to find its own rhythm, hoping it might beat in time with his. *Come back to me,* he seemed to be saying.

Chapter 36

Five days, nineteen hours, forty-two minutes.

That's right. I was still counting.

See the girl sitting in her office chair, lost in her thoughts, a pen cap in her mouth, nervously tapping her foot on the floor? That's me. Well, the new me.

Yet another version of Gioia.

I was the epitome of someone with PTSD. The symptoms were clear: flashbacks, panic attacks, depression, insomnia, heartburn.

I had them all.

The cause: abandonment.

For six days, I had been fighting with myself. Because if, on the one hand, I was crackling with hope that Christian and I could still get back together, there was also a part of me—a big part of me—that was convinced that the iPod was his way of saying good-bye.

Mr. Christian "Cover Boy" Kelly was gone.

I constantly checked Google Alerts, Twitter, E! Online. Nothing.

I monitored WhatsApp day and night. Christian had last been online two days before.

He hadn't called me; he hadn't written.

He had promised to be there for me. Always.

But when he walked out of Smile, he walked out of my life. For how long, I didn't know.

Fine, I got it. He was giving me the time I needed to regain confidence in myself so I could start a new relationship.

But then last night, I'd watched *Pretty Woman* for the thousandth time. In the final scene, when Edward scales the fire escape, he asks Vivian, "So what happened after he climbed up the tower and rescued her?" And Vivian responds, "She rescues him right back."

Christian had saved me.

He had made me smile, he had pissed me off, he had made me argue, and he had made me cry. He had made me . . . live. He had pulled me from the pit of despair I had fallen into after Matteo dumped me.

He had rescued me.

So, I thought, *maybe it's my turn to rescue him.*

I would go to New York and say, "Let's find the rhythm of our hearts together."

He had been courageous enough for both of us over the past few weeks, but now it was my turn to grow a pair. Have the courage to get on a plane and go to him, so we could face our demons together.

The courage to take risks.

For him.

For us.

The beep of a new email on my computer ripped me out of my Christian-saving fantasies.

I stopped tapping my toe on the floor and opened the message.

Oh. My. God.

It was from Christian.

I brought my face inches from the screen, hardly believing my eyes. Did PTSD symptoms include hallucinations?

I held my breath, and my heart began to pound in my chest. It really was a message from Christian.

Breathe, Gioia! Breathe.

From: Christian Kelly

To: Gioia Caputi

Date: June 15, 2014

Subject: (no subject)

Hi Gioia,

I'm sorry to have to write this in an email, but I've decided to get back together with Chantal.

It would be a waste to throw away what we built together because of one stupid mistake. Not trying would be yet another. I've decided to be with her.

I hope that one day you'll be able to forgive me.

Christian

Chapter 37

I was a terrible patient.

Gioia Rehab wasn't working, or maybe I wasn't trying hard enough.

It had been eight months—about thirty-four weeks—and I still hadn't recovered.

I'd tried everything. I'd deleted his phone number so I wouldn't check his WhatsApp status, I'd disabled Google Alerts. I avoided gossip sites and glossy magazines like the plague. I even blocked his emails.

Eight fucking months, and the dull ache in my chest would not go away.

Christian was everywhere.

I thought I had seen him in line to see *Fifty Shades of Grey*, and at the Gotha, at a farewell party for the Sounds, who were off to tour the US after a sold-out European tour.

But he wasn't anywhere.

I'd see Maseratis double parked on the street, and they'd still be there when I closed my eyes. It was as if Christian had been tattooed inside my eyelids.

I'd see his illegal smile tugging at the corners of his mouth; I'd sense his melty chocolate eyes on me and suddenly feel vulnerable and loved.

I could feel him. Everywhere.

I had forbidden everyone from mentioning him just so I wouldn't have to face the truth.

Maybe I'd never accept it.

Christian had chosen Chantal.

He wanted to try again with her—not trying would have been a mistake, he'd said. And what had we been? A mistake to forget about? I asked myself every night, staring into the darkness of my bedroom. Why had he ventured so far into my life if he had had no real intention of being a part of it?

The girls turned me around, peered at me, studied me from every angle, fearing I'd have a breakdown at any second. Bea, however, had moved into my place and created something like a witness protection program. She'd eliminated any reminder of him from my apartment and had even tried to drag me out to entertain me, but eventually realized it was impossible to get me off the sofa.

Me and my faithful pint of chocolate ice cream. That's all I had left. Especially since I had also banished music. Every song I heard reminded me of him, made me wonder if he would've liked it. But then, in weak moments, I couldn't stop myself from running into the bathroom at Dreamstart with the iPod he left me to listen to all our songs. So much for Gioia Rehab.

I was overwhelmed by the emotions those songs triggered. I'd feel his lips on mine, the warmth of his hands on my skin. I'd sit in that sad bathroom stall, my heart pounding, my breath shallow, and my eyes burning with the tears that I tried to hold back.

And the anger. So much anger.

I had known it that day in Barcelona: Christian was either going to save me or destroy me.

And it had been the latter.

I had read and reread his email countless times; I had checked the IP address; I had memorized every word. It was as if he had shot me point-blank in the chest. There was nothing beating. No heart left to beat with his.

So I clung to my rage and smothered him with it. I needed to blame him instead of myself.

I even threw away the notebook Melly had given me.

I had no story to write. No fairy tale, at least.

I probably wasn't meant to have a happy ending, like the kind in the fairy tales where the prince rescues the princess and they live happily ever after in their castle. Blah, blah, blah.

I had found out the hard way. Not all fairy tales have a prince as the hero. In the twenty-first century, the princess could save herself, as long as she had the spirit to start a new story. Her own. Maybe she wouldn't have the final word—but at least she'd be the one to start it.

How did that song go? Something about how every new beginning comes from the end of something before it?

It was a small consolation, but it was the only one I had. In addition to the established fact that Christian Kelly was an asshole emeritus. If I Googled "asshole," his bio and photos would be the first things that came up.

It was a whiff of Chanel No. 5 and the clicking of heels that informed me of Sabrina's arrival, but instead of fading in the direction of her office, they seemed to be moving in the direction of mine.

When I looked up from my computer screen, Madame Rottweiler was already standing in my doorway.

"Caputi, in my office. Now." She disappeared, leaving a cloud of perfume floating where she had stood.

I pushed back my chair, crossed myself, and walked off to the gallows.

I entered without knocking. I approached the glass table at the center of the room with four feet eleven inches of pure attack dog sitting behind it. As usual, Sabrina's face was obscured by her computer screen.

I only knew she was there because of the smell of her perfume and the tips of her black patent-leather shoes.

"Sabrina," I said, clearing my throat. I sat across from her and begged to that day's saint that she was in a decent mood.

The Rottweiler rolled her chair back so she could see me. "Caputi. I have an important new project for the agency, and I need you on it," she barked.

Yes, thank you, Sabrina, I'm fine. My family? They're fine. How's your nephew?

She cleared her throat and I snapped back to reality. "Our client specifically requested you, Caputi. I know you asked for a week off, but you have to deal with this before you can go on vacation."

Why thanks, Your Majesty!

"Okay," I said.

"For this one, the customer needs you onsite. Your expenses are covered. Flight, hotel, meals. Is there any reason I shouldn't put you on this, Caputi?"

Flight? I shook my head. "No."

"Good!" She hit the desk with both hands and turned back to her screen. "You leave in three days. You'll be away for a week, and then you can take off the days included under your contract. That way you can recover from your jet lag."

"Jet . . . jet lag?" Where was she sending me? Kamchatka?

"Yes, New York is six hours behind. It'll take a few days to adjust."

Did you hear that thud? It was my jaw and my heart.

Hitting the ground.

I was in shock.

"N-New York . . . ?" I stammered. My throat was so parched that I was doing my Marilyn Monroe and Britney Spears voice again.

Sabrina peered from behind her screen to look at me. "New York, the Big Apple, Manhattan . . . call it what you want."

She had gone back to looking at her screen, oblivious to the wave of emotion sweeping over me. You can ride a wave, or you can watch it coming until it sweeps over you. But Christian wasn't a wave—he was a tsunami.

"You'll be gone for a week, Caputi. Try not to make a mess out of things like last time."

"New York," I repeated. My brain's capacity for language had hit the ground with everything else. Jaw, heart, now brain.

At least Sabrina had not said the name "Sound&K." It could be for any totally normal client who liked my work. Did I mention what a success the Let It Be campaign had been?

"Caputi, what's come over you?" she blurted out, exasperated. "This client asked for you specifically. Don't look at me like that. I'm just as surprised as you are."

Thanks for the vote of confidence!

"Apparently, they were impressed by the Sound&K campaign and asked for you. It was their only condition."

Sabrina had taken Sound&K's name in vain.

Her nephew's company.

Her nephew Christian Kelly.

My Christian Kelly.

My heart pounding, I asked, "Why me?"

Sabrina rolled over to me with her chair. We locked eyes. The rottweiler in her was coming out.

"Caputi, if it were up to me, I wouldn't give this to you, but my hands are tied. The Sound&K contract is worth a lot of money—too much money—and if that means sending you to New York for a week . . ." She took a deep breath, as if she were trying to find the right words. "Then you will go to New York. Even if it's hard to believe they requested you."

"I can't . . . I can't . . ."

Gioia, construct a complete sentence. Subject, verb, object.

"I can't . . . I can't work from here?" I asked. My voice broke. It felt as if I had an apple in my mouth that I couldn't swallow. No air was coming in. I was probably going to die.

Sabrina raised an eyebrow, her patience reaching its limit. With the look she gave me, I expected the *Jaws* theme song to start playing.

"No," she replied dryly. "Caputi, are you feeling alright today?"

In my eleven months at Dreamstart, Sabrina had never, ever asked how I was. Just before Christmas I had dragged myself to work with a fever of over one-hundred degrees and she had said nothing. I could have shown up attached to an IV, and she still would have called me into her office and asked what took me so long to get there.

"Caputi?"

I snapped back to the present. "Yes . . . I'm fine."

"You need to get ahold of yourself, seeing as you leave in three days. I've arranged for all the documents you'll need."

"Three days?"

"Caputi, are you having hearing problems today?"

I shook my head. I had heart problems.

"We're done. You can go now."

She dismissed me with the usual wave of her hand. I stood up, thankful my legs hadn't joined the pile of body parts that were already on the ground.

I was going to New York!

Oh. My. God!

I would see Christian, the asshole who had called me a mistake. The only person on the planet who was a bigger asshole than Matteo. Because he had made me need him, and just when I had thought he was different—that our ending would be different—he had delivered the lethal blow. He had gotten back together with his ex. And he hadn't even had the balls to tell me in person.

I hadn't responded to his email. I didn't want to give him the satisfaction. He wasn't even worthy of my anger. I couldn't allow myself to give a fuck about someone who hadn't bothered to come up with a subject line for his email.

"Caputi."

I had reached the door when Sabrina said my name. With one hand on the doorknob, I turned to look at her. For the first time in my life, I witnessed Sabrina with her mouth twisted into something like a smile.

"Yes?" I asked hesitantly.

She stared at me for a long time over her glasses as I held my breath.

"Go to New York and bring back my nephew."

Playlist

"Happy," Pharrell Williams
"When You Say Nothing at All," Ronan Keating
"Strong Enough," Cher
"Stay with Me," Sam Smith
"Every Breath You Take," the Police
"The Blower's Daughter," Damien Rice
"Chasing Cars," Snow Patrol
"This Year's Love," David Gray
"I See Fire," Ed Sheeran
"All of Me," John Legend
"Poison & Wine," the Civil Wars
"Mirrors," Justin Timberlake
"For Once in My Life," Frank Sinatra
"You and Me," Lifehouse
"Photograph," Ed Sheeran

Playlist

Acknowledgments

Wow! I never thought I'd be thanking people for their help with my book. I've always flown high in my imagination, but never this high.

My first thank-you goes to my parents and my sister Barbara—my first reader—for their support, especially over these last few years. For always letting me dream and for always being there for the important journeys in my life. I know you're there.

Special thanks to Laura Ceccacci, my agent and gladiator. You once told me you'd raise hell, and you did.

Thanks to Frank Lang and all of Piemme for believing in me and my work, for making a reality out of a dream locked in a drawer I never thought I'd open.

Thanks to Paola Turani for your friendship and for being there for me with a WhatsApp chat, a voice message, or a like. Onward and upward!

Thanks to Carmen Bruni, Lidia Otelli, Jenny Anastan, Irene Pastorelli, and the wonderful writers I've met who have become my friends. Emanuela Torri, Sylvia Kant, Naike Ror, Victoria, Sabina Di Gangi, Chiara Parenti, and everyone I've met through blogging.

Thanks to the Consorelle and all the Mami girls for your wit and humor. I can always count on you to make me cry with laughter.

Thanks to Cinzia and Serena for cheering for Team Kelly.

A special thanks goes to all of you who have read and loved the story of Gioia and Christian. I am overwhelmed with your enthusiasm. My Facebook, Instagram, and Twitter have all been flooded with messages that keep me up at night wondering, "What next?" Your support has been essential. Thanks to you, I have learned to believe, always. Dreaming has no expiration date.

Be excited, let your imagination soar, and nourish your dreams. Never give up.

About the Author

Elisa Gioia was born in the province of Belluno, Italy, in 1984. With a degree in languages, she studied journalism after working for several years with the local paper. She enjoys all types of writing—an article, a story, a tweet, or a Facebook status. All are forms of release. She loves to travel, take photographs, and run marathons, but her greatest passion remains New York City. *The Hook* is her debut novel.

About the Translator

Photo © James C. Taylor

A resident of New York City, Hillary Locke studied Spanish and Italian literature and translates from the Romance languages into English. When she's not running along the East River or reading in Tompkins Square Park, she likes to travel around the world and listen to beautiful languages she doesn't understand.